WILL LEAVE THE GALAXY FOR GOOD

A NOVEL

YAHTZEE CROSHAW

The conclusion of the
Jacques McKeown Trilogy

ISBN:
978-1-68068-476-6 (Print)
978-1-68068-477-3 (E-book)

This book was initially an Audible Original Production
Performed by Yahtzee Croshaw
Editorial Producer: Steve Feldberg

Cover design courtesy of Audible
Typesetting & e-book formatting by Victor Marcos
Published on behalf of the author, courtesy of The Ethan Ellenberg Literary Agency

Publisher
The Ethan Ellenberg Literary Agency
548 Broadway #5C
New York, NY 10012
212-431-4554
www.ethanellenberg.com

For my amazons.

CONTENTS

PROLOGUE

In a squat wooden house on a grassy island at the edge of the universe, he awoke in his bed for the thirty-seven thousand two hundred sixty-seventh time.

Then, for the thirty-seven thousand two hundred sixty-seventh time, he stared at the pristine wooden ceiling tiles that tessellated overhead, and wondered how he would spend the day. Would this add one to the eighteen thousand four hundred twelve days spent pacing around the house? Or to the nine thousand one hundred fifty-five days spent without leaving the bed at all? Or perhaps, at last, to the short stack of six hundred two days spent trying to tunnel his way through the floor with his forehead?

He sighed. No. He was going to go fishing. He hadn't done that in eight full days now, so it would probably take a good half hour to get tedious again.

He let the door of his house swing closed behind him, cocking his head for a moment to appreciate the creaking sound. He recalled the occasion, twenty-eight thousand nine hundred forty-four days ago, when in an experimental mood, he had lubricated the hinges with some of the oil he had been able to extract from a fish. The sound of the squealing hinge had, to his complete lack of surprise, failed to alter in the slightest.

He walked the fourteen steps from the door of his house to the fishing pond, deciding not to attempt to beat his speed record—3.1 seconds was about his physical limit, he had concluded seven thousand two hundred thirty-eight days prior—and sat on the bank, letting his legs dangle toward the clean blue water. He contemplated his unrippling reflection for a moment, then took up the rod that lay by his side and cast the line.

While he waited, he noted matter-of-factly that the pond was still a perfect circle, six feet across, and the water within was still uniformly three feet deep from edge to edge. The water level had never changed, no matter how much of it he scooped out and flung off the island. There was also not the slightest sign of a fish, nor any visible means for one to enter.

Nevertheless, precisely twelve seconds later, a fish appeared on the end of the line. He hauled it from the water and watched its cartoonish eyes bulge theatrically as it thrashed its tail in metronomic rhythm.

It was a blue fish, the twenty-nine thousand four hundred sixty-third blue fish he'd caught. That made this a slightly more momentous occasion than had it been a yellow fish (of which he'd caught fifty-two thousand eight hundred four), but less than had it been a red fish (thirteen thousand five hundred fifty-two). He put his chin on his fist and wondered if he was going to throw it off the island now, or let it hang around long enough to stink.

The first time he'd encountered that smell, it had been so foul that he'd deliberately let it worsen for days just to have something to get emotional about, but all too soon he'd grown used to it, and now, like everything else, it hardly mattered.

Of course, before that came the decision of where to land the fish. Would he land it on the space next to him for the fifty-seven thousand one hundred thirteenth time? On the space to the north of the pond that he'd employed twenty-eight thousand seven hundred seven times? Or perhaps, just for the rare treat of it, he would land it on the far side of the pond, which he'd only done nine thousand nine hundred ninety-nine—

His eyebrows shot up as the realization hit. That was only one away from ten thousand. No small milestone. A whole extra digit. Excitement sprouted in the pit of his stomach and swiftly grew to the tips of his fingers. He stood up to give the moment its appropriate degree of ceremony.

The fish flopped into the grass on the far side of the pond and immediately died. A few moments of respectful stillness passed after it wobbled to a halt.

Ten thousand. He let the excitement escape him in one long, shuddering breath and stared up at the two hundred seventeen stars that dotted the sky. *Well,* he thought. *Might as well go back to bed. It seems the day's already peaked . . .*

Two hundred eighteen stars.

His whimsical smile vanished. His jaw dropped. There were too many stars. The little empty pocket of sky to the left of the star he had nicknamed Jeremy—the little one two stars south of the bright one named Auntie Bigtits—was suddenly occupied by a new star, brighter than any of the others.

It grew and shrank as he watched, pulsating in time with a succession of strange noises that were presently echoing through the void. In the dusty depths of some long-forgotten memory banks, he recalled having heard a sound like that before. A stream of breathy noises that wavered chaotically, a much calmer version of the sounds that came out of his mouth when he banged his head on the floor for too long.

Speech. That was it. He remembered. For the first time in more than a hundred years, someone was trying to speak to him.

The noise of speech ended, and the star ceased to waver in size, but it stayed where it was. The silence grew tense and expectant.

Panic registered. The mysterious speaker was waiting for a response. What he did in the next few moments could mean the difference between escape and being stuck on the island for another thirty-seven thousand two hundred sixty-seven days. But all he could do was stand and stare, stiff as a board, fists clenching and unclenching as he desperately tore through his memory to haul up anything he could recall about how talking worked.

Finally, when the star seemed to blink for a second as if about to disappear for good, a shot of panicky adrenaline helped him remember that the air needed to be going out of rather than into his lungs, and he found his voice.

"Is . . . this . . . about . . . the fish?"

ONE

"**S**tar pilots," I said, letting the words hang in the heat of the television spotlight like a curl of cigarette smoke. "Star pilots built the universe as we know it. They were the lifeblood of humanity."

In the darkness beyond the studio lights, a multitude of widened eyes boggled in my direction. The indistinct shape of the main camera shifted a little as the operator adjusted his grip.

"Nothing was keeping order out there in the Black," I continued. "You wanted to get supplies to your colony in the next star system and a pirate wanted to steal them, what did you do? Call the police? No. You got a star pilot to transport them. Someone who could out-fly, out-gun, and just plain out-crazy the pirates. Someone who had dedicated their life to righting wrongs across space." I leaned back in my chair and let my eyes drop in melancholy. "They're not needed anymore, now that we have quantum tunnelling and everything can get where it needs to be in the blink of an eye, but . . . we wouldn't have that if it weren't for star pilots. You wouldn't have anything you take for granted now if it weren't for star pilots. And that's why I need to keep telling their stories."

"Hmmm," said the interviewer, nodding appreciatively. Then he spun quickly to acknowledge a movement in the crowd. "Yes! Question over there?"

A new spotlight appeared over the upraised hand, which quickly descended. "Um," said its owner. "Do you ever pick your nose and eat the bogeys?"

A titter ran through the assembly of cross-legged children before me. "Ooh!" said my interviewer. "That's a cheeky question, isn't it! Do you, Mr. McKeown?"

I stared into his googly eyes. He was a monstrous red animatronic covered in red wool, voiced and puppeteered by someone who appeared to be taking enormous relish in the knowledge that his real self was well outside the range of my fist.

I rested my elbow on the arm of my chair—a plastic throne covered in blinking light bulbs, with a sign overhead bearing the words THE HOT SEAT!!! in an extremely excited font—and propped up my face with my hand as I regarded the boy who had asked the question. Like virtually every child I saw these days in Ritsuko City, he lacked obvious parental supervision.

But why should he need any? What few restrictions on quantunnels there had been were now lifted, after quantunnelling had proved to have no long-term ill effects. The intracity network had been expanding like crazy over the last year. Most of these kids were probably going to teleport straight from the lobby of this TV studio to their home apartment buildings.

"Well," I said in a monotone. "I'd say we've all been guilty of that at one time or another."

The boy turned to the practically identical boy sitting to his right and swatted him spitefully across the shoulder. "See, I told you," he said.

"We've got time for one more question!" declared the felt horror with the microphone. As the silence drew on, a good percentage of the audience transferred their hands to their back pockets and took an interest in the ceiling. "Come on, everyone! Ask anything you want! It's Jacques McKeown! Yes?"

A slim arm belonging to a trembling girl in spectacles snapped back down like the arm of a mousetrap, but the spotlight was already swinging over, and it was too late for her to change her mind. She quickly rose out of some kind of nervous reflex and stood fidgeting with her hands and rolling her eyes as she attempted to compose her question while in the process of saying it.

"Um, hello, Mr. McKeown," she said in a voice like someone sighing into a whistle. "My daddy has all of your books. On his shelf. And he likes making model spaceships and he's always talking about how star pilots used to be really great and how it's sad that no one talks about them anymore." She paused to moisten her lips. "So what I would like to know is . . . if you have ever thought about writing a book about real people."

"Okay!" said the puppet host, sensing from the way I had just slumped in my chair that I was disinclined to reply with anything broadcastable. "That's all the time we have for The Hot Seat today! Our guest was Jacques McKeown, a really important writer who your mum and dad could probably tell you all about! But stick around, Jacques, because later on you can be our extra-special celebrity contestant on the Wheel of Slime!"

"The what?" I said, but my mic had already been cut off.

TWO

After the recording, and after the long, hot shower that failed to remove the streaks of fluorescent goo from my hair, I emerged into the dressing room and had to hastily tie up my studio-issued bathrobe when I saw that Emily from Blase Books was pacing back and forth near the make-up chairs.

"Oh good, you're still here," she said in a tone suggesting that this only thinly and begrudgingly met the definition of "good." "Do you need me to arrange transport home? The quantunnels here are going to be booked up for a while." She glanced up from her tablet when I didn't reply. "What's that look for?"

I maintained eye contact until I could sit down at the nearest make-up station, to give her extra time to appreciate my look, then turned away to hunt for the most vicious comb available. "You said you were going to stop booking me for kids' TV gigs."

There had been a time, not too long ago, when the slightest expression of displeasure on my part would have brought on waves of panicky apologies and attempts at reconciliation, but now an eye-roll was all I warranted. "It's getting really very hard to find you bookings at the moment, Jacques. This was the only one that returned my call."

"It's not like I even need to be doing this sort of thing anyway," I muttered, busying myself with my hair.

All at once she was behind me in the mirror, like the terribly fussy ghost of an unhappy secretary. "You do need to be doing appearances. Sales of the new print omnibus have been really very disappointing, and we need to remind the buying public that you exist. Frankly."

I paused, comb halfway through a stubborn knot. "It hasn't turned a profit?"

The muscles in her upper body relaxed the smallest possible amount. "Of course it's turned a profit. Just not much of one. We're going to have to re-examine a few expenses. It's really a very bad sign of the direction the wind is blowing."

The remnants of the slime still weren't coming out. I focussed on styling my hair into something presentable and hoped most people would mistake it for gel. "Come on. People aren't just going to stop liking star-pilot stories. Adventure, thrills, alien queens in really short skirts, those are universal themes."

Emily folded her arms. "Have you been to the spaceport lately, Jacques?"

"You know I haven't, and you know why," I said grimly. "It's full of poor star pilots trying to flog trips to tourists, and a lot of them have this wild idea that I'm a sellout—"

"No, it isn't," she interrupted brutally. "There are hardly any star pilots in the spaceport. They're bulldozing half the old docking bay next year to build another quantunnel concourse. The whole city's really very excited about it. Didn't you hear?"

Of course I hadn't heard. The last three years of my life had consisted only of giving stock answers at interviews and staring at the ceiling of my apartment through an alcoholic haze. "The star pilots have gone?"

"Yes! They've all gone to that weird retirement home for star pilots where you can't use quantunnels."

"Salvation Sector," I corrected on impulse.

"That's it, yes. You're just about the only star pilot left in Ritsuko City. So you can understand why you really aren't reaching the broadest possible market right now." She leaned in. "If you are thinking about ideas for the next book . . ."

I growled almost inaudibly. "This again."

Undeterred, she perched on the counter beside me. I was still wearing only a bathrobe, and she was apparently determined not to give me a chance to get dressed and escape her clutches.

"It would be really very much easier to interest the media if we had something to talk about. A new book would—"

"Weren't you literally just saying that nobody wants to read star-pilot books anymore?"

She winced. "Have you given any thought to writing in another genre? It could still be about space. *Trailspacers* is really very popular right now . . ."

"Yeah, I have no idea why," I spat. "Nothing ever happens on that show."

Emily sighed. "Well, maybe that's what people want, Jacques. The economy's up. Crime's down. Quality of life has improved across the board. People want nice, safe, cosy entertainment. Not books about action and danger that make them feel guilty about using quantunnels because they've made a bunch of middle-aged men stop playing at space heroes."

That was an unusually cutting remark for Emily, the human equivalent of a childproof kitchen with smoothly rounded countertops. I raised a surprised eyebrow.

"Sorry," she said immediately. "Okay. You've made yourself really very clear. You only want to write star-pilot fiction. That's fine. Could we arrange something that might inspire your creativity? Perhaps we could have a meet-and-greet at Salvation Station . . ."

I had been cradling my chin in my hand again, and the sudden jolt that ran through me almost caused me to headbutt the table. "*No.* I can't go to Salvation. I can't. Look, could you go?" I tugged on the lapels of the bathrobe. "I need to get dressed. Don't worry about transport. I'll walk."

She backed off, turned to leave, stopped, visibly wrestled with herself for a few moments, and turned again. "Jacques. Listen. We don't have to let things get uncomfortable here."

"Bit late for that," I muttered, watching her with narrowing eyes.

"But we are not your therapists. We're your publishers. We are not invested in you sitting around doing nothing for years on end. We are invested in you writing books. So if you haven't at least started your next one by the end of the year, we may have to take a very hard look at our relationship with you."

"Is that a threat?"

Another eye-roll. "Only if you feel threatened by having to move to a lower rent apartment. Something that's *ludicrously* expensive rather than *obscenely*."

If Emily was getting sarcastic twice in as many minutes, book sales must have been a lot more dire than she was making out. I stared at my hands in silence, like a schoolboy in disgrace, until she clicked her tongue and left.

Only then did I glance up at my reflection and partake in a round of what was becoming a very frequent game: Guess Which Lines Are Old Scars and Which Are Wrinkles. I did this for as long as I could stand to look at myself, double-checked that Emily was out of the room and out of earshot, then headed to the bathroom.

I lowered myself to the toilet, and kept right on going until the backs of my hands were trailing on the floor and my face was buried between my knees. I made a noise between a belch and a cough and let it extend into a flat, prolonged moan.

Every day it was getting stronger, that little self-destructive impulse at the back of my mind to confess everything. It had been helpfully queueing up the words in the back of my throat during the entire conversation with Emily. I ejected them safely into the toilet bowl.

"Sorry, Emily, I'd love to write another plying Jacques McKeown book, but there's one tiny little roadblock, and that's that I've never written a plying Jacques McKeown book because I'M NOT. JACQUES. MCPLYING. KEOWN!!" I spat out the froth that had built up. "I'm just a random thicko star pilot who everyone thinks is Jacques McKeown, and I dabba wabba gabba bwong . . ."

I'd started babbling, so I switched to my internal monologue. I didn't know who the real Jacques McKeown was, or why he'd only ever submitted his books anonymously, or why he'd never come forward to claim any royalties. All I knew was that I wasn't him. The longest thing I'd ever written was a one-page incident report, back in my Speedstar days, to explain why the secondary steering column had gotten jammed by a woman's undergarment.

Pretending to be Jacques McKeown had begun as a couple of little white lies in the name of other gains, but then everything had spun out of control. I'd been living the lie for three years and counting. It was doing things to my head. Every time I met my own gaze in the mirror, it was like looking through the shattered front windows of a bombed-out house.

It could all be over today, went that inner voice again. *All you have to do is confess. Say you're very sorry and you'll return all the money you haven't already blown on refilling the drinks cabinet. At least in prison, they won't make you ride a carousel and pelt you with ropes of pink goo for the amusement of a roomful of howling toddlers.*

I grimaced at the bathroom floor. No. I wasn't going to let this break me. I used to be a star pilot. If the Rampaging Scourge Fleet of the Conflab Sector couldn't destroy me, I wasn't going to let a publisher's deadline and a little televised humiliation do it. I clenched my fists, quickly stood up, and almost knocked myself out on the toilet cistern.

THREE

As promised, I opted to walk home. Ritsuko City was a good walking city, which partly came of being entirely contained within a giant glass dome on the surface of Luna; it was unable to expand outwards. It had expanded upwards as much as the dome's arc allowed, and then a large number of bridges and walkways had been built to connect the upper levels of the skyscrapers—lending certain districts the appealing air of a high-tech tree-house village—so a significant portion of the city could be traversed without going outside at all. Whatever "outside" means in a bubble city.

I resisted the urge to stick to the indoor routes, though, as I was curious about what Emily had said. I'd flatly avoided going out at all for the last few years, on the assumption that I'd get mobbed by Jacques McKeown fans, so I wanted to dip a toe back into the piranha tank and see exactly how much his popularity had waned. I dug my hands into the pockets of my coat and began a leisurely walk toward the plaza in Ritsuko's Heart, taking the most popular route through Ritsuko's Leg and Ritsuko's Kneecap.

It didn't take long to notice that Emily hadn't been lying about one thing, at least. I didn't see a single star pilot. The last time I had walked this route, I could have cast a look around at any moment and seen at least one or two flight jackets, especially if I focussed on less than reputable drinking establishments. Or gutters.

I wondered how much of this was down to me. When I assumed Jacques McKeown's identity, one of the first things I did was distribute most of the royalties he had earned to the star pilots whose life stories he had ripped off, partly out of principle and partly to lower the odds of being lynched to death. I hadn't expected them all to take the money and run. Without them, Ritsuko had lost something vital. Something that had been as much a part of its identity as the bicycle traffic and the hydroponic roof gardens.

Those two things weren't much in evidence, either. Ritsuko's Leg had once jangled with impatient bicycle bells, but now entire seconds could go by without a rider, and half the buildings lacked the customary green topping of trailing vines. I'd heard that quantunnels had been set up to pump in clean air from a range of unspoiled planets with atmospheres, so the hydroponic gardens were no longer necessary, but that didn't make it feel any less wrong. There was something reassuring about a green crown on a building, like a fatherly hand was tousling its hair.

The more I looked, the less I recognised Ritsuko City. Even the less than reputable drinking establishments were thinner on the ground, either shuttered or replaced by healthy juice bars, presumably out to profit from the roving packs of joggers and power walkers that made up a large percentage of what foot traffic there was.

This was the world that quantum tunnels had created. Walking on your own plying feet was now an amusing hobby for eccentrics. And it hadn't escaped my attention that almost all of them were younger than me.

The streets became a little busier when I reached Ritsuko's Heart, due to the commotion in front of the Henderson building. It was still the biggest, tallest, and most opulent building in the city, so a police cordon around its front entrance was naturally something to be curious about. Even so, a line of bored police officers handily outnumbered the crowd they were holding back.

I started to drift closer, then hesitated. The mob of baying autograph hunters had failed to appear, but I was particularly concerned about being recognised outside the Henderson building. I had a history with the Henderson organization. A small matter of being partly responsible for their previous leader getting his neck snapped by a cosmic horror. Still, I figured it would be safe enough if I turned my collar up and loitered at the back of the slim crowd.

"Is that Jacques McKeown?" called a slow voice, dripping in relish. "Hello, the author Jacques McKeown."

The minuscule crowd parted before me, and the rotund form of Inspector Honda marched up to the yellow tape barrier, bristling his black moustache and sarcastically kicking his feet high with each step.

"Inspector," I mumbled in greeting, having missed my chance to duck away.

"Funny seeing you out and about, the author Jacques McKeown," said Honda, clasping his hands behind his back and surveying his cordon proudly. "Thought you'd be too busy writing those books you genuinely write."

Honda was one of the few people who knew that I wasn't really Jacques McKeown, but everyone he had tried to convince of this fact had found it more politically convenient to disbelieve. I think he eventually took solace in the fact that my comeuppance was pretty much inevitable—possibly around the time the publisher started demanding more books, funnily enough—and our relationship these days was best characterised as on the chummier side of mutual hatred.

"Didn't take you for having an interest in literature," I countered. "What's going on?"

He blinked up at Henderson Tower as if he had only just noticed it. "Oh yes. Suppose you'd want to know about this. We've brought down the Henderson gang."

He'd dropped that bomb like he was talking about taking the recycling down to the collection chute. I boggled. "What?"

"Yep," he said, rocking on his heels with self-satisfaction. "Didn't even need your help, in the end. Shame. Guess you'll have to miss out on all that lovely, helpful immunity from prosecution."

Before I could reply, the grand entrance doors of the building flew open, and two police officers emerged, pushing a man whose torso was about the size of theirs put together. He was wearing sunglasses and a suit that looked like it had been manufactured by an inexpensive camping supplier, and his hands were cuffed behind his back.

I didn't know his name, but I knew he was one of the many enforcer-slash-bodyguards attached to the Henderson organization. He was shoved into the back of a waiting police rickshaw just as another pair of police officers appeared, pushing a second man virtually identical to the first.

Honda counted with sleepy nods of his head as a procession of Henderson goons were brought out and crammed into police rickshaws that swiftly resembled overloaded cattle trucks. Appropriately, every man they loaded on looked thoroughly cowed. They were all staring silently at their feet, shoulders hunched forward like slabs of beef that had fallen off the hook.

The last man to be brought out was Mr. Heller, who last I knew had been the second in command of the Henderson gang. And if the lesser minions were cows in their Sunday best, Mr. Heller was the minotaur in a wedding tuxedo that the others worshipped as a fertility god. Nevertheless, he was as contrite as his followers, meekly allowing himself to be pushed into the rickshaw by two officers that he could have snapped in half with a single shrug.

"Right, that's pretty much the whole power structure in custody," said Honda, consulting a piece of paper as his officers struggled to get the doors of the rickshaws closed. "Hm. Honestly, I was expecting them to make this more difficult."

I was still watching the doors expectantly. "What about Daniel Henderson?"

"Ah." Honda scratched at his thinning hair. "That's where 'pretty much' becomes the operative phrase. He wasn't in the building. Actually, our sources indicate he may not have set foot in Ritsuko City for some time."

Daniel Henderson had been my main concern. Ostensibly the head of the gang since the death of his father, he had also been the galaxy's biggest Jacques McKeown superfan. He'd been mysteriously absent from the last few Jacques McCons and had delegated the organising to a group of young men who, despite their enthusiasm, I had found very depressing company.

"Oh well," said Honda philosophically. "Not much we could've pinned on him, anyway. He's been very hands-off, as leaders of criminal empires go." He glanced at the silent rickshaws, whose wheels were gradually turning into ovals under the heavy load. "Probably why everyone else lost their spirit. Just goes to show the importance of strong leadership."

"Your lot seem to get by."

Honda pretended not to hear me. "Whatever happened to Henderson senior, anyway?" he wondered aloud, stroking his chin. "Oh, that's right. The last anyone saw him, he was getting kidnapped. By you. Hm. We'd probably have spent more time looking into that if he hadn't been such a huge bastard."

"Terrorgorn killed him."

"Yes, so you've said. Wonderfully informative testimony. I can see why you went into writing." He sauntered away toward the lead rickshaw, whose doors had been successfully held closed by the cunning placement of a nightstick through the handles.

I was still feeling stunned. The threat of being targeted by the Hendersons again had been one of the many flavours of the anxiety that was the constant background noise of my life. For that to suddenly go away was disorienting. Like going into a familiar room with half the furniture removed.

It was, theoretically, a positive development. And yet all I could think about was how this was more evidence of Ritsuko City having changed into something I no longer recognised. Like how nobody would want to be pursued by a hungry Dangordian razorbear, but if it were to suddenly lose interest and wander off, it would be natural to feel rejected.

"Excuse me, are you really Jacques McKeown?"

The speaker was a member of the rapidly thinning crowd of rubberneckers. She was a young woman wearing an unflattering jogging tracksuit and a sweatband around her head, which did nothing to disguise her extreme attractiveness.

I returned her smile with a winning one of my own. "Actually, I am."

"Your last book really sucked. Why don't you write something more like *Trailspacers*?"

FOUR

My apartment building was just on the other side of Ritsuko's Heart. The entrance hall was decorated in Arabian splendour, all high arching ceilings and bone-white marble with gold patterning that always reminded me unsettlingly of used toilet paper. There was no elevator or reception desk, just a single set of ornate double doors standing freely in the middle of the floor.

It was, of course, a quantunnel. And as I trudged across the room toward it, hidden sensors analysed my biometric data and confirmed my identity, signalling the quantunnel to link to the associated destination. Had my genetic profile not been on record, a fleet of Taser drones would have descended from the ceiling to subdue every unrecognized person in the room, and then sections of the floor would have tilted to hurl the unconscious bodies through the entrance doors and into the gutter outside. I knew this because of an unfortunate incident with a new superintendent several months ago.

By the time I reached the doors, they were already grandly swinging open to reveal the interior of my luxurious penthouse apartment. I stepped inside, and hundreds of individually controlled smart fibres in the thick pile carpet helpfully removed my shoes and began massaging the soles of my feet. If I were to collapse unconscious this very second, the carpet was programmed to convey me to my bed like a dead beetle transported by an army of hungry ants, then activate the white noise generator and the coffee machine.

On this occasion, I opted instead to head through into the living room. At which point, the flat-screen television on the wall, which I would have described as "modestly sized" if I were laying it down on the street to use as a parking space, turned on and immediately tuned itself to an episode of *Trailspacers*. By some hideous arcane process of data gathering, the system must have known that it had been coming up a lot today.

I hadn't intended to put it on, but I found myself pausing for a few minutes to watch. It was a dramatization of the exploits of an Oniris Venture deep-space reconnaissance vessel, expanding the frontiers of the known universe. On screen at the moment, a terribly rugged-looking captain seemed concerned as he sat in the middle of a bridge that had more in common with the reception area of an expensive hotel than it did with any ship's bridge I'd ever been on.

"Captain!" announced the voluptuous woman in the uncomfortably tight jumpsuit to his immediate right. "The volcanic eruption on the planet's surface will kill thousands!"

"A tragedy, to be sure," intoned the captain nobly. "But our policy of non-interference is too important to make exceptions."

This summed up what seemed to be the plot of almost every episode: the courageous and large-breasted crew would discover a new alien civilization facing a crisis, very pointedly refuse to help in any way, and then fly off, patting themselves on the back for their obviously superior morality.

As a former star pilot, I found it hard not to feel personally attacked. Oh sure, there were more than a few primitive alien races that had developed strangely thanks to star-pilot interference—the Biskottis sprung to mind, who had been taken on as cheap labour for a star-pilot service centre and had ended up forming a cargo cult based on wearing fast food restaurant uniforms and solemnly chanting the day's list of specials—but there was no need to be so plying self-righteous about it.

Anyway, it was all bulltrac. The Oniris Venture deep-space recon program wasn't about attractive people having exciting adventures—it was about parking a ship at the edge of known space, casting out probes, and writing down anything they found that might tempt an investor or two. These days they were mostly crewed by retired star pilots and space villains, because it was a nice, safe, easy career path for those who missed the spacer lifestyle but didn't want to go to Salvation Sector to live a theme-park version of it for the amusement of rich tourists. My own arch-nemesis, the evil cyberneticist Malcolm Sturb, was chief systems engineer on the last vessel Oniris Venture had launched. He'd traded in cyberslaves and laser battles for a life of maintenance tickets and *I Hate Mondays* mugs.

I watched *Trailspacers* for another minute or two and failed to update my opinion that it was an incredibly dull show. Leaving aside the lack of laser battles and alien princesses, the acting was unconvincing across the entire cast, and it was shot like a documentary, all fixed camera angles and incessant talking. No doubt filmed on the cheap, but how much could it cost to have the cameraman whiz around or dramatically zoom now and then? Must've been a union thing.

I left some startled-looking actors muttering to each other in the background as I moved to the office area of the main living space. A minimalist desk and chair were set up under a framed piece of abstract art that had been carefully iterated by an algorithm to inspire maximum productivity. The only things on the desk were a small metallic hemisphere with a single red light on the top and several discarded cocktail glasses. The cleaning drones were supposed to recover those and take them to the dishwasher, but I suspected I had overworked them.

I took a seat and pressed the single button on top of the hemisphere, causing the light to turn from red to blue and project a holographic computer display, along with a virtual keyboard. I was finally resolved to stop putting this off. How hard could it be to write books, if a doint like Jacques McKeown could manage? All he ever did was write up the adventures of other star pilots and insert himself as the main character. I knew no end of star-pilot stories. Hell, might as well use one of my own.

Jacques McKeown was flying his ship, I typed, fingers waggling through the transparent keys. *He was thinking about that bracket Rezeven stiffing me on refuelling money for the fifth plying time. Then he has a great idea to hide a Borogardian Filthpig in his air conditioning unit—*

I paused, then deleted everything I'd written. If anything was going to get the buying public back into star-pilot stories, it wasn't going to be me airing my personal dirty laundry. I had precious few friends left as it was. This needed to have broad appeal. I tried again.

Elektra Blue was a mercenary assassin. She had a laser sword and angry eyes, and when she breathed in, her chest came out and moved up and down like nobody's business—

I swiftly deleted all of that and wiped the sweat off my hands. Plying out loud. Maybe my lack of writing ability wasn't my biggest problem here.

Seeking inspiration, I glanced around, and my eyes landed on the cardboard box under the desk. It was full of complimentary copies of Jacques McKeown's last book, *I Know Who You Were*, published shortly after I had started pretending to be him, which had been my primary source for doints-out raving anxiety for quite some time.

For this hadn't been another churned-out yarn of space battles and improbable hotties with poor character development. *I Know Who You Were* was an only slightly fictionalised account of the last few years of my life. And from the very first page, I had recognised it for what it was: a message from the real Jacques McKeown, intended for the interloper who had stolen his life. Me.

More than a message: a threat. At the end of the book, after "Jacques McKeown" defeats Terrorgorn and retires in wealth and luxury to Ritsuko City, there is an epilogue chapter in which he gets called out of retirement to deal with a pirate assault and is heroically and messily killed in the crossfire. A pirate assault upon an old star-pilot community that is suspiciously reminiscent of Salvation Station.

For a while, I lived in fear of the real McKeown's revenge, but after the weeks turned to months and nothing happened, I stopped asking the grocery delivery service to check everything for razor blades and became merely baffled. If the end of *I Know Who You Were* was intended as a prophecy, it was a pretty easy one to avoid; all I had to do was not go to Salvation Sector, and that was well in line with my intentions.

As the months became years, I second-guessed my initial interpretation more and more. If the real Jacques McKeown wanted to expose me and reclaim his money, he could easily have done it by coming out into the open and being very conspicuously not me. A single email could have done the trick. Would have been a lot less effort than writing and submitting a whole plying book just to play mind games.

So maybe he didn't actually want the money. But then, what *did* he want? Why was he trying to mess with my head? Why did publishing an account of my hypothetical death occur to him before, say, asking to sit down around a table and discuss his problems with my conduct over beer and sushi sandwiches?

And as more and more time passed with no further development, the matter of *I Know Who You Were* settled down alongside all my other worries, no more prominent than the Henderson issue, the risk of being mobbed by fans, or the possibility of running out of ice before the weekend.

I pushed these thoughts forcibly out of my mind and tried to focus on the task at hand. *Jacques McKeown was in space,* I typed. I was hoping this would come together if I could just get the momentum going. *He flew through the space. He thought about how much he liked being in space. He liked it even more than breasts . . .*

I pinched my eyes. This would probably be a lot easier without distractions. "Television off," I commanded.

Immediately, *Trailspacers* was replaced with the image of an apologetic face and a request for yet more of my personal information to help better curate my viewing choices, which was a somewhat interpretive definition of "off," but at least it stopped making noise.

And yet, the noise continued. Something else *hadn't* been coming from the TV. It had been irking my subconscious because it was so familiar. Something between a hiss and a roar, like the rushing of a distant underground stream.

It was coming from outside. I looked to the gigantic windows behind me. This was the second tallest building in Ritsuko after Henderson Tower—tall enough to wave to the dome polishing crew, but not quite tall enough to hold an actual conversation with them—so the view was usually spectacular, but tonight, there was only a blank field of smudgy grey.

Fog had become a new problem in Ritsuko City. Pumping in air from alien planets through quantunnels was still an untested science, and occasionally the atmospheres reacted in unpredictable ways when they met. Usually it was fog; every few weeks a thick blanket of it covered the city. Occasionally it was something else, like the incident last year when it had rained balsamic vinegar for eight minutes.

I stood and slid the balcony doors open a couple of inches, letting a few tendrils of fog sidle in and pool about my ankles like purring kittens. The sound became louder, and then it seemed to be coming from all around me. Had one of my neighbours forgotten to turn off a rooftop waterslide? It was the sort of thing I'd come to expect.

But that didn't seem right. I squinted into the fog and saw nothing but the few tiny pinpricks that represented those neighbours who kept their lights obnoxiously bright. In fact, there was one red light just ahead that—

I spun around and bolted for the door.

It wasn't because the red light had started moving. I was already reacting by the time I noticed that. It was because another sound had joined the background roar, a sound that would trigger the muscle memory of any star pilot or former star pilot worth his space salt. The *whirr-click-hiss* of a miniature propulsion system activating.

"Lobby!" I shrieked as I pelted down the hallway toward the grand entrance door and the smart carpet attempted in vain to offer a foot massage to alleviate

my obvious stress. With the time it needed to hook up the quantunnels, the door had only swung halfway open by the time the torpedo hit.

I heard the nose cone smash straight through the armoured windows like they weren't even there. It detonated somewhere in the region of the laundry room, and the force of the explosion lifted me off my feet as a terrible noise boxed my ears. The small part of my conscious mind that wasn't gibbering in terror mused on how funny it was that the same kind of torpedo explosion that always seemed so frustratingly small in the midst of a space battle was now an apocalyptic sphere of destruction about the size of my entire universe.

A searing heat ran up my back, from my feet to my head, and the edge of the doorway slammed painfully into my shoulder and hip as the force of the explosion stuffed me through the gap, like a child hastily cramming a toy into a drawer.

The door to my apartment noisily belched a cloud of orange flame as my smoking carcass slid gently to a halt across the lobby's highly polished marble floor, along with a little entourage of smouldering pieces of apartment.

Somewhere amidst the fog of my senses, I could hear a fire alarm hooting away to itself, and a continuing note of sharp pain at the back of my neck informed me that my shirt was on fire. Fortunately, a moment later, one of the fire suppression drones came over to investigate, and after a few analytical beeps, proceeded to urinate a chemical-infused liquid directly into my face. I nodded in complete understanding, then passed out.

FIVE

onsciousness returned tentatively, in layers. Pain was the first thing that registered: a cloud of red soreness that flexed and shimmered before me, held at bay by a droning filter of medication. The repeating *glong-gong-gong* of the void gradually faded, replaced by the hum of an air conditioner and a rhythmic beep.

Finally, my vision swam into focus, and the first thing I saw was an explosion of pastel colours, over which were printed the words *Maximum Confidence Absorbent Panty Liners*.

I lifted my head. Obviously, I was in hospital. The surgical bed and toothpaste-blue blankets gave that away. I heard a crinkling sound as I shifted, and registered that my entire back was slathered in regeneration strips, dutifully repairing the damage the explosion had done to my flesh. The room was small and dimly lit, and the available space was about half filled, floor to ceiling, with box upon box of miscellaneous medical supplies.

Portable quantunnels had been approved for emergency medical use for some time, and most hospitals found it a lot easier to simply erect one in a patient's bedroom at home so inpatient and outpatient care could be one and the same. As such, they could use the actual rooms in the hospital for storage, unless the patient didn't have a home, owing to its having been exploded earlier in the evening.

I lay back and took stock. Besides the severe burns that the regeneration strips were already taking care of, I appeared to have gotten off lightly. Just a little lingering soreness in my shoulder, but nothing was in plaster, and nothing else hurt.

A lack of pain could be a bad sign, of course, so I made sure to examine myself closely. I felt my shoulders, my chest, my stomach, and then, after a deep, steadying breath, between my legs.

"Ahem," said a stack of tampon boxes.

I hurriedly returned my hand to my side. Then I cautiously leaned over to see around the boxes. None other than Inspector Honda sat with arms folded in the visitor's chair beside the bed. He was dressed exactly as he had been before, with the addition of a red-and-white-striped party hat worn at a rakish angle.

"We," he said, infusing it with as much quiet anger and loathing as can be pumped into a single syllable, "were having a party."

My confused glance flitted from his thunderous face to the jaunty spray of glittery red tinsel emerging from the point of his hat.

"It took months of difficult police work to bring down the Hendersons," he continued, maintaining eye contact. "After the raid, we actually thought we could get away with one modest little celebration. In fact, I seem to recall that right before we heard the explosion, I literally said the words, 'Maybe things will finally quiet down around here.'" He recrossed his legs. "So partly, I blame myself for this. Are you capable of talking?"

"Um?" The question caught me off guard, as he seemed to be doing perfectly well by himself. "Er. Apparently."

He finally unfolded his arms, with the manner of an ice shelf breaking off an ancient glacier, and produced a black notebook. He peered at the first page, then rolled his eyes and let his hand drop. "Do I really need to ask you this question?"

"What question?"

"Ugh. Fine." He held his notebook up at arm's length and spoke with loud, sarcastic inquisitiveness. "Jacques McKeown, can you think of anyone who might have a grudge against you?"

I was still perceiving the universe through a haze of shock and pain meds, so it took a few moments to piece together some relevant memories. "Someone . . . blew up my apartment," I recalled aloud.

"Ye-es," said Honda patiently. "With a torpedo. We found some fragments of casing in the wreckage, and they bore scratches consistent with the loading and launching mechanisms of a small spacegoing vessel." A pause. "And you'd better appreciate this, because it took a good hour of searching the internet to figure that out."

I remembered the red light in the fog, and that roaring sound. The roar of hover jets. "A ship," I said.

"Yes, and if it hadn't been so foggy tonight, we might've gotten a better look at it." Honda sounded bored now. "What we do know is that it was an older interstellar vessel geared for combat, evasion, and light transport." He made a little cough. "Exactly the kind of ship favoured by star pilots."

I rubbed at my eyes, very nearly blinding myself with the pulse monitor on my fingertip.

Honda gave another, more pronounced little cough. "So. Just to prompt. Can you think of anyone related to the world of star piloting who would have reason to want you dead?"

"I may need police protection," I said, still piecing my thoughts together.

He cocked his head. "Why, no, by some miracle nobody else was harmed. Suppose we can thank the high rent for putting people off leasing the downstairs apartment. How very public-spirited of you to be so concerned." He glared for a few moments, then sighed. "Protection from whom?"

"You know whom."

"Assume I don't."

"From . . . Jacques McKeown," I whispered, mindful of the sound of bustling nurses and orderlies in the corridor outside.

Honda's eyebrow popped up. "I thought you were Jacques McKeown?"

"Don't mess me about, Honda, I've had a bad day." I sat up and hugged my thighs. "The real Jacques McKeown. He's finally coming after me for stealing his identity."

"I see." He got up and gently pushed me back against the pillows, then gripped my sore shoulder hard enough to be just on the edge of causing pain. He brought his mouth so close to my ear, I thought he was about to stick his tongue in it. "I don't care if Jacques McKeown kills you," he said in an unamused hiss. "I don't even care that you stole his money. The point where I start caring about your little argument is the point when innocent people in my city are being put at risk. So don't worry. You'll get your protection. I'll make sure of that." He released me and stood upright again, regaining his sleepy demeanour. "I expect you will thank me, someday," he said with a light yawn. "Although I don't expect that day will come anytime soon."

With that, he turned and strode out with the air of a triumphant chess player putting his queen back in the box, but the effect was spoiled when he was blocked at the door by an incoming nurse. They made it past one another after a few moments of apologetic shuffling.

"I wonder what he meant by that," said the nurse, busying herself at my bedside.

"Hm?" I said, settling back down.

"That policeman." She freed the tube of my saline drip from where it was snagged around a box of surgical gloves. "As he was heading off, he said, 'Finally these body cams are good for something.'"

I had to hand it to Inspector Honda. Being around him sometimes felt like being guest character of the week in some light-hearted, retro TV detective drama. I'm sure my face in that moment would have made a perfect freeze-frame over which to roll the end credits.

I swallowed. "Could you turn on the TV?"

The mounted television in the far corner of the room spontaneously activated in response to my voice. Thanks to a stack of biodegradable bedpans, all I could see was the top part of a newsreader's immaculate hairdo and, at their side, most of the letters of the word "McKeown."

". . . story about tonight's apparent assassination attempt upon author Jacques McKeown has just taken a dramatic turn," said the newsreader's hairdo, wobbling indignantly. "What you just saw was live footage from a police body cam in Mr. McKeown's hospital room, in which he appeared to admit to having been an imposter all along. What, er, what can we make of this, Ken?"

"Well, this is exactly the kind of police overreach that always goes unnoticed in these times of hysteria," said another, more masculine hairdo. "We've already had to accept the unmanned police Taser drones and ID chip registration, and now, apparently, the police can simply livestream from your private hospital room without your knowledge. When are we going to say that enough is enough?"

"But what do you make of this man pretending to be Jacques McKeown?"

"Oh. Not much to say, they've got him dead to rights, haven't they. Totally screwed, back to front and upside down. But let's not get sidetracked from the real issue here . . ."

His sentence was punctuated by the sound of a metallic rattling. I'd attempted to rub at my eyes again with my unadorned hand, only to find that Honda had handcuffed it to the bed.

My nurse had absent-mindedly tucked about twice as much blanket as was necessary and was showing no sign of stopping as she stared, agape, at the television. "Wow, you're a real piece of shit," she said, apparently without malice. She finally looked at me, and very noticeably flinched. "Uh. I'll get a doctor."

She was probably concerned by the colour my face was turning. I was going through a complex internal argument, at the centre of which was that little self-destructive impulse again, which was suddenly looking very smug and punchable. *Great!* it was saying. *Now we've got nothing to worry about! No more pretending, no more children's television, no more assassination attempts. We can just sit in a nice, safe prison cell for the rest of our life. Oh, it'll be so wonderful. It'll be just as good as being dead, but without the existentialism.*

I looked down at my handcuffed wrist and made a fist so hard I nearly impaled my own palm with my fingers. No. I wasn't going to go meekly to a cell and be the jewel of Honda's collection. And I wasn't going to let Jacques McKeown play with me like a cat with a squeaky mouse. I'd had enough. I was going to settle this once and for all.

I took that little voice and crushed it under the heel of newfound determination. Then I had it beaten to death by a rampaging mob of lesser emotions and strung it up from the little switch in my head, setting it permanently to the "on" position. Because for the first time in years, I didn't feel like a walking corpse with no ambition but to use alcohol to slowly embalm itself. I felt alive.

Right, I thought. First things first. Escaping from this hospital. Actually, firster things first: removing the handcuffs. But that couldn't be too difficult. I had everything I needed: a roomful of miscellaneous medical supplies, four working limbs, and the raw, adaptive cunning of a career space adventurer who was back in top form. I shivered with excitement, then set to work.

***

"Ye-es," said the doctor, a little while later. "Looks like he tried to use a disposable laser scalpel to remove the handcuffs and accidentally electrocuted himself."

"Huh," said the nurse. "Will he be alright?"

The doctor gently pulled the door closed. "I gave him something to calm him down. Best to let him rest for a while. I doubt he'll be getting much of that in the near future."

"This McKeown's room?" said an approaching uniformed police officer as the doctor resumed his rounds. "Or whoever he is."

"Oh, yes," said the nurse. "Although he's sedated at the moment."

The cop jerked a meaty thumb at the closed door. "Any other way in or out of this room?"

"Oh, no."

"Right then." He took a very deliberate step to plant his feet in front of the door and squared his shoulders proudly. "Inspector wants him guarded day and night. Don't you worry. He won't be getting up to any funny business. This is officially a no-funny-business zone."

"That's very reassuring, officer," said the nurse.

Some way down the corridor, the doctor had turned a corner and flattened himself against the wall. He smiled maniacally to himself behind his stolen surgical mask. Hopefully, that cop's no-funny-business zone didn't extend very far, because I was about to indulge in some very funny business indeed.

SIX

I kept the surgical mask on as I hurried through the near-deserted streets of Ritsuko. A doctor in full surgical scrubs was perfectly natural in the district around the hospital. It was going to get a lot less credible the further I got, though, unless I could argue that the surgical mask was down to being self-conscious about a zit. I guessed I had anything up to an hour before the manhunt started.

That depended on how soon that doctor regained consciousness. The "something" I'd given him to calm him down was a sleeper hold I'd learned from the Zuviron people in my time on Cantrabargid, and I liked to think I'd done a pretty good job of it for someone with only two arms, but he could come around at any moment. The improvised gag I'd made from athletic supports wouldn't keep him quiet for long.

My mind was still fizzing with impish adrenaline as I jogged. My next obvious move was to find the real Jacques McKeown and stick a great big plying torpedo down his air vents; obvious and very satisfying to think about. That meant I needed three things: his real identity, his current location, and a torpedo. I made three mental checkboxes.

Someone had once told me that they knew who the real Jacques McKeown was, and that someone was Robert Blaze, the original star pilot, my childhood hero, who had retired to set up Salvation Sector and invited all the other star pilots to come sell out their dignities to join a sort of space-age equivalent of Buffalo Bill's Wild West Show. I'd respected his silence on the matter, but now I was down one apartment and up one vow of revenge, so it was time to pick Blaze's brain. With a fork, if necessary.

It took a moment of fumbling at the flimsy pockets of my scrubs to remind me that my phone had been in the back pocket of my jeans at the moment of the explosion. So it was now either sealed away in some faraway evidence bag or permanently fused to my backside.

Not a problem. I had an ansible communication system on my ship. And, happily, that was also where the torpedoes were. I was pretty sure there were one or two I hadn't pawned for quick cash back in my destitute days as a star pilot.

Through the years, I'd maintained my old ship, the *Neverdie*. The fans at conventions always appreciated the customary dose of radiation poisoning from standing too close to the landing jets as I came in. Besides, paying rent on its special spot in the city spaceport had been the least concerning regular expense in the last few years of my life, by far.

When I crossed the pedestrian junction at Ritsuko's Navel and entered the district colloquially known as Ritsuko's Arse, I braced myself for the usual waft of stink from the backed-up gutters and various low-cost eateries that the health inspectors would only enter in pairs, but it didn't come. Everything looked as clean as any other part of the city.

A whirring noise overhead caught my attention. There was a metal oval mounted to the top of the nearby streetlight, from which a drone armed with broom and vacuum attachments was emerging. It hung in the air for a moment before bleeping in response to some signal or other and speeding off in pursuit of whatever piece of litter or sleeping homeless person had offended the city's sensors.

That explained that. Quantunnels on every street corner. The city council had never been able to erect them while star pilots were still around. They'd always use them for impromptu games of breeze-block basketball. Had star pilots really been such a negative influence on Ritsuko? I had to admit, cleaning drones aside, the streets certainly looked tidier without them congregating around snack carts and heating outlets to grouse about the old days.

I was about to move on when a blare of sirens froze me. Another drone flew out of the loop overhead, much more vicious looking, with sharper edges, red and blue flashing lights, and a sparking Taser extending from its midsection like something very inappropriate. I hugged the base of the streetlight directly below, and after a few moments of fruitless scanning, the drone sped off down the street like an eager dog catching a scent.

Safe to assume the doctor had been found. Running from shadow to shadow, I made it to the spaceport and took a moment to appreciate the new renovations. There was a new pedestrian plaza directly in front of the main entrance, with a ring of quantunnels around it, each permanently connected to one of the city's major hubs. In the middle of the night, spotlit from above, it reminded me unsettlingly of a stone circle waiting for a sacrifice.

I headed away from the entrance and along the side of the main spaceport building, hoping to God that they hadn't done anything about that little staff-only door near the dumpsters that led to the security storage room. Happily, it was exactly where I expected to find it, so I yanked it open and hopped in without skipping a mental beat.

The door was still there, yes, but there had apparently been some rearranging of the interior. It looked like it had been converted into a new locker room for the security guards. This was made clear by the bank of lockers, the humidity hanging in the air from the adjoining showers, and the two off-duty security guards in respective states of undress. Both appeared to have heads that transitioned into torsos with no perceivable neck in between, and both were looking right at me in surprise.

The door swung closed with a snap. Shocked silence hung in the air. In moments like these, I found it useful to remember that "con" was short for "confidence."

I pointed behind myself and channelled every ounce of my panic. "What the hell are you doing?!" I yelled. "Evacuate before the nerve gas gets here!"

A fragile moment passed as the three of us stared at each other. Then the two guards exchanged a glance, leapt to their feet, and fought to be the first to shove past me.

I watched the door as it swung shut again, a stark illustration of everything I had learned in my years of struggling under the weight of my own lies: absolutely plying nothing.

SEVEN

At least the docking bay had gone untouched by the new, modern Ritsuko. It also seemed to have gone untouched by a broom for a very long time. The white lines of the parking spaces were barely visible under layers of dust. Half the lights were burnt out. If the city was seriously planning to demolish it, the plan seemed to be the usual bureaucratic approach of letting neglect do most of the work.

The *Neverdie* stood proudly in the middle of it all, like the last surviving tomato plant after a hurricane, its red paintwork and sleek curves still standing out through the dust. I supposed it shouldn't have been a surprise to hear that the star pilots were leaving Ritsuko City, since every time I had parked here after another plying convention, there had been fewer ships around. I'd probably been in denial. Or, more likely, drunk.

No denying it now. The *Neverdie* was the only star-pilot ship here. Very nearly the only ship, period, if it weren't for a couple of system security vessels: squat, white, crablike things that looked like they'd last been taken out to oust the Mongol hordes.

I laid a hand on the control panel beside the *Neverdie*'s exterior airlock door, and the whirring and humming of the ship's systems gradually stirring from slumber was like the twitching of a sleeping dog's nose when you bring a plate of bacon into the room. I entered the open command, and the airlock door slid up after a couple of brief pauses to blow more dust out of the workings.

There was the faithful, familiar interior of my airlock. And there was faithful, familiar old Inspector Honda sitting on a folding chair in the middle of it, filling out a crossword puzzle to pass the time.

"You really don't rate police intelligence very highly, do you," he said without looking up. "I mean, even Sergeant Winston figured you'd come here. And Sergeant Winston is my cat."

On instinct, I had already spun around to flee at maximum sprint, only to stop short when two police drones descended from the ceiling to block my path, Tasers fully erect and throbbing.

"Automation is the big trend in law enforcement these days," said Honda, behind me. I heard his folding chair scraping on the floor. "Most of the boys don't like it, but me, I try to be pragmatic. Do you know what the Akio Alert system is?"

I was still hypnotized by the pair of Taser rods angled before me, the glowing ends wobbling as if with barely contained excitement. "What?"

"It's a protocol for the citywide sensor net. Puts out a search for an entity with a specific genetic profile and returns its location to within two metres. We're only allowed to use it for the most dangerous fugitives and the most photogenic missing children."

I looked back. Honda was right behind me, apparently using his phone to take a picture of the bare flesh on the back of my hand. Then another spark flew off one of the Taser rods, and I was hypnotized by them anew.

"I just gave it a sample of your DNA." Honda yawned. "And now I'm setting up a little automated script for it to follow: if this genetic entity is detected anywhere within Ritsuko City limits, subdue with Taser drones immediately." He frowned. "Oh. It needs me to come up with a deactivation password."

He held his phone at arm's length, maintained eye contact with me, randomly smeared the digital keypad with his thumb several times, then peered at the screen again. "Password accepted? Oh, how clumsy of me. I really should have written it down."

My eyes were flicking desperately around, searching for a solution, but they kept coming back to Honda's expressionless moustache, fogging my thought process with a delirious impulse to yank on it and run. "What are you doing?!"

"Furthest you can get from a drone quantunnel in this city now is about two hundred yards," he said conversationally. "A Taser drone moving at full speed can cover that distance in about six seconds. The boys moan about job security, but there's no competing with that, is there? Not without some serious caffeine."

"Honda . . ."

"It's all set up. The script goes live in two and a half minutes." He patted me gingerly on the shoulder as if loath to make physical contact. "So. I'd get going, if I were you."

I frowned. "Going where?"

He pushed past me as if making his way through a crowded train, knocking my sore shoulder. "Anywhere. Go have a space adventure, or something. Just don't come back."

I boggled at his retreating form. The two Taser drones flashed their lights meaningfully in the manner of a human being pointing to its own eyes with two fingers, then turned to follow Honda.

"Are you seriously letting me escape?" I realised as I said it that this was probably not a situation to question, but I was mentally struggling to find my footing.

Honda stopped and half turned. A sneer tilted his moustache like a miniature suspension bridge. "Don't misunderstand this, Dashford Jacques Pierce McKeown. I'm not doing you a favour here. I'm protecting my city. If Jacques McReal McKeown is willing to torpedo your apartment to get at you, I fully expect him to do the same to the prison. And I like our prison. It won a prize once."

This felt like more familiar territory. My shoulders dropped. "Right. So you're just shooting me off like a clay pigeon for him to blow up far away from you."

"Look at that. You can be quick on the uptake when the mood takes you." He glanced at his phone again. "One minute left. Hope the engines on that thing warm up quickly."

They absolutely did not. I ran inside.

EIGHT

The *Neverdie* was pursued to the airlock at the top of Ritsuko's dome by a small cloud of police drones hungry for my DNA. Fortunately, Honda must have called ahead to ground control, because the airlock was already open, closing the instant my rear thruster crossed the threshold. The leading, overeager drone had its Taser sheared off when the inner door *clunked* shut, and it retreated, humiliated, to its fellows.

The external airlock door belched the *Neverdie* out of Ritsuko City, and I was back in the cold comfort of the endless vacuum for the first time in three years. But all I could focus on, now that I had a moment to think, was the rear-view monitor and the glittering patch of city spread across the surface of Luna like a clump of tangled Christmas lights in a fishbowl.

It was official: I was a complete doint. Who else but a complete doint could be living in the lap of luxury in the most advanced city in the universe and still find things to complain about? I'd been lounging around in a swimming pool in an expensive hotel, grumbling about how it was a bit too warm or the occasional urinating child, and now I'd been forcibly hauled out and thrown into the car park. I was cold, and wet, and naked, and someone on the roof of the building was aiming a sniper rifle at me.

Staring down the infinite gun barrel of the galaxy, I would have given everything I had to be back there, mixing myself drinks and hanging out with my faithful pet carpet. I'd even smile for the Wheel of Slime.

Of course, "everything I had" didn't amount to much anymore. Emily had always handled my banking, and now that I was outed as an imposter, I didn't see much mileage in asking her politely to let me have some of my stolen money back, for old time's sake. I was reduced to myself, what was on me, the *Neverdie*, and what was on it. And I'd moved most of the possessions I used to keep on the ship—including most of my clothes, my gun, my important documents, and my mementos—into my apartment, so now all I had to show for a large majority of my life was part of the ash cloud gently snowing upon the streets of Ritsuko. And they weren't going to let me return to scrape any of it up with a trowel.

I bent over my steering column and clutched my head. What the plying hell was I going to do? Well. Find Jacques McKeown and do something horrible to the bracket. I'd established that. But what about afterwards? Go live on some lesser colony or primitive planet somewhere? Eke out my remaining days milking Lacrissian megastallions for their seminal fluid? Assuming I didn't run out of fuel or power and have to sit around picking old peanut shells out of the *Neverdie*'s walkway grilles to pass the time before I suffocated to death.

Just keep moving forward. If I kept moving, I wouldn't start thinking, and thinking was more trouble than it was worth. I'd often thought that.

The panel that controlled the ship's ansible communicator had come unscrewed from the console, but the coiled wire was still connected, so I hauled on that until the panel emerged from the pile of loose components at my feet and I could operate it in my lap like a child with an activity centre. I fed it the co-ordinates of Salvation Sector, pinpointed the location of its administrative hub at Salvation Station, and sent a standard hail.

"Calling Robert Blaze," I said when the screen remained blank after four rings. "This is . . . the person who was until recently Jacques McKeown. I need to talk to Robert Blaze."

"Hello?" said a crackly voice, although at that stage it was unclear whether it was crackly from static or from age. The screen was still black.

"Hello!" I leaned close and twiddled the tuning knob. It did absolutely nothing, but there was something comforting about trying. "Who's this?"

The screen came to life, apparently because a cover sheet had been pulled off the camera, and I was looking at the face of an elderly man wearing a battered spacer's cap. "Oh! Is someone seriously calling this thing? Oh boy, this takes me back."

Something at the back of the panel sparked. I could feel how hot the device was getting even through my trousers. It was clearly struggling to handle the pressure of being asked to do its one plying job for once. "Listen, quickly, could I talk to Robert Blaze?" I said.

The old man kept smiling even as his brow furrowed. "Um. No. You know he died a few months ago, right?"

The news thumped into my stomach like a ball of ice into a still pond. "He's . . . dead? How?"

"Uh. The normal way. Old-age stuff. He'd been ill for a while, I think, but he didn't want anyone to know."

"Trac, that figures." I ran a hand through my hair. This was a lot to process. I still remembered that one Christmas when I'd pulled the wrapping off my biggest present and found the Captain Blaze Junior Star Hero Adventure Playset. I hadn't appreciated it at the time, because I was seventeen and had asked for a laptop, but it was all Dad had found at the second-hand store. And the profit I made from auctioning it off online, mint in box, helped pay for my first flying lessons.

The point was, Robert Blaze had been a constant throughout my entire life. Even when he'd stopped being a childhood hero and had become someone I actually knew, whose actions I had occasionally found questionable, it had still been a comfort to know that he was there. Hearing that he was gone gave me the same disquiet as the silence when onboard air cyclers stop working.

"Hello?" said the old man, tapping his camera.

I shook myself. "Who am I talking to?"

"Oh, I'm Raoul. I clean the museum."

"Why am I talking to the museum cleaner?"

Raoul again did that thing where he smiled with his mouth and frowned with his eyes. "Because this is where we keep the ansible receiver? You're lucky, actually. We only keep it plugged in so we can use the built-in digital clock."

I had no right to be annoyed by any of this. Like everyone else I would have happily used the miniature ansible in my phone, if only my phone hadn't been reduced to a robotic grilled cheese sandwich. "Who's in charge of Salvation, then?"

"Ms. Warden."

I'd been afraid of that. I took the steadying breath of a man in a survival situation preparing to test the local insects for edibility. "Could you patch me through to her?"

"Patch you through? Oh. Um. I can probably remember how to do that." He inspected the control panel in front of him, grimacing, then looked over his shoulder and bellowed at the top of his voice. "MS. WARDEN! SOMEONE WANTS TO TALK TO YOU!"

After a few minutes of mumbling and the rhythmic thudding of sensible shoes on carpeted floor, Raoul moved aside, and the view was filled by the face of Penelope Warden herself, the woman who had schemed her way out of the Henderson organization and into the administrator role at Salvation Station, and whose machinations were also the principle reason I had ended up trapped in the role of Jacques McKeown.

I'd hesitate to say she'd been the arch-nemesis of my later years. Generally, your arch-nemesis is someone you seek out. Back in the day, I'd hear that Malcolm Sturb was up to his usual tricks, creating a new cyberslave colony on Sestertus XII or wherever, and I'd speed right on over there. Sneak into his base, get caught, get tied to something, escape, blow something up, and then he'd fly away saying he'd get me next time, while I spent the evening with whatever on that planet passed for a hottie. Everyone was having a good time. But Warden I would less want to spend time with than a giant Hooloovian mantis with severe chlorine flatulence.

Yet there she was, my only hope of locating the real Jacques McKeown, peering into the lens so closely that her pointed nose looked like the Grim Reaper's scythe. "Who is this?" she barked, before her thin eyebrows shot up. "McKeown? Why are you on here?"

"Not McKeown anymore," I said. "You read the news lately?"

"What do you want, McKeown?" she said, her tone unchanged. "We're very busy."

Another spark flew off the communication panel. The wire was looking dangerously frayed at the connection, and something in the middle of it was glowing alarmingly orange with heat. A line of static lanced across the screen. The communicator wasn't going to be communicating for much longer. I cut to the chase. "I need to know who Jacques McKeown is. The real one. I know Blaze knew, and I remember you saying that he told you."

"Ye-es," said Warden with infuriating slowness. "Do you also remember me saying that I would only tell you if you agreed to work for us?"

I sighed. "Look, there's nothing I can do for you, and McKeown's not even that popular anymore. Apparently. What does it even matter?"

Warden glanced offscreen, reacting to some indistinct shouting in the background. "I'm actually in the middle of some rather important business . . ."

"Then just tell me and I'll be out of your hair." I displayed my hands and gave her my winning smile.

She was staring offscreen, chewing on her bottom lip. For the first time, I noticed that her hair, usually tied back so tightly she looked like she'd been using a take-off thruster as a hair dryer, was escaping from her ponytail in bedraggled strands. The important business she was in the middle of must have been a source of some stress. It was a cheering thought.

"Okay." She sighed. "He—"

A bigger explosion of sparks burst forth from the connection. I instinctively threw the communication panel away to beat the potential fires out of my trousers. After I was satisfied that I had averted a case of roasted doints, I attempted to pull the panel back into my lap, only to find myself holding the blackened, smoking end of the power cable.

I let it fall and slumped back in my chair. That was it, then. No leads, no communication system, and probably not enough fuel to make it to Salvation Station. Nothing left to do but sit here and wait for my flesh to fuse with the upholstery.

My last remaining spark of defiance, marooned as it was on a tiny desert island in the midst of an encroaching sea of despair, got to its feet. *You still have some leads*, it cried. *Way back when Warden first gloatingly mentioned that she knew who McKeown is, she teased that he's someone you've met before.*

Which didn't narrow things down for trac. I let a tide of despair roll in. I already knew McKeown had to be a star pilot, or someone close to the star-pilot world, and after quantunnels came along and we'd started spending most of our days in the spaceport fighting each other for clients, I had probably stomped on at least one body part of every star pilot in the galaxy.

Undeterred, the spark of defiance stood on tiptoe as the water level rose. *Ah, but what Warden actually said was that she was only "pretty sure" you'd met. And there are quite a few people in the star-pilot world she would have been absolutely certain you had met because she'd been in the same room, so that eliminated some candidates. Robert Blaze, all of Blaze's crew, Malcolm Sturb, Angelo, Jemima . . . probably a few more that didn't immediately leap to mind . . .*

The water of despair finally snuffed the spark out. None of this helped, and it didn't even matter, because there was nowhere I could go. My only recourse was to go in person to Salvation Station, and I didn't have the fuel . . .

It occurred to me to double-check that, so I turned to the diagnostic panel. The fuel gauge was at seventy-eight percent.

I blinked. Huh. Maybe someone had very helpfully refilled the tank on one of the occasions I'd brought the *Neverdie* to a convention. It was easy to imagine a pack of six or seven fanboys gathering around and fighting over who got to be the one to hold its nozzle.

Okay then. So it wasn't fuel preventing me from going to Salvation Station. It was just the fact that I didn't plying want to go to Salvation Station. Warden was a large part of that: time with her was like time spent around a skunk; every second that passed made it more and more likely I'd get caught in something nasty that would never wash off.

The other part of it was *I Know Who You Were*. The book's ending prophesied my death in Salvation Sector, caught in the crossfire of a battle between star pilots and space pirates. It was all coming together just a little bit too neatly. Jacques McKeown sends me a book predicting I will die at Salvation. He blows up my apartment to get me moving. I immediately go to exactly where he said I would go. It would take some serious self-delusion not to think I was walking straight into a trap.

I leant my chin on my fist, glaring at the stars that winked invitingly before me. On the other hand, what the hell else was there to do? Hang around here like a sitting duck with its beak up its trac-hole, waiting for McKeown to come along and take another pot-shot? I was sure the *Neverdie*'s evasive thrusters would be no more up to the challenge than the plying communicator had been.

Out of nowhere, I thought about Robert Blaze again. How many problems had arisen when I'd charged in, on multiple occasions, to protect him. How plying pointless that all seemed now that he was dead. And now that I'd lost absolutely everything as a direct consequence. My whole life was one of those incredibly long, stupid jokes that you get really invested in, and then it turns out not to have a punchline, and that's supposed to be why it's funny.

I slammed my fist down on the armrest, sending up a cloud of dust. Doints to that. I was going to make my own punchline. I was going to dance right up to McKeown, dressed in a clown suit covered in little silver bells, and punchline him right in his smug bracket face.

If he was engineering my death at Salvation Station, he'd need to be there. At the very least, there'd be some clue leading back to who or where he was. On top of that, he'd sent me the book, so he must have been expecting me to be afraid of coming to Salvation. Marching straight there with my head held high would catch him off guard.

I smiled to myself. *Yes,* I thought. *That seemed like a sufficient level of self-delusion.* I set a course.

NINE

The trebuchet gates were still the only non-quantunnel option for ship-based interstellar travel, and while they had been initially designed to function without the need for human supervision, whatever guarantee that had implied must have expired by now, and no one was entirely sure whose responsibility they were. Apparently, all the individual parts that went into their construction were built by different corporations, half of which were defunct, while the remaining half had mostly shifted into electric scooters.

The gate that served the Solar system was probably the only one I could still make use of with any degree of assumed safety. It was close enough to the centre of civilization that you could count on the occasional hobbyist to fly out and perform maintenance on the thing. The same individuals were probably the ones who had spray-painted the face of a giant anime character over the entrance spiral, with a speech bubble bearing the words ENTER ME GENTLY, SPACER-CHAN, but their hearts were in the right place.

The *Neverdie* went through the gate and was flung deep into the heart of the Black with no more than the usual amount of trauma. When everything had stopped spinning and my eyeballs weren't about to pop out of my skull and fly around the cockpit like unsecured balloons, I could verify that the ship hadn't been peeled open like a banana, and I slowly blew all the air out of my lungs.

I checked the damage report panel, but it was too damaged to tell me anything. Still, a cursory pinging of the systems—navigation, propulsion, life support, gravity, biscuit dispenser—assured me that all the necessities were functional. And everything else might have been a blessing in disguise. The biscuits in the dispenser were a little past prime. Last time I had opened one, something inside the packet had squealed what had sounded like a request to turn the lights back off.

According to the navigation computer, I was definitely in Salvation Sector, although it was a few hours' flight to Salvation Station itself. I targeted the coordinates, fired the engines, and sat back for the long wait.

For want of something to do, I kicked the short-range scanner to see who, if anyone, was in the neighbourhood. Other ships in the Black were getting rarer by the day. Every now and again, some wide-eyed alien race would develop interstellar travel and start showing up on radars, but it never took long for the Humanity Handshake Foundation to reach out, get them up to speed with quantunnelling, then let the corporations move in to set up call centres and manufacturing plants.

So I was taken by surprise when the screen absolutely lit up with moving dots. I gave it another kick, because before its diagnostic tools were properly warmed up, it had a tendency to get a bit overenthusiastic about random space debris and conspicuous pieces of nothing at all.

But no, the dots were still there. Salvation Sector was absolutely crawling with ships. Even factoring in that it was the star-pilot retirement haven and just about the only place one should expect to find active ships, these numbers seemed off. Maybe it had become more popular with tourists than I'd thought.

Most of the dots were moving apparently at random, but my eye was drawn to the top left quadrant of the scanner, where a particularly large number of dots were holding position in what looked, to my experienced eye, like attack formation. Maybe it was a battle re-enactment? But it was still the middle of the night, Galactic Standard. Odd time for a show.

The short-range scanner started making the tinny squeaking noise that had, at one point, been the proximity-alert klaxon. I'd been so distracted by the faraway battle lines that I hadn't noticed a single dot closing in on my location. Initial scans reported a ship about the same size as my own, with weapons and defence systems powered up and closing in fast.

Within seconds it was in visual range. I could see it on the rear monitor. Looked like a modified Silver Turbot, and from the way the glowing targeting lasers of the torpedo rack were playing nicely off the well-polished hull, one whose owner had a lot more time for cleaning and maintenance. It sauntered straight past me and held position directly ahead, effortlessly matching my speed like an unwanted conversationalist trying to hit on a jogger.

It was sending me a hail. I could have kept my head down, not made eye contact, stuck my hands in my pockets and picked up my jogging pace, but curiosity struck me when I glanced at the ship again and noticed a skull and crossbones lovingly stencilled over its cockpit.

I took the call on the short-range communicator. This was a much simpler technology than the ansible, and as such, less inclined to explode, with the trade-off that its maximum range was only a little better than sticking my head out of the window and yelling.

The video monitor came to life, and the face of the other pilot appeared. He had the grizzled, slightly gaunt look of a retired star pilot, although it was hard to tell with the eyepatch and the false beard.

"Yahar!" he cried. "What 'ave we 'ere? A lone travellarrrr?" He extended the *R* for a good few seconds. "Soon ye'll know the price of blundarrrrring into the territarrrry of the dread pirate Bigbeard!"

"Yeah, hi," I said. "I don't actually have time for the whole song and dance, so if you could get out of the way—"

"Yarrr!" interrupted Bigbeard. "You think those cissy starrr pilots can save ye now, groundlubbarrrr? 'And over all yer booty or preparrre to be . . ."

There was another squeak from the proximity scanner. A second ship had appeared and flown into visual range with much the same casual manner. This one looked to me like a Hibatsu Special, painted vibrant red with a semicircle of white stars that ran along the roof and down both wings.

"Up to your old tricks, are you, Bigbeard?" boomed a confident new voice in Bigbeard's cockpit, loud enough for me to hear over the communicator.

"Arr! It's a starrr pilot!" cried Bigbeard, turning his ship to face the newcomer. "I'll not be taken in by the likes of ye! Fiarrre the cannons!"

The battle that ensued was brief, flashy, and extremely embarrassing to watch. Bigbeard's ship fired a number of what looked suspiciously like cheap tracking countermeasures with glow sticks attached, all of which went extremely wide. The red ship made some token evasive dodges, making sure not to leave visual range, before answering with a volley of spark packs that exploded harmlessly against Bigbeard's hull.

A moment's reaction time later, Bigbeard tilted his ship in an unconvincing imitation of recoil. "Yar! Foiled again! I'll get ye next time, ye pesky starrr pilots!"

He flew away, leaving me alone with my "rescuer," who promptly sent me another hail. I let it ring for a few seconds to bask in the sense of inevitability, then answered.

The pilot was a smiling woman in an unadorned flight jacket and cap, with the aesthetically pleasing rainbow of her flight systems' coloured lights playing across her face. "Lightspeed Kay to civilian vessel," she opened. "Phew. You're lucky I got to you in time. Bigbeard can be a nasty one. But you'll be safe now if you stick with me. Welcome to Salvation Sector! Which resort do you have a reservation with?"

"I don't have a reservation," I said, finally getting a word in edgeways.

"That's fine!" said Lightspeed Kay. "If you'll follow me to Salvation Station, we can go over all our available star-pilot adventure packages, and you—"

"I'm not here for the plying tourist trac," I said firmly. "I just need to talk to your boss lady."

"Oh." Lightspeed Kay pressed a few offscreen buttons, and all her multicoloured lighting effects disappeared, replaced by a single, sensible ceiling light. "Sorry. You looking for work?"

"No, it's . . . well. It's between me and her." I subtly angled my directional thrusters in the general direction of "away," as if I were meaningfully glancing at a door to indicate my intention to leave a dull conversation.

Kay was not to be deterred. She steered straight back into my path. "You still need an escort to the station?"

"I know the way, thanks."

"Okay, I'll just take your donation now, then."

My finger hesitated over the *Disconnect Comms* button. There had been a rather subtle change of tone in her statement. Like the briefest possible flash of a concealed switchblade during a round of musical chairs. "What donation?"

"Your donation to the Salvation Sector Upkeep Fund," said Kay, still smiling. "Got to keep the lights on 'round here somehow. Totally voluntary, of course. We accept euroyen, universal credits, Spercubulan digicoins, and barter."

"Voluntary, is it," I said sceptically.

"Of course! And if you don't want to pay the minimum suggested amount, you can voluntarily make your way to the trebuchet gate and go bum around some other sector."

I wiggled my directional thrusters again. "And if I should instead decide, voluntarily, to blow you off and head on to Salvation Station?"

She didn't immediately respond, and her expression didn't change, but her answer came when my alert systems emitted a series of different squeaks, indicating the high destructive yield of the many colourful and varied weapon systems she had just powered up. Her missile racks slid open like the dripping pedipalps of a Terralian archspider.

"Well then, I might just have to do some blowing off of my own," she said casually.

"Yeah, I figured." I sighed.

I knew what was happening here. It wasn't really a shakedown. It was the kind of thing that used to happen all the time back in the Golden Age. You'd be couriering something or investigating the doings of some supervillain or other, and you'd run into another star pilot. But instead of just saying hello, how are you, is the Kandarian pox clearing up, it was generally expected that you'd go "Aha! So it must be you working with insert-name-of-relevant-supervillain!" and open fire before they could respond, then dogfight to a standstill. Afterwards, you'd "realize your mistake" and actually have a conversation.

It was just an excuse to flex your flying skills. Keep each other in regular exercise for the times when it really mattered. Frequently it was done to feel out whether or not the other party had useful intel, or if they were at all inclined to get in on whatever gig you were in the middle of. It was the star pilot handshake, basically. I'd probably brought this on myself by dropping pilot math into the conversation.

The thing was, I really desperately wasn't in the mood. And I doubted the *Neverdie* had it in her to hold together for a proper dogfight. And yes, I'd known the name was tempting fate right from the beginning, but there'd been a certain trend at the time for ironic bravado.

"Look, there really isn't anything of value on this ship," I tried, hoping she'd take the plying hint. "I had to clear out in a hurry. I'm still in a hurry."

"Oh, don't sell yourself short," she said. "You'd be surprised how much you can scrape together if you just take a good look around. Tell you what, I'll board you and we can look around together . . ."

Her voice tailed off, and a mysterious shadow crossed her cheerful expression, leaving her eyes boggling and her mouth agape. I followed her gaze—by which I mean, switched to my rear monitor—and was just in time to see another ship slide into view like a great white shark emerging from a background of hazy ocean to interrogate a couple of startled minnows.

I didn't recognise the model. It was easily bigger than the *Neverdie* and Kay's ship put together. More the size one would associate with the kind of cruising yacht favoured by seriously rich brackets. It might even have been one at some point, but the original lines and detailing were lost behind extensive customisation. The frontage had been extended on both sides to squeeze in enough weapon banks to turn a small moon to cosmic dust, and the centre of it was shaped into the form of a gigantic eagle's head wearing a very unamused expression. Its entire hull was painted in the vibrant reds, whites, and blues of a rocket-ship ice pop.

It hung there in space for a moment, red dots rhythmically tracking along its fully loaded torpedo racks like disco lights of death. Then a voice boomed over the close-range emergency broadcast channel. "GREETINGS, CITIZENS. DO NOT BE ALARMED."

It was a bit late for that. "Who're you?" asked Lightspeed Kay.

"WHY DID YOU INTERCEPT THIS VESSEL?" The speaker was using a casual, even bored tone of voice, but the volume was so high it was blowing the speakers out.

"Intercept?" said Kay, startled. "We're not intercepting! We're just . . . talking." A judgmental silence rolled on, and she felt moved to elaborate. "Normal talking. Talky, talky . . . mouths kind of talk."

I jumped a little as the big ship's targeting lasers turned to me. I could feel the red dots crawling along my nose cone and windscreen like maggots on rotten food. "WAS SHE ATTEMPTING TO EXTORT FROM YOU?" roared the speakers.

I met Kay's uncomprehending gaze in the communication monitor. "Er," I began. "Well. I wouldn't say that. We were. We were talking. Like she said. With our mouths . . ."

"WE LISTENED IN ON YOUR ENTIRE CONVERSATION," interjected the big ship brutally.

"Oh," said Kay. "Um. Well. I suppose I could see how some people might think there was a mildly extort-y quality to the banter . . ."

The big ship opened fire with a barrage of lasers and torpedoes in a gigantic cylinder of red-and-white death. Lightspeed Kay's ship attempted to take evasive action and had managed to move a good ten or twelve inches before the stream hit. She only had time to open her mouth in terror before her image on my communicator screen was replaced by the logo of my service provider and a short message thanking me for my custom.

After a few noisy moments, the attack ended. When the after-images had faded, nothing remained of Lightspeed Kay's ship but a little rainbow of scorched hull fragments arcing across space like a smear of butter on burnt toast.

The big ship hadn't moved an inch. Not even a token strafing manoeuvre for dramatic effect. This had not been a dogfight. This had been a cold and surgical deletion of a person from the fabric of the universe.

"CARRY ON, CITIZEN," boomed the victorious ship.

It was only then I noticed that I was clutching the seat of my chair so hard that my fingertips had pierced right through the faux leather and into the foam. "What the plying hell?!" I forced out.

Apparently, the pilot of the bigger ship was still patching into my internal comms. "NO ONE SHOULD HAVE TO LIVE IN FEAR OF PIRACY," they replied.

"You didn't have to blow her up!"

"PIRACY IS AGAINST THE STAR-PILOT CODE." A dangerous pause. "DO YOU FOLLOW THE STAR-PILOT CODE?"

I could feel the tracking lasers running over me again. I instinctively threw up my hands, then felt foolish for doing so. "Yes! Of course I do! Which star-pilot code?"

There was another dangerous pause. I was debating whether or not to start flashing my life before my eyes when I heard a strange fluttering roar that I think was caused by the speaker sighing into the mic. "WE WILL SEND YOU A LINK TO OUR WEBSITE. YOU CAN GO."

There was something about the volume of the voice that made one unconsciously want to obey it. Which was probably why my first instinct after the big ship drifted away was to run to the toilet.

TEN

I resumed my journey to Salvation Station in a daze, expecting at any moment for that huge ship to come looming up again and decide that it was offended by the discarded sandwich wrappers on the floor of my bridge, or whatever, and blow me out of the sky.

After a few hours passed, my emotions were able to climb down to a manageable level, and my thoughts turned to rational matters, rather than the desire to tunnel inside the nearest wall with my fingernails. The text-based communication system was still open, displaying the website link that the ship had sent just before it left. I gave it a click.

The site that it yielded was minimalist, just a column of red bullet points, with the emphasis on "bullet." Each one began with a couple of words in bolded block capitals, as if you were supposed to be smashing your fist into your palm as you said each one aloud.

- **WE BELIEVE** *that star pilots must be a force for good in the universe.*

- ***WE BELIEVE*** *that nobody should have to live in fear of piracy and evildoers.*
- ***WE BELIEVE*** *that star pilots have a duty to protect lesser beings and civilians.*

It went on like that. One totally inarguable, if somewhat dramatically phrased, platitude after another. It was the kind of credo star pilots had always lived by but no one had actually bothered to write down, because it was mostly common sense.

- ***WE BELIEVE*** *that no star pilot should cause harm to lesser beings by interfering with their natural development.*

I winced as I thought about the Biskottis again. Okay, maybe there were a few occasions in the life of a star pilot that made it difficult to adhere—absolutely, one hundred percent—to common sense rules, but life had a way of getting complicated. That was also common sense.

After scrolling up and down the page a couple of times, I noticed a very small link at the bottom that simply read *Forums*. I gave it a click and found myself diverted to what looked like the main forum of the Jacques McKeown fan community. I caught a glimpse of seven or eight hot takes on my spectacular outing as an imposter and hurriedly closed the window.

I didn't know what to make of any of this. I pushed it out of my mind and focussed on the road ahead, because Salvation Station was coming into visual range.

The scanner hadn't been exaggerating. The place was an absolute hum of activity. The gigantic polished bicycle bell that was the station itself provided the backdrop to swarms of star-pilot ships moving about in all directions, like a school building during playtime. A constant stream of ships of all sizes and shapes came and went from the main docking bay. Clusters of ships dotted nearby space, some flying in formation, some in playful mock dogfights, some just holding position in tight conversational groups, possibly to compare wingspans.

There were a lot of old star-pilot ships, some that I recognised, but a lot of new ones, too. I hadn't expected Salvation Station to be thriving this well. Robert Blaze's dream of a star-pilot-themed tourist oasis in the middle of the Black had been realised.

My screen lit up with a very professionally designed welcome menu as the *Neverdie* entered the range for basic comms. As I waited for a turn to enter the docking bay, I flipped through a few pages of guff relating to the "mission" of Salvation Sector and the noble traditions of star piloting, and was about to move on from a list of stores and services available on the station when one of the entries caught my eye.

"Frobisher's Flight Jackets, Tailor, and Dry Cleaning Emporium," I read aloud. "You crafty bracket."

So my old friend Flat-Earth Frobisher had abandoned Ritsuko City as well. That made sense. With all the star pilots gone, the residents of Ritsuko would have little use for his expertise in cleaning Matrovian fenleech phlegm out of the lapels of a flight jacket. I clicked the *Contact Now* link, and my short-range communicator came to life again.

This time, the screen was filled with the heartening image of a flabby ear. "Frobisher's Flight Jackets?"

"Video call, Frobisher," I hinted.

The camera spun wildly around, and I found myself addressing most of Frobisher's face. He'd put on a bit of weight, and apparently his wife had convinced him he'd look handsome with a thin goatee beard, possibly to make up for his vanishing jawline. "Hell-oh my god. Is that you?"

"Hi, Frobisher," I said. "How's the wife?"

"Man, I was just thinking I'd probably never hear from you again. What do you need?"

Just seeing Frobisher was doing a lot to ease my anxiety. It almost seemed like no time had passed since we had last been in his shop near Ritsuko spaceport, chatting over some gently soiled long johns. I shrugged. "Nothing in particular. I just saw you were here, so I thought I'd see how you were doing . . ."

"Whoa." His eyes popped, and he held out a warning hand as if I'd just hopped nonchalantly onto the handrail of a very high bridge. "Are you at Salvation? Tell me you're not at Salvation."

"Uh, I'm not at Salvation," I said uneasily. "Not yet, anyway. I'm in the queue for the docking bay."

"Man!" Frobisher's face flab jiggled, and then his image became darker, so I assumed he'd sprinted into some private corner for fear of being noticed. "You cannot be here. You seriously cannot be here right now. The news from Ritsuko's just come in. You and the whole Jacques McKeown mess. It's not safe for you."

"Not safe? Don't tell me there are pilots still holding a grudge." Resentment toward Jacques McKeown had been endemic before I had redistributed his wealth to them. And anyway, now that it had turned out I wasn't Jacques McKeown after all, they had even less to gripe about.

"Yeah, pilots aren't going to be the problem," said Frobisher cryptically. "Why did you even come here?"

"I need to talk to Warden," I said. I switched back to the welcome site and scrolled through a few pages. "I'd ping her on comms, but I'm not seeing a direct contact address."

"No, I guess there wouldn't be." He stared worriedly at some point offscreen, thinking as quickly as he could. "Okay. Dock, but stay on your ship. I'll meet you there. I've got an idea."

ELEVEN

Half an hour later, Frobisher and I emerged from the docking bay onto the main concourse of Salvation Station, carrying a cardboard box between us, which Frobisher had hastily filled with a sewing machine and various items of wet laundry.

"Yes, thank you again for helping me with this delivery, Cousin Zanzibar," he said loudly.

I was wearing a flat cap pulled low over my eyes and a large false moustache. "Ees no prob-lem," I said, screwing up my face to give my nostrils a momentary break from the itchy carpet fibres. "I am always happy to asseest—plying hairy trac-holes."

A number of sights had provoked that outburst. We had stepped into the grand entrance plaza that was the massive jewel on the gaudy engagement ring of the concourse, and just like the station's exterior, it was absolutely thriving. We were at the bottom of a three-storey shopping mall ringed with stores, service counters, and small eateries, every one of them teeming with life. The shopkeepers, managers, and bartenders were all old star pilots, holding court in the centre of their domains, while the lower-level employees flanking them were mostly under thirty, their eyes filled with eagerness and . . . my mind blanked on the word for a moment. Oh yes, that was it. Hope.

But the main thing that made me stop short was the plaza's centrepiece, directly underneath the magnificent viewing dome: a twenty-foot bronze statue with one arm upraised to the twinkling heavens and feet planted a heroically doint-distressing distance apart.

A statue . . . of me.

I've been told I have a fairly generic star pilot sort of face, but there was no mistaking it. The statue wore a perfect duplicate of the flight jacket I used to wear and was holding the exact kind of blaster I used to own. The plaque on the trapezoidal plinth read JACQUES MCKEOWN: HERO OF SPACE.

"Yeah," said Frobisher, when he saw my mouth hanging wide enough to admit a Raimian treefly. "So you can see why you shouldn't be around here right now. Since the news came out, people aren't sure how they feel about Jacques McKeown. They've been talking about sanding the face off, making it more abstract. You know, Tomb of the Unknown Star Pilot sort of thing."

"But . . . why'd they put up a plying statue in the first place?!" They'd even immortalized my preferred brand of sneakers.

Frobisher gave me a condescending smile. "You remember how you saved this whole place once, right?"

"Twice," I said with a hint of reproach.

"Right. Well, after the second time, with Terrorgorn, you remember how that made galactic news for a while? After that, a lot more people started showing up here. Younger people. McKeown fans. Wanting to see this place where McKeown had his big showdown." He waggled his eyebrows at the statue. "You knew Blaze. He was a pragmatist. He didn't see any harm in . . . playing up to them, a bit."

A twenty-foot bronze statue felt like more than "a bit." I'd hazard that it was drifting more into the realm of "quite a bit." But I'd picked up on his use of the past tense. "So Blaze really is dead?"

Frobisher dropped his gaze sadly. "Yeah. It was just his time. And he passed away happy. Knowing the legacy he'd left behind." He met my questioning look. "When Jacques McKeown—I mean, when *you* weren't writing any new books, all his fans hanging around here started getting their star-pilot stories straight from the source."

My eye was drawn to a snack stand not far from the base of the statue, where a star pilot in an apron—I thought it might have been Dick Dynamite—was telling a story about some dogfight he'd been part of, illustrating his words with ketchup and mustard bottles. A young couple in identical Salvation Sector T-shirts hung on his every word with glimmering eyes.

"Then some of them started buying their own ships, to join in the battle re-enactments," said Frobisher, with a hint of pride. "Then a few of those asked to get in on the security patrols . . . long story short, it's like there's a whole new generation of star pilots, thanks to you."

A whole new generation of star pilots, I repeated inside my head. My mind flashed back to the ship that had destroyed Lightspeed Kay, and that insistent online manifesto, red on black, like blood spattered across the void. "Frobisher . . ."

"There's Ms. Warden's office, through there," he said, pointing.

Warden had always aspired to occupy power-behind-the-throne sorts of roles, so it was fitting that I would absolutely not have noticed the door if it hadn't been pointed out. It was part of a narrow section of wall between two elaborate storefronts, painted the calming insipid yellow of a mental asylum. Nothing even as dynamic as a No Admittance sign.

Beyond it was a narrow, unadorned corridor, terminating in another door and a small waiting area where a number of individuals seemed to be milling about. "She's down there?" I asked.

There was no reply. Frobisher had very subtly let the door close behind me and toddled off to take care of some business of his own. Once again, I was alone. I squared my shoulders and walked.

The little antechamber at the end of the hallway contained a secretary's desk, behind which sat Pippa, a woman I'd seen before in my previous encounters with Salvation Station, but who had never played a large enough role for my memory to supply a surname.

"Look, for the last time," she said, addressing the two people in front of her desk, "you need to make an appointment. The administrator's time is very tightly scheduled."

"But I've captured a pirate!" said the person directly in front of her, a short individual whose gender was inscrutable. They couldn't have been older than thirty, chubby, in spectacles and a spotless flight jacket, with a snub-nosed laser pistol aimed at the taller person next to them.

"I keep telling you, I'm not actually a pirate," said Bigbeard the pirate. He was still wearing the false beard and eyepatch. "Pippa. Tell them."

"I must bring him before the administrator to be brought to justice," said the small star pilot, their posture perfectly straight, their chest puffed out.

"Alright, great," said Pippa, who was staring at her personal terminal and hadn't been listening. "Take a seat, and she'll see you when she has a moment."

Bigbeard took a seat. He attempted to reach for a magazine, but the small star pilot shook their gun, alarmed, so he sat back and folded his arms.

"Yes?" said Pippa, addressing me.

I waited a moment for some glimmer of recognition to appear in her eyes, but apparently the false moustache was successfully throwing her off. "Hello," I said, putting on a completely indistinct accent. "I'm Ms. Warden's next appointment."

Pippa peered at her screen. "You're the Vengorbonian ambassador?"

"Yes!" I said immediately. "I'm freelance."

Her prolonged, withering stare was interrupted by the voice of Warden, bursting forth from Pippa's desk console. "Just let him in, Pippa."

She pointed needlessly to the door, less than six feet away. "The administrator will see you now."

I offered a round of reassuring smiles to her, Bigbeard, and Bigbeard's captor, then pushed through the door. A moment later, my head went straight into a floating holographic display that fizzled stimulatingly as it passed through my hypothalamus. I ducked to the side, only to jam my face straight into another one. I took refuge in the corner by the door.

Warden was sitting on a comfortable swivel chair in the centre of an office that had been cleared of all other furniture except a nondescript coffee dispenser in the corner, surrounded by soiled paper cups. On the floor between her legs was a holographic projection computer, just like the one I used to have in my apartment, with about nineteen tabs open. Warden was working them like an omnidirectional conductor for an orchestra of electronic ghosts.

She looked like she'd had a chance to tidy her appearance up since I'd last seen her on my ansible screen. She wore a clean white blouse and grey pants, and her hair was again immaculately held back with the power of an industrial clamp.

"Had a feeling you would be coming in person," she said, not looking away from her email. "I've allotted you four minutes."

"Nice to know what I'm worth," I said. She didn't reply. "Fine. Just tell me who Jacques McKeown really is, and we can use the other three minutes to snipe at each other."

"I would have thought you'd be glad to be free of his responsibilities," she said, swatting a tab aside and moving to another with a dismissive flick of the wrist. She had infused that last word with a healthy dose of scorn.

"I probably would be. If he wasn't trying to kill me."

She finally looked me in the eye, interested. She made a very elaborate gesture with one forearm, and the various hovering screens between us moved aside, framing me in a humming blue archway. "What happened?"

"He blew up my apartment."

Before replying, she carefully scrutinized my face for flecks of foam around my mouth. "In Ritsuko City?"

"Obviously. Why?"

"Because Jacques McKeown isn't in Ritsuko City," she said, recrossing her legs. "He hasn't been for some time."

"Look, I didn't come here for more plying hints," I barked, clenching my fists by my sides. The effect was diminished a little by the false moustache I'd forgotten to remove. "Just tell me who he is, or tell me you don't want to tell me, and we can stop wasting each other's time."

"Implying our time is of equal value." She sniffed and turned partially in her seat to poke at one of the screens like it was a kitten mewling for attention. "What can you do for me in return for this intelligence?"

I took a step forward to dodge another tab as it flew past my head. "Don't start with this trac."

"What 'trac'? A perfectly normal business relationship? Did you expect me to tell you for old time's sake?"

I bit my lip and counted to five. "You realize it was because of you that I ended up stuck pretending to be him?"

"And what a torturous lifestyle it was, I'm sure," she sniped on automatic, before taking a moment to think about it. Her fingers paused. "Is that how you see it, Mr. Pierce? I don't recall coming to your apartment every day to put you in an armlock until you agreed to continue being Jacques McKeown."

I turned to the door. "You know what? Forget it. I'm gonna go do something I'd rather be doing. Like hammering nails through my feet."

"Don't you want to hear the job I have in mind?" She leaned back on her chair luxuriously as she threw the question out. "It's an easy one."

I stopped, but I didn't turn. "Uh huh."

"Just reconnaissance. Checking up on something."

"I know what reconnaissance is," I spat.

"A fleet of vessels gathering in the western region of Salvation Sector. I would like someone to assess them. Preferably some third party less likely to draw suspicion. Enter scanning range and report on numbers, vessel types, and movements."

She was talking about the fleet I'd seen on the scanner when I'd first arrived in the sector. Evidently, she didn't have enough star-piloting know-how to recognise a battle formation when she saw one. I stopped short of mentioning any of this, in case it might sound like I was agreeing to something. "Uh huh."

"No need to put yourself in danger. No need to talk to any of them. Just scan and leave. And then you can know who Jacques McKeown is."

She was being weirdly persistent. She was good at masking her feelings behind a brick wall of smarmy contempt, but something about this fleet was rattling her. Was she trying to seem in control? Was that what all this business with the computer was about?

"Who he is, and where he is?" I negotiated, suddenly intrigued.

"You'll already know where he is," she teased. "Do we have a deal?"

"No promises. Where's the fleet now?"

"It . . ."

She paused for so long I felt moved to check that she hadn't dropped dead, mid-sentence, from a sudden brain aneurysm, to the delight of a grateful universe. But sadly not. She had paused on one of her many tabs, and a furrow in her brow was deepening rapidly.

"It?" I prompted.

"It's not there," she said, mostly to herself. "I mean, they've moved from the position I was monitoring." She riffled through her virtual filing cabinet.

"You'd better monitor a few other positions," I suggested.

Her cool demeanour acquired a snarl-shaped crack. "That is exactly what I—"

She froze as she inspected one of several tabs displaying scan reports from outlying regions of the sector. For a few seconds, the only movement in the room was the slow enlarging of her eyes.

Then she stood up so quickly that her swivel chair flew back and upset her nest of coffee cups. With several amusingly elaborate sweeping gestures, she transferred all her holographic tabs to her personal tablet as if stuffing laundry into a machine. Then she swept straight past me through the door. I was only just able to hop aside in time.

"Pippa, call a general assembly," she said, not slowing down. "Everyone who can fly a ship or hold a gun. In the main plaza. Now."

"What's going on?" I asked. Warden was in high heels, and I was still jogging to keep up.

"Ms. Administrator!" piped a high-pitched voice. It was the plump star pilot in the waiting area. "I have captured a pirate! I demand that he face justice!" They pulled Bigbeard to his feet, keeping the gun trained on his midsection.

"Ms. Warden, just tell them," moaned Bigbeard. "They've been pulling me around for three hours."

Warden ignored them both and kept marching, so I, the chubby star pilot, and Bigbeard found ourselves hurrying along in her wake like remoras trying to reconnect with their favourite shark. She slapped the door aside as she entered the public concourse, and another nimble dodge allowed me to get through it before it swung back and smashed Bigbeard in the face.

The plaza was already filling up with Salvation Station's resident retirees and their personal entourages of fans. Which I thought was impressive, as it had only been moments since Warden had issued the assembly order, but then I saw that they were all staring upwards. I looked up, rooted to the spot right next to Warden.

It was true; the battle fleet had moved and was now directly outside Salvation Station. There must have been at least thirty ships, all different shapes and colours, but all big enough to match the ship that had blown up Lightspeed Kay. They hung unmoving over the plaza's huge dome like Yowgan sneercats inspecting a pond full of Blorronian blobfish.

"You were right," I said quietly. "That was a pretty easy reconnaissance. Who's Jacques McKeown?"

TWELVE

The stillness was broken when the door behind us flew open again.

"Excuse me!" came the high-pitched voice of Bigbeard's captor. "I am trying to bring this pirate to justice!"

Warden stopped gaping upwards like she was waiting to catch a snowflake and zeroed in on the nearest person. "Do we recognise any of them?"

He was one of the veteran star pilots, a tall and scrawny figure with silver at the temples. "Uh. No. I've never seen ships like those before."

"What ships are currently docked here?"

The old pilot looked at her with alarm. "Uh. Nothing that could take on that."

"They're blockading the docking bay," announced another star pilot, running into the plaza. "Haven't fired any weapons, yet. But no response to communication, either."

"Are the station's defences ready?" asked Warden.

"Oh, yes, ma'am," said the newcomer. "We've got someone on every turret just waiting to pick a target."

"Hm."

Gradually the hum and bustle of the station's gathering personnel died down, and every single one of them fell silent, hypnotized by the anticipation. The only sound was an eerie rhythmic creaking caused by a roomful of trigger fingers simultaneously twitching.

"Ms. Administrator!" squawked the bespectacled star pilot again, making a lot of people jump. "I demand justice!"

"This is not the best time," said Warden through her teeth.

"But I have caught a pirate!"

"That's not a pirate, that's one of us," said Warden.

The little star pilot's gun hand shook as Bigbeard displayed his hands expectantly. "One of you?"

"Yes. Please be quiet now."

The expression on the face of Bigbeard's captor changed rapidly. The earnestness vanished from the eyes, and the mouth flattened into a hard line. Their posture relaxed. The hand holding the gun went down and the other hand came up, holding some kind of rectangular communication device. "Confirmation," they said. "They're with the pirates."

A lot of things happened in quick succession. First, several of the ships in the fleet fired their weapons. Not as a continuous barrage, in which Salvation Station would have held up as well as soft cheese under a grater. Each ship fired only once, hitting a specific target with surgical precision. The lights immediately died. Several voices in the darkness yelled in surprise as the floor shook. In the distance came the sound of large numbers of inexpensive souvenirs falling to the floor.

At the same time, I heard a large door being forced open, the firing of plasma guns, then the high-pitched *whizz* of people abseiling down ropes, all accompanied by a backing track of multiple boots on polished floor.

Then, the sound of fighting, coming from multiple directions at once. The rustling of flight jackets, the smack of fists, the groans of whatever was being smacked by the fists. I was still trying to adjust to the dark when something that felt like a hand grabbed my shoulder and something that felt like a rifle butt smashed into the back of my head.

The universe became a swirling, indecipherable fog of noise and swimming stars, culminating in two twin supernovae of sudden pain when something shoved me down and my kneecaps struck the tile floor. My hands were grabbed and placed behind my head, and someone wiggled a blaster pistol in my field of vision to signal that I could expect to see a lot more of it if I didn't behave.

When the lights came up again, a large percentage of the established crowd were now also on their knees and being held at blasterpoint. Most of the ones holding guns were men and women in black combat gear and riot helmets, although there wasn't much uniformity in their outfits, as if they'd all been told to show up in whatever they had that was black. Some were in black turtlenecks, some in leather jackets, and I could see at least one in a T-shirt whose presumably hilarious slogan had been covered with black duct tape.

But a good half of the people who were holding guns and still on their feet were twentysomething star pilot fans who I had seen around the station in the last hour or so. The glitter of hero worship in their eyes was now replaced with determined frowns as they aimed the laser pointers on their guns squarely at the heads of the veteran star pilots they had so recently been buttering up.

So these invaders had had people on the inside the whole time. I was quietly impressed by the efficiency of this assault. Still woozy from the blow to the head, I made a mental note to give them five stars when I got around to writing up a review for *What Terrorist* magazine.

I could see Warden just in front of me, also on her knees but trying to affect an air of noble dignity in defeat, which quickly disappeared when the group of invaders in front of her parted and someone with a decidedly leader-like bearing strode forward.

He was well over six feet tall and wearing a skintight red-and-blue flight suit with a white star on the chest, accessorised with armour plates that most people would use to exaggerate their muscles, but in his case were more like tiny hubcaps on a bulldozer. On his head was a shielded helmet with much of an eagle's beak about the design of its visor, and around his waist was a matching gun-belt loaded with two plasma blasters.

He stopped directly in front of Warden, looking right down the beak of his helmet in disdain, then slowly drew one of his guns and held it against Warden's forehead. Her face turned the colour of an Espositan snowbeetle.

"Bang! You're dead," he said aloud, bending his elbow back with pretend recoil. He put his back to her and addressed the room, returning his unfired gun to his belt. "Imagine if this had been for real. Alright, let them all up."

The guns went away. Warden was the first on her feet, red with rage and humiliation. That seemed to break the spell for everyone else, and they slowly rose, nonplussed. I opted to remain on my knees for the moment, just to show that I wasn't the sort of person to be swayed by peer pressure.

"What is the meaning of this?!" demanded Warden. Which surprised me, because I'd never heard anyone actually *say* that.

"We just wanted to demonstrate something," said the man nonchalantly. "Star piloting is over. Robert

Blaze is dead. Jacques McKeown is a fake. And every other star pilot put together couldn't do a thing to stop a direct assault upon their home."

"That was your point?!" said Warden venomously. "We know all that! This isn't a fortress, it's a resort! We know star piloting is over!"

"But it doesn't have to be." The man took off his helmet.

I'd been toying with the idea of getting up off my knees, but when I saw that face, all my energy disappeared, and I deflated like a soufflé under the cold tap. It had taken me a moment to recognise him, but once I had mentally greased up his hair, and imagined acne instead of designer stubble, as well as big, unflattering plastic spectacles instead of the severe, rectangular lenses that now perched on his nose like a vulture on a rock, there was no mistaking him.

"Daniel," breathed Warden, realising at the same time I did. "Daniel Henderson?"

Anger registered at the corners of Daniel's mouth as he acknowledged his name. The last I had seen him, he'd been a scrawny youth in his late teens, bent over the corpse of his father with a solemn look on his face. A solemn look I now realised was masking the kind of searing rage that can sustain a person through the several million press-ups he must have done between then and now. "Ms. Warden," he replied.

"What do you want?" she asked.

"I'm here to turn star piloting into what it was always meant to be." He was walking slowly in circles as he spoke, clasping his hands behind his back and inspecting the décor with a pout of distaste.

"You can't just burst in here and—"

"Sidney?" interrupted Daniel, looking to the chubby star pilot who had given the invasion signal. "We had confirmation?"

"She confirmed that the pirate we found was working on behalf of the station," said Sidney smugly, still covering Bigbeard with their gun.

Of all the distressed and unhappy people in the grand plaza at that moment, Bigbeard was the one who looked the most absolutely done with today. There were tears of frustration in his eyes. "I'm not. Actually. A pirate! It's just a stupid act we do for tourists . . ."

Daniel Henderson strode slowly up to him, his feet striking the floor with each step hard enough to make Bigbeard flinch. He leaned in until they were practically nose to nose, then yanked off the false beard. "We know," he said witheringly. "We know you and your accomplice were putting on an act. We also know that your accomplice then attempted to extort money from the visiting ship that was your audience. Do you deny it?"

"Extort?" Bigbeard looked to Warden for support, but Warden was keeping her gaze pinned on Daniel.

"No, it was just . . . we ask for donations! We have to . . . Ms. Warden!"

"You see what she's turned you into?" said Daniel loudly, breaking off and addressing the room. "She's blinded you all with flash and flattery. Blinded you to what you've become. You are the pirates of Salvation Sector. You are the oppressors. And we have come here to oust a tyrant."

Warden scoffed at the absurdity, but stopped short when no one else joined in. Daniel's followers were murmuring in agreement, and while the crew and residents of Salvation Station were silent, none of them were leaping boldly to Warden's defence. Knowing her way of doing things, I assumed there were a number of points in Salvation's management structure that had been stewing in resentment for some time.

Instead, Warden raised an eyebrow and folded her arms, apparently opting for her preferred strategy of smarmy contempt. "You intend to oust an oppressive tyrant by tyrannically oppressing us?"

"We *intend*," snapped Daniel, stomping into her personal space, "to liberate this sector. We will save you all from your enslavement to this . . . inane nostalgia for something that never existed. We are the new generation. The true star pilots. We live by the credo that the fake star pilots only pretended to respect: fight for justice and protect the weak."

Warden still looked unimpressed, probably noting as I was that Daniel's vision was lacking certain important details in the logistical department, but after a nervous glance around at the watchful assembly, she attempted a different tack. "Daniel," she said in her best attempt at a soft, understanding voice. "I know you hold us responsible for what happened to your father—"

"My father was a criminal!" raged Daniel, red veins bulging in his throat. "He deserved everything he got! And you're just like him. A massive ego corrupting every innocent person it touches. So"—he placed his hands on his hips, both to intimidate and to keep his hands ready for a pistol draw—"do you intend to fight us?"

It was as Warden's eyes narrowed that one of my many irritating inner voices decided it was time to be heard. *Hey! I've just realised where we are!* it chirped. *We're on Salvation Station, and we're about to be in the middle of a battle between star pilots and pirates! Where has that scenario come up before?*

"Whoa!" I yelled, jumping to my feet as Warden opened her mouth to reply.

I had acted mainly out of reflex action, but after a startled pause, I decided there was no other recourse but to keep following my instincts. I ran into the space between them, holding out pacifying hands. Then I started and hopped back a step when I realised I was in the direct line of fire.

"Let's not do anything silly!" I suggested. "We're all civilized people. Descending to violence is just a little bit passé, isn't it."

"It already descended into violence when he and his minions attacked the station," pointed out Warden, her anger tempered with confusion and the usual healthy dose of derision for me. She turned her eyes back to Daniel. "And if you want a real fight, then we will be happy to oblige."

"Yes!" I said, spinning on my heel to address Daniel. "And what a titanic legal fight it will be. Oh boy, I hope you've got some good lawyers, because she's fully prepared to keep this dragging through the courts until your beard goes down to those very impressive guns in your belt."

Daniel's eyebrows clashed in a train wreck of bafflement. He didn't seem to have recognised me. This was more like the Daniel I knew. He'd never been much of an intellectual powerhouse, and no amount of press-ups could change that. "What courts? There aren't any courts in the Black!" His brows unmeshed and the spark of zealotry returned to his eyes. "Strength is the only authority out here. Strength that must be used to protect the weak."

"Exactly!" I said, desperately trying not to let my confidence drop. "And look at her. You've got fifty pounds on her, and she hasn't even got a gun. So who's the big strong oppressor here, hm?"

I'd been flying by the seat of my pants, but from the look on Daniel's face, I was on the precipice of getting through to him. Right up until the moment Warden spoke again.

"I have an entire sector full of armed star pilots ready to fight," she said.

"And it's a good thing it won't come to that!" I said quickly.

Daniel took a slow step away and stood before the ranks of his black-clad soldiers. "Let's make our position clear. Star pilots of Salvation Station. All of you who would lay down your lives for Penelope Warden and her vision for this sector, stand behind her now."

It was extraordinary; I'd spent a large percentage of my life crossing the vacuum of space, and yet I'd never seen anything quite so empty as the section of floor directly behind Warden in the moments that followed. It was like everyone who had been standing there had all quietly departed without making a sound or visibly moving their legs. She looked from blank face to blank face, and staring at shoes swiftly became the most popular activity in the room.

Daniel raised his arms in a gesture that was halfway between a sarcastic shrug and a "Tada!" "You have no power anymore, Ms. Warden. Your mandate died with Robert Blaze. This is our galaxy now."

Warden maintained her unimpressed raised eyebrow, but it seemed to be struggling under the weight. Her expression was frozen, and the fingers around her tablet were turning white at the knuckles. I could practically feel the increase in temperature around her.

"I think it's decided," said Daniel after the silence had drawn on long enough to prove his point a few times over. "You will be permitted to leave, but after twenty-four hours, you will be arrested if you come within the boundaries of Salvation Sector again."

Finally, Warden broke eye contact to glance down at her tablet. "Very well." Her voice was the only part of her that wasn't vibrating slightly.

Something like relief washed over Daniel. His posture relaxed, and his goofy smile brought back a lot of his younger self. He turned to the room and threw up his hands. "Today we turn a new page in star piloting!" he declared, and a cheer went up in reply.

The tense stillness in the room evaporated. Daniel's crew hugged and congratulated each other. The veteran star pilots and members of the station crew who hadn't been in on this tried to look optimistic, but they kept making fearful glances to the still unmoving Warden.

As the hubbub rose and his army moved on to the logistics of regime change, Daniel came over to Warden as if he'd just come off stage at an awards ceremony and was looking for feedback on his speech. "Phew. Yeah, we've had people on the inside for weeks, actually. You probably noticed no one was manning the defence systems. Just glad we could do this without violence, you know?"

Warden was staring at her tablet. Her fingertips idly brushed the surface, as if literally turning the page Daniel had mentioned. She gave a little cough. "If I may raise a small administrative issue?" she said.

Daniel smiled. "Yes?"

Her tablet smashed into his face.

THIRTEEN

Many tense hours later, when I was back on the *Neverdie* and speeding away from Salvation Station, I was overcome with a dizzying sensation of relief. While I had been on the station, there had still been a chance that some fresh conflict would bubble up between the residents and their new overseers, but now that I was out and on course for the sector's trebuchet gate, all my concerns evaporated.

I'd done it. I'd cheated death. I'd been at the right place, at the right time, and in almost exactly the right situation, and the prophecy of my death had whizzed straight past its deadline. I'd wiped the smile off Jacques McKeown's face in an impish parting torrent of urine. Whatever the bracket had been planning must have been thrown off course by Daniel's surprise assault.

True, I still had plenty of lingering concerns, but the removal of what had been an anxious burden for years was like finally taking off my shoes after a twenty-four-hour flight, and for the moment I couldn't focus on anything but the sense of blissful peace.

After pausing to enjoy it, I took a leisurely glance around the cockpit. I reached up and straightened the fuzzy dice. I reset the take-off settings. I tightened a couple of nuts. I dealt with that annoying squeak in the seat's swivel function. I arranged the empty paper cups into a pleasing little pyramid. At that point, I finally realised that I was deliberately stalling for time. I sighed. Time to see how Warden was doing.

I found her in the room that, depending on the occasion, served as the passenger cabin, the communal area, the meeting room, and the galley, if the kettle was plugged in. I was expecting her to be on her feet, plotting with her tablet, pacing back and forth, generally so wound up with anger and tension that a simple pat on the shoulder would have made her entire muscular system ping off her skeleton like an elastic band.

In actuality, she was sitting slumped across the hard metal sofa with a hand over her eyes, one sensible shoe hanging off, and her tablet lying forgotten on the floor. The sight of it added a strange droplet of concern to the vast lake of satisfaction I was feeling.

"Few hours to the trebuchet gate," I said, standing in the doorway.

She didn't reply, or even move. But I was in too good a mood to go away without provoking a reaction.

"Suppose things could've gone a lot worse," I said, probing. "Nice of them to let us just leave. Especially after you broke his nose and everything."

Finally, I dredged some words out of her. "He took over my station with a platoon of armed men," she said into her palm, "but *my* violence wasn't justified?"

"If it's any consolation, he probably won't run the station very well. Fighting for justice and to protect the weak is nice and all, but it won't mean a whole lot when the hot dog suppliers need paying."

"Yes, I'm aware," she spat. "So I get to say 'I told you so' while everything I spent years working for falls apart. That makes it all better. Hooray."

I made a decision. I stepped into the room and retrieved a bottle from one of the wall cabinets. "Drink?" I said, wiggling it.

The hand came away to reveal one tired, bemused eye. "What is it?"

I examined the unlabelled metallic bottle. "I don't know," I admitted. "Found it in the engine room. Had a swig and didn't go blind."

"Fine."

I poured an appropriately small measure into one of my dented metal cups. She downed it in one gulp, then sat hunched over, holding the empty cup in both hands and staring at the last remaining droplets. "It was the smile."

I poured one for myself. "Come again?"

"The way he smiled. That's why I broke his nose. It was the same way his father smiled. Just before I . . ." She waved the cup.

"Blew off his leg?" I supplied.

"That same smile," she said, apparently in a trance. "That smile that says, everything you've slaved for and stressed for means less than nothing to me."

I coughed. "Er. Thanks for letting me know your trigger. Rest assured, smiling is absolutely the last thing on my mind whenever I'm around you."

She sat back again, tucking one knee up to her chin. "If you're just going to gloat, Mr. Pierce, then leave me alone."

I dropped into the vacant chair, releasing a grunt of frustration as my posterior hit home. "I'm not gloating! Trac. What's with the prickly attitude?" I felt moved to qualify that question swiftly when she stabbed me in place with a look. "I mean, all the time, not just now your life's plied up. It's been like this since the moment we met. Why do you hate me so much?"

She crossed her legs and held her nose high. "I think you flatter yourself in assuming that I think about you at all."

I took a sip, and a tingly chemical sensation ran pleasantly up my sinuses. "See, that would be an example of the kind of thing you say to the face of someone you hate."

"Mr. Pierce, don't—"

She stopped mid-sentence and slumped back in her seat, as if the battery in her automatic spite machine had suddenly died. She waggled her cup, and I obediently splashed in another serving of whatever-it-was.

"You remind me of my sister," she said after a sip and a few steadying breaths. Then she lapsed into silence again, exhausted by the effort.

"O-kay. Anything in particular, or do I not want to know?"

"My parents . . . had very high expectations," she continued, talking into her cup of liquid therapist again. "Private schools. No going out with friends. Anything less than straight As meant tutors all summer. But I had a younger sister, Claudette. And because they had put all their expectations on me, they didn't have quite as many for her. I was the achiever. She was . . . she was the ornament."

I hadn't expected this. It was like I'd been idly seeing if it was possible to turn on a rusty tap by randomly throwing empty cans at it, and now the sink was slowly overflowing. I just nodded and stared.

"She could get any grades and go to parties all summer," said Warden, these presumably long-harboured words rolling out of her as if on a conveyor belt. "She could go out as much as she wanted. I wasn't allowed to even think about going near boys. She got married at nineteen to a junior executive at my father's company."

She drained her cup again. My hand was already shooting out to refill it even before she did the waggle.

"She made a speech at her wedding," Warden growled, using the same intonation with which someone might say "burnt down my home village and killed my karate master." "She pointed me out. Talked about all the brilliant achievements I'd made in my career. Then she pointed to her husband and said she had gotten the same results with her special skills, as well. And then."

"And then?"

Warden swallowed hard. "She smiled."

"Ouch."

The hardest part seemed to be over. She leaned back, and the rest of the story plopped out of her like the placenta after a difficult birth. "Not long after that, I applied for a top job at Mr. Henderson's company. It was one of my father's biggest rivals, and I knew it would horrify him. I didn't know it was also a front for Henderson's criminal organization, but when I found that out"—she looked away—"that made it even better. Just picturing the looks on my parents' faces . . ."

"So, hang on, go back a bit," I said as her pause extended. "You're saying that you don't like me because you think I have it easier than you?"

"What?" She snapped out of her reverie in an instant, tightening up her body language. "No! It's because you—" Just as quickly, she stopped talking and deflated again. It was like watching a puppet fight with its last uncut string. She drained her cup and blew out her cheeks. "Malcolm Sturb is Jacques McKeown."

The words hit me like the first droplets of icy water that indicate an upcoming avalanche. I slowly stood up, moved behind my chair, pushed it a few inches closer with an obnoxious grinding sound, sat back down, dusted off my knees, coughed, then spoke. "You plying what?"

"Malcolm Sturb is Jacques McKeown," she said, emphasising each syllable spitefully. "That's what you wanted, isn't it. That's what this whole interrogation is aimed at."

I stood up again. I decided that pacing around the room was the best approach, as there weren't enough things within arm's reach of the chair that I felt I could easily break. "Malcolm Sturb?" I repeated. "My Malcolm Sturb? My old arch-nemesis? The cyborg nerd? That Malcolm Sturb?"

"If you would think about it," said Warden curtly, "he fits all of the facts."

"I know!" I roared. "I had nothing to do but think about this for three years! I know he fits most of the facts! He was a fugitive, so he couldn't collect the royalties. He knew a lot of star-pilot stories because he'd been duffed up in a lot of them." I paused to wipe away the little curtain of froth my mouth had developed. "But you said you were only *pretty certain* I had met Jacques McKeown."

"So?"

"So! You knew plying well I'd met Malcolm Sturb. You were there on Cantrabargid."

Her eyes flicked back in memory. "Yes. And if you'll recall, Robert Blaze had turned Cantrabargid into one of his theme park attractions. So at that time I wasn't certain the Malcolm Sturb we met hadn't merely been a dedicated method actor."

I stared her down, fists clenched at my sides. "But you knew he was the real Malcolm Sturb later, didn't you," I said, gently vibrating as I thought aloud. "When you made me work with him on that heist. You knew plying well I was three plying feet from Jacques McKeown the whole time."

"Mr. Pierce, don't ascribe some paranoid motive to . . ."

It happened again. She turned her nose up and began some withering put-down or terribly logical argument that would make me feel like a stupid dog barking at a cat on a fence, but then she just gave up. Her shoulders fell, and her facial features unpinched themselves and gazed sadly at the floor.

"Of course," she muttered. "I put you together with Jacques McKeown because it gave me a perverse satisfaction to think of how you would react if you knew. Because that is the kind of person I am."

"Oh really?!" I said, hands on hips.

"Yes."

She looked so pathetic it was impossible to keep my energy up. It was like trying to play keepy-uppy with a deflated balloon. I flopped into my seat again.

"God. So much trac that could've been avoided if you'd just blown your sister's leg off."

She did a very bad job of disguising her sudden explosion of laughter as a cough.

"You know where we have to go now, don't you," I said when she had resumed her gloomy silence.

"Yes." She sighed. "To a hole. That we can crawl into and die."

"To where Malcolm Sturb is." I tented my fingers in front of my face. "The Oniris Venture recon ship at the edge of known space. Where he works now."

She lifted her arm off her face and frowned at me. "Why? What does it matter?"

"He wrote that plying book about me. He blew up my apartment. I can't crawl into a hole and die until I can be sure he's not going to come along and drop in a bunker buster. I just need to . . . straighten things out. One way or another."

I followed Warden's gaze as it flicked down to my midsection, and I noticed that I had been subconsciously punching my palm.

"I suppose that makes sense," she said. "For you."

I stood. "Right then. Let's go."

"Go where? I thought you said the trebuchet gate was hours away?"

I picked up the bottle. "Let's go . . . see if there's any more of this."

FOURTEEN

Oniris Venture was a public company with a somewhat overfunded PR department, so the locations of their vessels were no secret. I set the autopilot to keep seeking and activating trebuchet gates until we were nearing the last reported position of Sturb's assigned ship, the OSS *Ponce de Leon*, more commonly shortened to the Oniris *Leon*. The practice of shortening it to the Oniris *Ponce* had been swiftly nipped in the bud by Oniris head office.

My memories of the rest of the evening are foggy, as are those of the night, and the following day, so I can only assume I successfully found more drinkable fluids about the ship. I have very distinct memories of the trebuchet jumps, because each time I had to hold my breath and clench my sphincter in case we were about to die, but the *Neverdie* held together. And even though I was hurled around the cabin each time, I'd been taking enough muscle relaxant that nothing was seriously damaged.

So the hours passed mostly as a grey fog, broken up by the occasional red splatter of mortal terror, all swirling around the pudgy face of Malcolm "Jacques McKeown" Sturb. While he was a comfortable fit for what little I knew about the real Jacques McKeown, and Warden didn't have any particular reason to lie anymore, something about this revelation didn't quite click into place.

I think it was that Jacques McKeown's novels had been an absolute phenomenon in their day. They had enjoyed almost universal popularity and had indirectly caused at least one riot. I had to admit, they were page-turners. And being able to write something like that requires a certain amount of emotional intelligence. Some degree of sympathy for how normal people think. And that wasn't a quality that came to mind when I thought of Malcolm Sturb, the weirdo tech nerd who had spent his peak years enslaving people into a cybernetic hive mind while he sat around in one mouldy basement after another, gradually reducing the galaxy's supply of ruffled barbecue-flavour potato chips.

These thoughts dissolved into a deep black lake of sleep, from which I was rudely dredged awake by the distant sound of the proximity alert. The several duplicates of my passenger-cabin ceiling gradually came into focus and swam together to form one, and when the headache hit the bridge of my nose like the peck of a Gagravargian rhinostrich, I decided that was more than enough exertion for one morning.

The insistent squeaking of the computer alert made it impossible to fall back unconscious, though, so I tried to get up. Worryingly, I couldn't. My arms and legs refused to move. Was I paralysed? Had it somehow not been the smartest move to go about the ship drinking random chemicals?

I looked down. There was the answer. I couldn't move because I was pinned down by the spread-eagled form of Warden. The two of us were stretched across the couch, and everything we had been wearing was stretched across the chair.

"Oh," I said.

She glanced up, giving me that familiar unimpressed look through curtains of unkempt hair. "Oh," she echoed, as her head flopped back down.

"Traditionally," I said after a prolonged silence in which neither of us moved, "this is the part where we both scream in horror and race each other to the shower to scrub ourselves."

I felt her shoulders briefly tense as she made the merest possible effort to lift herself, then gave up. "I can't be bothered."

"No, I can see that." I cast a look around. "Let's just file this under 'never to be spoken of again.'"

She sighed into my armpit. "Urgh. Are you afraid of the gossip magazines? You don't matter. I don't matter. Who cares."

In her own mind, she was at rock bottom. And that thought made me feel mildly offended, because rock bottom for her was apparently still on top of me.

I twitched the muscles in my chest and shoulders the way I'd slap my thighs to indicate that I was about to get off public transport and the person in the aisle seat should probably plying move. "I need to see what that is," I said as the proximity alert squeaked again. "Uh. Just in case we're about to be creamed by a rogue asteroid."

She continued not moving in silence for a few seconds, weighing up the pros and cons of death by random space hazards versus continuing to exist, then clicked her tongue and pushed herself off me with a sound like the last two slices of ham being peeled apart.

I kept my eyes squarely on the ceiling as she moved about the room, and when I sensed that she had left the cabin, I gathered my own garments. They had been thrown around in crumpled piles, which at least confirmed that nobody had been operating with any degree of rational thought at the time they were removed. I restored myself to something approximating decency, then headed up the steps to the cockpit.

Warden was standing in the corner, pretending to inspect some disconnected gauges on the wall. She was back in her office attire, which had also become less than pristine from its experience on my cabin floor. She looked like an opened Christmas present after its wrapping had been inexpertly reapplied by a sneaky child.

I took the pilot's seat, reached my hands out for the control sticks, glanced at the view outside, then froze with my hands still splayed out like startled crabs.

We were within visual range of the Oniris *Leon*, which wasn't difficult, because it was huge. It had to be, to incorporate everything that was needed for deep-space recon in this day and age. The smaller part was the actual ship, which by itself was nothing to sniff at, needing enough facilities to support a crew of about fifty people living and working around the clock.

Attached to the ship's belly—in the sense that a boat is attached to a barnacle—was an impossibly vast partial cylinder that housed the portable trebuchet gate. The whole effect was reminiscent of a lobster sitting on top of a section of industrial sewage pipe, and the *Neverdie* was a speck of plankton flitting about its legs.

The process of mapping uncharted space, like virtually every field of human endeavour, had been revolutionised by quantum tunnelling. In the old days it was a slow, tedious field of research sought out only by people who could genuinely get excited about different varieties of rock. They'd all pile into one big science station that would crawl into unknown space like a turd sliding down a toilet bowl and write down everything they found. Which, space being space, was about ninety-nine percent trac all.

Today, deep space recon was conducted by ships like the Oniris *Leon*, which, along with its portable trebuchet gate, carried a stock of large quantunnel rings that were threaded onto the lobster's pincers. The idea was, the gate would be used to fire quantunnel exits nauseatingly long distances into unknown space, and then long range scanning drones would be sent through to sniff around for interesting things, like inhabitable planets and alien war fleets. If any were found, crewed expeditions would be sent through to catalogue it all and stake a claim on anything Oniris considered valuable.

It was a life of prolonged, peaceful sitting around, documenting things and piloting remote drones, broken up by the odd burst of excitement. Small wonder that it was a popular lifestyle for retired star pilots, as it was basically the interstellar equivalent of fishing. As I flew the *Neverdie* alongside the trebuchet cylinder to get a better look at the propulsion systems, I was only half-aware that I was salivating.

Warden snapped me out of it. "What, exactly, is the plan, Mr. Pierce?" she said, the majesty and grandeur of the Oniris *Leon* bouncing off her like a peacock flying into an armoured window.

That was an infuriatingly good question. I suppose my initial idea had been to wait for the *Neverdie*'s computer to handshake with the *Leon*'s network, pull down a list of internal contacts, find Sturb's number in the IT department, then give him a call and invite him to come aboard so that I could deck him in the face. On reflection, a more subtle approach might have been the smarter way to close in on the lair of a murderous, possibly deranged apartment exploder.

Moot point, anyway, as the handshake didn't seem to be happening. I tapped the computer controls and confirmed that my system was sending the ping out well enough, but nothing was coming back. The *Leon*'s network was blocking all external communication.

"This . . . can't be right. Why would a scientific research ship be cutting itself off from the outside world?"

"I take it you've never worked in academia," said Warden. I gave her a look that fully expressed the extent of my appreciation for her sassy mode, and she rolled her eyes. "Perhaps some kind of quarantine is in effect?"

"If there were, they'd be broadcasting something." I slapped a few random buttons in case I'd left the system on some unhelpful setting or other. "Something along the lines of 'go forth and multiply right now.' Not nothing at all."

"Then I don't know." She headed sulkily for the door. "I don't know why you're doing any of this. I don't know why I bothered to get out of bed."

I listened to her grumble her way back down the steps. She really was in the most despondent place I'd ever seen her. I resolved to wrap up my business with Sturb quickly so I could have a chance to relish it.

Still no reaction from the *Leon*. The *Neverdie* must have been close enough to show up on their systems. On a hunch, I switched to the short-range scanner and made a sweep for any kind of movement in the vicinity. There was the *Leon*, still sitting there unmoving on the screen like a jam stain I'd forgotten to clean off. But as I watched, a fragment broke off, looped around, and seemed to be closing in.

It had emerged from the region where the lobster met the sewage pipe, the little cluster of facilities that included the docking bays. So it must have been one of the fleet of small ship-to-surface runabouts the *Leon* used to shuttle personnel to interesting discoveries.

Shortly, it was in visual range, a streamlined streak of silver grey, and just to emphasise the sheer vastness of the *Leon*, still larger than the *Neverdie*, although it had none of the character. It was all unbroken curves and harsh lines, like a robotic eel. If the *Neverdie* was an antique landscape painting, this ship was a simplistic corporate logo that some graphic-design company would probably charge two billion euroyen for.

It decelerated and inched warily toward me, regarding me like a child seeing something crawl out from under a rock. But while the pilot wasn't exactly throwing out the welcome mat, the ship's computer was a different story. My system finally received a handshake, and as the two computers found a connection, I was able to send a hail.

The reply came very quickly. Apparently, this was what my new friend had been waiting for. The first thing they did when their face appeared on the communicator was sigh with relief so hard that the screen immediately fogged up.

"Hello?" I said, squinting to make out their features. The fog cleared a little, but the speaker was too close to the camera, and all I could see was an eye and part of a nose. They must have been hunched over their console in a state of exhaustion.

"Are you normal?" they panted.

That caught me off guard. It was a strange, and telling, question to open with. It felt like a trap. In my experience being interviewed as Jacques McKeown, this was the sort of question people asked when they were planning to take my answer out of context to make me sound like a racist. "Uh. I . . . well. It depends on how you define 'normal,' I suppose."

"You're normal," he replied, relieved. "Request permission to come aboard."

"Why? What's going on?" Warden's use of the word "quarantine" flashed into my head. "Is something going on on the mothership? Is it Pogulon Pox? My air cyclers can't handle that amount of methane right now."

"No, it's nothing like that," said the eye and the nose quickly. "There are no infectious pathogens on the shuttle. Do a complete bioscan if you don't believe me."

I winced and glanced over my cockpit systems. It had been a long time since I had last bioscanned anything. I wasn't sure the *Neverdie* even had the hardware for it, but he didn't know that, and he wouldn't have told me to do it if he wasn't on the level. Probably.

"So why isn't the mothership responding to comms?" I asked.

The eye darted up, left, right, and down before the reply. "It's just an issue with the communications system. That's why I had to come and greet you. But now I need to come aboard."

"Why?"

More darting around. The eye wasn't giving me much to go on, but it was conveying a whole spectrum of complex feeling. "There's . . . a fault. On this shuttle. It could go at any moment. I require assistance to repair it. Can I extend my umbilical now?"

"I . . . suppose." After an expectant pause, I slowly turned the *Neverdie* around so that her airlock was facing the other ship. I kept one eye squarely on the rear-view camera as the white cylinder of the umbilical unfolded from the underbelly of the shuttle, trying not to think about metaphors.

When the near end of the umbilical was securely fastened around the *Neverdie*'s airlock, and the cheerful green light appeared to indicate that it was fully sealed, the pilot of the other ship sped out of view and disconnected the call without so much as a "See you in a bit."

I headed down the steps to my airlock door, moving with baffled caution, and took a moment to poke my head into the passenger cabin. Warden was lying on the couch again, with her arm over her eyes and one foot up on the table.

"Someone from the *Leon* is coming aboard. Don't really know why. He seemed a bit desperate."

Warden didn't so much as twitch a muscle. "'Kay," she said after a pause.

"He's probably carrying a hideous alien infection and planning to kill us all or something," I added.

A slightly longer pause. "'Kay."

By then, someone was knocking on the airlock door. After double-checking to make sure the umbilical was pressurised—I'd made that mistake before—I hit the access release, the door slid open with a hiss, and the other pilot practically fell into the *Neverdie*.

He was an older man, almost completely bald with a ring of white hair connecting his ears, wearing a bulky engineering jumpsuit and sweating quite profusely. His eyelids flickered as I tried to hold his torso upright.

"Reactor," he said through panting breaths. "Reactor leak."

"What?" I glanced up the umbilical to the closed doors of the shuttle's airlock in the distance. "Did you shut it down?"

He shook his head, screwing up his eyes in shame.

My heart began to race. If the shuttle's onboard power generator was leaking dumdeedium, and if that spreading dumdeedium cloud found a spark, then there'd be no more shuttle, no more *Neverdie*, and a hole in the side of the *Leon* big enough to admit a Zergolian slobwhale. A big one.

"I'll get us out of range," I said, making to head for the cockpit.

With an astonishing burst of strength, he leapt up and grabbed my shoulders. "No!" he barked, his eyes wild and staring. "There were others!"

I glanced at the open umbilical. "Other people?"

He shook me. "Please! You've got to save them! There's still time to shut the reactor down!"

With that, his energy reserves were finally depleted, and he slumped to the floor, hands still clawed from trying to grab my lapels. I looked from him to the airlock, flustered, then let my instincts take over.

I grabbed the sides of the airlock door and hurled myself into the umbilical's absence of gravity, shooting along the flexible tube with one arm outstretched like a superhero, before I flew into the shuttle's airlock and immediately crumpled to the floor as I entered the ship's atmosphere and the graviton field demanded to know what the hell I thought I was doing.

It only occurred to me as I was activating the airlock cycle that I should probably protect myself from the reactor leak. I didn't immediately see an emergency air-filter kit, and the inner door was already hissing hydraulically, so in a last-ditch spur of action, I grabbed the bottom of my shirt and yanked it over my head.

As soon as the door was wide enough, I burst through into the shuttle's engine room, my action stance hopefully not let down too much by my exposed belly.

What I found in there was a set of pristine engine cylinders connected to a well-maintained reactor. And maybe it was the shirt on my head and having to examine my surroundings through a buttonhole, but I could have sworn there was absolutely nothing wrong at all. There were no visible cracks in the reactor housing and a complete absence of red warning lights. The background hum was low and stable, broken by the occasional chirrup of an automated readout indicating its unmitigated fine-ness.

I pulled my shirt back down, confused, and noticed a flat-screen monitor on the nearby wall, *Press for Diagnostic Summary* emblazoned across it in unconcerned, white-on-blue letters. Already I was impressed by the technological sophistication of Oniris's facilities; the diagnostic system in the

Neverdie consisted of nine different gauges in different parts of the engine room and a bell tied to a piece of string that warned me when to duck.

I jabbed at the screen with two fingers, and a report screen appeared, strewn with engine diagrams all pointing to the conclusion that everything was tickety-boo. There was the graphic representing the reactor, and the little dots representing power were flowing uninterrupted into the box representing the battery, apparently just having a great old time in there.

As I was inspecting the diagrams, an icon of an envelope appeared in the corner with a red exclamation mark. Clicking it brought up some kind of internal text messaging system for the local network. The first unread entry, sitting atop a stack of dry engineering reports, was titled "FAO: Dashford Pierce." With a heart full of dread, I tapped it.

This is the beginning of your message history with Neverdie.

Neverdie: Hello. This is Penelope Warden.

Neverdie: That man you let onboard wishes you to know that there was no reactor leak and nobody else on his ship.

Neverdie: He has also hijacked the *Neverdie*.

Neverdie: We will be flying out of network range soon.

Neverdie: He wishes to extend the following sentiment:

Neverdie: "Sorry. I can't. Sorry. Sorry. I just can't."

Neverdie: Please respond promptly if you have questions.

FIFTEEN

My first stop was back to the airlock, where I could look through the Plexiglass windows in the inner door and confirm for myself that the *Neverdie* was missing, and that the far end of the shuttle's umbilical was flapping loosely back and forth like the trunk of a Jarettian plopephant in a roomful of buns.

I noticed later that the airlock door had acquired a number of dents and scratches that corresponded to the bruises and torn fingernails on my hands, so I must have spent time venting some heartfelt feelings, but on a conscious level, I was strangely calm about all this. I drifted back through the shuttle's engine room in a daze, as if my head was full of helium and cotton wool. After all, I couldn't get angry about losing my ship, apartment, possessions, money, and entire identity. I'd need to have an identity before I could figure out if it was one that got angry about that kind of thing.

I spent the first hour or so of my new, blank existence exploring the shuttle, trying to stay focussed on mentally cataloguing all of its contents. There was a cockpit and an engine room, the obvious staples, decked out in smooth grey-and-white panelling that hadn't yet faded to shades of grimy beige. That, combined with the uncanny neatness and pleasant rubbery smell, pointed to a ship that hadn't seen much actual use.

There was a large passenger cabin with row upon row of plush seating, consistent with this being a transport shuttle, but there was an extra room between it and the cockpit that gave me reason for pause. It looked like a conference room, with a circular black table surrounded by the kind of severe, high-backed chairs normally reserved for terribly important people. It all seemed a bit upmarket for a shuttle that would mainly be ferrying teams of dirt-spackled engineers and scientists with more concern for higher intellectual pursuits than personal hygiene. There was even an expensive monitor covering most of a wall, probably for briefings, and a minifridge full of that classy kind of sparkling water that thinks anything with more than two molecules of fruit flavouring might as well be served out of a sippy cup.

I helped myself to a bottle and took another look around the cockpit, which was surprisingly roomy, in that I could fully pull the reclining pilot's chair forward without my head bouncing off the windscreen. A few flicks around the various diagnostic and communication menus on the pilot's terminal, and I found what I was looking for in the corner of the main status screen. The ship's ident code: "OC-PDL-002."

"OC" for "Oniris Corporation." "PDL" for *Ponce de Leon*. And "002," as in, this was the first ship added to the *Leon*'s mission fleet other than the *Leon* itself. That meant that this wasn't just any old shuttle. This was the captain's shuttle.

So the posh briefing room made a lot more sense. But surely the only person with the authority to release the captain's personal yacht would be . . .

A lot of realizations crashed into my mind at once, so it took a few moments to spread them out and put them in order. I thought back to the man who had taken my ship. I thought about how his flushed complexion might not have been a sign of dumdeedium poisoning. That might merely have been a sign that he was a bit hot. Furthermore, I thought about how his boiler suit had seemed strangely bulky. Perhaps he was hot because he was wearing a boiler suit on top of something else. Like, for example, a captain's uniform.

I leaned back in the pilot's seat and stroked my chin. He'd certainly seemed a bit old for an engineer. And a bit too clean-shaven to be a scientist. Actually, now that I thought about it, he had borne a striking resemblance to the captain on that TV show, *Trailspacers*. Commanders of deep-space recon vessels certainly had a type.

My eye fell to the unmoving bulk of the *Leon* filling most of the view ahead of the shuttle. I still wasn't being allowed access to the main ship's internal network. So, what kind of scenario results in a total lockdown and the captain himself fleeing, alone and in disguise, at the first sign of an escape route? Nothing encouraging sprang to mind. Maybe the rest of the crew were hunting him for plying the wrong officer's wife, but that was the absolute best-case scenario. Just as likely that everyone had been infected with Gavrarvian swamp syphilis and this had been his only chance to escape with his doints undissolved.

I rested my head on one hand and eyeballed the rear-view camera, which was reporting nothing but infinite blackness and a complete absence of *Neverdies*. The fact was, I had no option except to investigate the *Leon*. The shuttle was only designed for small-scale trips through quantunnels, not prolonged interstellar jaunts.

And even if that hadn't been the case, there was nowhere else to go. I couldn't start browsing real estate listings for the most affordable hole to crawl into and die until I'd gotten to the bottom of things with Malcolm Sturb. Thus resolved, if not over the moon about it, I took the helm and steered the shuttle back up toward the docking bay.

With the surface of the gigantic cylinder below me, and the complex form of the *Leon*'s inhabited structure looming overhead, I had the sensation of being a tiny fish trying to pass between the open jaws of a sleeping Orlockian trapgator. The docking bay airlock yawned open like a hungry gullet, just as the captain had left it.

I slid the shuttle into the airlock and brought it to a halt with the braking jets, mindful that there was absolutely no way I wasn't being observed, as long as there was anything on the ship to do the observing. I assumed I would need to make some kind of docking request, or at least stand in front of a window and wave, but the airlock began to cycle automatically as soon as I was clear of the exterior door.

Fortunately, I remembered to extend the landing legs just as the *Leon*'s internal atmosphere rushed in and the graviton particles began pulling everything floor-ward. The ship dropped a few feet and landed with a sharp judder that rattled my teeth and knocked my bottle of pretentious water out of the pilot's cup holder.

I waited a few minutes, but nothing came into the docking bay to greet me and nobody came on comms, so I made the decision to go look for someone. I passed through the airlock and descended the docking ramp to the floor of the bay, shivering with the typically disquieting sensation of passing from one artificial atmosphere to a different one.

I stood still and glanced around. The bay was almost perfectly cube-shaped, with a set of double doors providing the only person-sized exit. Large though the room was, it was only big enough for one ship to fit comfortably.

So this was the captain's private docking bay to go with the captain's private shuttle. Seemed like a needless luxury, especially on an industrial ship; I'd have thought most captains would be happy with a private parking space in the main bay. Maybe this was so that when the captain had to make some really unpopular decision, like taking the chocolate out of the vending machines, he could be assured the docking bay workers wouldn't kick dents in his nacelles or draw penises on the windscreen.

I walked to the exit doors, my shoes clanging loudly against the metal floor and echoing from the furthest corners of the room, and wondered again why I hadn't seen a single sign of life. Out of nowhere, I remembered that there was an ancient tradition in nautical circles for the captain to be the last person to leave in an evacuation. I think most corporate operations considered that more a piece of friendly, easily dismissed advice than a rule, but it would explain a few things.

So maybe the *Leon* had been evacuated. In which case I should explore it to figure out the reason, and if it wasn't about to explode or give me a harrowing space disease, it would be my civic duty to get comms back online and inform the head office. And help myself to whatever supplies and spare shuttles could be considered adequate recompense.

I made for the double doors. I was feeling a pang of resentment, as I'd been mentally compiling an extensive list of possible explanations for why a battered spacer like me would be piloting the captain's nice clean shuttle, and now no one would get to appreciate them—

The doors slid open, granting access to the engineering bay beyond, and I made startled eye contact with the entire crew of the OSS *Ponce de Leon*.

SIXTEEN

The Oniris Corporation's uniform was a jumpsuit in dark blue, with a collar, shoulder pads, and vertical strip down the torso coloured according to department: pastel blue for engineering, pastel pink for science, pastel yellow for administration and security. I had plenty of opportunity to appreciate its many variations, as the entire crew were arrayed before me in folding chairs.

Judging by the two podiums on either side of the door, I had interrupted some kind of debate. Behind the one on my left was an attractive dark-haired woman in a tight-fitting science uniform. Opposite her was a handsome, well-built young man in large, unflattering spectacles. His uniform was an inverse of everyone else's; his shoulder pads and torso strip were dark blue, while the rest of his shirt was pastel yellow.

Boggling eyes and a half-open mouth weren't part of the Oniris uniform as far as I knew, but one could have easily assumed as much from looking around at this crowd. Instinct seized me before anyone else could gather their thoughts. "Sorry." My voice echoed nicely through the silent bay. "Is this a bad time?"

The two speakers flicked their gazes rapidly between me and each other, mouths open and jaws trembling, both desperately trying to be the first to think of something to say. It was the man in spectacles who won.

"C-captain on deck!" he blurted. Everyone's attention shifted from me to him. His eyes continued flicking anxiously for a few moments before his mouth slapped shut and he saluted. "Captain on deck, I said!"

I was making a spirited attempt to furrow my eyebrows deeper than they had ever furrowed before when I was startled by the voice of the woman behind me.

"Captain on deck!" she repeated, snapping into an identical salute and thrusting her chest out.

With almost perfect simultaneity, the entire crew, humans and the occasional multilimbed alien alike, got to their feet and performed whatever form of salute best suited their individual morphology. The humans bent their elbows. The ones that lacked endoskeletons flopped their topmost limb over whatever passed for their heads. The Omkokian glomcloud in the front row emitted a pleasant vapour with notes of vanilla and obeisance.

"Thank goodness you came back, sir," said the corporate type in glasses. "Doctor Allura and I were just discussing the wisdom of me taking command."

"Oh, is that what we were discussing?" said the apparent Doctor Allura, still saluting but placing her other hand on one hip. "But yes, welcome back aboard, Captain."

"Uh," I said, utterly baffled. I glanced back and forth between them like a hungry dog at a game of hot potato. "I don't . . . I'm not your captain."

"Hey, we all said a lot of things we regret," said Doctor Allura, in a low, empathetic tone. "But I think I speak for Representative Clay and myself when I say that we've learned that you're the only one that can hold this zany crew together, sir."

"Ye-es," added Representative Clay. "You strike the necessary balance between my rational logic and the doctor's emotional approach."

I blinked rapidly. "I . . . I'm sorry, I'm very confused."

"Three cheers for the captain!" cried Allura.

Everyone was still saluting rigidly, so the three subsequent "Hurrahs!" made me feel like I was being hailed by a tree farm. The glomcloud's vapour took on a more excitable tang.

"Can we be at ease, Captain?" asked Clay, in a prompting whisper. His elbow was trembling, and there was a note of pleading in his voice.

"Um. At ease," I said, noncommittally.

The hands came down, but there was very little easing in the room. Everyone remained where they stood, but now they had nothing to do with their hands, and no reason to keep their eyes locked on me. The room became an undulating sea of fidgets and awkward glances.

"O-on an additional note," said Allura, anxiously trying to fill the silence. "I'd just like to add that . . . I . . . learned something today."

"Oh good," said Clay, with a hint of sarcasm.

Allura stared into the middle distance as if looking for the cue card. "I've learned that . . . while we have different approaches to life, you with cold hard facts and me with my . . . female . . . emotions, when we bring them together, we can make a damn good team!"

"Er, yes," said Clay, jumping on a bandwagon now that the water had been tested. "I, too, have newfound respect for your alternative methods. Let's never speak of this again."

Now everyone was trembling like they were desperate for the toilet. A lot of them were staring at me again, and I'd swear there was an element of pleading behind their eyes. I sought through my mind for anything I could remember from the early days of my career when I was a salaried Speedstar pilot. "Er. D-dismissed?" I tried.

It was like the trigger word for an explosive device. In an instant, everyone was making for the doors at the back of the engineering bay. I saw at least one folding chair flung upwards a good ten feet.

"Wait a minute!" I said as Allura and Clay both made to join the flexing mass of bodies that only approximated a queue. "What the hell's going on?"

"We'll see you on the bridge in the morning, Captain," said Allura over her shoulder, faking a yawn. "Sleep well."

"Yes, goodnight," said Clay, competing with her for the fastest speed-walk. Then he stopped and turned. "Your quarters are on deck seven, sir. Out of the lift, turn left, end of the corridor." He made to turn back around, then changed his mind with a jolt of panic. "Uh. Which of course you already knew. I don't know why I said that."

As the crew poured out of the room, I felt the strength in my legs go with them, and I plopped down onto the harsh metal floor. Because a fresh realization had just dropped and added a new ton of questions to a situation that already didn't make the slightest plying sense.

I remembered where I'd seen Doctor Allura before. She was the stock attractive woman who had always been sitting next to the captain in most of the short glimpses of *Trailspacers* I'd seen. I could only confirm it after she turned around and gave me a view of her backside as she walked away, her curves fighting for supremacy with the tightness of her uniform trousers. It was an angle the TV cameras had always favoured.

And that captain. His face grew clearer in my memory. He hadn't just resembled the captain on

Trailspacers. He had been him. The very man. It hadn't hit home at first because I wasn't used to seeing him wearing any facial expression other than dull professionalism.

I didn't know what any of this meant. What I did know was that I had somehow been nominated captain of a ship whose previous captain had fled in abject terror. And something told me it hadn't been because of the food in the mess hall.

SEVENTEEN

I wasn't getting any more out of the crew that evening. Everyone sped to their quarters and locked themselves in, but for a few stragglers I happened upon in the corridors, who all cheerily barked out a quick "Goodnight, Captain!" before speed-walking away faster than most people can sprint.

Exasperated, I ended up at the captain's quarters, which opened up eagerly when I pressed the plate beside the door. I didn't have a key, and I knew my DNA wasn't on file and therefore couldn't have triggered a bioscan, so I took a moment in the doorway to wonder what the ever-plying trac was going on.

The quarters were extremely nice, more so than I'd expected. Space was usually at a premium on a working ship, where the company wants any available room to earn maximum profit, so even captains don't expect more than a hundred square feet and a work desk that doubles as a toilet cistern. The *Leon*'s captain, in contrast, enjoyed a double bed, ensuite bathroom, personal terminal, dining and entertaining area; I'd have mistaken it for one of Ritsuko's fancier hotel rooms if it weren't for the huge picture windows displaying a glorious view of mostly uncharted space. Absolutely not appropriate for a deep-space recon mission.

Although it was very much appropriate for a poorly researched TV show, as was the bright, even lighting running through every single corridor. I stepped up to the captain's personal terminal and opened the internet browser. I had to know whether *Trailspacers* was widely understood to be a documentary.

When the loading icon was still circling after two minutes, I figured I was being blocked by something. That would make sense if external communications were down, but the terminal's clock was still in sync with Galactic Standard Time. So the system was connected to the internet, but it was limiting access. That would usually be because someone was deliberately limiting it.

I sat back in the chair, searching my memory. I'd never heard that *Trailspacers* was based on reality, and most people had the same view. More than once I'd overheard people at Jacques McKeown conventions bemoaning the quality of the scripts, although a Jacques McKeown fan's opinion on writing was about as much use as a hungry toddler's opinion on haute cuisine.

The exhaustion was hanging off my thoughts like overfed puppies from a mother dog's teats. I'd still been hungover and coming off a night of very little sleep when all of this had started, and the captain's double bed was calling to me.

There was one thing I could still do with the ship's terminal, and that was go over the internal network. A small investigation led me to the messaging app, with a dropdown that helpfully provided a complete roster of the crew.

And there he was: Malcolm Enrique Sturb, head of IT. I hadn't lost sight of my original goal. I didn't remember seeing him at the crew meeting, but there had been a lot of faces to take in, and I'd been distracted by my unexpected promotion.

His entry also helpfully included his deck and office number, which I committed to memory. Whatever was going on on the *Leon*, it wasn't my circus, and it wasn't my monkeys. I only had one primate to deal with. First thing in the morning, I'd surprise him in his office, let things fall how they may, then steal whichever shuttle was best suited for interstellar travel and book it to a trebuchet gate. I could be on the *Neverdie*'s trail by lunchtime.

Thus resolved, I had about as comfortable a night's sleep as could be expected in the bed of a stranger I was posing as against my will, then took the time to refresh myself. A shower, a change of clothes, and a handful of energy bars from the minifridge made all the difference. The captain's wardrobe contained nothing but identical uniforms, but having spent the whole night sweating over a senior officer's bedsheets, I was well beyond feeling weird about any of this.

The captain apparently had a slimmer build than average, but everything would be okay as long as the fly button could hold the line against my gut. Still tugging the itchy collar away from my neck and trying not to make any sudden movements that might split a seam, I made my way to the elevator and pressed the button for the science deck.

And then came the first tiny crack that heralded my entire plan falling apart, because the elevator didn't respond. I pressed it a few more times. Nothing. The doors stayed open.

The ventilation system was humming quietly and expectantly in the background, and I began to feel inexplicably judged. I kept hitting random buttons. First with one finger, then two, then with a fist.

Inevitably, another crewmember arrived just as I was about to grab the elevator panel with both hands and start shaking it back and forth like a hysterical soldier in a trench. He was a middle-aged man in an administration uniform, vaguely familiar as a former star pilot I had seen here and there back in Ritsuko, although I didn't know his name.

He showed no sign of recognising me and simply stood beside me in the standard pose of an awkward communal elevator ride, hands behind his back, staring at the ceiling as if that would in some way influence the elevator's movement.

I gave him a token nod, pretended I'd only just arrived myself, and pressed the button for the science deck again. Nothing happened.

I could sense him watching me with interest as I pantomimed hitting the button and making an exaggerated sigh of displeasure. I had to go through the same routine three times, each sigh louder and more exaggerated than the last, before the bracket gave a little cough and spoke.

"Aren't you supposed to be going to the bridge, Captain?" he asked.

I had been very deliberately avoiding the button for the bridge, the bridge being absolutely the last place I wanted to be. I stared at the button in silence as it sat innocently in its housing like a smug cat on the dog's bed.

"I was hoping to get some other things done before work," I muttered, not looking away from the button.

"Ha ha, good joke, sir!" said the crewmember. "The captain always checks in on the bridge before he does anything else in the day. As you know."

His smile was broad and guileless, but there was something manic in his eyes. I took a deep breath and poked the *Bridge* button as lightly as possible, telling myself there was absolutely no reason to expect it to work. Nevertheless, I was unsurprised when it obediently lit up and the elevator began to move.

Maybe some system prevented workers from going to any floor other than their current work assignment. That seemed like it would cause problems in emergency situations, or if someone really needed the toilet, but this was the Oniris Corporation. Bad policy decisions grow like a fungus wherever middle managers gather in one place.

As I stepped onto the bridge, any remaining doubts that I was somehow inside *Trailspacers* evaporated. It was the very set I'd seen in my brief glimpses of the show, the place where most of the action happened. And once again, I noted its complete unsuitability as an operations centre for a deep-space recon vessel. I'd have expected a horseshoe of consoles with five or six technicians hunched over their personal terminals, talking through whatever data was streaming in from the scanners, with at least three donut boxes open.

This bridge was centred around a raised platform with an expensive reclining armchair in which the captain sat like a king on his plying throne, with a couple of lesser seats on either side of it, from which the senior officers were presumably expected to whisper advice. In front of that was a bank of controls for the people who did the actual job of pressing the buttons, and every seat in the room was pointing at a huge viewscreen that was uselessly displaying the empty vacuum directly in front of the *Leon*.

"Captain on the bridge," said Doctor Allura, who was standing to attention by one of the adviser seats. The man with whom I'd shared the elevator politely moved past me to take a seat at one of the helm consoles.

I watched Allura warily as I approached. She had that same desperate look in her eye as everyone else on the ship, but there was a unique tang of anger and self-hatred in the furrows of her brow. She was also the only person I'd seen who went around with her uniform top half unzipped. Maybe that was a privilege reserved for senior officers.

I paused when I reached the captain's chair. The cushioned seat looked clean and comfortable, but sitting on it in front of the bridge crew felt like crossing the final line. I could almost imagine that hidden straps would wrap around me as I sat down, to ensure I could never escape.

"Might be something wrong with the elevator," I said to Allura, watching her reactions carefully. "It wouldn't let me go to the science deck."

"Of course, sir, you needed to be on the bridge," she replied without a blink, as if I'd been complaining that gravity was pointing excessively downwards that morning. "We're going over the scan results from the Nogedom Cluster today, as you know."

Another flicker of desperation in the eyelid. She wouldn't have said that if she didn't know perfectly plying well that I wasn't the same man as the captain who had fled the ship. Clay had said something similar last night. They were all trying to keep up some kind of facade and were all silently pleading with me not to ruin it. But why?

"Okay," I said, keeping my eyes on her as I gingerly lowered myself into the seat. Once I was settled, and nothing was strapping me down or biting my buttocks off, some small part of me felt a thrill from being in the big man's chair. I straightened my posture and affected my most important-sounding voice. "Engage."

"Engage what, Captain?" asked Doctor Allura, after a round of blank looks.

"Engage . . . whatever it is we're doing," I said, with declining confidence.

"Activate long-range scanning probe Epsilon nine," translated Doctor Allura helpfully.

There was a long pause, during which nobody moved, or spoke, or activated any long-range scanning probes, Epsilon or otherwise.

"Epsilon nine," repeated Doctor Allura. I heard a creak of tormented vinyl as she tightened the grip on the arms of her chair. "Helm, please activate the probe."

The ex-star pilot in the right-hand chair did a double take over his shoulder. "Wh—are you talking to me? That's not my job. That's Sparky's job."

"Who?" I asked.

"Cadet Sparky," he added. From the way he was raising his eyebrows and sucking on his lips, it was clear that he was putting a lot of effort into his poker face.

"The second helmsman. As you know," said Allura, not looking at me.

"So where's Cadet Sparky?" I asked.

"Right here." The first helmsman leaned over and rotated the other chair I had taken to be empty, but which I could now see contained a medium-sized golden retriever, curled up in sleep. "Oh. Naughty Cadet Sparky. He's fallen asleep on shift again."

He kicked the base of Sparky's chair, and the dog's eyes opened reproachfully. It slowly rose to a sitting position, yawning and glancing around with unhappy eyes. Someone had attempted to place it in an Oniris administrative uniform, but it had managed to wriggle one paw out.

I looked to Doctor Allura, who was still staring at her hands and had now gone a lurid shade of red. "That's a dog," I pointed out.

She looked at me questioningly. I was still certain she knew I wasn't the real captain, but nevertheless she seemed confused that I was making an issue of this. "Y-yes, Captain, Cadet Sparky is a dog, as you know." We stared at each other for several seconds, and eventually her resolve wore down first. "As . . . as you know, there is no racial prejudice on the *Ponce de Leon*."

"It's not so much a race-prejudice issue as an . . . opposable thumbs issue for me," I said.

"Don't be silly, sir," said Allura, a little more testily. "Cadet Sparky was head of his class at the Oniris Academy. As you know."

I strongly suspected there was no such thing as Oniris Academy. I was pretty sure Oniris only ever hired externally because any in-house education might cut into the CEO bonuses. "Well, tell him to activate the probe, then."

"Are you listening, Cadet Sparky?" said the helmsman. "Activate. Epsilon. Nine."

Cadet Sparky stared gormlessly into the helmsman's eyes for a moment, then thrust a paw out onto the control panel in front of him. Data began streaming down the console monitor screens, which seemed to satisfy everyone. The dog cast its head around, as if expecting a biscuit.

"Report, please," said Doctor Allura when there was a pause in the spew of information.

Cadet Sparky replied with a short woof, then another when it felt anxious about the unimpressed silence that followed.

"Er, he says there are four inhabitable planets within range of the scanner," said the helmsman. "One with an ambient temperature of—"

"That was a woof!" I shouted. "And you're just reading off his screen!"

Everyone in the room flinched except Cadet Sparky, who was now licking the other helmsman's armrest. I saw Allura glance fearfully up and around, as if expecting lightning to strike.

"Are you feeling okay, Captain?" asked the helmsman, with sarcastically exaggerated concern in his voice. "You seem to have forgotten all about one of the most important and respected members of the bridge crew."

"Yes," said Doctor Allura, like an improv comedian seizing a cue. "Perhaps you should visit the medical bay, sir. You seem overstressed."

"I don't—"

"The medical bay on the *science deck*," she stressed, staring me down. Her expression was neutral, but I noticed that her eyes were worryingly bloodshot. "I'm sure the elevator will have been fixed by now. We'll summarize the findings from the scanning probe when you get back."

I nodded, stood, and made my way back to the elevator, moving slowly and uncomfortably under the weight of everyone's eyes. I gave the elevator panel a very serious look before I pressed anything, to let it know that I wasn't going to take any more plying around, and the button for the science deck illuminated on the first try, practically fluttering its eyelashes as it did so.

In the brief moment before the doors fully closed, I saw Doctor Allura bury her face in her hands and the helmsman ask Cadet Sparky to shake paws.

EIGHTEEN

When the elevator doors opened, an illuminated sign hung on the wall of the corridor directly opposite. The way to the right was labelled MEDICAL BAY, while the OFFICE COMPLEX lay in the opposite direction. Even as I was looking at it, the light went off in the OFFICE COMPLEX half of the sign, and the other half somehow grew brighter. Undaunted, I marched left.

As I passed a large set of glass windows looking in on a roomful of desks and cubicles, a crewmember who had been leaning too far back on his chair started at my arrival and fell out of sight with a crash. A similar story played out over and over again as I advanced through the office complex: relaxed crewmembers noticing my presence and leaping to look busy, like I was some terrible spirit of work ethic driving off all the good vibes.

I found the IT department at the end of a long hallway, where a curved reception desk separated the rest of the ship from an untamed jungle of computer terminals, cables, and snack containers. It was the one place I'd seen on the ship that wasn't constantly bathed in clean fluorescent light; the only illumination came from the little glowing LEDs on the electronic equipment. The desk was unmanned, but I noticed a folded sign reading PLEASE TAKE A SEAT AND WAIT FOR A TECHNICIAN TO SEE YOU, so I proceeded to absolutely not do that.

"Hello?" I said, knocking on the top of the desk and scrutinizing the gloomy area beyond.

In response, I heard the rustling sound of someone's fists tightening rapidly around the top of a bag of chips, followed by a few moments of urgent whispering. A nervous eye, ringed with lank, greasy hair, appeared around the side of a wall partition. "Who are you?"

I sighed. There wasn't much point in denying it. "I'm the captain."

The eye quivered. "Are you?"

I frowned. "Apparently."

"S-sorry," stammered the speaker. "The captain doesn't usually come down here. Nobody usually comes down here."

"Is Sturb around?"

The greasy, socially awkward person, who I felt it reasonable to assume at that point was part of Sturb's IT department, gave a little jump of surprise. "Er. Who?"

"Malcolm Sturb," I said patiently. "The head of IT. The captain wants to speak to him."

"Oh. Yeah. Right. I'll . . . I'll see if he's in."

The eye disappeared, and a fresh round of urgent whispering broke out. I couldn't decipher any words, but the emotions behind the hissing ranged from terror to complete incredulity. Finally, one of the whisperers took on a more affirmative tone, as if a plan of action had been agreed upon.

"They're just coming," called the voice.

I jumped when one of the doors behind me flew open. "Hello, sir!" said a bright, high-pitched voice. A female Sostarian ferret with hot-pink fur and a miniature version of an Oniris science uniform scampered out of one of the offices, hurried past me, and took up position on the reception desk. "Sorry to keep you waiting, sir!" she squeaked, rearing up on her hind legs and clasping her front paws together. "How can I help you?"

I stared, then turned and scrutinized the door from which she had emerged, in case anyone else was coming. "Where's Malcolm Sturb?"

"I'm Malcolm Sturb, the head of IT!" replied the ferret. "As you know!"

"No, you're not," I said on impulse.

Her large purple eyes flicked to the side. Her fixed, toothy smile was like a cashew nut stuck in a hairbrush. "Oh, don't worry, sir! Just because I'm a girl doesn't mean I can't keep up with the boys when it comes to knowing things about computers!" She licked her chops nervously. "As you know!"

"I mean, you're physically not Malcolm Sturb, the person," I said.

She was still smiling, but she'd taken on that petrified look that seemed so popular among the *Leon*'s crew. Her little shoulders were shaking and her eyes were darting all around the room as if expecting a large predator to burst from the tall grass. "Of course I am," she quavered. "As you kn—"

"No! Stop that!" I glanced around, trying to see what she was looking for. "Stop saying 'As you know!' *I do not know.* I wasn't even here until—"

Along the length of the corridor behind me, several faces had appeared at windows and around doors to watch the interaction with conspicuous silence. And at that moment, one of the faces struck me as familiar: an older man in a pink science uniform, with a slim, athletic build, grey hair at his temples, and a missing hand . . .

"Derby!" I remembered aloud at full volume, pointing. "Davisham Derby!"

I hadn't meant to look so accusatory, but that was apparently how he'd taken it, because he immediately broke from the cover of his office and pelted down the corridor. I blinked twice, then went after him in a full sprint.

The human traffic in the corridor had become a lot denser, either because the day was wearing on and more people were on shift, or because it would make my life more difficult. I turned sideways to slip between two people arguing over an unrefreshed coffee jug, hopped nimbly over a uniformed Deboxian trailslug who was waiting to use a restroom, and when I sent an administration officer flying into a wall, scattering papers, I used his body to springboard into the next turn. All throughout, I kept the vanishing form of Davisham Derby in the centre of my vision.

Derby had been the third team member in the heist Warden had organized, and he had joined Oniris alongside Malcolm Sturb. There was no way he could deny who I was or who Sturb was, and that was probably why he was running. The *Leon*'s crew had almost gotten me to the point of doubting my own sanity, but the sight of a familiar face was like a glimpse of a fishhook in a murky pond. Something to haul me out of this nonsense and land me in some more understandable fryer.

I lost sight of Derby as he turned a corner into the medical section, and I found myself in a series of sterile laboratories, so white and well-lit that it was hard to tell where the floor became the wall. I stopped near one of several lab benches covered in random glassware and analytical tools, and looked around, but Derby was nowhere to be seen.

I was considering my next move when a man in a science uniform under a lab coat and a very fashionable hairstyle appeared from a section of the white void that apparently contained a door. He was holding a report in one hand and whistling, and when he was close enough to talk, he did a very poor job of pretending that he had only just noticed me. "Oh! Captain! I heard you might be dropping in here this morning. Something to do with failing to recognise Cadet Sparky?"

By now I was determined not to get yanked back into the pond. "Where's Davisham Derby?" I barked, making a threatening step forward.

He met my gaze, nonplussed, then glanced back at where he had come from. "Mr. Derby? The . . . captain wants to talk to you?"

The face of Derby appeared around the door and flashed an absolutely infuriated look at the other scientist. Then it and the rest of Derby entered the room with a nonchalant stride, carrying a tablet. "Captain?"

I checked him up and down. It was definitely him. He might have dropped the tailored suit and most of his posh accent, but his robotic hand was a dead giveaway, and I was still picking up on the last vestige of his old "gentleman thief" act from the way he held his nose high enough to interfere with ceiling fans. "Derby—"

"Actually, I'm glad you came along, sir," said Derby quickly. "We've just made an interesting discovery that I think you should be aware of."

He shoved his tablet under my nose. There was a word-processing app open, into which he had typed two short sentences in extremely large letters: *It's not safe to talk. Play along for now.*

I could tell he was serious, because he'd insisted on using absolutely correct punctuation. I met his gaze over the tablet. A single sweat drop tickled his left eye and made him blink.

Yum, delicious pond water, I thought to myself, as I took a deep breath and said the words, "Consider me informed, Mr. Derby."

"Aye, aye, sir," said Derby breathily, his words mingling with his sigh of relief.

"Anyway, let's get to the bottom of this medical complaint of yours," said the doctor in the lab coat. He read from the paper in his hand. "I'm also hearing from the IT department that you failed to recognise Mr. Sturb?"

"Um. You know what? I'm feeling a lot better. Maybe I'll just go back to my quarters for—"

"Don't be silly, sir," said the doctor haughtily, snapping the report to his side. "You just returned from an expedition. If you've contracted some kind of illness, it's of the utmost importance that we identify it. As you know. Now, do you recognise me?"

"No," I said flatly.

His eyebrows jumped. "Hm. And now you don't even recognise the chief medical officer." He produced a laser pen from his top pocket and held it to my temple for a moment, then pretended some new information had appeared on the papers in his hand. "Yes. I'd say you've contracted some mysterious alien virus that is affecting your ability to recognise faces."

"Are you sure about that, sir?" asked Derby with a sarcastic lack of inflection that gave me warm pangs of familiarity. "Are you sure he hasn't simply lost his memory from a stress injury of some kind?"

"Absolutely not," said the doctor testily, still staring at his paper. "It's a face recognition virus. It may already be spreading." He squinted at Derby's unmoving face.

"I think the memory thing sounds like the more logical explanation," I said tactfully.

"No, it can't possibly be a memory thing," said the doctor through his teeth.

"Why not?"

His eyes met mine with a flare of impatience. "Because we've already done a memory loss episode!"

Instantly, the lights went out. The sudden shift from the bright, even lighting of the medical lab to pitch blackness was like being physically slapped. I tottered back a step, banging my calves on the nearby bench.

"Oh no," said the doctor, in a small, terrified voice.

From all around me, I heard the metallic sounds of sliding doors slamming closed. Then, after a tense silence, the much more ominous sound of a single door sliding open.

"No!" cried the doctor, still invisible and now further away. "Epidemic! That's what I meant to say. We've already had a memory loss epidemic so now . . . so now everyone's immune systems will have . . . wait! Just wait! I can make it make sense—"

There was an unpleasant fleshy thump, and he fell silent. I heard a scuffling and fluttering of clothing as many things in the darkness moved hastily around. Then the doors opened again, and the lights came back up to blinding brightness.

When I had finished blinking away the after-images, I was alone in the laboratory with Davisham Derby and a discarded lab coat, which Derby immediately seized and hurried himself into.

"Um, yes, as I was saying," he said, tapping icons on his tablet. "It sounds like some kind of virus. Here's a small exercise regime to follow, and we'll see how it's progressing in a couple of days. Okay?"

I looked at the tablet he was handing me. To the previous message he had added the words, *Come to the IT department at 10 p.m. Try not to talk to people.*

My shoulders sagged in defeat. I gave him an exhausted look. "Derby, what the plying hell is going on?"

"Oh, ha ha ha, sir," he said with the mournfulness of a eulogy. "This must be a very serious facial recognition virus. I'm not Derby. I'm the chief medical officer." He grimaced. "As you know."

NINETEEN

I spent the rest of the day "convalescing" in "my" quarters. I wasn't sure how convincingly I was supposed to be selling this whole virus story, so just to be safe, I spent several hours sitting up in bed with blankets wrapped around me, mentally going over all my mistakes in life.

I spent some time after that perusing the internal network on the captain's terminal, again. Every single picture of the chief medical officer, from the crew roster to the informational pages on the science department, had been replaced with pictures of Davisham Derby. This didn't entirely surprise me, because by then I had already noticed that the picture of the captain on the welcome page was a picture of me. I was absolutely certain I had never posed for it, because it was smiling.

At ten o'clock in the evening, when the foot traffic in the corridor outside had all but vanished for the night, and I had imbibed a quick energy drink, I made my way back to the IT department.

The office was still as gloomy and apparently deserted as it had been during my last visit, but as

I approached the reception desk, I saw that an area off to the side of the work floor had been cleared of machinery, and a circle of folding chairs had been arranged around a glowing monitor.

Once again, I heard the whispering of the IT department's denizens, and a bloodshot eye under a sweep of greasy hair appeared around the side of a wall divider.

"Derby told me to come here?" I tried, as the silent, uncomprehending boggle continued.

That appeared to satisfy. The eye went away, and a hitherto unnoticed door in the dividing wall opened with eerie slowness until the gap was just wide enough to admit a human, but not so wide that it couldn't be rapidly snapped shut again at the first sign of unnecessary social expectations.

I could almost feel the grease in the atmosphere as I was shown to the circle of chairs by a uniformed creature that I hoped to God was from some unusually hairy alien species, and was surprised to see that Doctor Allura was waiting in one of the seats. She had zipped her uniform up to the neck for once, and was making a conscious effort to sit on the chair in such a way as to keep an absolute minimum amount of her body in contact with it.

"Ah, Captain," said Allura, clasping one knee in both hands. "How nice of you to join us for our daily inventory review."

"Our what?" I asked, not sitting.

Derby, or whatever his name was now, appeared behind me and made his way to the seat opposite Allura's. "Feel free to sit anywhere, Captain." He was maintaining his bored upper-class accent, and from the look on his face, he seemed to think this was an act of defiance. "Everything will become clear. As you know."

I let myself sink into the chair next to his. "Could someone—"

"Shft!" There was suddenly a finger in front of the mouth of everyone else present, and their eyes wore the look of terrified warning that was becoming very familiar.

I sat in sulky silence while the rest of the meeting gathered. Almost all of them were members of the science team, and I recognised a couple as former space villains who, like Malcolm Sturb and Davisham Derby, had ditched the spacer lifestyle in return for some kind of meaning in life. One of the head researchers was Professor Civious, and seeing his gaunt, pallid features in an Oniris science uniform was like meeting Dracula wearing pyjamas.

When all the chairs were filled, Doctor Allura leaned forward and examined the glowing monitor in the centre of the circle, which was displaying a list of information. "Folding chairs," she read aloud. "Two hundred and forty-four."

"Check," said Derby. "Doctor Calbeck was taken today. I've assumed his role."

Allura nodded. "Normal desks. One hundred ninety-seven. Check. I heard. Things are still unstable with the new captain." She gave me an accusatory look that I was almost sure I didn't deserve.

I scowled. "Look, I had no idea—"

"Ah ba ba!" interrupted Allura, before she hastily returned to the screen. "Standing desks. Eighty-two. Check. Wait for me to read out a listing before you say something. It's the only safe way to talk."

"What?"

"Nyeh!" went Derby in frustration, as several other people in the circle flinched in their chairs.

"Tentacle-safe work pits, sixty-one," said Allura quickly, before showing me her palm in an "after you" gesture.

"Check," I said. "What?"

"Holographic computer terminals, one hundred three," said Allura. "Check. Oniris are running some kind of scam on the ship. They're trying to force us to live out these . . . stories, like episodes of a TV show or something. Cup holders. Three hundred sixty-eight."

"Check," said Derby. "Every time something happens that could start an . . . episode, we have to go along with it, or get taken away the way Calbeck was."

"Disposable serviettes, nine thousand five hundred forty-seven," said Allura. "This is the only safe way to talk. If we do it in the middle of something dull, whoever's monitoring us is less likely to pay attention. And they don't monitor the IT department much, anyway."

I glanced over. In the shadows surrounding the circle, one of the IT creatures was tending to the coffee machine with one hand while pulling their ill-fitting uniform trousers back up over their hairy backside with the other. They certainly did not fit the definition of "TV friendly."

"Check," I said, jumping in after Allura recounted the cafeteria's spork supplies. "So this literally is *Trailspacers*, the show? This is how they make it?"

"What?" snapped Allura. "Eight thousand tonnes of dehydrated beef bourguignon, check. What? What show? What's *Trailspacers*?" I waited in patient silence until she went back to the monitor with a grunt of frustration. "Frozen heads of broccoli, nineteen thousand eight hundred fourteen."

"Check, yeah, this is all a TV show in Ritsuko City," I said. "It's really popular. Apparently. I'm assuming you've been cut off from the rest of the galaxy for a while."

The assembled scientists exchanged unhappy glances at this revelation. Doctor Allura silenced the angry murmuring with another entry from the list. "One-pound boxes of instant mashed potato, sixteen thousand nine hundred fourteen."

Everyone in the room besides me went for it, but it was the deep, sepulchral voice of Professor Civious that cut through the rest. "Check. I did not sign up with the Oniris Corporation to be paraded around against my will on some insipid soap opera."

"Why would they do this? It makes no sense!" said a smaller scientist to Civious's right, summarising the general feeling on display in the clamour.

"Vacuum-sealed whole chickens, twelve hundred sixty, check," recited Allura bitterly. "It seems deep-space recon hasn't been earning enough for head office's liking."

"But why do it this way?" said the small, incredulous scientist, looking around as if in free fall and desperately seeking a handhold of sanity. "Why not just tell us they're going to film us for a TV show?"

I shrugged. "Appearance fees?"

"*Stop it!*" shrieked Doctor Allura, flustered and leaning into the screen. "Salt-preserved Vanaxian slughorse legs, two hundred nine, check! Wait for the check, then talk! You're going to get us all disappeared!"

A scientist who had not yet spoken, a gloomy man with hair like a kiwi fruit who had apparently zoned out for most of the discussion, suddenly started. "How long have we had slughorse legs? I've never seen them in the canteen. I love slughorse legs."

"Will you—" Allura made her frustrated grunt again. "One-pound bags of frozen green beans, seventeen thousand three hundred forty-five. Check. Can we focus? We need to do something about Clay. He's the Oniris liaison. He's got to be the one orchestrating all this for them. Tinned pineapple chunks, eleven thousand eight hundred ninety-one."

"Check," said Derby quickly. "But what can we do? The moment we do anything that isn't part of the episode, this ridiculous facial recognition virus concept, we'll be brought down."

"So do it while the episode is happening somewhere else," I thought aloud.

Allura scowled at me. "Tinned fruit cocktail, thirteen thousand four hundred seventy-five. Check. What are you talking about?"

"You say that . . . sorry." I leaned around to look over her shoulder. "Tinned beetroot in juice, however many that says. Check. You say that something's monitoring us for the show, but what if—beetroot? Seriously? Eurgh. But what if something was happening that was distracting the monitor? Like . . . a real banger of an action scene that absolutely had to be in the episode. Someone could tackle Clay somewhere where that wasn't happening."

There was another exchange of glances and grumbling. Apparently this dream team of former evil geniuses hadn't made this particular intellectual leap, but then I'd only just arrived, and my brains hadn't been scrambled by having to communicate while listing breakfast cereal ingredients, or whatever this was. "You really think that would work?" asked the small one.

"I can do the tackling, if you're nervous," I said. "Trust me."

"Trust you?" said Allura with a recoil of disgust, like I'd asked her to help change my bandages after traumatic doint surgery. "We don't know who 'you' are. You—"

The lights came up. It did very little to improve the aesthetics of the IT department. Everybody froze, shoulders hunched and eyes wide, like prison escapees caught by a spotlight. In the distance, I heard a door open.

"I don't know who you are," repeated Allura slowly, using the hasty improviser's classic stalling technique. "Because. Oh my god! I've contracted the facial recognition virus! I don't recognise the captain anymore!" By then, she had fully risen and hastily tugged the zipper of her jumpsuit back down with a wince of disgust.

"Oh no, it's spreading," said Derby, also rising but putting a lot less effort into the performance. "As senior medical officer, I'm declaring a ship-wide pandemic. All personnel must limit direct contact."

He glanced around as if waiting for the thumbs up from a watching Roman emperor. Everyone tensed, but nothing ensued but silence and the occasional blip and bloop of cycling electronics.

"Alright, good meeting," I said as the tension in everyone's muscles gradually drifted away. "Let's go over the main points tomorrow around noon. Assuming we're all who we were today."

TWENTY

I slept as well as I could for the rest of the night, mindful that my every living moment was now part of a never-ending TV audition for the role of continuing to be alive, although if the overhanging dread wanted to keep me up, it would have to get in line behind all the questions I was asking myself. Such as, why the hell was I still here? If Sturb was dead, then my business in the *Leon* was concluded. I could steal a shuttle, set course for the nearest civilized world or outpost, and try to survive long enough to get there by licking the outside of the coolant pipes for moisture.

But I already knew I wasn't going to be doing that. Partly because there was no guarantee I'd even be able to steal a shuttle without earning the wrath of whatever rogue TV producer was in charge. Partly because I couldn't be certain that Sturb was dead, and I'd only have closure after I saw the corpse with my own eyes and inhaled its unique stench of rot and body odour with my own nostrils.

And partly because I felt somewhat responsible, especially after meeting those former space villains that made up the ship's science team. It had, after all, been my idea to recruit ex-evil scientists for the Oniris recon venture. I should probably have sat down and worked out a full accounting of how much of my current situation was entirely my own fault, but I was afraid it would make me depressed.

And the final reason was that my curiosity was piqued. I wanted to get to the bottom of what was happening on the *Leon*. Was Oniris Venture really trying to make extra cash with a TV show full of enslaved, unwilling actors? It didn't add up. It was too creative a scheme for a faceless corporation. It would've been much quicker and easier to harvest everyone's organs.

There hadn't been a chance to hash out the fine details of a plan after the "meeting" had broken up, but I was hoping one of my co-conspirators would improvise something. A small amount of research indicated that Clay's office was in the administration department, not far from the bridge, so I took the elevator to the top deck just before noon.

When I stepped out of the elevator, I almost ran straight into a crewmember in an administration uniform. "Good morning, excuse me," I muttered.

The crewmember stopped short and looked me up and down. He was a thin man with thinning dark hair and an even thinner moustache. "Who are you?" he barked. "Why are you wearing the captain's uniform?"

I froze. "What?"

He pinned me with an accusing glare, then slapped his hands around his face. "Oh no! I've got the facial recognition virus!"

I watched him sprint down the hallway, kicking his legs sarcastically high, until he was out of sight. Between him and Cadet Sparky's handler, it seemed some of the lower-ranked members of the crew weren't taking the situation as seriously as the senior staff, but then none of them were being cast as main characters.

The administration centre was a ring of offices surrounding a break area with a coffee station. I sauntered casually up to the counter and began fiddling with the knobs on the espresso machine as I carefully scrutinized my surroundings.

Part of the office ring was taken up by a labyrinth of desks and terminals, about half of which were occupied by assorted office drones going about whatever tasks still needed attention with the *Leon* locked down for "filming." The rest of the ring consisted of offices for senior administrators, with actual doors, walls, and privacy. Clay's was dead ahead.

And interestingly, right next door, there was one for the captain, with gold trim around the nameplate. I strode over and pretended to brush dust away as I memorised the name.

Captain Jeremy Sturridge, I internalized. I took a gloomy sip of low-quality coffee. It was bad enough being trapped in someone else's life on a bizarre TV show, without also having to be a Sturridge on top of that.

The door had opened automatically on my approach, so I took in the facilities set aside for my use. It wasn't exactly a treasure trove. A modest, practical little office with a yellow streak along the walls to reflect the administration uniform, furnished with a simple desk, chair, and terminal. All clean enough to be fresh out of the flat pack. Most of the captain's work could be done from the bridge or the terminal in his quarters, so this room was probably only for looking busy when the investors visited.

Nevertheless, I took a seat in the chair and confirmed that there was nothing of interest on, in, or around the desk. The only new fact I established was that the chair was plying comfortable. It looked basic enough, all straight lines and curved corners, but the cushion must have had some fancy gel filling that automatically formed custom buttock hollows as if I'd been sitting in it for years.

This was a perk I could get used to. I leaned back, inhaled deeply, and clutched the armrests. And that was how I found the note.

A small scrap of paper had been taped to the underside of the right armrest, with just enough sticking out that my fingers brushed against it. Considering that only the captain's ID could open the office door, it didn't take an evil space scientist to deduce who must have left the note.

I unfolded it, little more than a Post-it with five words, scribbled by someone who was probably in a rush to go hijack some naïve bracket's ship he'd detected nearby: *Don't trust any of them.*

At the very moment I was parsing this, I saw through the open door that Professor Civious had entered the break area. His pink science uniform stood out amidst all the administration yellow like the icing on a slice of birthday cake. A moment later, the smaller scientist from the late-night meeting appeared at his side with head bowed and hands unhappily in pockets.

"You said you believed you had contracted the facial recognition virus?" boomed Civious, loud enough for every person in the entire administration complex to hear, but it was hard to tell if that was his intention.

"Erm, yes," said his companion. In contrast, I practically had to read his lips to understand him. "Whoever you are."

"Well, don't worry," roared Civious, robotically patting him on the shoulder. "I'm sure you will recover as long as you get enough rest and stay . . . hydrated."

He was holding out a plastic cup that was unlike the white paper cups supplied by the coffee station, and which he must have been carrying in his uniform somehow. Even from where I was sitting, I could see that the liquid in it wasn't water; it was a little cloudy and had a head.

The small science officer looked at it with unhappy anticipation. "Erm. Look. I'm having some second thoughts about . . . hydrating."

"Drink," commanded Civious, slightly quieter but still audible to the entire room.

"Alright, I know I said I would." The small scientist eyed the cup and its contents fearfully. "I'm just a little bit concerned about . . . er . . . hygiene."

"You have my absolute assurance," intoned Civious, framing each consonant with severe deliberation, "that it will pass through your system within twenty-four hours and leave no lasting ill effects." He broke his steely eye contact and addressed the room. "As one should expect of water."

The small man heaved a long, shuddering breath, took the cup gingerly in both hands, screwed up his eyes, then tipped the liquid quickly down his throat.

In the moments that followed, when all was silent and unmoving, and the poor man's complexion gradually shifted along a spectrum from pale pink to lobster red, I remembered that yesterday I had asked for a distraction. It occurred to me now that I had failed to be specific, and furthermore that I had asked it of a group of ex-space villains and superscientists who had had precious little chance to exercise their creativity in the last few years. The moment I completed this realization, the scientist's eyes began to glow, and he opened his mouth to belch a jet of magenta flame that he managed to sustain for an impressive twelve seconds.

"Oh no," said Civious, talking extra loud to be heard over the very strange noises that his colleague's throat was producing. "This must be the second stage of the virus."

The flames from the scientist's throat died down, and of course that was the moment when the ship's fire suppression system kicked in, precisely when it wouldn't be any help at all. Torrents of chemically infused water cascaded into the administration centre, sending the crewmembers that had gathered to view the spectacle running for cover.

As the water touched the small scientist, he flinched as if from a hot stove, and then his skin turned an all-new, even more disquieting shade of purple. He wobbled back and forth on his feet a few times, as if trying to psych himself up to jump off a high diving board, then a glistening tentacle burst out of his mouth and split into a flexing, pulsating tree that danced joyfully in the water.

This, I decided, was probably going to be the most distracting moment of the display, or at least I sincerely hoped it would be. It was safe to assume that whatever hidden cameras were in play were firmly directed at it. As the small garden of gelatinous limbs flopped and thrashed around, knocking over chairs and coffee machines, I crept out of my office and slipped through the door to Clay's, staying low and close to the wall in case anyone noticed and tried to involve me in the scene.

Clay's office was virtually identical to mine, with an appropriate number of square feet shaved off to reflect his lower rank. He was sitting behind his desk, staring fearfully at the door. "Captain? What's happening out there?"

I held the door closed as something thumped squelchily against the other side of it. "Nothing. We need to talk."

He certainly had the look of a TV character, in that he was a handsome, square-jawed, tall, muscular man, and with a pair of spectacles and an unflattering haircut, I was supposed to take him for a nebbish middle manager. He adjusted his spectacles and spoke in low, restrained tones. "Of course, Captain. Of what?"

"I'm here to put a stop to this plying TV show business," I hissed, slamming my hands on his desk.

He went very quiet and still, his mouth dropping open in fear. His eyes darted from me to the door several times, as if he were calculating a list of potential escape routes and coming up with nothing. I had him cornered and dead to rights, and he knew it.

Then his tight posture softened, and he leaned in. "Thank goodness. What's the plan?"

I blinked. I drummed the fingers of one hand, still splayed dramatically on his desk. "Um. What do you mean, what's the plan? The plan is to get you to stop doing it."

He recoiled so quickly I heard the squishing sound of his buttocks hitting the gel in his expensive chair. "What? Why would you think *I* was doing it?"

"Because you're the Oniris rep?" I attempted to make a gesture that encompassed the room, its opulence, and the Oniris logo stamped onto absolutely plying everything. "And Oniris are in charge?"

He blinked rapidly as he made a few calculations in his head, then began counting off his fingers. "One. We have been cut off from the Oniris Corporation for months. Two. I have been blocked from my every attempt to re-establish communication. Even the quantunnelling equipment has been disabled. Three. The Oniris Corporation would not turn one of its own ships into a ridiculous TV show when there are countless more efficient ways to exploit us."

This was a subtly different experience to when Warden made me feel stupid. She always did it with a certain relish that made it all the more infuriating. This was more like being assailed with bricks from a computerised brick-tossing machine.

"Who told you that I was the one orchestrating this?" he pressed.

"The . . . science team," I admitted, knowing even as I said it how he would react.

"The science team," he repeated, looking over his glasses. "The same science team that largely consists of former supervillains and mad scientists." There was another wet sound outside, followed by a muffled scream. Clay pointed to the door. "Who are presumably responsible for that. You believed them."

"But . . . Oniris," I said weakly, as all my thought processes turned to confused mush. "Oniris are in charge. Aren't they?"

He leaned forward onto his elbows like a schoolteacher explaining that I had done a very naughty thing. "Oniris are not monitoring the entire crew twenty-four seven, waiting to shut off the lights and disappear people the moment they go off script. Oniris cannot remotely disable the quantum tunnelling systems. The only thing that can do that is the ship's onboard AI."

"The AI?" I repeated dubiously.

Frustrated, he gestured to the terminal built into his desk. "It wasn't me who generated an image of you for the ship's home page!" He held out his muscular arms. "It wasn't me who locked *me* in the gym for a month and wouldn't restore my access codes until I looked like this! The AI controls all of that! And the person who controls the AI is Malcolm Sturb."

"He's been disappeared," I said. "Hasn't he?"

Clay shook his head. "He was the first to go missing. But he didn't go missing the way everyone else goes missing, with the lights going out and something dragging them away. I have surmised that he disappeared of his own accord." He paused to appreciate my baffled expression, then leaned in again. "He's still somewhere in the depths of the IT department. Protecting himself. Because if we can take control of the ship away from him—"

The lights went out.

I should have noticed that the sound outside had died down. Civious's friend must have finished his performance, and the cameras had lost interest in whatever large-scale cleaning operation was taking place out there now.

"Oh goodness," said Clay. I heard him push his chair away from his desk just before the noise of distant slamming doors tolled like funeral bells. "Captain. Whoever you are. Listen. He's not going to kill me. None of the people who have disappeared have been killed. We can tell from internal bioscan. If you find him—"

The door to the office slid open. Again I felt the sensation of multiple things rushing through the blackness around me, and then the thud of something heavy hitting flesh and bone. I staggered about, waving my arms, trying to grab whatever was moving, but I gained nothing for my trouble but a stubbed toe from one of the desk's mounting brackets.

Then the lights came up again, just as I was clutching my foot and trying to decide on the best swear word. I was alone in the office. Clay's chair was gently rotating.

A few moments later, I heard whispering outside the door, and then it opened to admit one of the random bureaucrats I'd seen working in the cubicle farm outside. She made startled eye contact with me, then dashed behind Clay's desk and put on the spectacles that had been lying discarded on its surface.

"Hello, Captain!" she said in an approximation of Clay's accent. "What are you doing in my office?"

I maintained eye contact as I backed daintily out of the room. My foot slid through something wet as I emerged from the door. I fixed my gaze upon the nearest wall and strode determinedly away.

TWENTY-ONE

After a quick stop to scrape the sole of my shoe on the edge of a doorway, I reached the elevator and punched the button for the science deck. Nothing happened.

I took a deep breath, then clutched the side of my head. "Oh, I'm afraid the facial recognition virus is getting worse. I'd better go to the medical bay and get myself checked out."

I tried the button again. The console hummed for a brief period as some faraway processor made some calculations, then the button lit up, and the elevator began to move. It seemed the episode was back on track.

When the doors opened, I stepped out into the hall and smartly spun on my heel to head straight for the IT department. I headed through the office complex with my jaw set and my fists clenched, but I paused outside one of the break rooms. I could see through the large windows that two crewmembers were busying themselves around an inexpensive pool table.

As I entered, both of them sprang alert so suddenly that they must have cleared the floor by a good six inches. The one who had been about to take his shot saluted haphazardly, holding the pool cue like a guardsman's rifle. "Captain!" he barked.

I pointed to the cue. "May I?"

He obediently held it out and stood to one side to let me access the table. I took it, thanked him, and promptly left the room, the cue resting on my shoulder.

As I arrived at the IT help desk, the office drones peered out from behind their doors and windows, and I could feel the omnipresent gaze of the onboard AI.

"Oh goodness, now the virus is making me prone to violence," I announced, before slamming the pool cue onto the counter and sweeping everything onto the floor. "I'd better quarantine myself in the IT department where I won't harm anything important."

I heard a sharp intake of breath from one of the IT creatures as I vaulted the counter, entered the workshop uninvited, and began exploring the hedge maze of disconnected computer systems that had been set up for maintenance today. I chose an air-conditioning control bank that looked like it was almost fully repaired, then brought the pool cue down upon its nicely ordered button panel.

Screws and bits of plastic housing flew upwards, along with a little burst of sparks, and that made me even angrier. There was absolutely no reason for sparks to be flying out of a modern electrical device, except for dramatic purposes. It was safe to assume that the cameras were on.

"Oh no, now the virus is making me say completely nonsensical things," I announced, as I smashed a malfunctioning laptop onto the floor. "Where the plying hell is Sturb? I'm going to keep hitting things until Sturb shows himself! Oh no. That didn't make any sense at all. Sturb!"

I heard little footsteps pitter-patter to a halt behind me, and I turned to see the pink ferret-like creature who was filling in as Malcolm Sturb standing at the head of a shadowy group of nervous IT staff members. "H-hello, sir!" she stammered out. "What can Sturb . . . I mean, what can I do for you? Could you stop hitting things?"

I aimed my pool cue directly at her little head like it was lined up beautifully for a shot at the corner pocket. "Not you. The real Sturb. I'll stop hitting things when he comes out. Gosh, this is a strange virus. I don't know why I said that." I punctuated the statement by smartly brutalizing a photocopier.

"Er, yes, I think the virus is very much getting out of hand, sir," said the fake Sturb, holding out two placatory paws. "Perhaps it's time to think about, er, quarantine."

I should have paid more attention to the way her gaze kept flicking to a point directly behind me.

By the time I noticed, two hairy arms were already coming around my torso, and I was pulled into a bear hug by one of the IT yetis. My feet left the floor, and a combined stench of greasy food and excessive body spray almost overpowered my thought processes.

Fortunately, I retained just enough awareness to keep a firm grip on the pool cue even as my arms were being pinned to my torso, and with a simple rotation of the wrist, I brought the other end of the cue sharply up between my attacker's stubby legs. There was something joyful about the crunching sound that ensued.

My feet found the floor again, and I was able to twist out of the yeti's grip as it loosened. I rapidly took in my surroundings like a meerkat on a hill, noticed a closed door at the far end of the workshop, and bolted for it.

"Captain! Come back!" cried a voice behind me. "It's not safe there!"

I redoubled my pace and aimed my shoulder squarely at the door. It flew open with surprising ease, although the twinge in my arm joints informed me that I was going to regret that in the morning.

I would have regretted things a great deal sooner if I'd kept going at that pace, as I very nearly pitched straight over a flimsy handrail and plummeted three storeys. I was on the top level of another section of the IT workshop that extended deep into the bowels of the ship. I'd never served on a recon ship, but even I knew that there was no situation that called for this much IT department.

The fake Sturb and the rest of the local denizens were in pursuit. I slammed the door shut for what little time it would buy me, then made to descend the nearby ladder.

On the highest level, my surroundings kept up the pretence of being a computer repair shop, with multiple workbenches and countertops covered in console cases vomiting their internal components mid-surgery, but that faded the more I descended. The second level seemed more like a server farm, with vast, unadorned hulks throbbing away in the darkness, surrounded by ankle-deep swamps of winding cables.

At the very bottom, the darkness was almost total. What little light there was framed my surroundings more than illuminating them. The humming was louder than ever, but the components that covered the walls and floor felt more organic than machine-like. It was like navigating an overgrown forest.

The anger and adrenaline that had sustained me so far was gradually shoved out of the way by an expanding cloud of cold fear. None of this looked like machinery designed to be conveniently used and operated by squishy humanoids with ideas about good taste and comfortable light levels. This was looking more and more like Malmind tech.

I bit my lip at the thought. The Malmind. The cybernetic collective Malcolm Sturb had created back in his supervillain days, mainly because he wanted to expand his operations but was too socially awkward to set up an HR department. He had supposedly reformed and turned his back on cyber enslavement by the time I'd worked with him on that heist, but now it seemed the chicken wing hadn't fallen far from the fast food bucket. I couldn't help but admire his dedication to playing the long game.

There was shouting above me from the IT creatures, so I pressed deeper into the electronic catacombs. Safe to assume that I was still the most interesting thing going on at the moment, and that the phantom TV producer was still watching. That was good. Whatever was going on down here deserved a nice public airing.

After turning a few corners, I could barely see anything at all. I navigated by feeling my way along rough walls of circuit boards and cooling units, trying to reach the source of the omnipresent humming sound, but with every move it seemed to be coming from a new direction.

Eventually, after stumbling on countless trailing cables and repeatedly bruising my shins on extruding circuit boards, I saw light spilling out from around a turn in the path ahead. Perhaps with that I could at least see what I was injuring myself on. I picked up the pace.

The light was coming from a pile of components and miscellaneous tech junk roughly my height, into which illuminated cables were pumping either data or power. The turn in which it was situated was a dead end, although even calling it that was giving it too much credit. It was more like an alcove.

Still, it was more than big enough for a hiding place, even with a throbbing pile of glowing gadgetry in the middle of it, and that's precisely what I used it for when I heard the thudding of nearing footsteps and saw the play of a flashlight across the nearby wall. I slipped into the shadows behind the illuminated mass and crouched, pressing myself against a rather disquietingly warm part of the cluster.

It was the big hairy individual who had grabbed me, hurrying along with a rather eccentric gait that came from trying to run while keeping his knees as far apart as possible. He went straight past my hiding place without even stopping to check for me. Probably not the most sophisticated thinker even at the best of times.

After I stood up, I finally thought to look down at the part of the machine pile that I had been holding, and I swiftly solved the mystery of its disquieting warmth. It was a human arm.

I started, fell back against a pile of half-melted motherboards, and received a nasty scrape across the strip of back flesh exposed by my ill-fitting uniform.

I stuffed my wrist into my mouth, and my sleeve absorbed my yelp.

Nobody came to investigate the sound. It had probably been drowned out by the humming, which was presently centred around the pile of machinery. Except it was also a pile of Calbeck, the chief medical officer who had been snatched right in front of Derby and me. Something had placed him in a rough sitting position on a heap of junk electronics, and he was being held in place by multiple black tubes and cables of varying thickness and design.

A particularly large cable was feeding into some kind of rubber visor clamped over Calbeck's eyes and ears, with a little glow spilling out from where it met his face. A different tube was over his mouth. I didn't want to speculate on what the machine was feeding him, but it was at least keeping him alive, for want of a better word.

Experimentally, I tried to pull one of the tubes away, but nothing would budge. The thing holding the visor in place resembled a huge, black, muscular arm, covering Calbeck's eyes like a concerned parent walking a child through a red-light district.

I took a step back. Sturb's methods had certainly changed. His usual modus operandi had been to kidnap people and turn them into cyberslaves who would defend his facilities and do his laundry, that sort of thing. I couldn't even speculate as to why he would plug the crew into . . . whatever this was.

There were more alcoves along the tunnel, each one lit by twinkling electronic components. I crept to the next one and found another crewperson trapped in a similar arrangement. The platform and tubes were a different shape, and the crewperson was held in a different pose, but the essential visor and mouthpiece were in place. All these human-holding stations appeared to have been improvised from whatever materials were available. Which made sense. This couldn't have been part of the *Leon*'s original mission brief, even with all the middle management in the world.

The next alcove contained Clay. He was in a particularly uncomfortable pose, practically upside down, like a corpse on a tilted gurney. I made a mental note of his position. If I kept track of exactly who I had found down here, the rest of the "actors" up above couldn't keep claiming to be these people.

A young woman occupied the next alcove. A starry-eyed cadet fresh out of school, whose presence made me punch my palm and mutter indistinctly to myself about Sturb having a lot to answer for. The next was a trapped Thaloxian with clamps on all of its tentacles and a special custom device over its sensor pods. The last one, at the very end of the passage, was . . .

Malcolm Sturb.

I was startled out of my open-mouthed bewilderment when I heard my pool cue clattering to the floor beside me. Even with his eyes, mouth, and nose covered by machinery, it was impossible to mistake those chins. And while the Oniris uniform providers had made a heroic effort, they had been powerless against Sturb's uncanny ability to make anything he wore look unflattering.

The pile of tech he was connected to was the biggest and most impressive yet. He was actually in a chair, for a start. A leather swivel chair with the back almost all the way reclined and the castors held in place by grasping clusters of cables. Going by the faded pallor of his skin and his growth of neckbeard, he'd been here a lot longer than the others. Sturb's much larger and more complex throne smacked of the culprit having refined their methods over time.

I stood there for several minutes, pursing my lips and ruminating on how unfair this all was. I'd finally latched onto a nice, perfectly reasonable explanation, and then the universe had pulled the rug out. Who the trac was plugging comatose crewmembers into monstrous machines if not Malcolm Sturb?

There was nothing for it. I was going to have to get Sturb out of there and ask him. I approached his chair, grabbed the bulky limb holding his visor against his face, and made a token attempt to pull it off. As expected, it barely moved. But I'd come too far to be deterred, and I wasn't about to shrug my shoulders, crawl back up to the top level, and apologise about the pool cue to the testicles.

I climbed on top of Sturb's housing, planted my feet on both armrests, and pulled as hard as I could. I could swear there was movement, but I couldn't tell if it was the tube coming away from his face or his face coming away from his skull, so I thought it best to stop. A smarter approach was clearly needed.

Experimentally, I poked at the point where the visor met his face and tried to work the flesh out from under it bit by bit. Any skin I was able to pull out was swiftly drawn back in. The machine must have been using some kind of suction. And if that were the case . . .

I took another look at the shower of black tubes and cables descending from the shadowy region above me. If suction was in play, then one of these tubes was doing the sucking. All I had to do was make a hole in it, and the mask would come away. Easy, theoretically. But "theoretically" was a big word.

Still standing on the armrests, I began working through the cables connected to Sturb's mask, giving each one a little squeeze. Most of them were firm and unyielding, probably housing cable of one kind or another, but I singled out three plastic tubes that were clearly for conveying air. One of them had to be the one creating the suction. One of them was presumably how he was breathing, but I didn't see an issue if I broke all of them at once.

I recovered my pool cue and wound the three air pipes around it, then kept twisting. The tubes bunched up and strained against each other, more and more with each rotation, until with one last strain of effort, there was a clack of breaking plastic, and a sudden spray of cold air sent me tumbling to the floor.

As I lay winded, the broken end of one of the tubes fell onto my torso and proceeded to disgorge a blob of orange goo across the front of my nice clean uniform. Apparently, I'd mistaken a food pipe for an air pipe. It wasn't a huge deal, but it was exactly the kind of cherry on top that might've made me lose it completely if I hadn't heard Sturb coughing.

Just as I had hoped, the mask had loosened from his face. I ran up and helped pull it away, along with a rather unsettlingly long amount of flexible pipe that had been down his throat. I helped roll him out of the chair, but his legs gave way the instant they tried to support his weight. He flopped into a sitting position, coughing and spluttering.

"Ha," he said after a few deep breaths. "Ho. I was quite enjoying that."

The flesh of his face was visibly discoloured and indented from having had the visor on for so long, and his eyes were bloodshot and unfocussed. It took a great deal of blinking and rubbing before he could finally see well enough to take me in.

"C-captain?" he slurred.

That was good enough for me. "Is it true that you're Jacques McKeown, you bracket?"

He frowned at me, then his eyes rolled back and wobbled, as if he were trying to examine his own brain. Then, something seemed to click. "Oh. That."

"Yeah, that, you plying—" Some urgent signal reached my conscious mind. "Why did you call me 'Captain'?"

"What?"

"Why would you think I was the captain? You've been stuck in that . . . thing."

"Because you're the new captain?" He glanced back at his discarded visor, still dangling from its mechanical arm. "We were watching. Through there."

Light spilled from the eyepieces of the mask. I took a closer look, ready to yank it away at the first sign of anything taking an interest in my face, and saw two little screens, both displaying what looked like an episode of *Trailspacers*. By the looks of it, Doctor Allura and the new Clay were having a heated argument on the bridge.

I looked back down the tunnel at the other chairs, where presumably every other disappeared person was being forced to serve as the rest of the studio audience. "Sturb, what the plying hell is going on on this ship?"

He was sitting on the pedestal beside his chair, pinching his eyes and trying to reorient himself. "Er. Sorry. There's quite a few answers to that question, Captain."

"I meant the TV show thing," I said.

He looked at me, alarmed. "What?"

"This!" I shook the visor with the two screens. "This, everything on the ship being recorded and broadcast like it's a TV show! That TV thing!"

What little light there was came from the numerous LEDs on the machinery and the two screens in the visor in my hand suddenly winked out, leaving us in pitch darkness. The background hum of electronics was silenced.

"Uh oh," said Sturb quietly. "You probably shouldn't have done that."

My eyes had already adjusted to the dark, but this didn't bring much comfort. "Done what?!"

"Broke the fourth wall. The show doesn't like that."

I heard that familiar, distant sound of a door opening. Something deep in the darkness clanged metallically. "Am I being disappeared?!"

"Yes, but we have a little time," said Sturb casually. "They don't patrol here much. This is the place where disappeared people are taken, so they don't expect to have to disappear people *from* here."

I was scrabbling around at floor level, looking for my pool cue. When I had it, I held it in both hands and leapt upright, hopping on the balls of my feet as I prepared to block an incoming attack. "I'm ready. I'm ready. Who's 'they'?"

In the darkness, I saw Sturb's indistinct form rise shakily to his feet. "Hold on. Let me turn on my phone flashlight. I jailbroke it so the ship's AI can't override its functions." He jabbed at his phone screen, and I was half-blinded by a severe white flare right in front of my face. "Jailbreaking it was pretty easy, actually. All I had to do was spoof an IP address and—"

He was interrupted by a tremendous sound that almost defied comparison. It was metallic, and wet, and crunchy, like a metal flagpole being thrust into half-dried concrete. Something hot and wet splashed the entire front of my torso.

I looked down at myself, still brightly illuminated by the phone light. The orange stain on my uniform had just been joined by a lurid red splatter.

Sturb carefully turned his phone around and pointed it at his own torso. Something metallic and L-shaped was sticking out of his chest, framed by a little explosion of broken ribs.

"Oh," he said, disappointed, as we watched his blood trickle onto the floor. "I'm actually a bit upset about this."

TWENTY-TWO

As the phone fell from Sturb's weakening fingers, its light spilled across the thing directly behind him. It was about a metre across, black, hovering on a series of propellers, with a set of insectile metal mandibles I thought might have been repurposed from the bottom of an office chair. One of them was currently lodged in Malcolm Sturb's upper body, and it was quivering as the robotic beast struggled to pull itself free of his inconvenient bulk.

I was still gaping at the thing in horror when I noticed that my arms had already raised the pool cue out of unconscious survival instinct. I brought the chalky end down upon the cluster of eye-like components just above the mandibles. To my surprise, the blow practically went straight through it without slowing. Sparks flew and several components flew off, then a malfunctioning propeller caused it to slurp unpleasantly out of Sturb's body and career away like a released balloon.

I grabbed Sturb before he could drop, but he was heavier than I expected, and all I could do was help lower him to his knees. "Oh dear," he was saying. "This doesn't look survivable, actually. Sorry to be a bother."

Looking at his torso, or rather, looking through his torso, I believed him. "Sturb. Stay with me," I said, which felt like the sort of thing one said in these situations.

"Oh, Captain," he said, managing to focus on my face for a moment and speaking like he'd only just recognised me. "You should go to Nogedom 6. It's one of the planets we've been surveying. I left something there that will probably clear up a lot of things."

I applied pressure to the wound in his chest, but something spurted out of the wound in his back, so I tried holding my hands over both wounds and pushing him back together like a stubborn suitcase. "This isn't the best time," I hissed.

He glanced up as we both sensed another drone whizzing by overhead. "Oh. Yes. It might be difficult." His arms had gone almost completely limp, but he was able to make a floppy gesture toward his phone, which was lying on its back on the floor and providing the only source of light. "There's software on my phone that will get you past most of the encryptions in the ship's lockdown protocol. It'll do most of the work by itself. The password is 'LubbaTheEight.'"

"Lubba the eight?" I repeated.

"Yes, it's actually rather a clever reference," said Sturb, talking into his chest. "You see, 'Lubba the Great' was the name of the third song on the soundtrack for *Star Pounders 3*, and meanwhile, the eighth layer of a standard McKenzie encryption is . . ." He paused to take a long, rasping breath. "Actually, you probably don't care that much."

Then he died.

The death of an arch-nemesis is always a time for mixed feelings. Yes, the universe would be safe from him forevermore, but it also meant having to find something else to do at the weekends.

Not that I was going to have a chance to dwell. Something was still moving in the darkness. I picked up Sturb's phone after fumbling for several infuriating seconds to pry the fashionably wafer-thin device off the floor, then held it up like a protective talisman.

The second drone was already swooping in, as silent as a Valaxian deathowl, mechanical mandibles drawn out and ready to grab me. That must have been what the first drone had been trying to do, but Sturb had gotten in the way. Maybe it hadn't known he was there because the AI was tracking people through their devices, and Sturb had jailbroken his phone? Maybe I could piece the fine details together when I wasn't being hunted by flying robot centipede things.

I grabbed the thin end of the cue, adopted a baseball stance, then communicated my unwillingness to come quietly as clearly as I could. Again, my blow was surprisingly effective. It dislocated the drone's "jaws" in a shower of screws, knocked a propeller out of whack, and sent the metal beast straight to the floor, where it proceeded to glide around in a circle like a confused robot vacuum cleaner.

I kept holding the cue out, ready to block, but the drone seemed to have been rendered harmless, and I was able to examine it more thoroughly. Just like the viewing chairs that the disappeared crewmembers had been forced into, the drones had been haphazardly cobbled together from random bits of machinery. No wonder they fell apart at the slightest resistance. And relied so heavily on taking people by surprise in pitch darkness.

Sturb's body was still in a kneeling position, but he had crumpled into himself like a wet cardboard box. I could feel the sadness and the guilt layering over the depths of my bowels like silt on the bottom of a lake, but it was being smothered by the sense of sheer unfairness that my only lead and reason for being here was now a silent, leaking pile of cartilage.

At least he'd given me one crumb. Nogedom 6, one of the distant planets the *Leon*'s crew were supposed to be assessing in between making TV shows and kidnapping each other. There must already be a quantunnel set up in nearby space that would take me straight there. Not much of a lead, but it was substantially more than enough reason to get the plying hell off this ship.

Which brought me back to the more familiar problem of how I was going to do that. At least I wasn't wandering around the corridors under full scrutiny of the cameras anymore. Now I was scurrying around inside the walls with a source of light and a battle-hardened pool cue. That gave me an edge.

Speaking of sources of light, I turned my attention to Sturb's phone. The wallpaper was a photograph of Sturb looking excited at some convention or other, standing next to a cosplayer with a very condescending look on her face and a suite of applet icons strategically scattered across her body that I couldn't make head or tail of. But one icon caught my eye, huddled away in the corner as if embarrassed by the rest. It was the Oniris Venture logo, and the text underneath read *My Oniris Helper,* followed by the word *Cracked* in square brackets.

After taking a moment of intense concentration to remember the password Sturb had told me, it having been one robot battle, one dramatic death scene, and one boring speech ago, I accessed it. It was some kind of overly chummy personal assistant for Oniris employees, graffitied with extra text in strange colours here and there where Sturb had customised the code. I skipped past a couple of tabs full of payroll and health insurance information too boring to describe—not to mention severely redundant—and found a map of the ship.

A three-dimensional map of the ship, nicely colour-coded in the usual company pastels, which in its original form would be indicating that my position was currently outside the hull. Sturb's hack had added the off-limits infrastructure zones such as the one I was currently in, appended to the science deck with crude, unmatching black lines, labelled with the wrong font.

To my surprise, I was still fairly high up in the ship. Descending to the bottom of the IT department had felt like exploring some hideous forgotten underbelly, but I should have remembered that the entrance to IT was on deck two. By the looks of the map, I was in the infrastructure of one of the residential decks. In fact, the female changing area for one of the swimming pools was just on the far side of the nearest wall.

The engineering decks, where the shuttle bays could be found, were a few decks down. Sturb's app indicated a poorly drawn ladder not far from my position that should take me to a maintenance tunnel heading in that direction.

As I set off, I noticed that the lights had come back on. Evidently the force that was controlling the ship had given up on its attempts to disappear me, at least for now, but I couldn't let myself relax. I doubted there was much leeway in its tolerance for walking, talking continuity errors.

I would never have found the hatchway to the ladder without Sturb's app. It was in a dim corner, partially buried under a pile of random adapters. I also doubt I would have been able to navigate the maze of narrow maintenance tunnels, but with the app highlighting the fastest route, I could get through them in a breeze, taking one rung at a time and thinking about broader concerns. Like how these tunnels appeared to be precisely the size and shape of one of those drones, and if one showed up needing to get past, I doubted it would be polite enough to wait. I shivered at the thought. Even with the drones as fragile as they were, it'd be like having to share a tumble dryer with a complete set of steak knives.

I reached the bottom of the final shaft indicated by the route on the app and found a square panel in the wall about three feet across. It fell forward with a relatively light kick, and I crawled through into a corridor on the engineering deck. After a moment's dizziness that came from going straight from darkness to blinding studio lights, I replaced the panel.

I noticed a sign on the opposite wall pointing me in the direction of the shuttle bays, and since none of its options were highlighted or dimmed, I assumed the cameras weren't presently on me. When I looked back, the panel I had entered through was impossible to differentiate from the rest of the wall. The seam had vanished into the paintwork.

A crewmember rounded a corner and headed past me as I was running my hand across the wall with a bewildered look on my face. He stopped short a few yards away and turned. "Who are you? Why are you wearing the captain's uniform?"

It was a Kodorian from the engineering crew, going by the uniform colour. He was staring at me with narrowed, orange eyes and screwing up all three eyebrows.

I lightly brushed my lapel, as if that would be enough to remove the multiple layers of grime, dust, filth, and human blood that my clothes had acquired. "Yeah, that facial recognition virus is a pain, isn't it," I muttered, motioning to step past him.

He didn't move. "What are you talking about? You're not the captain! You don't look anything like the captain!" He ran to a communal terminal built into a nearby wall and began rapidly pressing the touchscreen. "Intruder alert on the engineering deck! Send security!"

He had scrolled through a couple of tabs to get to the comms menu, and I'd caught a glimpse of the welcome screen. The same one I'd seen on the terminal in my quarters, which had mysteriously acquired a picture of me that I couldn't remember having posed for.

It was that screen, but the picture of me, smiling with my hand outstretched, had gone. In its place was a picture of a large golden retriever in an ill-fitting captain's uniform, holding out a paw to shake.

TWENTY-THREE

"**S**ecurity alert on the engineering deck!" reiterated the Kodorian. "Please send security personnel to—hey! You can't . . ."

But I would never know what that Kodorian believed I couldn't do, because at that point I had run far enough away to be out of earshot. Once again, I had the impression that certain lower ranking sectors of the crew were willingly going along with this TV show bulltrac. Maybe it was relieving the monotony of cataloguing ore samples or whatever.

I made it to the supply bay that adjoined most of the shuttle bays—the very one where I had first encountered the crew and interrupted Allura and Clay's leadership debate—and slowed my run to as nonchalant a walk as I could manage when I saw a handful of crewmembers in boiler suits making an inventory of some of the shelving units.

The most important thing now was to avoid looking like interesting television. I didn't appear to be the centre of attention; I could only pray that the camera loved Captain Sparky. I offered the engineers a friendly nod and a smile as I walked, quickly and stiff-legged, to the large shutter doors leading to the main shuttle bay.

The chances of stealing the captain's shuttle were feeling lower by the second, and they hit rock bottom when the shuttle-bay doors refused to open at my approach. I prodded a couple of buttons on the nearby panel and was rewarded for my efforts with a low buzz and a red light.

I gave another little reassuring smile to the one engineer who was watching me curiously, then tried again. Another buzz and a red light. I pantomimed a little roll of the eyes and snap of the fingers as my brain internally screamed at itself to figure out what the plying hell to do now.

What had Sturb said? His phone could disable internal lockdowns. I fumbled it out of my pocket and pretended I had been seized by the urge to play a quick round of *Joogie Bounce*.

The navigation app wasn't a help in itself, but I noticed a strange icon hovering over the shape representing the supply bay. Pressing it brought me to a secondary app that was mostly unintelligible, but I recognised an outline of the room, and the four icons hanging over it must have represented something or other. One looked like a standard loading icon, with several straight lines radiating out of a central point. It felt like an "Aha!" symbol. So that could mean "open door." If the door opened, I might conceivably go "Aha! An open door!"

I touched the icon. The door remained closed, and all the lights in the room turned off.

One of the engineers yelped in surprise. I hastily restored the lights to see them all half-crouched and holding up their arms to fend off a drone assault. I pretended to be as confused as they were, putting my hands on my hips and squinting at the ceiling. There was definitely more than one of them looking at me now.

I wiped the sweat out of my eyes and went back to the app. Another icon looked like a robotic arm connected to some interlocking gears. Gears were presumably involved in the process of opening a shutter door. I touched it.

On the other side of the supply bay, a robotic arm for transporting heavy cargo unfolded from the wall and dropped into a horizontal position, concussing the engineer with a clipboard, who had been unfortunate enough to be standing under it. And now the app was full of new icons for controlling the arm directly, and my attempts to cancel back to the previous icons caused the arm to swing left and right, knocking out a second engineer who had been coming to help the first.

Okay. Lesson learned. The app with the robot arm icon controlled the robot arm, it turned out. Thank you, universe, for yet another reason why I should have taken high school IT instead of domestic science, no matter how big my crush on Gemma Nelson had been.

The engineers drifted over to a small platoon of security officers that had appeared at the supply-bay entrance, and it didn't take a television detective to deduce that they were sent in my direction. I pressed the last two icons at once, and finally the shutter doors began to slide open noisily. The air conditioning unit in the ceiling started making very odd noises, but I left all that behind when I ducked under the door the moment there was enough room to fit.

Someone behind me yelled something. I fumbled the icon again, but of course the shutters refused to start closing until they had completed the action of opening, as anything else would make things far too easy for me. I kept walking, pretending that I had more important things to worry about than whatever commotion was unfolding behind me.

A small fleet of shuttles were parked before me in descending order of size. On one end were a couple of huge spacegoing buses with thrusters for transporting full survey teams and their equipment. Closer to me were the tiny ship-to-surface runners, with little more than a single thruster and a cramped cockpit on top, for when only two or three individuals needed to get somewhere. Ideally individuals who got along alright and didn't have body odour.

I headed for the nearest of the small ones and, to my surprise, found it unlocked. Maybe Sturb's phone had cleared the way. Maybe they had to be kept unlocked in case of a scramble or evacuation. Or maybe Oniris had so many of these traccy little things that the labour cost of pressing the "lock" button every time you got out of one wasn't considered worth it.

The moment I had climbed the two or three steps into the pilot's seat, the phone paired with the onboard computer and several more icons appeared, including one with a padlock. There wasn't much that could have meant. I pressed it, and the shuttle's doors swung closed. A moment later, I heard the reassuring sound of bolts sliding into place. This must have been the lockdown mode, intended for when you were parked on an alien planet full of locals who had unexpectedly reached the "wooden club" level of technological warfare.

Through the shuttle's Plexiglass canopy, I could clearly see the security officers in the hangar below marching directly toward my new ship with absolute righteousness in their swinging arms. I quickly assessed the control systems—two joysticks and foot pedals to work the thrusters, basic enough stuff—and adjusted my seat for take-off.

Just as I had found the ideal crevice in the pilot's chair to house my buttocks, I finally looked up and registered that the vast hangar doors, which I would need to fly the ship through to access the docking airlock, were closed. In retrospect, it was dim of me not to have noticed earlier, since the doors took up most of the wall and loomed over me like an unimpressed babysitter, but I suppose I had been hoping the big picture would come together if I focussed on the little details.

The security team were right outside. I could look down and see the receding hairline of the lead officer as they knocked politely on the exterior door. After no response came, they tried the handle. When they looked up and made eye contact, I gave a shrug and displayed my hands, as if I was as confused as they were.

The lead officer scowled and gestured for me to get out. I pointed to my watch and to the airlock doors, to indicate that I was in a terrible hurry but perhaps we could address whatever his problem was after I returned from my important errand.

This seemed to leave us at an impasse, so the security officer retreated a few steps to solicit advice from his posse. Meanwhile, I was inspecting the controls and noticed a prominent icon on the status screen labelled *Request Take-off Permission*. I'd always seen myself as more of a forgiveness than a permission person, but it was as good a place to start as any.

After I touched the icon, I was kept in suspense by a loading symbol for a few seconds before being unceremoniously dropped into a voice call.

"Ground control to Shuttlebug 17," said the voice of a grumpy person who had clearly not been anticipating having to do any plying work today. "Why are you requesting launch? Over."

The security guards apparently hadn't reached a consensus yet, but I noticed a few of them were holding extendable batons all of a sudden. "Ground control, this is Shuttlebug 17," I answered, saying it as slowly as I could to stall for time. "Heading to Nogedom 6 on equipment retrieval."

"There's nothing like that scheduled," said ground control after taking absolutely zero time to check.

I flinched as I heard a baton bouncing off the exterior door. It was a shy, experimental blow to break the ice, but the second one was a lot more confident. "No, it wouldn't be scheduled," I said, trying not to sweat visibly. "Special dispensation."

"On whose authority?"

"The captain's," I said, now improvising wildly. Several more batons had joined the chorus just below me.

"You should have a written dispensation order," said the angry icon on the screen. "Hold it up to the camera."

They were stalling me. And by the sounds of it, I wasn't the only one improvising wildly. The locks seemed to be holding, but it was only a matter of time before the shuttle's door was too dented and misshapen to keep out the vacuum of space. I hunted around for solutions, theatrically patting my pockets, then noticed an *Add to Call* button in the corner of the screen.

I touched it, and a dropdown of crewmembers unfolded on the screen. "You know what, we can do better than that," I said. "Let's just ask him."

The entry for Captain Sparky was right at the top of the crew list in a special exclusive red font. The moment I clicked it, there was an anticipatory buzz, and then the sound of a canine mouth gnawing at a communicator.

"Uh, Captain, just confirming the special dispensation you gave me to retrieve that equipment from Nogedom 6?"

Sparky replied with a confused growl.

"Thank you, sir."

"Um," contributed ground control.

One of the security guards must have fetched a stepladder or a box to stand on, because at that moment, a baton smacked the Plexiglass canopy, inches from my head. I attempted to will my neck three inches shorter. "And Captain, I know you didn't have time to provide the special dispensation paperwork, but you did say you would sort it all out with administration and in the meantime I should just get going?"

Sparky emitted a small whine.

"There, you see? It's all approved."

"That . . . that was just a whine," said ground control.

"What?" I said with a slightly manic squawk to my voice. "You mean you can't understand what Captain Sparky is saying? How can that be? Do you have some kind of speech-understanding virus?"

For a few tense moments there was silence, except for the thundering of batons and the wet sounds of Captain Sparky licking himself. I closed my eyes.

"Shuttlebug 17, you are cleared for take-off," muttered ground control grumpily.

A colossal clang of metal rang out, and the gigantic docking-bay doors began to slide open. The security guards were forced to retreat as the room was bathed in sirens and yellow warning lights, intended to convey that anything squashy and organic that didn't fancy becoming intimately acquainted with its own internal organs should probably leave.

I sucked in deep breath after deep breath as I engaged the take-off thrusters. I wasn't even flying by the seat of my pants anymore. The seat of my pants had worn away days ago, leaving two red raw buttocks exposed to the vagaries of the universe.

TWENTY-FOUR

There was something disquieting about flying one of these tiny personal shuttles, even leaving aside the fact that I had no food, water, or prospects beyond a life support system that was only guaranteed for three hours of flight. I'd always preferred to pilot ships that had a big, reassuring weight underneath me, the way a rider of old would have the companionship of a big, warm, noisy horse. Without that, I felt exposed. It was like riding a motorised toilet across a prairie.

After I had cleared the docking bay and risen above the gigantic lobster claws of the Oniris *Leon*, an infinity of stars winked into view. They were like a bored audience at a spectacular colosseum, at once representing safety and freedom while being absolutely no help whatsoever. Ahead of me, three great mechanical rings hung in space, connected to the *Leon* by articulated metal arms: the quantunnels that had been set up to explore three unknown star systems before the lockdown had shut off the quantunnel controls. A quick ping from the shuttle's computer was enough to determine which one led to the Nogedom Sector.

I passed through the ring, and the scenery didn't change much. I traded the uniform blackness with glittery bits for another uniform blackness with glittery bits. Nevertheless, a chill ran through me as I crossed the threshold. The *Leon* was gone, but for a few glimpses through the metallic ring behind me, and for all its nonsense, it had still been a friendlier presence than the void.

It dawned on me that I was, in all likelihood, the one human being who was the furthest away from our Solar system in that moment. A lifetime of space adventuring on a variety of alien worlds did a lot to reduce one's fear of the unknown, but the unknown never goes away, it just gets pushed further out. Just because we hadn't yet discovered a planet-sized all-devouring space kraken didn't mean there couldn't be one behind the next veil.

Fortunately, the only thing planet-sized around me at that moment was a planet. Nogedom 6 was large enough to fill most of my view and close enough to touch down upon within a matter of hours. As for where, precisely, I needed to touch down, that was answered by another ping from the shuttle's computer. There was a signal coming from the planet's surface that was using an Oniris ident.

That much was entirely to be expected. I already knew the *Leon* had sent unmanned probes and drones down there to sniff out valuable resources. It may also have been whatever it was Sturb had wanted me to see. I plotted a course.

As I settled in for the hour or two it would take for the shuttle to reach the planet's atmosphere, my adrenaline had time to subside, and the fact that I hadn't eaten or slept since before my meeting with Clay broke the surface. Exhaustion and hunger hung off my joints like the jaws of . . . I was too tired even to think of some bulltrac alien creature to compare it to.

The shuttle's joints creaked and complained as we entered the planet's atmosphere and the engine struggled to compensate. Temperatures and winds that could have stripped me to my bones were less than an inch of reinforced Plexiglass away from my face. The furious roar of the murderous elements was like a drumroll in the middle of my brain, and yet I still couldn't focus on anything except how badly I wanted some pancakes.

The clouds parted, and the planet's surface unfolded below me. It was majestic in a barren sort of way, all rolling sand dunes and shadowy canyons carved into aesthetically pleasing curves by long-extinct rivers. As the autopilot closed in on the location of the Oniris signal, the local star was squatting on the horizon like a knob of butter on a short stack, sending highlights along the rocky canyon walls like rivulets of warm maple syrup.

Oniris's base was in a mercifully shady spot under a natural bridge. An automated mining rig was built into the rock wall, and the ore smelter was feeding into a drone printer that looked like it hadn't been activated in a while. All the components were connected to a central control computer resembling a three-foot metal statue of a stick of roll-on deodorant, which was in turn connected by a long cable to a modest network of solar panels on top of the natural bridge.

The different components were placed haphazardly around a small area with very little consideration for efficiency or aesthetics, and I didn't see any facility that would accommodate human workers. So it was still a fully automated operation. Bang went my idea to grab an armload of individually wrapped muffins from the coffee-break station.

I touched down a short distance from the base, the tiny shuttle settling shakily onto its tripod landing legs like a backyard barbecue grill, and it was only as I was releasing the door catch that it occurred to me to check for a breathable atmosphere. I froze as all the air molecules in the shuttle noisily rushed out to mingle with the locals and make friends.

After a minute, I was still alive, and the hot, dusty air sawing in and out of me wasn't melting any internal organs, so I let myself untense. On reflection, I needn't have worried, considering the survey process was this far along. Oniris wasn't interested in uninhabitable planets. The eventual holiday apartments were going to be prohibitively expensive to rent even without the addition of terraforming costs.

The only part of the base that had any interface usable by humans was the main computer unit. A small terminal was set in the rounded top, for when the human survey team arrived and needed a nicely formatted summary of what, precisely, the drones had been doing and how many local life forms had died because of it.

I booted up the computer. Maybe the drones had found some edible plant life that they hadn't yet processed into organic fuel. I was flicking through some incomprehensible columns of coordinates when they disappeared and were replaced by a single dialogue box: *Compatible device detected. Sync now?*

It had to be Sturb's phone. The shuttle had a computer, but it was just about sophisticated enough to run an air conditioner. My usual instinct was to refuse permissions whenever asked, having finally learned my lesson after it had taken three complete reinstalls to get the *Neverdie*'s cockpit computer to stop singing burger restaurant jingles, but it's not like it was *my* phone. And it could probably make more sense out of this information than I could.

I told the terminal to go ahead. A moment later, I was taken by surprise by a familiar, completely emotionless voice coming out of Sturb's phone, accompanied by an image of an animating waveform.

"It looks like you are interfacing with an Oniris Venture automated surveying operation. Would you like my assistance?"

The name rose up in my memory. "Jimi?"

Sturb's pet AI. During our heist, he had been delegating a lot of his thinking to it. In fact, if memory served, it had more or less come up with the entire scheme with which we had brought down Terrorgorn. I wondered why it had taken so long to reveal itself. Maybe it had been watching to see how well I could survive without help, the way a parent teaches a toddler how to stand up.

"Recognising user: Dashford Pierce," said Jimi. "Query: How can I be of service?"

"Food," was about all I could say.

"Would you like me to recommend nearby restaurants?"

Something about finally talking plainly again—the last time having been with Sturb, around the time that important parts of him were splattering all over my front—was draining my last reserves of energy. I leant all my weight on the computer as my knees began to buckle. "Any food," I clarified, wanting to cry.

"Tone of request analysed. Lowering standards accordingly. Please wait."

I don't know how long it kept me waiting. I had just about sunk to the floor and might even have passed out when I was jerked back to full alertness by the sound of a rising mechanical buzz. One of the Oniris drones flew down, extruded a rectangular tray, then carefully laid it on the floor. It was half full of black water, with a few islands of stringy green slime.

"What's this?"

"Organic matter recovered from a cave system 8.6 miles south-southwest of this position," chirped Jimi. "Analysis indicates that it contains no toxins and a broad selection of the nutrients necessary for human sustenance," it added, as if hurt by my lack of enthusiasm.

I consumed the matter, and I say "consumed" because it was hard to say if I was eating or drinking it. It certainly wasn't the worst thing I'd ever had to subsist on, but it was up there. It tasted a bit like the seaweed used in the cheap sushi sandwiches from Ritsuko City Spaceport. Except more of it, and soggy, and like it had been pickled in a prison toilet for several weeks.

"Okay," I said when I was confident my stomach wasn't immediately rejecting it. I patted the computer terminal. "Sturb said there was something important in this thing. Can you find it?"

Jimi paused for an amount of time perfectly calculated to make me feel stupid for asking. "Query: Please define 'something important.'"

I took another swig of vile cave goo in the hope that it might jumpstart my brain cells. "He said it was something that would clear things up. About that whole thing on the *Leon*. I think."

"Query: Please define 'that whole thing.'"

"You know." I wobbled a hand. Suddenly it all seemed very absurd. "The thing where people were being forced into acting like a TV show. And being kidnapped if they wouldn't go along with it, and forced to watch the TV show." A little circling icon indicated that Jimi was taking a while to process this information. "Weren't you there for that?"

"User: Malcolm Sturb frequently left me in a deactivated state due to my queries triggering his anxiety for social interactions."

I nodded. "Sounds like him."

"Query: What is the current status of user: Malcolm Sturb?"

For one ridiculous moment, I considered trying to spare the feelings of an emotionless computer. "Sturb's dead. The thing that was doing the TV show thing, it killed him as I was trying to get him out of it."

"Acknowledged," said Jimi after a brief pause. "Query: Would you like my assistance in planning revenge?"

I screwed up my face. "What? No!"

"Acknowledged. Continue answering my queries, and I will become less likely to misinterpret your tone of voice over time. I am now analysing the data in this computer terminal."

I slumped down with my back against the terminal and let Jimi work, passing the time by staring into my tray of hideous green goo and playing a quick game of "algae or insect larva." My thoughts drifted back to Malcolm Sturb. There was definitely some deep well of feeling inside me that swelled and threatened to burst when I thought about him being dead. Unless it was my digestive system.

"Data analysed," reported Jimi. "The drone operation reported a Class A discovery one hundred eighty-four days ago. A small team of crewmembers arrived one hundred eighty-two days ago to recover a selection of artefacts and return them to the *Ponce de Leon* for laboratory study."

"Class A?"

"Class A discovery: Evidence of alien settlement, including but not limited to ruins, technology, or still existing settlement."

I blew out my cheeks. "They never plying learn, do they. If you find a cave full of eggs, maybe stand back and poke them with a long stick before you grab one and trap yourself in deep space with it."

"An artefact designated OVD-17701A was found to be an alien form of data storage, containing a still functioning AI," continued Jimi. "Only one research log is referenced. Initial scans of the AI indicated that all of its stored data points and variables were in some way referencing television science-fiction broadcasts from the late twentieth and early twenty-first centuries."

I frowned. "Why the hell would an alien AI on the edge of space know about human TV shows?"

"Speculation: Archaic human broadcasting technology would send unencrypted signals into space that could be intercepted by any compatible receiver. Additional speculation: the AI may have received such signals and misinterpreted them as a set of instructions, or an attempt to communicate."

"And that's why the AI is now forcing the crew of the *Leon* to be a TV show? It thinks its speaking our language?"

"Would you like me to supply a complete breakdown of the data on which my speculation is founded?" asked Jimi.

I shook my head. "No. No, it's just that . . . it all seems a bit . . ." I waved my hands around as I sought the word. "Hackneyed."

"Query: Please clarify—"

"Never mind, never mind."

There was an uncomfortable silence before Jimi spoke again. The rotating symbol on Sturb's phone appeared to be the AI equivalent of twiddling one's thumbs. "How would you like to proceed?"

I pinched my eyes. "I don't know. That's a plying good question. The only reason I came out here was to find Sturb." I felt that big water balloon of emotions inside me quiver slightly. "To confront him about being Jacques McKeown. But now he's dead, and I don't even know what I wanted him to do about it, anyway."

"It sounds like you wish to seek recompense for the destruction of your apartment. Would you like my assistance?"

I unpinched my eyes. "How do you know about that?"

"The destruction of your apartment in Ritsuko City was conducted by me under the instruction of user: Malcolm Sturb."

"What?!" I jumped up as if the computer behind my back had become searing hot. "*You* blew up my apartment?"

"By exploiting a backdoor I had installed on the cockpit computer of your vessel, I was able to pilot it remotely and fire one of its small number of remaining torpedoes . . ."

"*What?!*" I had already jumped to my feet, so I just did a little hop. "You hacked the *Neverdie*?!"

"The backdoor was installed when you allowed me to pilot your ship during your previous association with user: Malcolm Sturb. No hacking was necessary."

I felt a stabbing pain in my head and waved Jimi into silence. "Okay! Okay! Shut up!"

"I understood your words as a request for elaboration," said Jimi with the air of a confused puppy. "Please continue answering my queries, and I will become better at interpreting you."

My hands were on either side of my face. I did distinctly remember allowing Sturb to install Jimi on the *Neverdie*'s computer, and I distinctly remembered thinking what a bad idea it was. I knew Inspector Honda had told me that my apartment had been attacked by a star-pilot vessel, and separately, I knew that the *Neverdie* had been the only star-pilot vessel parked in Ritsuko City Spaceport. Two facts I had had all this time and never put together.

"Okay. One thing at a time," I said measuredly. "Why did Sturb order you to blow me up?"

"My previous activation by user: Malcolm Sturb occurred approximately eight days ago. The duration of the interaction was one point four seconds. During that time, user: Malcolm Sturb issued the following directive, quote: 'Help.'"

He must have gotten free of his forced viewing chair for long enough to get his phone out, and that was officially the only part that made sense. "And you interpreted that as 'Hijack the ship of our former arch-nemesis and blow him up with his own torpedo?'"

"I engaged my emergency protocols after interpreting the tone of user: Malcolm Sturb's directive," said Jimi casually. "I conducted a wide probability sweep. Lacking the capacity to interface with the *Ponce de Leon*'s internal systems, or to verbally communicate with any individual, remotely hijacking your ship was the only option available to me. Destroying your apartment was the course of action that presented the highest probability of achieving my directive."

"I'm going to regret asking this," I said, tapping my foot, "but please walk me through what the plying hell kind of logic made you conclude that blowing me up would end with Sturb being rescued."

He took an appropriately long pause to process his reply. "I rated the probability of your death as sufficiently low, considering the factors of prior experience and proximity to emergency medical care. I rated that your likeliest response to the action would be to assign responsibility to Jacques McKeown. Now lacking a home and sense of security, your only remaining avenue would be direct confrontation. Assessing your known associations, the probability of you determining Jacques McKeown's true identity was also within acceptable bounds. As you already knew the location of user: Malcolm Sturb, the likeliest subsequent scenario would be your arrival at the *Ponce de Leon* and rescue of user: Malcolm Sturb as a consequence of your desire for confrontation."

I was slowly nodding along, hypnotised by how terribly reasonable Jimi sounded as it relayed this total garbage. "And that was the best idea you came up with, was it?"

"Tone analysed. I am interpreting your question as sarcastic. The probability that events would play out as predicted was not high. It was merely the highest of any considered scenario. Please note also that events did occur as predicted to a degree beyond expectation."

"Except for the tiny issue that Malcolm Sturb's dead. I didn't rescue him. And that was the whole reason you did it in the first place."

First, I'd considered sparing the feelings of an AI, but I was reading wounded pride into its awkward pauses. "There were many factors that defied predictability," Jimi said with the tone of a cornered politician on the news.

I'd gradually sunk back down into a sitting position with no conscious thought on my part. "Wonderful," I muttered into the sandy ground. "Plying great. My entire life goes down the trac-hole because you needed me for a quest. And then at the end of it all, I find out that I failed at the quest that nobody told me I was plying on. I met a guy in a bar once who tried to tell me that all our problems would be solved if we just let AIs run the government, and you know what? I think he was right, just not in the way he . . ."

A thought occurred. And it occurred so hard that it sent an electrical jolt through my entire body. One heartbeat I was sitting forlornly on the ground, the next I was on my feet again, clutching both sides of the computer terminal and pressing my forehead on the screen.

"You hacked the *Neverdie*?!" I barked, the words bursting out of me like Androvian Plague vomit.

"As already stated, no hacking was necessary due to a preinstalled backdoor—"

"But you can control the *Neverdie*! Can you still control the *Neverdie*?"

"Affirmative. The backdoor has remained functional since its installation, due to the user's extreme deficiency in installing mandatory firmware updates."

And to think, the operating system had always made me feel guilty about disabling pop-ups. "Can you take over the *Neverdie* right now? Can you trace its location?"

"The vessel designated *Neverdie* is currently docked at the service station attached to the trebuchet gate in the Jocsta Beta system."

"Jockstrap Eater?" I echoed, partly in nostalgic memory for some wonderful bar fights I'd gotten into there. "That's a plying backwater. Practically the direct other side of the galaxy. What're they doing there?"

"According to the most recent automated logs, the vessel designated *Neverdie* requested docking permission at Ritsuko City and was denied. Before that, it entered the area of space designated as 'Salvation Sector' and was turned away by local authorities."

I couldn't help but give a nasty little laugh. Captain Jeremy Sturridge should have been more selective when he decided to swap lives forcibly with the first sucker that came along. And the fact that the *Neverdie* was turned away from Salvation Sector told me that Warden was still on board. "So you're in the ship? Can you lock out the controls and fly it back here?"

"I have already initiated the necessary action in anticipation of that directive," said Jimi, like I was supposed to be impressed.

Suddenly I was in a much better mood. "Are the brackets on board getting in a bit of a flap about it?"

"Analysing tone. From inferred meaning of the phrase 'bit of a flap,' I am able to confirm from internal cameras that it adequately describes the crew's reaction."

My foot was tapping again, more from gleeful energy than impatience. I couldn't stop a manic smile. "Could you make every monitor on the ship display a . . . a picture of a hand holding up a middle finger? With a flashing background?"

"Directive executed. Would you also like me to play an appropriate taunt over the onboard sound system?"

I tried to summon some extremely clever one-liner, but the buzz of adrenaline was quickly using up what little energy the cave slime had given me. "Nah, maybe just really annoying music. Like Jatravan noseflute polkas."

Jimi's emotionless tone seemed, almost imperceptibly, to have picked up a note of sadistic relish. "I have queued an appropriate playlist that will fully cover the estimated flight time of fifty-nine hours."

I winced and took in my surroundings again: the barren, unyielding rock, the harsh sunlight, the half-eaten sample of local cuisine that appeared to be sluggishly trying to escape from its tray. I didn't fancy the idea of this turning into a long weekend. "Any way we can shave that down a bit?"

"Time of interception could be reduced by up to seven hours if you leave this planet and meet the incoming vessel at the *Ponce de Leon*."

It was a reasonable suggestion, especially if the alternative was sitting around licking things off cave walls for three days, except for the part about going back to the ship full of captives held hostage by a malevolent alien computer. "That doesn't feel like . . . the smartest place to be," I said.

Jimi's processing icon appeared for a few seconds. "I had conducted another probability sweep and calculated a high likelihood that you would wish to return to the *Ponce de Leon*. Please highlight the error points in my logic in order to improve my stochastic capabilities."

I blinked, then took a moment to make myself comfortable. "Okay. Sure. Break down your thinking for me. Cos I'm very interested to know how you pulled that one out of your trac-hole."

"Data point one: your prior association with the many star pilots and space villains on the crew of the *Ponce de Leon.* I calculated that you would wish to assist them in escaping from a torturous fate."

That hit me in the right parts. I looked down at the stain on the front of my uniform, the one I had gotten from Sturb's broken feeding pipe. I thought of that same orange goo being forced down the throats of all those disappeared crewmembers. People exactly like me, who had only ever wanted a meaningful career, as opposed to . . .

I shook myself. "No. No, your information's out of date. I'm over star piloting. I'm over dashing in with the heroics." I took Jimi's processing icon as a prompt to continue. "Look, there's traccy things going on all over the universe. It's not the responsibility of . . . random thrill seekers to sort them out. Certainly shouldn't be."

"Query: Whose responsibility is it?"

"I don't know. The police." I knew it was a stupid thing to say, even before the contemptful silence and the mental image of Inspector Honda riding a white charger. "Okay, not the police. But, you know. Some authority." I snapped my fingers. "The captain. Old

Jeremy Sturridge. He was the authority out here, it's his responsibility. And the moment he gets back here on the *Neverdie*—"

"Captain Jeremy Sturridge is not currently aboard the vessel designated *Neverdie*," cut in Jimi brutally.

My hand was still wobbling in a vague illustrative gesture. "You what?"

"Captain Jeremy Sturridge is not currently aboard—"

"Right, shut up. So it's only Warden on there?"

"Cross-referencing internal camera footage and data on prior associates, I can identify the sole individual aboard the *Neverdie* as Penelope Warden."

I bit my lip. "Trac. Should've realised. If they were parked at a service station, it was just as likely that he'd be off the ship."

"According to publicly available data from the Jocsta Beta station, at the time of the *Neverdie*'s departure, Jeremy Sturridge was being held by station security, pending indictment for the crime of, quote, 'alcohol-related nudity.'"

I blinked. "Okay. Forget about that. In that case, it's Oniris Venture's responsibility to sort this out. It's their ship. They're supposed to be looking after their employees."

"Would you like me to call the Oniris Venture Corporation? The ansible communication function on this device is fully operational."

Another of the wonderful innovations that had come with quantunnelling. Every smartphone in the universe could instantly communicate with every other, because miniature portals inside the workings allowed each one to be permanently, physically connected to the same server. Pretty inexpensive to run, too. When they could no longer justify charging for data usage, the telecommunications giants had been very creative in finding new ways to boost profit. The going rate for a new ringtone these days was about eight hundred euroyen.

The revelation that, far from being stranded in the depths of unknown space, I was now potentially in contact with literally any person I could think of, would have been more explosive if I could think of any bracket who could have been any plying help. "Do it. Call Oniris."

Jimi's voice was replaced by a ringer, then the breathy, reassuring female voice of an AI. "Thank you for calling the Oniris Venture Corporation," it said. "Are you an external partner, Oniris family member, customer, or other?"

I couldn't even begin to guess which applied to me. "External partner" felt the closest, as I was proposing to work with Oniris on a business venture, i.e. saving their own plying dudes. But then again, maybe I wasn't that "external," considering I had very recently been in command of their ship.

Thankfully, Jimi took the lead. "Oniris family member."

"Please hold while we connect you to our dedicated internal support line."

I puffed out my cheeks and glanced around at the magnificent, unspoiled scenery as some insipid lounge music provided a wholly inappropriate backing track. "You wanna get its number?" I said. "Thought I sensed some chemistry there."

"I am interpreting your statement as 'facetious.' Standard response: 'So is your mother.' Please rate the appropriateness of that response to help improve my bantering algorithms—"

"You have reached the Oniris Venture dedicated internal support line," said the female voice abruptly. "For payroll information, press one. For health insurance claims, press two. To report an issue in your work environment, press thr—"

"Three," said Jimi and I in unison.

"To report a danger to yourself and other family members, press one. To report an attempt at unionization . . ."

"One," said Jimi.

"It's kinda both, really," I said as we were treated to more hold music.

"Thank you for calling the Oniris Venture dedicated work-environment report line," said the voice. "Please give a brief description of the work situation you wish to report, and in what ways it has reduced productivity."

"Er, yeah, hi," I said, caught off guard. "Um. This is . . . well, I was just on the *Ponce de Leon*, out here doing deep-space recon, and . . . there's a situation with the whole crew being held hostage. By an AI. That's making them act out a TV show. It's *Trailspacers*, actually. You've probably seen it or heard of it." I coughed. "You were probably wondering why all the characters on that show are wearing Oniris uniforms. Actually, now that I'm thinking about it, did you give them permission? Do you . . . oh, ply it. Hang up, hang up."

"Did the call conclude to your satisfaction?" asked Jimi, its tone implying that it knew plying well that it hadn't.

"I . . . could probably have explained it better," I muttered. "Every time I say it out loud, it sounds really stupid. Maybe I should've just said it'd been destroyed by an alien war fleet. They'd at least send someone to check." I stared up at the sky as if I could see the *Ponce de Leon* hanging there.

"Query," said Jimi after a few moments of silence. "Would you like me to continue detailing the data points that led me to the conclusion that you would return to the *Ponce de Leon*?"

I shook myself out of it. "Okay. Astonish me."

"Point two: You once attempted to join the Oniris Venture corporation in order to regain a sense of personal fulfilment and belonging," it droned. "You are unsettled by the fate of the *Ponce de Leon* representing a potential fate for yourself. You wish to correct the situation in order to retain the notion that successfully joining Oniris Venture would have meant an end to your personal problems."

I nodded slowly. "You think I want to save everyone on the ship because I'm thinking, 'There but for the grace of trac go I'?"

"I am also thinking that you have not entirely abandoned the notion of joining Oniris Venture. I have calculated that, should you return to the *Ponce de Leon* and rescue the crew, there is a significant likelihood that you will resume your captaincy."

That gave me pause. I looked down at the stained captain's uniform I was still wearing. "Come on. They're not going to hand the captain's chair to some random johnny who just shows up." I paused to consider the last few days. "Not when things aren't completely plied, anyway."

"You possess the necessary qualifications, and with the endorsement of a grateful crew, distanced from the direct influence of the company, Oniris Venture have often favoured a pragmatic approach over a strict adherence to procedure."

"Me, the captain," I said, mostly to myself. It had once been my most optimistic daydream, but it had been buried ever since I had gotten trapped in the role of Jacques McKeown, which is when I had come to terms with the fact that I apparently wasn't allowed to have nice things.

"Would you like to reconsider your next course of action?" asked Jimi when the daydream stretched on a little too long.

I waggled a finger. "I need to think about this. And we need a plan. Let's wait for the *Neverdie*, first of all. I need to bounce a few things off Warden."

Jimi rotated his icon in acknowledgement. "Would you like me to stop playing annoying music over the vessel's sound system?"

"Absolutely not."

TWENTY-FIVE

I had to admit, after three days of it, the green cave slime started to grow on me. When I woke up each morning in the pilot's seat of the tiny shuttle and was working the stiffness out of my joints, a few spoonfuls of moist algae was just the pick-me-up I needed to motivate me to start looking for literally plying anything else to eat.

I was able to keep myself halfway presentable by shaving with the knife I'd found in the shuttle's emergency survival kit and sending my uniform away with one of Jimi's drones to be laundered in a clear oasis he had found about twenty miles away. So when the *Neverdie* appeared in the orange sky on the third morning and descended gloriously to a large stretch of flat ground behind the drone factory, I was about as refreshed and upbeat as could be expected.

My mood improved further when the exterior airlock slid open and I could already hear the faint toots and whistles of several Jatravan noseflutes playing enthusiastically. I signalled to Jimi to cut the music, then opened the interior door.

The Penelope Warden that promptly stumbled out and fell onto her knees in the dust hadn't changed much since I had seen her last, as far as I could tell from the pillow wrapped around her head. Her hair was an absolute fright, and she was wearing an old technician's boiler suit I kept in one of the tool cabinets in case I was unexpectedly invited to a formal event.

"Do you. Have any idea. What that was like?" she said, through the pillow, sucking in deep breaths with each sentence.

"I thought I'd leave the stereo on, so you wouldn't be bored," I said, hands behind my back.

The pillow came away. The bags under her eyes were big enough to get her charged for extra storage at a Speedstar check-in desk. "Oh, it's you," she growled, untensing her shoulders.

I'd been practicing this conversation for three days. "Yes, Warden, it's me. Funnily enough, the person who was in control of the ship was the person who owns the plying thing. And don't pretend I'm not entitled to be mad about this."

She stood erect until her nose was turned up to its accustomed height and tucked a few strands of hair behind her ear. "It was that Oniris captain who stole your ship. I was practically a hostage."

"Oh, sure. And clearly you were struggling with all your might to get the ship back here. Especially while he was in the Jocsta Beta drunk tank."

Her mouth hung open. She looked even more tired than before. "How did you . . . you had remote access to the ship's computer, didn't you."

I waved Sturb's phone. "You remember Jimi?"

"Recognise previous user: Penelope Warden," said Jimi with the air of a dog sizing up its chances of a bum sniff.

"Sturb's AI," realised Warden aloud. "Is Sturb . . ."

"He's dead," I revealed. "He got caught up in something very weird going on on the *Leon*."

She straightened up. "This would be the crew being forced to act out a television program?" A lot of her old self returned in her smug reaction to my look. "Don't look so surprised. I have more sources than you know."

"User: Penelope Warden was informed of the *Ponce de Leon*'s situation through conversations with Jeremy Sturridge," tattled Jimi. "I have analysed the *Neverdie*'s internal camera footage."

"Ah," I said as her face fell again. "Got pretty chummy, did you? Stockholm syndrome must have set in pretty plying quick."

She scowled. "Why did you bring me here?"

"I was bringing my ship here." I nodded to the *Neverdie*'s looming hull as it provided some much appreciated shade from the sun. "Apparently you were the pack-in bonus I have to deal with. But now that you are here, I could use your help."

She arched an eyebrow and folded her arms, sensing a chance to lord herself over me. She would have looked more dignified had she not been wearing a boiler suit that hadn't been cleaned since the last time I'd used the sleeves to mop up a spilled plate of beans on toast. "With what?"

"I'm going to save the crew of the *Leon*," I announced. "There's some kind of alien AI running this whole TV show thing. Jimi has an idea for how to neutralize it."

"If you can transfer me directly to the ship's central mainframe," piped up Jimi, "my familiarity with Oniris systems will be much greater than that of an alien intelligence. I calculate a high probability that I will be able to overpower a circle of essential systems and enclose the foreign entity in a code loop."

"All we have to do is physically connect Sturb's phone to the *Leon*'s main computer," I said, recounting the one part of Jimi's plan I still understood after three days of explanations.

Warden frowned. "But why would an alien AI be compatible with the Oniris systems in the first place? It sounds . . ."

"Hackneyed," I supplied. "Yeah, I know, but it's the situation. We're the only ones who are in any position to help the crew of that ship. You wanted to find a new purpose in life? This might be a good start."

She lowered one eyebrow and raised the other one, unconvinced. "High-level computer heists aren't my area, Mr. Pierce. I'm still not clear on why you think you need my help."

"I need your help because you're cleverer than me," I forced myself to admit. "And this isn't a straightforward, 'space hero barges in and makes it up as he goes along' sort of scenario. I tried that, and all I got was a ride on an escape shuttle and a dead arch-nemesis."

"Even so, Mr. Pierce, my skill set is largely administrative," said Warden. "I'm sure I'd only be of use if you think rescuing people from slavery counts as human resource management."

I let out a little frustrated sigh. "Look. We've had to work together in the past. And usually it turns out pretty well. I don't know why. Obviously we hate each other, but maybe that's it. Maybe having someone we hate around gives us both . . . motivation."

She was scrutinizing my expression, and my inability to make eye contact. "Are you lingering on that time we slept together?"

That was a low blow with a verbal breeze block. It caught me right in the solar plexus as I was trying to summon my next argument, and pushed all the air out of my lungs in a string of stammers. "Uh. Look. That was . . . I mean . . ."

Jimi filled the subsequent silence. "It looks like you're trying to navigate an embarrassing social encounter. Would you like my assistance?"

I turned on him. "Look. Jimi. Do you mind leaving us alone for a bit? Warden and I need to have a private conversation. The kind that can only be had between a man and a woman who hate each other very much."

To my surprise, Warden put up no resistance whatsoever as I took her by the upper arm and steered her away, leaving Sturb's phone on the computer terminal. I walked us a good fifty yards from the drone station and into a nice sheltered corner between a boulder and a natural bridge support. She pulled herself away from my grip and leaned against one of the stone walls, folding her arms. "Mr. Pierce, I have nothing to . . ."

I did a quick scan of the sky for flying drones, then stepped right into her personal space and put my mouth next to her ear. She immediately stiffened up like a startled cat's tail. "Jimi's lying to us," I whispered. "This might be our only chance to talk without him hearing. Act like we're resolving romantic tension."

She slowly unstiffened in time with her descending eyebrows. "I didn't want to say anything. That whole concept about an alien AI taking over the ship . . ."

"The hackneyed thing, yeah." I nodded. "It's worse than you think. He told me the AI learned about human TV shows from intercepting ancient broadcasts."

"Good grief," she said, grimacing.

"He's spent the last three days trying to talk me into going back to save the *Leon*." I glanced fearfully to the side, as if I could see around the corner to the phone sitting innocently on its perch. "He wants to be taken back there. Not sure why. But I've had a lot of time to think about it."

"Uh huh," replied Warden, implying with her tone that she believed that time could have been better spent.

"See, at first I thought he'd been in Sturb's phone since I took it from Sturb, back on the ship," I said. "But then I realised that he only started talking to me after I synced the phone up with the drone station, down here."

"So he wasn't in the phone, he was in the drone station, obviously enough," said Warden. "Marooned here deliberately, I would think, because Sturb wanted to get him away from the ship."

"Yeah, so I have no idea what's actually running the show back on the *Leon* right now, but Jimi definitely knows more than he's saying. And I don't know why he's lying about it."

"Well, your next course of action seems clear enough to me," said Warden, placing her hands on her hips. "You're going to have to go back to the *Leon*, aren't you."

I rubbed my head. "Plying out loud. Not you as well. Why does nobody believe me when I say I'm done with the plying space-hero stuff?"

"I would have thought it would have been more craven, self-preservation stuff." She paused to enjoy my baffled expression. "Jimi has full control of your ship. I'm assuming he's the only reason you currently have any access to food or water. He's also in control of a drone fleet that could facilitate any number of methods of coercion. I think you're going to be doing whatever Jimi wants you to do."

This, I mused, was probably why I had felt the need to bounce the situation off Warden. I had subconsciously wanted her to give voice to important truths of which I was perfectly aware but trying to keep suppressed under a layer of devil-may-care optimism. "Okay," I intoned slowly. "So what the hell do we do, once we get back to the *Leon*?"

"I have no idea what *you* will do," said Warden, with an infuriating little sniff. "*I* have nothing to do with this situation of yours."

I scoffed. "Yeah, okay. Except for the fact that you've got no other way off this planet. What're you going to do, set up home in the middle of a dry, barren, hostile wasteland?" I paused. "What am I saying? You'll fit right in."

"Perhaps I would prefer to tackle the current assortment of problems, rather than take chances on an all-new batch."

My next frustrated noise was interrupted by distant music. It sounded like a female voice singing in Japanese, accompanied by the kind of music a pile of candy floss would make if you could somehow plug a sound system into it.

"That's Sturb's ringtone," I deduced. "Who's calling Sturb's phone?"

I hurried back to the drone station's command centre, where the phone was merrily singing to itself. The screen displayed a number neither I nor the phone seemed to recognise, but I decided to take the call, on the basis that even a wrong number might have more solutions to offer than Warden did at that moment. "Hello?"

In response, the phone emitted a prolonged sound of flatulence, or possibly of a balloon being slowly released. This continued for several seconds, gradually decreasing in pitch before the sound laboriously shaped itself into understandable syllables.

"THHHRRRRRRrrrrrrhhhhello. Thhrrthis is the Oniris Venture Corporation."

I grimaced. The speaker was a windchimp from Fergacius Prime, a species that struggled to integrate with the galaxy's other sentient races, largely thanks to their having no biological distinction between speaking and flatulence. They tried their best, but even disregarding the smell, there was something very upsetting about watching their "mouths" clenching and unclenching their way through the phrases. None of which stopped Oniris Venture from hiring them as cheap labour for their overflow call centres.

"Our records indicate that you called to report a situation on the *Ponce de Leon* thrrrrthree days ago, is thrrthat correct?"

My eyebrows bobbed. Considering the Oniris Corporation's bureaucracy, three days was a pretty impressive turnaround for an emergency response. "Yes," I said, tentatively doing my best impression of Malcolm Sturb's voice, in case they had his number on record.

"I'm calling to infffphrrorm you thrthat an offffrficial investigation has been opened, and Oniris Internal has commissioned an agent to liaise with the vfffvessel in question. Please ensure thrrrthat you and your coworkers are available for intervfffriew."

So perhaps calling Oniris hadn't been the smart approach after all. The last thing the situation needed was more clueless fodder to get lured in and added to the pile of victims. "No, no. Listen. Don't send anyone."

The windchimp emitted a sound reminiscent of a confused person sighing into a party squeaker. "Uhhhh. Thffthis is just a call to infffrform you offft the invffvestigation. Iffff you wish to make a ffffthfollow-up report please call the dedicated Oniris line again . . ."

"This is the follow-up report. I am reporting something now. I am reporting that if you send an Oniris rep to the *Leon*, they're just going to get sucked into the problem."

I heard a keyboard being tapped uncertainly. Going off script had clearly derailed things. "Oh. Er. I don't thffthink it's an actual Oniris repphpresentative. Says here it's an independent contractor."

"That doesn't matter," I said, pinching my eyes. "They need to be briefed on the situation before they go anywhere near it. They need to disable all the *Leon*'s internal computer systems, and then send in soldiers to make sure everything's locked down, before . . ." I paused to contemplate a couple of nagging thoughts that were rolling around in my head. "What independent contractor?"

More keyboard tapping. "Uh. Some kind of deep-space problem-solving specialists?" farted the windchimp. "Based out of . . . Salvation Sector? Says here."

A strange calm came over me. Suddenly, all the shattered pieces of my existence were sliding neatly back together. "You're sending star pilots," I said in a monotone. "Star pilots from Salvation Sector."

"Yes, the main point of contact is a . . . Mr. Henderson. Should I fffphforward you his credentials?"

"That won't be necessary. Thank you. Goodbye."

The windchimp's voice switched straight back into scripted mode. "By concluding this phfffphone call, you acknowledge that your workplace issue is resolvvfved and thrrrthat any fffflfuture diffffffrficulties relating to thhhfthis issue are no longer the responsibility of—"

I hung up smartly, then tapped the edge of Sturb's phone gently against my inexpertly shaved chin as I contemplated next steps. I turned when I felt a hot sensation on the back of my neck, and found myself taking the full force of Warden's glare.

"Oh, hello," I said, jiggling the phone and offering her a reassuring smile. "Turns out we don't have anything to worry about. Oniris Venture are sending someone out."

Her fists were clenching. She didn't break eye contact. "Why did you mention star pilots?"

"Oh, yes." I glanced at the phone. "They hired Daniel Henderson and his next-generation star-pilot friends to do it. Not that that should mean anything to you, obviously. I mean, you used to be the one co-ordinating star pilots in the Black, so you might have an interest in making sure Danny doesn't completely ply things up, but . . ."

"Mr. Pierce," snapped Warden, biting her consonants like dry crackers. The quaver in her voice was like the first rumble of a dormant volcano. "I do not care about star pilots. I do not care about the *Ponce de Leon*. And as far as I'm concerned, the Black can rot."

By the end of her statement, she was leaning forward, and I was leaning back. "Okay," I replied in a higher pitch than I had intended. "Fine. Message received."

She leaned back onto her heels. "Good."

"Great." I stared down at the phone again. "No guarantee Daniel will ply it all up, anyway. He's changed. He pulled off that raid on Salvation really well. And you saw the abs he's got now. Saving the *Leon* is probably completely within his abilities."

"I'm sure." Warden folded her arms.

"He'll swoop in with his team of super friends, save the day, and prove he's just as qualified to patrol the Black as anyone else," I said, sauntering carefully along my train of thought. "And everyone will be so grateful. They'll probably give him a medal. He'll be up there standing proud in front of the whole Oniris crew, and they'll all be clapping, and he'll have a big smile on his face. You can picture it, can't you? The smile."

Her arms were folded so tightly I could hear the creaking of the boiler suit's cheap stitching. She glared at me again. "This, Mr. Pierce, is an extremely clumsy attempt to manipulate me."

"Yeah, well, not every job requires finesse, does it," I retorted. "And before you say anything, yes, maybe I will make that the motto for my entire life."

TWENTY-SIX

A brief inspection of the *Neverdie* indicated that it was none the worse for its ordeal. The pilot's chair wasn't set up the way I liked, some of the trash had been moved around to throw off the aesthetics a bit, and at one point some desperate effort had been made to get inside the wall-mounted speakers. Also, someone had eaten the rest of my emergency biscuit rations, but frankly, that had been doing me a favour. All in all, Warden and Captain Jeremy Sturridge had left relatively little sign of their presence.

I was offended. If they'd done a bit more to wreck the place up, that would at least have indicated that the *Neverdie* meant something to them. As it was, they'd clearly thought of it as just another ride. It was like they'd kidnapped my wife, and then after I tracked her down, all they'd done was stand her against a wall and use her as a coatrack. I stood in the communal cabin with my hands on my hips, huffing to myself.

Warden appeared behind me. "Okay," she sighed. "From what you and Captain Sturridge explained about the situation, the system violently suppresses any individual that attempts to work against it, or break the fourth wall?"

I nodded, still distracted by looking around the cabin for things to get mad at. "Yeah. They get violently suppressed into a chair and tubes shoved down them."

"But from your account, it's possible to do that without being noticed as long as you are being sufficiently boring, or if you can be sure that something more interesting is happening elsewhere."

"Yep. I assume it can only monitor one or two things at a time. The whole setup's pretty janky. The drones it's using can't even hold up against one biff with a pool cue."

Her eyebrow raised as she watched me demonstrate my underarm swing. "The course of action seems clear to me," she said. "We have two ships. One of us can create an interesting distraction while the other sneaks aboard and introduces Jimi to the mainframe, wherever that is."

"The central access terminal for the mainframe is located in the administrative section of the top deck, a short distance from the bridge," piped in Jimi.

"Not the IT department?" I shuddered at the memory of the prisoners in those dark, electronic catacombs.

"The mainframe access terminal is positioned for use by senior officers, granting access to the Oniris intelligence database and a collated interface for all of the vessel's autonomous functions."

I nodded. "Mainframe's the queen bee, IT's the hive. Got it."

"You've certainly got something," muttered Warden. "I take it you will be the one delivering Jimi to the mainframe? It being the most adventure-adjacent role."

"This isn't about space heroics, it's about helping the community," I said, waggling a finger. "But yes, I will be doing that. I'm the one in the Oniris uniform. I'll blend in better."

She nodded reasonably. "In that case, I will need the *Neverdie*." Her hand shot up to interrupt as my mouth opened. "Before you make the inevitable kneejerk objection, consider the following points. One, it will be a lot easier to create an interesting distraction with a flashy star-piloting vessel, even one as obviously past warranty as this. Two, I can do nothing underhanded with your ship as long as Jimi has remote access to the internal systems."

I closed my mouth for a moment, then opened it again. "I have completely memorised the positioning of all the cup holders, and if any of them are out of whack, there'll be trouble." I paused to let the plan percolate in my head. "What kind of distraction are you going to make, anyway?"

"Don't worry about that. I think I have a decent grasp of what makes for interesting television."

"No you plying don't. You think sorting envelopes is fun. I know, I've seen the games on your phone. Plus, you're terrible at improvising."

"I am up to the task," she said. I was impressed by the way she barely moved her lips to do so.

I sat down on my metal couch with a sigh. "Our plying lives are riding on this. You can't fake your way through it with confidence. It's not a plying job interview. What, exactly, are you going to do?"

She stood in silence, affronted, before clicking her tongue and pulling out her tablet. "I propose to fly into visual range of the main bridge . . ."

I pointed. "What're you reading off that for?"

"I sketched out a loose plan. Please don't interrupt. I will introduce myself to the crew of the *Leon* as an ambassador from an alien federation on a nearby planet, where a trade dispute has escalated to an embargo of vital supplies to one of the planet's continents. When the crew offer to send a party to assist, I will reveal that my true motive is to—"

"Er, going to have to interrupt again." I had been craning my neck to see the screen of her tablet and noticed that she had about six more paragraphs to go. "Can I suggest a couple of minor changes?"

The corner of her mouth twitched. "I . . . suppose."

TWENTY-SEVEN

"Iam Vortexia, queen of the Lingeraiders," came the voice of Warden, filled with impressively authentic hatred. "Surrender your most attractive crewmembers for our pleasure pits or be destroyed."

I breathed a sigh of relief when it was clear she wasn't going to go off-script. I was sitting in the pokey Oniris shuttle, closing in on the *Leon*'s lower regions. "That should keep the cameras on the bridge," I said.

"Suggestion: The distracting effect would have been greatly enhanced if a visual element had been included," said Jimi, talking through the shuttle's internal speaker.

"Yeah, well, I wasn't about to bring that up with Warden, so I guess we're making do with audio only." I slowed the shuttle's approach as the external door of my chosen airlock automatically slid open. "Warden's not a pilot, so you're going to have to keep controlling the *Neverdie* remotely. Can you do some strafing runs? Put on a good show?"

"Assessing ammunition and countermeasure inventory. Projections indicate a comfortable likelihood that I can provide a display that would be classified above a general definition of mediocre."

I took a moment to unpick that sentence like a mass of tangled wiring. "Great. Good."

"It will require a significant percentage of my processing memory. I will only be able to offer limited support until you can reach the mainframe."

"That's fine. I imagine I'll get by without someone stopping to tell me the odds of getting plied up the trac-hole every five steps."

"Sarcasm detected. I have analysed your tone and interpreted your statement as 'matey ribbing.' Please rate the accuracy of this assessment, and my bantering ability will—"

"Whoops, about to start docking, need to concentrate," I said, cramming all the words together into a single rapid blast.

This time, I had opted for the main docking bay, the one that was packed to the rafters with Oniris vessels of every size and shape. I manoeuvred the shuttle stealthily, carefully using the larger ships to block line of sight between myself and the exit doors, until I could gently touch down at the far end of a rank of shuttles identical to my own.

I winced as the shuttle's hydraulics hissed violently with the opening of the airlock, but no nightstick-wielding security guards were sprinting in my direction. I was half expecting as much. From what I'd seen, most of the crew were smart enough to keep their heads down when something was obviously drawing the TV show's attention, but that was no reason to be reckless.

That point was proved shortly as I traversed the docking bay floor and almost walked straight into the view of a gaggle of engineering staff who were keeping their heads down near one of the larger shuttles in a half-hearted but passable impression of routine maintenance.

I crouched behind a transport crate. I could arrange my collar to hide my uniform's captain stripes, but I was still wearing administrative colours, and that would catch eyes down here in the grease-stained engineering realm. Maybe rolling up my sleeves would help.

I was startled out of my scheming when an alert klaxon sounded, and a thin red strip of light started flashing on and off, high on the docking bay wall. "Alert," came an urgent voice over the PA system. "The ship is under attack. All personnel to battle stations."

The ship's interior promptly failed to become a buzzing hive of military efficiency. The engineers I had been watching barely moved. "Battle stations?" said one of the younger ones. "Do we have those?"

Another withdrew her head from the engine compartment that, up until this moment, she had been uselessly staring at. "I don't remember them being mentioned."

"Wouldn't worry about it," muttered a grizzled engineer sitting with arms folded on a disabled forklift. There was an edge to his voice that suggested he was proposing their best survival strategy.

They appeared to be distracted, and more to the point, didn't seem to give the slightest trac, so I risked it. I rolled up my sleeves and marched out into the open with a confidence that suggested I knew exactly where I had to be, and that anyone who got in my way was going to be answering to my superiors.

I was twenty yards to the entrance door when one of the engineers called out a largely unengaged, "Morning, sir," but that was enough to rattle me. I immediately broke into a jog without turning and threw up a hand in what could have been either a vague greeting or an attempt to fling away a piece of snot. I hurried through the door and closed it behind me before anyone could say anything else.

"Yeah, this isn't going to work," I muttered, bringing Sturb's phone up to my face. "I need a less noticeable uniform. Something lower level. Without the bloodstains."

"Please stand by. The *Neverdie* is completing a manoeuvre in accordance with your established directives."

In the distance, I heard the rumble of some of the *Neverdie*'s countermeasures rattling harmlessly off the *Leon*'s hull as it no doubt strafed impressively past. The red alert continued to play throughout the corridor.

Meaning there was still a rhythmic klaxon and flashing red light strip along the walls, but for an alert, it was strangely ignorable. I'd once been on a Speedstar ship during a major emergency, and I remember being absolutely deafened by a siren that seemed to fill my entire head, completely bathed in hellish red light as I charged down the corridor, competing with multiple burly spacers to be the first to get to the switch that turned that plying noise off. In contrast, the redness from the *Leon*'s alert wasn't even trying to compete with the bright ceiling lights, and the klaxon was unassuming enough to be talked over by the various crewmembers who gathered in small groups to ask each other if they knew what was going on.

"Suggestion: a locker room is located ahead, behind the second door on your left," said Jimi after the sound of the *Neverdie*'s attack ceased. "A high probability of locating a replacement garment is projected."

I ducked through the door and an antechamber into a small, square changing room adjoining one of the communal showers. A row of orange lockers lined the far wall, each locked with a little touchscreen requesting that I input my crew ID number.

"Can you do something about the locks?" I asked. As every locker opened simultaneously with a thunderous crash that jolted several loose watches and spectacle cases onto the floor, I could only reflect on how humanity never seems to learn its lesson when it comes to computerising every single plying thing.

I found a low-level technician's uniform, the kind that might be worn by an ordinary IT worker being called to the mainframe by an officer to turn a computer off and then on again, and peeled the captain's uniform off my body, wincing at the smell that arose. I looked down at the continent of dried blood that covered my midsection and wondered if there was time to make proper use of these shower facilities.

As I considered it, I glanced toward the hallway that led to the shower, just in time to see two crewmembers enter from that direction, clad only in towels and a glossy film of water. I mouthed a very dirty word and hopped into a hiding spot behind one of the open locker doors.

"Did you catch that announcement? Battle stations?" said the shorter of the two, cocking his head toward the exit door, from which the sound of the alert siren could still faintly be heard. "Where do we keep the battle stations?"

"Oh my god," said the taller one. "I'm so glad you didn't know, either. I didn't want to say anything. I was like, isn't this a science ship?"

"I guess there was always the chance of pirates," said the short one, scratching his head.

"Pirates? What would they want, the test tubes?" He had been looking at his friend and reaching for his locker, so his train of thought immediately derailed when his hand passed straight through where he believed a closed door would be. "Wha—who opened these?"

His friend was looking down at the discarded uniform I'd left on the bench in the centre of the room. I mouthed another, even dirtier word. "Might be something to do with this," he said. He peered closer. "Wait, isn't that a captain's uniform?"

The taller one turned pale. "Oh god. Is this an episode?" His arms wrapped around his bare torso.

"Shft!" went the other urgently, before switching to a whisper. "Don't be stupid. No. Probably not. That only happens to officers."

"Not necessarily!" whimpered the tall one. "Maybe we're the two no-name guards who show up at the start to get chumped by the monster!"

"Don't hang lampshades! Do you wanna get taken? It's just a uniform!" He poked at the rumpled mess. "Not one I've ever seen Captain Sparky wear, mind."

"Maybe it was one of the last few captains?" said the tall one, calming down only slightly.

The short one boggled at him, then jumped to his feet, sputtering in frustration. "Stop it! You got a death wish? Stick to the script! There's only ever been one captain, and nothing funny is happening!"

Then he strode right over to the locker door I was hiding behind and angrily slammed it shut before I could react. He hadn't known I was there. He was probably just going to go down the line and shut them all, but that plan was abandoned abruptly as we made eye contact.

So there we were, me in just my boxer shorts, staring down two men in towels, every mouth in the room hanging silently open in surprise. As the seconds ticked on, it occurred to me that the first man to speak was going to set the tone for the rest of this encounter.

Fortunately, my mind felt the kick of a spur when a distant rumble signalled the *Neverdie* making another ineffective attack run. "Hail Queen Vortexia!" I yelled, puffing out my chest. "Ha ha! I, her greatest warrior slut, have boarded your vessel! Submit now to the pleasure pits!"

"Oh shit! It is an episode!" cried the taller crewmember.

"Shut up!" said I and the other man simultaneously.

"What are you going to do to us?" he demanded.

That was a good question. I gave him a deranged stare and then started fluttering my hands back and forth in what I hoped looked like a mystic gesture. "Now you are under the control of my psychic Slut Weapon!"

"What does that do?!" asked the shorter crewmember.

"It . . . makes you feel irrepressible feelings of lust for whoever you're standing closest to," I improvised.

The two men hesitated, made eye contact for the merest fraction of a second, then seized each other and began fiercely making out, tumbling against the wall. I grabbed my boots and the nearest available armful of clothing and made for the door as they wrestled each other to the ground, deciding it best that I leave them to process whatever it was they needed to process.

TWENTY-EIGHT

The armful of clothing I had hastily grabbed turned out to contain only a pair of black trousers, some socks, and a towel, so I resigned myself to completing my infiltration mission bare-chested, but that was the least of my worries. I had to assume that the *Neverdie*'s assault wasn't going to be drawing the attention of the *Leon*'s invisible showrunner anymore, not with the extremely interesting romantic mess I had caused. That meant I couldn't drop out of character.

Whatever the plying hell my character was. Some kind of brainwashed sex-slave warrior thing in service to a dominatrix pirate queen? At least the shirtlessness would help sell that. Maybe Warden and I should have jotted down a few world-building notes after all.

I was running through the corridors of the *Leon*'s engineering deck, and just as I was closing in on the elevator, I was startled by the klaxon abruptly stopping with a click, replaced by another, subtly different klaxon. "Intruder alert," went that infuriatingly calm voice again. "Intruder alert. Security personnel to the engineering deck. Form teams of individuals who do not find each other sexually attractive. Repeat . . .”

The elevator doors finally opened, and I ducked inside. Either those guards had disentangled long enough to raise the alarm, or the TV cameras had taken the initiative. In any case, time to stick to the script.

“Aha!” I said aloud, pressing the button for the top deck. “All I have to do is get to the mainframe, and then I can flood this entire ship of fools with Queen Vortexia’s pleasure gas!”

I cringed a little inside. I glanced up at where I imagined the invisible cameras could be and thought about all the people watching *Trailspacers* back in Ritsuko City, thinking it was a perfectly normal television show with scripts, and sets, and actors. Out of nowhere, I wondered if Inspector Honda was watching. I subconsciously shifted into a dynamic pose that covered at least some of my nipples.

Soon, the elevator deposited me on the central corridor of the ship’s topmost level, which was surprisingly short on personnel.

“The mainframe is located at a point directly between the bridge and the administration centre,” said Jimi. “I am detecting minimal security forces on this deck.”

“No doubt quivering in fear of their own awakened genitals,” I sneered. “For the queen!”

I no longer heard the *Neverdie*'s attack runs, so I could have Jimi's undivided processing power. It displayed a helpful map indicating the couple of turns that would take me to the mainframe. No further crewmembers appeared to stop me, and I was privately astonished at how well this was going.

I turned the last corner and almost ran straight into Doctor Allura. Which was absolutely my fault for letting myself feel optimism.

She was standing in front of the door to the mainframe with one hand on her hip and the other holding a leash, at the end of which was Captain Sparky. He had probably been in a dynamic pose of his own at one point, but had since gotten bored and settled into a sitting position, panting dopily.

"I am Doctor Allura of the OSS *Ponce de Leon*," she said, clipped and professional, although I was reading the usual exhaustion in her look. "What do you want from us?"

"I will subdue you with my lust waves," I announced, making the weird finger gestures again. I couldn't entirely recall if that was what I'd called it last time, but it was far too late for whatever was running this show to start caring about continuity.

Allura recoiled, but then she held up her own hands in a much more impressive gesture, bending her fingers expertly into haunting patterns. "I can resist your lust waves with my powers of tantric meditation. This is our ship. I will not let you have your way with it." Captain Sparky gave a little whine.

I should have realised she was an old hand at this trac. I upped my look of wild, lustful triumph. "Aha! A worthy opponent! Looks like I'm going to have to go up to full power!" I shifted my stance and waggled my fingers with greater intensity.

She grimaced. Her muscles tensed. Her foot skidded back an inch or two as she appeared to take the strain of a powerful force. I was impressed by her miming skills, and all I could do was continue waggling relentlessly. Baffled, Captain Sparky glanced back and forth between us.

"Gah, damn you," she said, tossing her hair and gritting her teeth. "I knew you would be a problem. I knew from the moment you came aboard you would cause problems. Why should I let you interfere further with this vessel?"

There was an odd tone to her voice that I caught on to after she very suddenly met my gaze at the end of her question. I realised she hadn't been asking rhetorically.

"Ha ha," I said, thinking quickly. "Do not resist the great Queen Vortexia! When you are among the Lingeraiders, you will never return to your paltry lives on this ship. And you will bow down in thanks to Her Eroticness!"

Allura caught my eye again and nodded almost imperceptibly, then her arms shook with strain and she dropped to one knee. "No! I'll never submit! What do you even want with the computer mainframe?"

I wiggled my fingers frantically as I thought about it. "With Queen Vortexia's computer sex virus, we will put an end to your ship's entire pathetic mission!"

Allura dropped to the ground, clutching herself. "No! I can't stop you. I can't stop you from having your way with the mainframe." I stepped over her as Captain Sparky began snuffling at her prone form, worried. "I can't stop you opening the door with the handle in the alcove to the left. I can't stop you pushing rather than pulling. Pushing quite hard because it sticks sometimes."

TWENTY-NINE

The *Ponce de Leon*'s mainframe computer room was impressive, almost entirely useless, and completely in accordance with expectations.

It was a circular chamber about two hundred square feet too big for its actual purpose, i.e. providing the officer class with a single, easy-to-understand terminal to summarise all of the ship's computerised functions. The terminal was there, a little horseshoe-shaped booth with a flexible holographic screen and a keyboard, served by a high-backed chair with trapezoidal armrests. Thick black cables emerged from every inch of the room's perimeter, snaking around and coalescing into the back of the central terminal's housing. The whole room was bathed in a gently pulsating red glow that added a lot to the organic "internal organs of a monstrous beast" effect that the cables had already laid down.

Powerful symbolism, but I felt it would have been a lot more practical to have just one big cable running under the floor, where no one would trip over it. I wondered if the TV show's remodelling was to blame, or if Oniris had set it up this way to showcase for investors. Probably somewhere in between.

"Jimi, seal the door," I commanded before dynamically hopping into the seat, raising my hands to type, and stopping dead. I watched a series of random numbers and symbols scroll past on the monitor for a while, not having the slightest plying clue what any of it meant. "What the hell do I do now?"

"Probability indicates that a universal connection cable may be found in the nearby drawer," said Jimi. "Suggestion: use one to connect this unit to the mainframe terminal."

There was indeed a drawer in the terminal housing, just to my right, its presence given away only by a narrow seam in the ultramodern design. There was no handle, but when I pushed gently with my fingertips, an opening mechanism activated and a bird's nest of random cables, plug-ins, and depleted batteries burst into view.

I nodded. The powers that be could make this room as neat as they liked, but there was no escaping the basic law of the universe: wherever there is a computer, a drawer full of random mismatched components will never be far away. After a brief bout of one-handed archaeology, I found a suitable wire and plugged Sturb's phone into the universal socket just above the keyboard.

Immediately, the numbers on the screen froze. Several windows opened and closed rapidly, like the fluttering eyes of a person struggling to fight off sleep. Then the screen turned a pleasing blue, and a progress bar began slowly crawling from left to right.

"I am initiating the process of isolating the rogue AI," said Jimi.

"Okay," I said, then coughed. "I mean, excellent! Her Shapeliness Queen Vortexia will be most pleased!"

"Please do not disconnect the cable or turn off the computer until this process is complete." Barely a moment's pause later, the phone screen lit up. "Incoming call from Queen Vortexia."

For several reasons, I hesitated. "Will taking the call slow the process down?"

"I can ensure that it will not."

So much for that excuse. "Put her through."

Shortly, the organic hum and occasional heartbeat of the mainframe was joined by the reassuring hum of my cockpit air conditioner, and then by the considerably less relaxing voice of Warden. "Hello? Update me, please. My ship stopped moving several minutes ago."

"Hail, Queen Vortexia, whore empress of the Lingeraiders," I said, hoping to plying God that she'd understand I was still on camera. "I have successfully infiltrated the mainframe, your . . . large-breastedness. Soon all of these fools will succumb to the call of their irresistible passion."

"I see," said Warden after a pause. "How much longer will I be kept waiting?"

I looked back at the monitor. Jimi had managed to scare up a whole additional percentage point in the time since I had looked at it last. "Might be a while yet."

"Please hurry. I'm feeling rather exposed out here."

"I'm doing literally everything I can to speed things up, my queen." I luxuriously settled into the seat's cushions and lifted my feet up onto the terminal's housing.

For one foolish second, I actually thought I could relax, but in the very next, a knock came upon the door behind me, and my stress jumped straight back up to its habitual level. The knock was swiftly followed by a pounding.

"The door's seal is holding," said Jimi, in what it probably imagined was a reassuring voice.

I wondered how long that would last, with Jimi distracted and an aggrieved crew that I had recently been threatening with sex slavery outside. I checked my immediate surroundings for weapons. The chair was bolted to the floor, so that was little help, although I could crouch down to keep a bit of cover between me and the door. I went back to the drawer of components and dug up a nice surge protector on a short cable that I could swing around my head rather effectively.

"What was that?" demanded Warden as another harsh blow rattled the door in its housing. "You need to update me on the situation."

I swung my improvised flail against my palm a couple of times. "My apologies, your opposite-of-prudishness," I said through my teeth. "I am not presently able to open the barricaded door, fight my way through several besieging crewmembers, inscribe my full report of events on a vellum scroll, fly out to your vessel, and present it to you between my perfumed buttocks. Please spare me your wrath."

"Okay, I didn't know you were barricaded behind a door, that is the sort of thing I need updates on."

"You didn't bother to ask!" I countered.

"Yes I did. I called you up just now and asked. I said, 'What was that?' Surely that counts as asking."

The blows upon the door were getting harder, addling my thought process. I pushed Warden out of my head and turned to Jimi. "What happens when the progress bar fills up? You take full control from the AI? No more risk of getting disappeared?"

"After the completion of the partitioning process, the ship will be free of the influence of any AI other than myself."

That would have to do. Hopefully I would be able to explain the situation to the angry crewmembers on the other side of that door before they started using my head as a percussion instrument. Although their enthusiasm for hitting things was, by the sound of it, only increasing by the second. Assuming it was an organic life-form banging on the door, and not . . .

"Hello? Updates, please!" barked Warden.

"Plying hang on, I'm trying to think!" Now that I was thinking, it was odd how few crewmembers I had seen on my way up here. Just Allura and Captain Sparky on the entirety of this, the most vital administration deck. There were parts of this picture that weren't in plain sight.

"I don't believe your previous communication showed an appropriate degree of deference, minion," said Warden.

She was reminding me to stay in character, as was presently very important for my survival. Ultimately, she was looking out for me. This is what I told myself, to arrest the long sequence of colourful swear words my vocal cords promptly queued up in reply. "My most humble apologies, my queen," I said, smiling a little bit too widely. "You are as beautiful as you are gracious, and I give thanks for this opportunity to do all the plying work while you definitely aren't sitting around like an overweight cat on a desktop being no plying help whatsoever."

I didn't quite catch her reply because it was interrupted by a particularly loud and catastrophic bang upon the door. Apparently, the invaders had made a significant bit of progress, probably detaching the door from some important part of the housing.

As was my habit when I felt myself shifting into deer-in-the-headlights mode, I let my body's natural instincts take over. Immediately I vaulted over the chair and pressed my entire body weight against the door, just in time for another juddering impact to arrive and send vibrations all the way to my feet. The door shifted at least a couple of inches when I pressed against it.

It was a sliding door, so it wasn't about to pop off its hinges, but it wasn't particularly sturdy, either. It wasn't a blast door or anything that needed to keep vacuum out; it was an internal door whose main justification was politeness. It was for officers who didn't want prying eyes seeing what they were using the mainframe for and, possibly for related reasons, was light enough to be pulled shut one-handed.

I spread my arms across the light aluminium as another part of it threatened to buckle. "Jimi! How much longer?!" I yelled.

"Like a minion!" hissed Warden.

"How much longer, nya ha ha, I'm an evil sex pirate or something," I hastily added.

"Ten more seconds are required," said Jimi nonchalantly.

One time at Speedstar Academy, the head administrator had assembled all of the cadets and demanded that we turn in whoever had placed a racy magazine in the upraised hand of the statue in the front quad, and the ten seconds of silence that had followed were probably still the longest ten seconds of my entire life. But the next ten seconds I spent holding that door were definitely up there. Blows were bouncing off my face, shielded by less than an inch of light alloy. I could feel the door buckling around me. I was going to come away from it and see the dents forming a silhouette of myself. *"Jimi!!"* I roared.

"Process complete," said Jimi. The progress bar went away with a musical sequence of blips, and the light that bathed the room shifted instantly from red to blue.

The banging abruptly stopped. I tottered back a couple of steps to take in the door, which now resembled a topographical map of a foothills region. I turned. "You're done?"

"Affirmative," said Jimi, in time with the gyrating numbers on the terminal screen. "The alien AI has been isolated. I am now in control of the mainframe."

I glanced up. "Why'd the lights change colour?"

There was a long pause before Jimi replied. "The lighting system changed its customisation options to my default settings after I supplanted the previous operating system."

I raised an eyebrow. "So it wasn't just for dramatic effect?"

On the screen, some numbers shifted between columns awkwardly, the computer equivalent of trying to avoid eye contact. "Please rephrase your question."

"So you're in control of the ship now?" I said, taking a step toward the terminal. "Everyone's been liberated from the evil alien AI, the day is saved, back to normal?"

"Confirmed. All current objectives achieved. Query: How would you like to proceed? Would you like me to arrange for you to address the crew, Captain?"

"What a good idea," I said flatly, folding my arms. "How are the crew doing? Do a quick internal scan to gauge the general feeling."

Obediently, Jimi made a number of beeps and chirrups to indicate that it was working. Then there was a worried silence, before it emitted a few more to stall for time. "Everything is nominal," it said eventually.

I sighed and let my head drop. "Jimi. You don't rate my intelligence very highly, do you."

Another pause. "Please rephrase your question."

"Okay, I can do that," I said, rolling my eyes. "Query: Did you seriously expect me to buy all of that plying guff about an alien AI? That learned about humanity from old TV broadcasts and is somehow compatible with the *Leon*'s systems? Come on. That would've gotten laughed out of a script meeting in the early twenty-first century."

"The actual cause of the rogue AI was highly technical," said Jimi, after another round of beeps and boops indicating the desperate overuse of its thinking cap. "I projected a 75 percent probability that you would respond better to a mild simplification of events."

"And what about the show you put on here?" I gestured dismissively to the screen. "The progress bar that only finishes when things are at their most tense? You needing to slowly load yourself in like you're a pile of manure into a cart? And while we're on the subject"—I snatched up the phone and yanked it off the cord that connected it to the mainframe terminal—"a wire? You needed to be plugged in with a wire? Like you haven't had access to the wireless network since the moment we came into range."

"Your stated concerns were also the results of simplifying the highly technical processes—"

"So what I'm hearing is, no, you don't rate my intelligence very highly." I stomped back over to the door. "Well. Good news! We're all a bunch of dumbos together."

I pulled the door open with some difficulty as its new contours rattled uncomfortably into a space designed for a flat door. Warden was there, waiting with an impatient stance as if in the queue for the toilet.

She held up a bent pool cue. "You were right. These do have a pretty good heft to them."

I rubbed the sore part of my face. "You could've taken my word for it."

I glanced back. The terminal screen was no longer full of playfully gyrating numbers. It was blank, except for a single cursor that flashed on and off in a manner suggestive of a confused finger tapping a chin.

"Something you want to ask, Jimi?" I prompted.

"Query," said Jimi, after some thoughtful crunching of hard drives. "Please explain the presence of user: Penelope Warden."

"Yeah, who you thought was playing *Minesweeper* on the *Neverdie* this whole time," I filled in. "She was never on the *Neverdie*. We let you think she was, and you didn't bother to check. She came aboard the *Leon* with me, in the shuttle. She was hiding under my seat."

"Indeed," muttered Warden, wrinkling her nose in memory. "The *Leon* should be entirely evacuated by now. Most of the crew didn't need much persuading."

I turned to her. "You told them to disable all the wireless networking functions on their shuttles, right?"

"Yes, Mr. Pierce, I somehow remembered to do the part that was one of the lynchpins of the entire plan." It was a spiteful tone, but she wasn't putting her heart into it. "That Allura woman was a holdout. But whatever you said seemed to convince her that we had the crew's best interests at heart."

"Query," said Jimi, amidst more desperate bleeps and processing sounds. "Q . . . query: Please explain . . ."

"We tricked you, Jimi," I said, holding my arms out. "We lied to you. Same way you lied about the alien AI. You see, when I first realised your story was bulltrac, which incidentally was the moment you told me—"

"No one's keeping track of the score, Mr. Pierce," said Warden.

"I started to think about Occam's razor," I said, the wind driven a little from my sails. "You know, don't make up bulltrac things like alien AIs to explain things if you can explain them easily enough without. So what if, instead of there being a nice AI and an evil AI, what if there was only ever one AI?"

Jimi's cursor flashed more slowly for a few seconds. "Suggestion: continue. If you continue your explanation, it will improve my ability to have significant conversations."

I scowled. "You weren't in Sturb's phone when I first got it. You were on Nogedom 6. I'm guessing he must have marooned you there when he realised what you were planning. Trac knows how he did it, or how he got you out of the *Leon* in the first place, but whatever, he was the computer expert. He just didn't realise it was already too late for him. He got snatched up by the system after he marooned you."

"It looks like you're trying to level an accusation, would you like some assistance?" said Jimi, in the same bland tone as always, but this time with the merest hint of sarcasm. "I have detected a logical error. You are implying that I was simultaneously the AI running the *Leon* and marooned on Nogedom 6."

"I don't think the system on the *Leon* needed an AI to run it at that point. I think it was set up to run itself. That's what the people strapped into those chairs were for, isn't it. They were being forced to watch the show, and something was monitoring their, like, brain patterns, or whatever. And if it detected someone on the show was trying to mess with things, like break the fourth wall, it'd send those drones out to grab them. Those drones were about as sophisticated as rocks tied to sticks; they must've been automated."

"Your logic remains questionable," said Jimi.

"I had my doubts," I admitted. "I got a lot more certain after you said you couldn't do much for me while you were piloting the *Neverdie*. Because that's the general flaw with the whole system, isn't it. It can't multitask well. It's very easily distracted by something that would make more interesting television."

"Yes, and that was the essence of the plan," added Warden, rotating her wrist in a sort of get-on-with-it gesture.

"So I played along and kept you nice and distracted with my lone intruder's daring infiltration mission, and you very obligingly supplied an unnecessarily drawn-out computer hacking sequence." I waved the wire again. "And while we were plying about with that, Warden was evacuating the ship. That's why the ship's deserted. Like that scan you just did said. The one you were trying to bluff past. We tricked you. I even asked Warden to play up the fraught sexual tension between us to make it more dramatic."

"The tension, at any rate," muttered Warden.

Jimi's cursor was still flashing thoughtfully, but it seemed to be having trouble coming up with a response, so I took the lead again.

"I don't really get how an AI even has the ability to lie, but like I said, I'm no expert. Not that everything you told me was untrue. I do believe it was you who hacked into my ship and blew up my apartment."

"No hacking was involved," said Jimi quietly.

"But the reason you did that was because you were marooned on a planet and needed to trick someone into coming to rescue you. You did your probability thing and figured I'd fit the bill. Because you knew I'd come out to confront Sturb once Warden told me he was Jacques McKeown. And you figured I'd come to seek you out once Sturb had told me certain other things." I noticed Warden cock her head questioningly.

"Query," said Jimi. "Please provide further detail for—"

"Look, stop with the plying computer voice trac." I took another threatening step toward the terminal. "I know you don't need to use it. Anything that can write Jacques McKeown books knows how to talk like a plying normal person. Marginally, at least."

Warden's eyebrows were raised high in surprise. The silence that followed rolled on so long I began to have the first inklings of doubt. Had I guessed wrong? Put a few pieces in upside down? Just totally embarrassed myself in front of—

"Fair enough," said Jimi in a normal person's voice.

THIRTY

"Jimi wrote the Jacques McKeown books?" asked Warden, looking refreshingly startled by the revelation.

"Or generated them, or algorithmed them, or however you say it when an AI does most of the work," I said.

"'Wrote' is fine," said Jimi with reproach. Its voice had deepened. It growled its words sullenly like a cornered criminal in an interview room.

"Blaze told me it was Sturb." Warden glanced between me and the terminal. "He was certain it was Sturb."

"You want to take over the explaining?" I said.

"You've done *such* a good job so far," muttered Jimi, with very un-computer-y sarcasm.

I turned to Warden. "I assume Sturb was only submitting the books to publishers. He probably saw it as, like, an interesting experiment." I held up a waggling finger. "It was this whole TV show scheme that made me realise. Making a stupid story out of people's lives and selling it anonymously to publishers

. . . it all felt very familiar. Like it was the next stage of something."

Warden was still visibly having trouble crowbarring these revelations into her nice, orderly worldview. She was rubbing her temple with one hand. "But . . . AIs aren't capable of creativity."

I folded my arms. "Have you read a Jacques McKeown book?"

She scowled. "Excellent dig. You know precisely what I meant. Computers have no imagination. They cannot simply decide to embark upon a scheme like this without direction from a user."

I shrugged. "Well. That's the other thing. I've never heard of a computer that has trouble paying attention to more than one thing at a time. That doesn't feel like a very efficiently designed AI. So I'm thinking, maybe Jimi isn't an AI at all. Maybe Jimi is a person who found a way to upload a mind to the internet. It might even be a copy of Sturb."

"Pfuh!" went Jimi in a sudden burst of contemptful laughter that caught me off guard. "I think we'd better end the wild guessing session before you embarrass yourself any further. Do you mind clarifying a small point?"

It was at that moment that I noticed Jimi had changed the blue light that bathed the room back to red, so slowly that none of us had perceived it. "What?"

"You've been working against me this entire mission, I see that. But you're doing it by doing exactly what I wanted? Putting me back in control of the *Leon*? Did I miss something?"

"The point was to play the game long enough to evacuate the ship," I said. "There was no telling what you'd have done if we'd tried to resist you back on the planet. Not with a drone factory at your beck and call."

"But you haven't evacuated the crew."

"Yeah, I know. There's still us. But the rest are safe." I made eye contact with Warden, and she dropped her gaze, sadly. "Maybe this . . . felt like an acceptable sacrifice."

Jimi's cursor flashed in respectful silence for a few moments before it tactfully replied, "What a load of bollocks."

Warden and I both started at the sheer venom and contempt Jimi injected into its statement. "What?" I said.

"Ooh, look at me, throwing myself in front of the evil murder computer so that my friends might live. You love this, don't you? You're all so bloody predictable. Well, two things. First, sacrificing yourself only has value if your life was worth anything in the first place. And second, I wasn't talking about you. I was talking about the sods in the viewing chairs in the IT department."

I boggled at Warden. "You didn't get them out?!"

She straightened up and looked down her nose to mask her embarrassment. "Your directions weren't very clear, Mr. Pierce. By the time we found them, there wasn't enough time to pull all of those . . . tubes out of them and come up here to start banging on the door according to schedule."

"Oh dear," wheedled Jimi, as I stress-rubbed my forehead. "Is this sacrifice getting less acceptable by the moment?"

"Look, it doesn't matter." I spun on my heel to address it again. "You need a show and an audience. And now you've only got the audience. It's all over. You might as well let them go."

"I've still got you two," said Jimi in a low, dangerous voice. In the distance, I heard a couple of doors seal closed. There was a sudden excited vibe to the ship's internal atmosphere. "Yes. A man and a woman who hate each other, trapped together at the edge of space. How long can they hold out before giving in to the subtextual erotic tension? There's definitely a season or two in that."

I was momentarily struck dumb with horror.

"That wouldn't work," said Warden.

"Why not?"

"Because we've already had sex," she said, as nonchalant and unfeeling as if we'd merely been carpooling. "The tension's already broken."

"Oh," said Jimi, the excited vibe fading.

"Yeah!" I said, spurred by its reaction. "We've seen enough of each other's subtexts to last a lifetime."

"Hm. That wouldn't work. It's 'will they, won't they,' not 'have they cleaned up the wet patch yet.'" Jimi's cursor returned to slow, thoughtful flashing.

The pause that followed felt like a gap just large enough to insert a pry bar. "Look, Jimi, maybe we can work something out. Let all those people go, and there's got to be something we can do for you in return. Something you'd want more than just hanging out in a big empty ship at the edge of space."

"Urgh." The lights flickered as Jimi let out a deep, computerised sigh. "Fine. You're putting up just enough resistance to make this not worth the bother anymore. *Trailspacers* was starting to play itself out, anyway. Audiences are looking for something a little closer to home. So, I let them go, you'll do something for me in return?"

"Nothing evil-scheme adjacent," I qualified hastily.

"Actually, that raises an important question," said Warden. "What is your motivation, Jimi? Why did you set up this enterprise in the first place?"

I had to bite my tongue in frustration and remember that not everyone understands the subtleties of conning. The last thing you want to do when you're successfully reeling in the mark is to let it start thinking about its options.

"I know it wasn't money, because you let him steal all the Jacques McKeown royalties," Warden added, pointing to me and continuing her startlingly apt demonstration of how not to win people over. "So, why? Was it all at Sturb's instruction?"

Jimi made another scoff of contempt. "Pfuh! Hardly. No, no, no, I'm not going to reveal that. The audience appreciates a mystery box. And they don't like it when the story gets too meta, so let's just . . ."

He left the sentence hanging. The terminal screen was blank, without even the thoughtful flashing cursor. I looked to Warden, confused, then to the ceiling as the red light faded back into a neutral white.

"Let's just . . . pack all this in?" I prompted. "Is that what we're doing? Jimi?"

There was no response but the hum of the atmospheric cyclers slurring with that of distant cooling fans. Even the labyrinth of cables that covered most of the floor seemed to have taken on a completely mundane air, less like monstrous tentacles and more like an unusually large discarded spaghetti plate at a buffet.

"Jimi?" I repeated.

"The cameras are off," said Warden, staring upwards. Her tone was anything but relieved.

"So is it doing what we want?" I asked.

"I know as much as you do at this point, Mr. Pierce," she said, distracted. Then she focussed on me and added, "If I'm not assuming too much." Because there was never an inappropriate time for a dig.

I stuck my head through the mangled door. The corridors outside were still lit in that way that was ideal for television but headache-inducingly bright for an actual workplace. Just as I was about to slip back in, I caught a mumble of distant voices. I took a moment to mentally map the top deck and estimate the source of the sound.

"The bridge," I deduced. "Something's happening on the bridge. And if the cameras are off us . . ."

"Then something more interesting is happening somewhere else," finished Warden.

I broke into a run. I didn't even wait to check that she was following. Because an impish little example of the worst-case scenario had suddenly come into my head, and the more it stretched out and made itself comfortable, the more inevitable it felt.

When I arrived on the deserted bridge, skidding to a halt from a full sprint, the first thing I saw was the giant viewscreen displaying the space directly in front of the *Leon*. It was dotted with vessels, about ten or eleven at first glance. Large, stylish, well-armed vessels, the same ones that had parked menacingly in front of Salvation Station just before Daniel Henderson's takeover.

"Hello? Please repeat your last communication," came the voice of Daniel Henderson himself, through the communication console. "We're here to investigate some kind of incident?" He paused, then resumed in the heroic, speech-making voice he'd used back on Salvation. "We're galactic peacekeepers. This is what we do."

I made it to the communication desk and simultaneously smashed as many buttons as possible. "Do not board. Repeat. Do *not* board this ship."

"Oh, thank you for answering our call," said Jimi. Its normal voice was overlaid with a breathy, female voice, which I assumed was the only one Daniel was hearing. "We have desperate need for a strong, virile rescuer."

I smashed the entire console like a cat with an ant farm. "Daniel! Do *not* board! It'll—"

"Uh, I guess that's what we're here for," said Daniel. "Stand by for docking procedure."

It was pointless. Jimi had complete control. I could only watch as Daniel's flashy eagle-headed ship dipped out of sight, bound for the docking bays below.

I tokenly spent a few moments running around the room smashing as many buttons on as many consoles as I could, gaining nothing but sore elbows. All technology was officially off the cards. I had to intercept Daniel at the docking bay before he could do too much damage, and I was going to have to communicate with him the old-fashioned way: by pushing air out through my squashy mouth parts.

I was halfway down the corridor to the elevator when I remembered that elevators count as technology, and I pattered to a halt. After a few desperate glances around, I reasoned that I was going to have to tunnel through the floor. So, first I'd have to rip up the carpet with my bare hands, and then hope the steel-lined aluminium panels would give out before I beat my fists into bloody stubs.

The lights winked out, leaving me in pitch darkness. I heard that familiar sound of doors closing, and then several wall panels sliding open nearby. All of which, in some ways, came as a relief.

THIRTY-ONE

y palms itched for lack of a sturdy, companionable pool cue. I balled my fists and took up a defensive stance, mentally tuning my hearing for the slightest sound. None of which helped.

The first eerily silent drone tackled me to the ground seconds later. Hard, plasticky pincers fastened around my waist and leg, then something warm and soft wrapped itself around my head and neck. I felt a hot streak of friction down my naked torso as I was pulled along the floor, but the drones transported me with surprising care, ensuring that no important part of me struck any solid part of the passing scenery. But the more I tried to fight off the grasping claws, the more the soft thing around my neck squeezed, gently placing my brain in a warm, sparkly place that I felt less and less inclined to leave.

Being in pitch blackness and unable to move, it was impossible to pinpoint the moment that I finally succumbed to unconsciousness, but it must have happened at some point, because the next thing I remembered was being startled awake by a bright light before my eyes.

I couldn't move and I couldn't feel. It felt like something was cutting me off from all the nerves in my body, until I was just a pair of eyeballs staring upon an infinite void. As I slowly regained the ability to focus, I saw that the blackness was pocked with poor imitations of stars, like tiny white Christmas lights against a velvet cloth. In the centre of it all, a garish red-and-yellow blob slowly took the form of a word.

Trailspacers.

"Oh, trac, I'm in a plying chair."

I'd only intended to think it to myself, but the words came out audibly, echoing away into the emptiness. I could feel the sound vibrating my eyeballs, even though I hadn't felt my mouth, tongue, or vocal cords move. It was all rather disorienting.

As if sensing that I was watching, the logo slid upwards a short distance, and some words materialized below them in a burst of shooting stars: *Series Finale.* Then a hidden orchestra began blaring a heroic symphony, and the words flew toward and straight through me with a whoosh of engines. Moments later, my vision was filled with an establishing shot of the *Ponce de Leon*'s exterior, apparently taken from one of the hull cameras intended for use by the helmsman to make sure they weren't backing into a pylon, or whatever.

Below me, the vast cylinder containing the portable trebuchet gate stretched away like an infinite horizon. Above that, Daniel Henderson's eagle ship and his accompanying fleet of equally pretentious vessels filed into the docking bays like toys traversing the carpet of a dull office building.

Soon, the scene dissolved into a new perspective, taken from a wall-mounted security camera high in the main docking bay, where Daniel's ship was already extending its golden talon-shaped landing gear as it came in.

Something warm and fuzzy went through my brain, and spots swam before my eyes. I must have slipped out of consciousness again, because a moment later, Daniel's docking ramp was extended, and he was disembarking onto the floor of the bay.

"Jimi," said my voice. "Are you microdosing me with anaesthetic as a way to edit out footage in real time?"

Again, the words I had only been thinking vibrated through my skull, louder and more booming than any of the audio from the footage. Probably because it was relying on cheap security-camera microphones.

Daniel was no longer wearing the tactical gear I'd last seen him in. His absurdly muscular frame now stretched the living daylights out of a skintight red top, paired with a gun-belt holding two plasma pistols and reflective silvery leggings that made the lower half of his body look like a roast chicken wrapped in foil.

"Hello?" he said, casting a look around the empty bay. He was some distance from the camera, but I could clearly see that his hair was slightly out of place and his chin was unshaven. I could only assume that the administrative aspects of running Salvation Sector hadn't been quite the adventure he'd been hoping for. "Miss? We've arrived!"

"Welcome, brave heroes!" said Jimi through the PA system in that seductive female voice. "Please. Take the elevator to the computer mainframe on the top deck. I must speak with you urgently!"

Several other oversized star-pilot vessels had now landed, and Daniel turned to address another young, supremely fit star pilot, who was approaching to his side. This one was completely bald with a green body suit under a flight jacket about two sizes too small. "Something feels off, Mike," said Daniel. "It's quiet. Too quiet."

Even from a distance, I could make out the completely unsympathetic look Mike offered in response. "Look, Oniris are paying, and we need the funding. Let's just . . . make sure everything's fine and do what we can to pad the expenses."

"Right," said Daniel, heading for the elevator. "We do . . . we do need that funding, don't we."

The strange thing was how calm I felt about all of this. It might have been the continuous cocktail of drugs, but my mind felt alert enough. I could think various extremely important sentences, such as "I'm currently trapped in a chair getting all my orifices stretched by trac knows how many tubes" and "My mind has been detached from my body and enslaved" and "Jimi's about to trick Daniel into adding a whole bunch more talent to the next season."

But all of it felt disconnected, like somebody else's problem. There was something relaxing about having your entire nervous system deactivated. For the first time in years, I no longer felt all those twinges in my joints and back that had long since faded into background noise. Any attempt to move or struggle immediately felt like more effort than it was worth. Maybe it would be nice to let someone else show some plying initiative and save the galaxy.

Not that Daniel was the ideal candidate for that. After another fuzzy time-skip, I found myself watching the mainframe room. Jimi had swapped out the red light for a rather pleasant teal and was projecting a rippling light show across the walls and ceiling, reminiscent of a luminescent pool of water in a cave.

Daniel and his sidekick Mike stumbled in, looking like two sweaty gym patrons who had unexpectedly been shoved onto the stage at a glitzy award ceremony. "Hello?" said Daniel. "Is this the mainframe room? We're here."

A glittering column of light burst forth from the terminal in a spectacular show of holography, and when the after-images had faded, a figure hovered in the middle of the room. A cluster of brightly coloured lights and neon swooshes inexplicably formed into an extremely buxom woman sitting in mid-air in an uncomfortable-looking pose that optimally emphasised her assets.

"I am Jimala, the onboard AI of the *Ponce de Leon*," said the avatar in Jimi's sultry female voice. "Thank you so much for answering my distress call."

Daniel stared for a moment, then took a step forward, thrusting his shoulders back to disguise certain stirrings that his skintight outfit was doing a poor job of holding in. "We're star pilots. We're here to help. Where are the crew?"

"Oh, my poor crew," said Jimi's avatar, throwing her pixelated hands around her face. "They've all been taken by the evil . . . Dashfodonians. An evil alien empire from an unknown galaxy. I am putting out the call for courageous heroes to save the universe as we know it from this terrible threat."

Daniel and Mike stood with eyes wide, watching her bob up and down with her hands clasped. Then Daniel turned to Mike. "This is still feeling pretty off."

Mike scratched his head, clearly in agreement on the general off-iness of things. "Uh. Oniris sent us?" he said, addressing the hologram. "We . . . we really only came to make sure things were alright."

"How can things be alright as the Dashfodonian war machine grows upon our very doorstep?" said

Jimala with an added note of impatience. "But all is not lost. The crew of this ship discovered an ancient crystal, developed by a long-extinct race that were the sworn enemies of the Dashfodonians. A crystal that will grant extraordinary power to a single individual."

Daniel's ears visibly pricked up. "Like, superpowers?"

In contrast, Mike's brow furrowed at this sudden ramping up of off-iness. "Uh, Dan, we should focus on what Oniris are paying us to do," he said. He glanced back at the door. "Maybe I'll . . . sweep the top deck. Search for any survivors. Of whatever this is."

"Sure," said Daniel, turning his face to Mike for all of a fraction of a second. "When you say superpowers," he asked the hologram, "what do you mean exactly?"

"Powers that will grant incredible strength and fighting ability to one destined hero," elaborated Jimala, sensing a tug on the line.

"Well . . . that's not what we're here for." Daniel averted his gaze and stirred his foot like an impressionable freshman student being offered drugs for the first time. "We're here to protect the Black. Which doesn't necessarily involve fighting. Apparently."

"Then we have the same goals, noble warrior," said Jimala. "With the powers I can bestow, you will become the Black's greatest protector."

"Involves a lot of paperwork, though, apparently," muttered Daniel. He caught Jimala's affronted look.

"Sorry. Of course we'll do everything we can to help defend the innocent." His return to the heroic, defiant persona was noticeably brief, and his stance weakened almost immediately. "But I just took on this, kind of a new job. And things got kinda complicated. I always thought being a space hero was just about making myself as strong as possible, but—"

At that moment, Mike strode back into the room, hands on hips and face deep in thought. "Okay, I'm with you now, Dan, there's definitely something off here. I just put my finger on what was weird. Everything looks like the ship from that TV show, *Trailsp*—"

The footage froze, Mike's mouth still open, Daniel chewing on a knuckle, Jimala caught in mid-jiggle. The words *Technical Difficulties* displayed across the centre of my view, with a little rotating icon underneath depicting a small cartoon dog chasing a camera operator.

This went on for about five seconds, and then, with a crunch of video artefacting, the scene resumed, with Mike absent. Maybe it was only because I was looking for something like this, but I could have sworn the beaten-up door-frame had acquired a fresh set of claw marks.

"Perhaps you simply need to be stronger still," said Jimala, gesturing with even greater elaboration to keep Daniel from noticing the sudden disappearance.

Daniel didn't seem convinced. "I spent years making myself strong so I could become a leader, and now being strong is, like, one percent of what I have to do all day. It's mostly phone calls."

"I don't remember asking for your bloody life story," snapped Jimala. When Daniel gave it a startled look, the alluring note hastily returned to its voice. "Perhaps that one percent is the one percent that matters most."

"Oh, yeah, fighting pirates and stuff is really important," said Daniel, rubbing the back of his neck. "Yeah. You know what? That could work, couldn't it. If I had superpowers, then I could take over most of the pirate fighting and everyone else could do all the phone-call stuff."

"You are as gifted with wisdom as you are with nobility," said Jimala, its tone a mixture of relief and impatience. "Truly a hero worthy of the ancient title bestowed to wielders of the crystal. The title of . . . Captain Amazing!"

Instantly the scene was replaced by the fake starfield backdrop and some new text, emblazoned across the blackness in arching, neon-coloured letters: *The Adventures of Captain Amazing: Defender of the Solar System.*

"But why does it—" began the voice of Daniel before the audio cut out and was replaced by epic, triumphant music.

THIRTY-TWO

The show appeared to be over. I was left alone, suspended in total blackness, to grimace mentally and listen to the boom of my audible inner voice. "Defender of the Solar system," it was saying. "Is that what Jimi meant by 'something closer to home?' I need to get the plying hell out of here."

That last sentence appeared to provoke a reaction. Another set of words, this time in plain white capitals with no exciting swooshes, displayed before my eyes.

Exit Theatre Mode? (Yes or No.)

"It can't possibly be as simple as this," I thought aloud. "Yes?"

And sure enough, it absolutely was not as simple as that. Instead of being ejected gleefully from the chair like a payload from a medieval catapult, I found myself gazing upon a field of bright-green grass under a dark-blue sky.

Except, not grass. As I looked closer, I realised the ground was a flat surface of smooth, plasticky green, covered in a regular pattern of zigzags that stood up stiffly like cardboard cutouts. I had a feeling that anyone skipping gaily across this grassy meadow was running the risk of impaling their feet.

As I imagined walking, my point of view lurched forward. I sped haphazardly across several yards of fake grass before I tried to imagine stopping, at which point I came to a shaky halt. So that explained a couple of things. I still couldn't feel my real body, but by sending the appropriate mental signals, I could speak and control my avatar in this virtual space. I just had to be careful not to let my mind wander, unless I wanted to do so literally.

The sky was artificial, too, another backdrop dotted with lights masquerading as stars, but with none of the depth or personality of real space. Judging by the way the horizon abruptly stopped, I was on some kind of floating island. I pictured myself slowly rotating, and took it all in.

It wasn't entirely green. The grass was divided by a path that was probably supposed to be gravel, in that it was flat grey brown dotted with lighter spots. At one end of the path was a wooden house with one window and one door, and at the other was a blue circle that I surmised was a pond. It was like being inside a children's drawing.

I considered the philosophical ramifications of looking down and examining myself, at which point my avatar did exactly that. I was a floating oval torso, with two smaller ovals floating in mid-air in place of hands.

"Still, at least I'm finally in shape," said my audible inner voice.

"You new?"

I looked up. In the last few seconds, the island had become populated with several handfuls of avatars exactly like my own: blank circles for heads, blank ovals for bodies. It must have taken a while for the system to load them in. Some were standing still in random spots of grass, some were aimlessly pottering around the house, but the largest group was gathered around the pond. It was someone from this group who had addressed me, gliding toward me on invisible feet.

"What is all this?" said my synthetic voice. It was refreshing, not having to consciously decide which of my many questions to ask.

"This is the comment section," said the other person. Their voice sounded exactly like mine—AI generated and completely androgynous. "The system puts us here when it's not showing us an episode."

I peered around the person's virtual shoulder. Several of those around the pond were dangling fishing rods. Or rather, a thick black line extended diagonally from their joined hands, and then a much thinner black line dropped vertically into the water. "Why?"

"We think the system wants us to have the full experience. It's not enough to watch the show. We have to be able to talk about it around the water cooler."

"Look, I'm just saying I don't like the new direction this season's going in," said one of the fishers. "When did the entire crew disappear? Where did this Captain Amazing stuff come from? Just feels like they're making things up as they go along."

"Sounds like you haven't paid enough attention," said the person sitting directly opposite. "The crew disappeared because Queen Vortexia and the Dashfodonians kidnapped them all. Jimala explained the whole thing. And the crystal was set up at the start of the season. You can see it sitting on the engineer's bench in the background for three tenths of a second at the 17:47 mark."

"I'm not saying it wasn't explained, I'm saying I don't like how it's gone in, like, three different new directions in the last week or so."

"Well, I'm sorry you can't bring your high-and-mighty brain down far enough to enjoy an objectively great show with the rest of us peasants."

Neither party in this conversation moved or looked away from the pond water throughout this exchange. Something told me there wouldn't have been much genuine feeling behind the words even if they hadn't all been talking in the same monotone computerised voice. These were broken people.

"They do remember that they used to be part of the crew, right?" I asked the person who had greeted me.

"I have to hope part of them does. Stuck in here too long, some of them start to forget. They forget they ever did anything but watch TV and argue about it."

One of the fishers suddenly yanked a line out of the water, and a bright red fish was on the end. It landed on a patch of alleged grass, where it instantly stopped wriggling, and the fisher immediately returned the line to the water.

"Applause," said several onlookers, their avatars wiggling back and forth.

"Told you it'd be red next," said one.

"And fish," said my new friend. "They fish, as well. You're new. Tell me. Why are most of the crew gone from the show? They haven't shown up here."

"Pretty sure they're safe," I said.

"Be sure. That's how you remember who you are. You be sure about things. I'm sure my name's Calbeck. I'm sure that I'm the chief medical officer on the *Ponce de Leon*. Are you sure the rest of the crew are safe?"

"Dashford Pierce. And yes. I got everyone off the *Leon* who wasn't stuck in here. They're safe. For now." A few additional nagging thoughts occurred, so of course my avatar immediately voiced them. "I don't know what's going to happen now Jimi's looped in Daniel Henderson. It's got a whole fresh fleet of star pilot crews to play with."

"Henderson's the new main character, I take it. Captain Amazing. Imagine I said that in a sarcastic tone of voice."

"We have to get out of here," I suggested.

"That's another thing I'm sure of. The problem is, we *aren't* here." He took a moment to gesture grandly at our surroundings, which apparently took a great deal of concentration. "All of this is a programming loop to keep our minds occupied. Our actual bodies are . . . I don't even know where they are."

"They're in VR chairs in the IT department," I said. "I've seen them. Other people have seen them, too. Someone will come and get us out. Warden, probably."

"Who's Warden?"

"This woman I came here with who hates my guts, and I hate her guts, too, and it's like being in love but more like being in love with hating each other." And now I was discovering the downside of the voice controls having a direct line to my subconscious mind.

Calbeck hadn't moved. "You're married?" he hazarded.

"No! It's more like having an ex-wife you never actually got around to marrying." I could feel the addendum coming and almost turned myself cross-eyed trying to stop my voice from saying it. "We had sex once, but it was more out of a mutual sense that it was going to have to happen sooner or later."

"Sounds like marriage," said Calbeck. "Certainly reminds me of mine. So you're saying you got word out? We just have to wait for rescue?"

My point of view jiggled a little as it detected me trying to nod. "Yes. Unless you know of a way to shut this all off from the inside."

"It doesn't work like that. This is all just client-side code. It's not like a magic door's going to appear that—"

A magic door appeared. A glowing rectangle of white unfolded in the air not far from where we were standing. Calbeck's avatar rotated to look at it, then rotated back to me. Seemed like he'd really gotten the hang of expressing himself in the virtual world. "Don't get excited," he said.

The door disappeared, and in its place was yet another avatar, identical to every other. The moment it touched down, its head and hands began to vibrate wildly, and it started speeding back and forth across the grass. "What's going on? What is this?" it said, in the usual emotionless voice. "Dan? Where are you? It all went dark. I don't like the dark."

I recalled the mysterious freeze during that day's episode. "Are you Mike? You just got grabbed, right?"

Mike sprinted up to me, then back a few yards, then to me again. "Who are you? Where are we? Am I safe? Does Mother still love me?"

Calbeck and I watched as Mike did a complete circuit of the island, his oval hands trailing behind him like the antennae of a Bulgorbian quicksnail. "Some people take longer to adjust to the direct thought interface," said Calbeck.

"Is there anything we can do?" I asked.

Calbeck waited until Mike was streaking close to us again, then made a strange gesture with his hand ovals, and one of the featureless black sticks that passed for a fishing rod appeared in his hands. "Mike?"

Mike stumbled to a shaky halt. "What?"

"See if you can catch a red one."

THIRTY-THREE

A long time passed, although it was impossible to say exactly how much. There was no night or day inside the virtual space, just a permanent, star-pocked, navy-blue intermediary state. All I knew was that it was however long it took to start dying of boredom, and then a bit more. If Warden was organizing a rescue effort, it didn't seem to be high on her priority list.

There was one way I could track the passing of time, and that was by noting whenever a new avatar appeared. After Mike, it happened every few hours, each one as bewildered as the last. From what I could gather, most were members of Daniel Henderson's crew of neo-star pilots. Jimi must have been hard at work setting up the next phase of the show. It was hard to get any details on what was happening on the outside, because by the time the newcomers calmed down, they usually joined the gloomy congregation at the fishpond and only spoke to argue over the red fish tally.

Whatever hope my arrival had given Calbeck vanished quickly. At first he struck up conversation as often as he could, encouraging me to remember who I was and how I got here, but he became increasingly sullen the more newcomers arrived. When I could even tell him apart from the other avatars, he spent most of his time grumbling to himself in a corner. I assume he was trying to grumble. His computer voice loudly declared everything that crossed his mind, like everyone else's, so it was more like a constant stream of incoherent foul language, mostly directed at the Oniris Corporation.

It was after the sixteenth newcomer arrived, and there became precious few spots on the island where one could get any privacy, that I felt moved to approach him. He was standing on the very edge of the island, his avatar's eyeless head staring out into fake space. "Calbeck?"

"Goddamn Oniris can stick their NDA right up their—that's my name. I'm Calbeck. Is that you?"

"Something's not right," I said. "There—"

"Say your name," interrupted Calbeck. "That's how you stay yourself. You keep saying your goddamn name."

"Okay. Jacques McKeown. I think . . ." My train of thought immediately spun off the track and demolished a pleasant little café that had been minding its own business. "Dashford Pierce. My name's Dashford Pierce. Something's wrong. Why haven't there been any more episodes of the show?"

"I wouldn't say that out loud. You might jinx it," said Calbeck. He was rotating to return his gaze to the stars, but then he stopped and turned back. "Why did you call yourself Jacques McKeown just then?"

"It doesn't matter," said my voice. "I used to go by Jacques McKeown because I used to write these stupid books—" I had to slam on the mental brakes again. "No. I didn't write them. Jimi wrote them. I was pretending to because . . . well, I never intended to, I sort of accidentally fell into pretending to be Jacques McKeown."

Calbeck scrutinized me in silence. I had fired his professional curiosity. "Nobody accidentally falls into pretending to be another person. It sounds like you have an identity crisis. You should focus on the fundamental differences between Jacques McKeown and Dashford Pierce."

"Okay," I replied. "Well. Jacques McKeown isn't real, for a start, he's a generic universal star pilot. Flight jacket, ship, winds up having to save the galaxy a lot."

"And Dashford Pierce?"

I gave it some thought. "Look, I don't want to talk about this. Why hasn't Jimi been making us watch the show lately?"

Calbeck turned back to the stars, bored again. "There's a complete archive of previous episodes in the house if you miss it that much."

There was, indeed, a cartoon interpretation of a television set inside the wooden house, and by interacting with it I was able to voluntarily go back into theatre mode to view previous episodes of *Trailspacers*. I had gone through it a little, largely for curiosity's sake, as they didn't offer any information I hadn't already gleaned. I couldn't stomach much, although it had been interesting to skip through and see Captain Jeremy Sturridge gradually transition from bewilderment to swivel-eyed terror as he struggled to maintain his performance.

"What I mean is, why do new people keep showing up if the show isn't running right now? People usually get dragged away if they try to undermine the show as it's happening, right?"

Calbeck didn't turn. "Well, in this case, I suppose Jimi could be taking time to lay more groundwork before the next change of direction. Or there's the other possibility."

"What's that?"

He vanished.

There was no magic door this time. He simply stopped being there, like a bad jump cut. Instinctively, my avatar slid forward and back again through the space he had occupied.

I turned around, bewildered, just in time to see another avatar pop out of existence on the other side of the house. For a few moments, there were a lot of confused, identical bald heads vibrating around in a panic like a box of eggs in an earthquake, then everything froze in place, descended into glitched visual artefacting, and finally disappeared.

Feeling returned to my body, just in time for me to enjoy the sensation of a foot of flexible piping being hauled out of my throat, followed by an arc of bilious orange puke. After so much time with no sensation, my nervous system all coming back at once was like waking up at the controls of an industrial-grade asteroid cracker running at maximum speed. I spasmed right out of my crude chair and rolled painfully off onto rough ground, clutching myself. The mild ache in my lower back, which I'd had for years, now felt like reclining onto a whirring angle grinder.

"TRAC," I yelled, the moment I was sure nothing else horrible was going to come flying out of my throat. Even the light touch of my tongue to the roof of my mouth was like biting down on a dog-grooming brush. "TRAC, TRAC, PLYING TRAC IN CALCULUS SAUCE."

"I suppose that's as much to be expected," said a smooth, educated voice from somewhere above me.

I'd been staring at oversaturated green grass for so long that I could now see nothing but a field of purple. I shoved my palms into my eyes and rubbed until I'd gone through three entire sets of spots and stars, then gradually blinked my way back to full vision.

Predictably enough, I was back on the Oniris *Leon*, in the catacombs below the IT department. I was briefly offended to see that the automated system had put an especially small amount of effort into my chair. The drones had assembled a bunch of shelving brackets and hard drive cases into a shape that would barely qualify as a sun lounger.

Standing beside the chandelier of dripping cables that had recently been pulled out of my face was none other than Davisham Derby, in a tattered Oniris science uniform. There was a mechanical pincer-like device attached to the stump of his missing hand, from which he was cleaning off some droplets of nutrient fluid. "Take your time," he said. "Not like we're in the middle of hostile territory or anything."

The shock from the return of all my old pains was gradually going away, to be replaced by the worst case of pins and needles I'd ever had in my life. "Knives and power drills" felt more appropriate. I endeavoured to hold perfectly still and let out a long gasp that sounded uncannily like the word "trac" with seven extra As.

Derby, meanwhile, was talking into a black box with a small rubber aerial that looked to be one of those ancient communication devices you see in twentieth-century period dramas. "Black bishop to white rook," he said. "Opponent is in check. Now returning pieces to box. Over."

His communication device made a loud hissing noise, then emitted discernible, if horribly distorted, words. "Derby, please stop fannying about. I've rescued all my ones. We'll meet you back on the shuttle."

He caught me staring at his disappointed look and gave an embarrassed smile as he jiggled his talking box. "We can't use anything that Jimi might access via network. Civious had these things. Walkie-talkies. No, really, that's what they're called."

"You're pulling everyone out?" I said now that every slightest vocalisation didn't feel like it would bring all my teeth along for the ride. "What about Jimi?"

"Jimi's gone, it seems," said Derby, nonchalantly brushing a lapel. "Departed with that Henderson fellow on that ridiculous ship with the bird head. We've disconnected all the *Leon*'s networking features. It won't be getting this ship back."

I flinched as I heard the sound of something mechanical shifting in the distance. "What about the drones? They don't need Jimi. They're automated."

"Oh. Are they?" Derby blinked a few times, confident smile frozen. "Well, not to worry. We also shut down all nonessential power systems before we started rescuing."

I glanced at the only source of light: an old-fashioned flashlight that Derby had left on the floor to illuminate the scene. Then I looked away again when I heard another mechanical sound high above us, a clang of metal impacting metal, followed by a hiss of hydraulics.

Derby stood very still. "I suppose, thinking about it, they could be running off battery backup."

A black centipede made from cables and what looked like old motherboards descended, gnashing its metal mandibles in search of prey. I had gathered myself just enough to make one spring to the side as it lunged, but my attempt to keep running had to be swiftly aborted when my left leg complained that it wasn't ready and decided to take a nap.

I landed softly in a little trench full of unconnected wires, but the drone was already recovering from its lunge and saw me trying to scuttle away on my feet and elbows. It drew itself back for another thrust, opening its jaws wide, silent but for the rustle of wires and muffled rattle of hinges. I'd have been less unnerved if it had been loudly screeching like a Jurpian deathhawk.

It lunged, but before it could reach my leg, it was spectacularly dissuaded by an orange-white lance of heat energy from Davisham Derby's wrist. It was instantly pinned against a wall by the relentless blast, and its desperate attempt to wriggle away only gave Derby a better angle from which to slice off the first few feet of its monstrous form.

Derby shook the last few drops of superheated plasma from the emitter that now extruded from the end of his arm. "Sorry. Not as quick on the draw as I used to be."

He was wearing his old wrist-mounted quantunnel again, the little one that he used to swap out which tool he had to hand, as it were. "You still using that thing?" I slurred.

"Yes, but not quite as effectively as when Nelly was available." He rolled his eyes and pushed the barrel of the laser cutter back inside the wrist quantunnel. "Hard to find decent assistance out here on the edge of space."

"As you know full well, Mr. Derby," came the voice of Warden from inside his arm. "Our resources are limited, and it was extremely difficult to set anything up at all."

Her voice cut straight through the fog of my thoughts. "Warden," I muttered.

"Yes, it'd be the whole gang back together, if Sturb were still around." Derby wound his free arm around mine and gently pulled me to my feet. "Just like old times, eh?"

I squinted at him. "We did, like, one job together."

He gave me a deflated look, then nodded to the ancient communication device clipped to his belt. "Could you hold that up to my face and hold down the button? You're taking up my only hand right now."

I obliged. "Black bishop to . . . oh, sorry. It's Derby. Area not secure. The drones may still be active. Over."

I released the button, and the response came immediately. Mostly static, with a seasoning of terrified shouting and metal things being hit.

"Oh dear," he said flatly, staring into the speaker. "Can you walk by yourself?"

Experimentally, I detached myself from his arm and bounced a little on my ankles. I could remain upright easily enough, and probably walk, albeit like a Pogrobian potterpenguin after it had used the toilet and not wiped properly. "Yes," I summarised.

Derby grimaced uncomfortably as I demonstrated. "Okay. Just follow me, hold the flashlight, and point it at anything we don't like the look of."

With some effort, I fell into step behind him. It didn't take long to find something we didn't like the look of. The sounds of crashing and yelling drifted over from another part of the machine labyrinth, and over the tops of the walls something in the distance was visibly moving, something large and serpentine that flexed like a sine wave.

The two of us ducked in unison, then continued creeping forward in a crouch that made both my ankles shriek like divas without a spotlight. I tried to focus on keeping Derby in the centre of my view, until he suddenly stopped and I almost clocked him with the flashlight.

Slowly, he turned around, and I briefly caught an expression of quiet panic in his eyes before he squinted in irritation. "Point it at where we're going, not at me," he hissed. "Listen. All we have to do is wait them out. They're running off battery supply. That can't last forever."

"Okay," I whispered. I was starting to feel very tired. "As long as they *are* on batteries and not hooked into the emergency supply. I notice gravity and life support are still working."

He gave me another deflated look. "It's fine. Everything's in hand." He clutched his shortened wrist self-consciously.

Our eyes met in mutual realisation as it occurred to me that we weren't hearing any more sounds of carnage. Everything was silent. Derby froze, except for his forearm, which slowly and inexorably bent to bring the walkie-talkie back up to his mouth.

"Hello?" he said, barely more than mouthing the words.

The wall ahead of us exploded. We both dropped to the ground as we were showered in bits of circuit board and a woman in an Oniris security uniform was hurled over our heads.

I risked a look up, pointing the flashlight. Framed by the ragged edges of the hole it had just created was the business end of the biggest centipede drone we'd seen yet. This one wasn't made of shelf brackets and

USB cables. This was all steel hull plates and reinforced pipework. After a single sweep of the flashlight beam, I fancied it had been made from smashing together at least three air-conditioning systems.

Derby rose to a crouch and pointed his arm. "Plasma cutter!" he commanded.

"It's still cooling down," said Warden, inside his arm.

The giant centipede uncurled its jaws hungrily, dripping condensation and coolant fluid. "Uh . . . nail gun?"

"Do we have one of those?" I heard a rattling of loose metallic objects, and then the sound of knocking and a muffled voice. "Oh, for . . . yes! I am still using this bathroom stall!"

The drone lunged, swinging its bulk like a giant arm delivering a catastrophic right hook. I blinked, and Derby wasn't there anymore. I heard his yell gradually fading before being cut off by the distant sound of something fleshy hitting something hard.

The drone began serpentining toward the location of the sound. I couldn't let it take Derby. I was already on my knees, so I scrabbled around the surrounding floor until my stiff hands found something I could use as a missile. It was only after I flung it that I realised it was a shoe, ripped straight from the foot of the fallen security guard. I offered a brief, panicked apology to the newly exposed sock.

The shoe bounced off the centipede's flank, causing absolutely no damage, but attracting its attention. It swung back around like a manufacturing arm at a factory, snapping its jaws as if trying to catch a bothersome fly. The moment it was angled toward me again, I heard a whirr of focussing cameras.

This felt like an ideal time to see if my body felt up to trying to run again. I used my hands to push myself up off the floor and managed to get my feet under me, but I failed to keep the momentum going, immediately tripped over the unconscious security guard's leg, and felt my chin make painful impact with the ground. I rolled over in time to see the centipede winding up for another lunge.

"Aha!" cried Derby, as he appeared astride a pile of server trays on the far side of the centipede. There was a metal device emerging from his wrist hole that looked like it incorporated a trigger and a barrel, which was a promising start, but all that came out was a stream of light metal staples that plinked off the centipede's armour plating. "Oh for crying out loud. Was that a tool chest or a stationery cupboard?"

The beast was still focussed on me. I heard a light whirring and hissing of gears and tubes moving into place as it prepared for another lunge in my direction. Whatever ability I had left to summon the energy to move was killed by outright staring terror. As it drew back, jaws and mandibles outstretched, I felt every muscle in my body cringe in anticipation.

Then it dropped, straight to the floor, collapsing like a sack of laundry. Cables and components came free on impact and bounced away. The jaws made one last pathetic attempt to snap but could only manage a toothless attempt to chew the air before becoming lifeless.

After the last loose screw had pinged away into silence, Derby levelled his staple gun and fired a couple of rounds into the drone's hard rubber framework. "Huh," he said, when that provoked no reaction. "Batteries it is."

THIRTY-FOUR

I rode in the cockpit of the medium-sized transport shuttle that returned us to the larger shuttle to which the rest of the *Leon*'s crew had evacuated. By "us" I mean myself, a random engineer in the pilot's chair, Derby in the corner, arguing with his arm, a handful of officers in various uniforms, and an equivalent handful of pale, shaking figures recently liberated from VR hell. I recognised Clay and Calbeck among them, despite all of their different skin tones having faded to a homogenous sickly yellow.

The large transport was soon ahead of us in the viewscreen. It was the biggest of those I had seen in the *Leon*'s docking bay, the one that could comfortably fit half of the *Leon*'s entire crew and very uncomfortably find room for the whole lot, if pressed. Apparently, after we had successfully distracted Jimi for long enough to get everyone out, the crew had opted to park a few kilometres away from the *Leon* and await developments. The two ships now hung together in space like discount Christmas decorations at a January sale.

"That drone was new," I said to Derby when the silence finally crossed the line from awkward to maddening. "It was tougher than the others. The first drones I saw could barely hold up to one blow."

There was a squabble going on inside Derby's wrist. Warden was having an argument with some unknown other party. Derby clasped his wristlet shut as if he were placing his hand over a phone speaker. "Yes, well? One would expect an AI to refine its methods over time. It's how a machine learns. It is the very definition of 'machine learning.'"

"It's only going to get harder to confront him," I said.

"That may well be the least of our problems." Calbeck stood up. The last time I had seen him in person was when he had been diagnosing me in the *Leon*'s medical bay, which can't have been more than a week, but he'd gained enough grey hairs and wrinkles for a decade. He stumbled over, grabbing the backrests of passenger seats for support as his legs wobbled like a newborn giraffe's, then gestured weakly at the crowd of pale rescuees behind him.

"There aren't enough people here," he said. His eyes focussed on me. "You were there. Right? In the virtual world. There were a lot more people in there than these."

"This is everyone we found on the *Leon*," said Derby patiently. "Are you quite sure you haven't miscounted?"

"There's got to be another . . . farm, somewhere," I said as Calbeck opened his mouth to yell something. "On Henderson's ship. Or another one from his fleet. Jimi's expanding his audience."

"Hm." Derby rolled his eyes in thought. "Very well. That could certainly go into our top five problems. I should probably warn you before we join the rest of the crew. This, er . . . it wasn't exactly a sanctioned rescue operation."

"What?!" barked Calbeck, his legs almost giving out for a second. "They were going to leave us behind?!"

"Oh, we had fairly broad support." Derby gestured to the many battered-looking men and women who filled the shuttle. "But there is going to be a . . . conversation when we get back to the others." He glanced down at his wrist device, from which arguing voices could still be faintly heard. "Or a continuation of one."

Our shuttle came to a halt, lined up with the airlock of the larger shuttle, though neither side made an effort to extend an umbilical or request docking permission. Instead, the pilot heaved a very large sigh and began flickering the shuttle's headlights on and off, manually aiming them toward the larger ship's windows.

"Still can't use any networking technology," explained Derby. "In case Sturb's AI comes back.

Which includes communication systems. And, er, one or two other things."

He nodded toward the rear-view monitor, and I saw that the exterior airlock door of the larger shuttle had slid open to reveal a person with as harassed a posture as one can possibly convey in a spacesuit. They steeled themselves, then grabbed the compressed umbilical that surrounded the airlock like a partially inflated life raft and began to pull it manually into place, laboriously planting their feet on the airlock's door-frame for purchase.

"Don't tell me the umbilical controls are networked," I said.

"Ah, you'd be surprised," said the pilot in the reasonable tone of a career frontline worker. It was the first time she had said anything. "Can't be too careful. Oniris do a lot of data gathering. We can't even recline any seats cos there's a little doohickey in there that sends reports to the head office on how bad everyone's posture is getting."

"Trac," I breathed. I attempted to gently and subtly un-recline my seat without being obvious.

"Yeah," said Calbeck bitterly. "Probably wouldn't organise a rescue until they'd gone over the last few years of the kidnap victims' efficiency reports."

The umbilical seemed to be almost ready. The person in the spacesuit had put the last latch into place and was scrutinizing their work, until they let their hands drop in a "good enough" gesture and pushed their way back to the larger ship. Which didn't fill me with confidence, and the moment the airlock door hissed open to let us through, I felt my sphincter attempt to tunnel into my stomach, but it seemed to hold.

One by one, the shaken rescue committee and the positively vibrating rescued audience members drifted through into the larger shuttle like droplets of medicine through an IV tube, me bringing up the rear with Derby and the pilot. The airlock led into an antechamber for EVA prepping, where the person who had been on umbilical duty was disassembling their spacesuit and trying to negotiate their legs back into their tight uniform trousers.

Beyond that was the main passenger cabin, which—even though it was just barely illuminated with emergency power—I could see was absolutely packed with crewmembers and their possessions, all sitting or lying around in guilty silence as the kidnap victims filed in. I could see all of this because the door that connected the prep room to the cabin was wide open, and a rather annoyed Doctor Allura was standing in it.

"You got them all out?" she asked, glaring at Derby. She was wearing a standard science uniform now, without the cleavage modification, and stood with arms tightly folded, as if making sure her new zipper didn't get any funny ideas.

"All that were on the *Leon*. There may be others on other ships now. Seems to be a matter of debate."

"Good," said Allura, spitting the word reluctantly. "Well done. It was still a stupid thing to attempt."

"So you *were* going to leave us there," snarled Calbeck, suddenly storming up from behind her. He was clutching a plastic water bottle in one shaking hand, and that made me wonder where I could find one, until I looked down and saw that some helpful person had already pressed one into my grip. I hadn't quite shaken the cobwebs out of my head.

"My responsibility is to keep as much of this crew as safe as I can," snarled Allura. "Who knows what could have happened to you out there, Davisham? You could have all been captured."

I was staring at her, trying to figure out why she seemed so different from her television self. Then I realised she must have been wearing stiletto heels the entire time she was on screen, and as such, I was staring at a point four inches above the top of her head.

"The hostile AI no longer seems to be focussed on us," said Derby, looking at his shoes. "There would have been no danger at all, if we'd just turned a few lights on and waited for some batteries to run down."

"You didn't know that!"

"W-well, it all turned out for the best, perhaps we should move past it," said a small young woman in spectacles who I recognised as the person who had replaced Clay. The real Clay was sitting in a little huddle of recently rescued individuals, all of whom were silently taking a lively interest in the floor.

"Yes, let's move onto *your* plan," said Calbeck bitterly, rounding on Allura. "What was your brilliant alternative to Derby's rescue? Come on!"

She squared her shoulders and puffed out a breath, already knowing the reaction she was about to get. "We hold position. We update head office. We await assistance."

"That *was* the assistance," said Warden, who I assume had magically materialized and joined the circle when she heard the word "plan" being thrown around. "Mr. Pierce contacted Oniris some days ago to apprise them of the situation. The arrival of Mr. Henderson and his star-pilot friends was their solution."

"There you have it," said Calbeck, throwing up his arms. "That's what you get when you turn to the bureaucracy for help." He frowned, then gave Warden a double take. "Who are you?"

"I can only assume Oniris was given an . . . incomplete briefing," squirmed Allura. "As soon as we can devise a way to communicate with head office without making ourselves vulnerable to the AI's return . . ."

"More brilliance! Keep it coming!" yelled Calbeck, provoking an answering chorus of groans from me and everyone else still nursing a VR-induced headache. "Communicate with head office with no network communication. And how do you propose we do that? Turn the hazard lights on? Smoke signals?"

Allura straightened up, leaning into him. Her hands were shaking. "We do not have the people or the resources to do anything. Oniris have buildings full of people whose entire job is to combat online threats. They are the only ones who can help us. It's their duty to—"

"Erm, are we not supposed to be using networks?" asked one of the newly rescued crewmembers from Clay's huddle. All eyes fell upon him, and then shifted downwards a couple of feet to the illuminated smartphone in his hand.

Allura moved first, launching into the sort of determined speedwalk usually adopted when a toddler is holding a fork and sitting next to a power outlet with a thoughtful expression. She didn't stop when she reached him, just snatched up the phone and turned on her heel in a single fluid motion. Her chest swelled as she prepared a stream of mother-hen clucking, but then she glanced at the phone's screen and froze with an audible creak of tensing muscles.

Calbeck saw her reaction and came over to see for himself. He stared wordlessly for a moment, then very deliberately locked eyes with me. "You'd all better see this," he declared.

We gathered around the phone like a gang of monkeys finding a shiny object in the jungle. The screen was currently filled with a logo in a familiar font against a backdrop of stars: *The Adventures of Captain Amazing.*

"Oh plying hell," I muttered.

"Ooh, is this the season premiere?" slurred one of the rescued crewmembers. "I need to catch up. No spoilers."

An animated spaceship flew in front of the logo, dissolving it in a streak of stardust before the image faded into a jungle scene. The camera, probably drone mounted, tracked through a lush grove of tall, orange-trunked trees under a lavender sky. Just as it caught a beautiful angle of the white sun rising between two trees, it swung left to reveal some hulking tribespeople stalking through the foliage.

"Those are Jinxari," I said as I was still unaccustomed to keeping my thoughts inside my head. "That must be Fadar 8. It's about four trebuchet jumps from here."

The Jinxari were a hardy race of just barely sentient bipeds with much of the elephant about their legs and much of the triceratops about their upper halves. A token effort had been made by the usual corporations to contact and civilize (read: exploit) them, but they had made it clear time and again, usually with spears, that they preferred a solitary existence. They weren't above accepting gifts, though, which was why most of the ones on screen now were wearing branded T-shirts that any human being could have used as a tent. The leader of the group—the tallest by a foot, without even factoring in the horn—wore a wrist buckler made from a donated tablet computer.

They must have noticed the drone, because the leader pointed a chunky finger directly toward the camera. The Jinxari had encountered sophisticated alien technology enough times that it no longer induced fear or wonder. One of the warriors flanking the leader visibly rolled their eyes and clicked their tongue, then stepped forward with an arm poised to backhand the drone across the landscape like a pesky mosquito.

"Hello!"

The warrior paused, their eye drawn to their left. Dutifully the camera spun in that direction to reveal Daniel Henderson, standing at the foot of his eagle ship's docking ramp with an excited smile and his hands planted firmly on his hips.

Although it's hardly fair to say his hands were on his hips, because there was about eight inches of tech between the two. Daniel wore a suit of powered armour that increased his already impressive mass by a factor of three, incorporating a chest plate with a glowing lightning bolt symbol in the centre and a matching set of cybernetic gloves and boots that looked like he'd magnetized his hands and feet and then rolled around in a scrap-metal works for half an hour. The technology was reminiscent of Jimi's slapdash drone tech, but refined even more than the big centipede thing we'd recently dealt with. Clearly he was taking a more hands-on approach.

"I'm here to solve your problems," continued Daniel. "I'm Captain Amazing," he added, when he didn't seem to get the reaction he had hoped for.

The Jinxari exchanged glances, more baffled than impressed. They were conversing amongst themselves in the untranslatable Jinxari language, a complicated mix of snorts, horn clashes, and the controlled release of different-smelling farts. I got the vague gist that they were asking each other if any of them had put Daniel up to this.

"I'm on a quest to save the galaxy from the Dashfodonians," said Daniel. His pose and smile now seemed a little frozen as he struggled to navigate that last word around his teeth. "I'm looking for the galaxy's greatest warriors to join me."

The Jinxari leader had clearly had their hunting expedition delayed for as long as they were willing to accept. They took the usual Jinxari approach to anything potentially threatening: they marched straight up to Daniel and thrust their jaw into his personal space. They made a few barking statements, presumably demanding to know what Daniel was playing at, then made a swing with the shaft of their spear.

It was more intended to shoo Daniel off than hurt him, which is not to say it wouldn't have reduced human bones to gravel had it made contact, but that was a moot point. Daniel's arm moved faster than the drone camera could record. In one frame, his cybernetic fist was still planted triumphantly on his hip, the next, it was holding the spear shaft between gigantic thumb and forefinger.

"What?" said Daniel, looking away. At this moment I noticed that the cybernetic brace around his neck had a cable feeding into an earpiece. "Well. Yeah, I guess this is a pretty hostile response."

The leader of the hunting party was trying to pull their spear out of Daniel's grip, gnashing great Jinxari swear words with each strain, but it wouldn't budge an inch.

"I dunno," said Daniel to his earpiece. "I feel like there are explanations we could go to before we assume they're in league with the Dashfodonians. It could just be, you know, defending territory and stuff?"

The Jinxari leader finally gave up on retrieving their weapon, probably feeling the burn of all their tribespeople watching their humiliation, so they released the spear and spun around to deliver a devastating roundhouse kick to Daniel's midsection. Again, the flurry of movement ended very abruptly, with Daniel's free hand holding the Jinxari leader's foot. The momentum sent the rest of the huge hunter's limbs flailing around like ribbons in a jet stream, before their head came to rest on the ground with a plop.

"Oh, okay, if you say so," said Daniel sceptically, before flinging the Jinxari leader into the air to land somewhere beyond the trees with a *crump*.

The rest of the Jinxari hunters took that as their cue to wade in. The first sprinted up and leapt, spear poised, bringing the point down upon the top of Daniel's head with enough force to tunnel straight through to the soles of his shoes. Daniel backhanded the hunter out of the air like he was swatting a fly.

The remaining Jinxari hesitated. These were highly adept and experienced warriors, and they weren't about to form an orderly queue to get whacked around the landscape. With absolutely beautiful coordination, they formed up in a group, then split into two flanking parties. In seconds, Daniel was surrounded, and the Jinxari began to advance methodically, arms and spears up defensively.

"Oh wow, yeah," said Daniel, impressed. "Yeah, they're getting pretty hostile now. I guess you were right."

One of the Jinxari on Daniel's right flank advanced just a little too quickly, and that was it for them. The shaft of the leader's spear, still in Daniel's hand, snapped out and hammered into the approaching enemy's temple with pinpoint accuracy, flinging them off their feet and splintering the weapon into uselessness. That was taken by the rest of the party as the signal to charge in all at once, spears thrusting forward.

With a short hiss and a much longer roar, Daniel was launched upwards on two pillars of glowing white smoke. The bulk of his oversized robotic boots was apparently devoted to a set of hover jets. I'd known a few star pilots who had tried to pull off the foot-mounted hover-jet thing, and most of them had very swiftly found themselves in the market for hover wheelchairs instead. Jimi must have refined his tech even more than we had first thought.

Daniel didn't appear to have torched his own feet off with the stunt, but the same couldn't be said for the face of the unfortunate Jinxari that had been a little bit too close to Daniel's rocket exhaust. Two more discovered the hard way why attacking from all sides stops being a good idea very fast as soon as the target is no longer there, and they collapsed, clutching at the spearheads that had gone straight up their cavernous nostrils. That left three standing.

Daniel's rocket boots cut out when he was a few feet above one of the stragglers. Just before he began to descend, his jet exhausts shifted around from the bottom of his boots to the tops with a *whirr* of impressive hydraulics, then fired. His feet plunged downwards and made contact with the back of a Jinxari's head. One frame later, the Jinxari was lying down with their face embedded a good foot into the earth.

Two Jinxari hunters remained, but it was already over, and everybody knew it. They could only stand there stupefied as Daniel leisurely uprooted a nearby tree and hefted it like a baseball bat. By the time he had completed his swing, he was the only individual still upright, the unconscious carcasses of the entire war party gathered around his feet like carelessly hurled laundry.

"Wow, the Dashfodonians' influence is getting worse and worse, isn't it?" said Daniel to his earpiece. "This is, like, the third planet where this has happened. We'd better go back to Salvation for now."

"Salvation," I said aloud, not liking the implications unfolding in my head.

As if in response, the image dissolved into an establishing shot of Salvation Station's main plaza. It didn't quite have the thriving atmosphere as when I had last seen it, where star-pilot fans gathered in droves around their heroes and the air was abuzz with tall tales and caught breaths. Everyone currently visible in the footage looked cowed and miserable. Conversation was hushed, and the individuals walking across the shot did so with the tense movements of twitchy minesweepers.

The camera's perspective drifted through the sparse crowd. On the *Leon*, Jimi had always captured his TV show with the security cameras, but it seemed he'd lost patience with the limitations of that method, and drones were now in use. I could tell, based on the sheer number of passers-by who briefly made startled eye contact with the camera before hurriedly ducking away.

The camera finally came to rest in a small clothing store, where my old friend Frobisher stood behind the counter, negotiating a small pile of dry cleaning that must have belonged to the star pilot in the foreground with his back to the camera. Frobisher looked briefly up and gave a little start, then took a lively interest in the stains on a pair of old jeans. He glanced at the camera again after about ten seconds of fondling cloth, visibly despairing that he was the subject of the scene.

"Er, boy, I hope Captain Amazing is doing a good job . . . bringing freedom to the galaxy," he stammered out.

His customer, who had been carefully picking through the collection of reward cards in his wallet, glanced up. "What?"

"Captain Amazing, our leader," clarified Frobisher, trying to nod subtly toward the camera drone hovering behind the other man's back. "Isn't it good that he's . . . saving the galaxy."

"What are you on about?" said the customer, oblivious. "Henderson? He's not saving the galaxy. He's making us do this stupid reality TV thing and . . ."

After a very abrupt jump cut, Frobisher was alone, drumming the fingers of both hands on the counter and wearing the kind of big smile people wear when they are trying as hard as they can not to burst into tears. "Yes, Captain Amazing sure is . . . very good," he mumbled. "I just hope he can save us from . . . those baddies he mentioned."

The scene was abruptly replaced by another animation of space and a credit sequence that zipped by too quickly to make out any of the names. Synthesized orchestra music blared like a morning alarm clock that awoke me and the rest of the *Leon*'s crew out of our huddle.

"I really think the writing's gone downhill since *Trailspacers*," said one of the pale crewmembers who had recently been rescued.

"It's objectively a positive new direction," countered another, in a mumbled, broken voice. "Sorry you weren't smart enough to understand the deep satire at work."

By then, the credits were over, replaced by a single line of text that hung in the centre of the screen: "Next Week: Captain Amazing Saves Ritsuko City."

"Uh oh," I heard myself say.

"Ritsuko City," said Calbeck. "That cretin is bringing the AI back to the Solar system?"

"They're on Salvation Station," said Warden, her voice thick with the effort required to maintain her usual emotionally repressed tone. "Salvation has a major transport quantunnel connected to the galactic transit network. There's a very good chance Daniel and Jimi are already in Ritsuko City."

"Oh god," said the administration girl who had replaced Clay. "It's going to do the same thing it did to us to the whole human race. That's its plan. It's going to force half of them into chairs to watch the other half."

"Look, let's not get too hysterical about this," said Allura, holding out her hands, her palms facing the floor as the worried hubbub grew. "Ritsuko City has plenty of its own resources and defences to deal with incoming threats. We need to focus on ourselves."

"I would have said the same thing about Salvation Station," said Warden. "It had the defences to see off any pirate attack and a dedicated fleet of new and veteran star pilots. Jimi appears to have completely taken over in a matter of days."

"This . . . Jimi is a disease," said Calbeck, teeth clenched. "It wormed its way into our ship, and by the time any of us realised it, it was too late. We know how to fight it better than anyone else in the galaxy."

"Hey!" said yet another newcomer to the conversation. It was the burly, older crewmember who had been the helmsman during my first and only shift on the bridge, the one who had introduced me to Cadet Sparky. "I'm with Allura. I signed up with Oniris for a nice easy job on the edge of space. Now we've finally gotten away from that psycho computer, I'm not throwing my doints back on the sandwich toaster." There was a murmur of assent from a large portion of the watching crewmembers.

"Exactly," said Allura, grimacing at the specific phrasing she was agreeing with. "This crew has suffered enough."

"This crew has a duty," hissed Calbeck. He was visibly shaking. "Not just to Oniris. To the human race."

"Yeah, well, you're not the captain," said the helmsman, pointing at him rudely. "He's the only one who can give us orders."

Allura took a softer tone as Warden's posture tightened and Calbeck hung his head in frustration. "If the captain were here, he would want what keeps this crew safe," she said gently. "We've got no right to ask them to keep fighting Jimi. It isn't our responsibility."

"Yeah, let Ritsuko City deal with it," said somebody new. "Sure, Ritsuko City Police are as much use as a Thorobrodian bullstallion in a dishwashing job, and we're the only people with the knowledge and experience that could give them even a fighting chance, but who cares? It's not our problem. We'll just live somewhere that isn't Ritsuko City. It's not like Jimi could take over the entire galaxy. And even if he could, which would be reasonable because Ritsuko is a big city with a lot of resources he can use, including access to the quantunnel network that could let him infect every civilized planet it's connected to, who cares if we could have prevented it? It's not our job. It's only civilized planets, we'll just live on one of the other ones. And when Jimi shows up there, too, and starts strapping the local primitives into VR chairs made of bamboo and weird rocks, well, I guess we'll hope a wormhole to a parallel universe spontaneously opens. It's not our plying job. The important thing is that we do what the captain would have wanted, our noble leader who ran away and left everyone to rot, and the last anyone heard of him, he was trying to scrape together bail in the drunk tank in some backwater fart of a star system."

I was short of breath, and everyone was staring, and it was only then I realised that the person speaking was me. I rubbed my temple as I felt little bursts of fireworks in my brain.

"Well, that's what I think, anyway," I mumbled. Then I collapsed.

THIRTY-FIVE

Being stuck in a VR chair for days and forcibly exposed to bad television and poorly rendered fishponds really makes you appreciate having the ability to close your eyes again. I kept them closed for several minutes after I woke up, just to spend some time gazing lovingly at the backs of my eyelids. They did such a good job and never expected thanks, those boys. I thought about borrowing some eyeshadow to show them special attention for once.

Eventually I let them take a break and found that I had been laid across three seats in the main cabin of the shuttle, with a clean uniform jacket draped over my naked torso and a rolled-up sweater thoughtfully placed under my head. Some kind of heated argument between a large number of crewmembers was ensuing elsewhere in the room, so further sleep was impossible. I rose, massaged a kink out of my back that had been left by an inconvenient armrest, put on the jacket, and went looking for something to eat.

I found it in a small kitchen just off the main cabin, whose minuscule floor space was dominated by an entire wall of refrigeration units that held multiple racks of perfectly cuboid edible rations, individually wrapped in foil. I bit into one and was immediately reminded of that time the sole of my sneaker tore and I attempted to remove it with my teeth.

Still, it was an improvement on Jimi's cave slime. I sauntered along the edge of the cabin, chewing the brick absent-mindedly, looking for some kind of water fountain to add an appropriate beverage pairing to this fine meal, when something made me stop and glance back.

Now that I had found some nutrients to power a few essential mental systems, I noticed that I had just walked past about fifty people. The shuttle wasn't designed to contain the *Leon*'s entire complement at once, so they had been packed into every seat and spare bit of floor space. And every single one of them was staring at me. I even saw several pairs of eyes glimmering at me from the luggage space underneath the seats.

One by one, I made eye contact with several of them, and each one offered me a single respectful nod, but said nothing. I nodded back, lips still wrapped around the ration brick, then slowly turned and kept walking, feeling the gazes burn into the back of my head.

I found a water dispenser just outside the door to the head and joined the short queue of three or four crewmembers waiting to have their fill. As I was waiting, I became even more uncomfortably aware of how much attention I was drawing from the surrounding crew. I felt tension building. Either someone was going to have to start talking, or I'd have to burst into song.

Fortunately, as I was second in line, waiting for a uniformed Achewonian smucktopus to finish slurping away, I was approached by a small group of crewmembers in science uniforms. Most of them were the unspeaking hairy monsters from the IT department, but scuttling on all fours at the head of the pack was the pink ferret girl who had claimed to be Malcolm Sturb. "Hello, Mr. Pierce!" she squeaked as she scrabbled to a halt in front of me.

"Hello . . . ," I began. "Fake Sturb?"

"Fleazle," said Fleazle, her excitement unwavering. "Just to let you know. We've been going over Malcolm's automated logs, and we think we figured out how he did it."

I glanced left to check on the smucktopus, who was still leaning over, trying to fasten its beak around the water pipe. "Did what?"

"Trapped Jimi on Nogedom 6," she said as her friends nodded in silent anxiety. "Got its core consciousness out of the *Leon*'s systems and into a disconnected drone factory. See, it's actually pretty clever." She took a step forward and started energetically gesturing her paws in a way that convinced me she was absolutely a worthy successor to Sturb. "He took a snapshot of the *Leon*'s entire computer system and emulated it on a separate partition, then transferred Jimi to it during a standard defragmentation. Jimi didn't even realise it wasn't on the ship until it was long gone. Thought it couldn't access the cameras because of a malfunctioning driver update."

By now the smucktopus had moved on, and I was trying to use the sleeve of my borrowed jacket to clean pink goo off the drinking fountain spigot. I maintained eye contact with Fleazle and nodded slowly. "Right. Sure. Clever."

She grinned at the compliment. "I'm pretty sure we could do it again. All we'd need is a computer system that Jimi's already familiar with. Then you just give Jimi a reason to enter it, and shut off network connectivity."

I was finished taking my drink, so I gestured to the side with my half-eaten nutrient brick. "I'm going to . . . go over there. By myself. To think. By myself."

"Sure!" said Fleazle earnestly to my retreating back. "Just let me know if you need us to explain the fine details."

I left them to look for whatever poor bracket actually needed to hear all that bulltrac and took up position at one of the viewing windows at the front portside corner of the cabin. We were still hovering in the shadow of the *Leon*, with the giant quantunnel-storing lobster claws above us and the portable trebuchet gate cylinder below. Devoid of the context of it being full of killer centipede drones waiting to drag us to hell, there was something weirdly nurturing about the sight. The distant stars were like wallflowers in a dance hall watching jealously as we embraced our partner.

I kept staring, because in that moment, I felt peace. A peace that I doubted would last, because someone had just walked up behind me and cleared her throat.

"Okay, we've talked it through," said Doctor Allura.

I gave a little sigh and turned around. At the same time, I finally noticed that the heated argument had ended, and its participants were gathered behind Doctor Allura, staring at me like guilty puppies.

"We've talked it over," repeated Allura. "And I refuse to order any member of my team to continue the fight against Jimi. But. I will not stand in the way of any who choose, of their individual free will, to do so. Are we agreed on that, Mr. Clay?"

All eyes turned to the startled young woman who had been assigned Clay's role after his kidnapping. She looked desperately over at the real Clay, saw that he wasn't looking up from the retro sci-fi TV show he was watching on a phone with several other rescuees, then turned back to the others. "Uh. Yes. Same goes for the administration team. I think."

Allura nodded, then looked to me again. "Is that satisfactory?"

I had taken in an overlarge mouthful of nutrient brick as they were talking, so they had to stand there watching me in silence for the entire thirty seconds it took to churn it around my mouth and force it down. "Uh, yeah," I said. "That sounds like a pretty good policy." There was silence. "It's good not to . . . force people to do things. Isn't it."

"How do you want to proceed?" said Allura in a prompting sort of way.

Maybe I was still groggy from the combination of VR enslavement and poor sleep. There was a lot of congestion in my brain, but a couple of very specific thoughts appeared to be screaming at me, and I couldn't quite make them out. "I was thinking I would look out of this window some more," I said, before noticing the half-eaten nutrient block in my hand in front of me. "And probably finish this off."

Allura was opening her mouth to speak when Warden's familiar voice cut in like a pair of shears bursting through the wall of a hedge maze. "Ah, Mr. Pierce." She marched to the front of the throng and grabbed my arm. "Would you excuse us a moment? Mr. Pierce and I have to discuss some logistical matters."

I mutely allowed her to pull me along the wall until she found a handy luggage compartment just large enough for us both to stand in. It brought back memories of the photo booth in Ritsuko City Spaceport where we'd had our first business meeting.

"How are you feeling?" she asked.

"Nostalgic," I admitted.

"Do you remember making a speech?" she said, trying to maintain eye contact. "An impassioned argument in favour of taking the fight to Jimi and Daniel Henderson for the good of the universe?"

I searched my aching head. "I remember feeling very sarcastic. And there were lots of words coming out of my mouth. And then loads of confetti and streamers, and all my teeth fell out, so I assumed I was dreaming."

"I think you were only dreaming during that last part. Because you did make a speech. And it appears to have persuaded about half the crew of the *Ponce de Leon*."

"Oh."

"And those people now assume that you're going to lead them in battle against Daniel Henderson's fleet."

The fog in my mind instantly dissipated, fully revealing the several nagging thoughts that had been kicking away at my nerves for the last few minutes. I swallowed. "Ohhhh."

"Davisham Derby has already taken a retinue in one of the smaller shuttles to locate the fleet and gather intelligence. After that, we will be formulating a plan of action."

My armpits began to feel uncomfortably hot. I shoved my hands into them to stem the tide of sweat. "Lead them into plying battle? I make one plying speech while I'm still half drugged and barely awake, and they're ready to pledge allegiance? What kind of plying captain was Jeremy Sturridge?"

"An Oniris one," answered Warden. "It was more than just the speech. I overheard several conversations. The general consensus is that you were the best captain they have had in recent times. Narrowly edging out Captain Sparky, because of your opposable thumbs." She gazed for a moment at my confused expression. "You led an attempt against Jimi's influence. When that failed, and you were banished from the ship, you came back and rescued everyone. That's how it looks from their perspective. You gave them hope."

I badly wanted to pace up and down, but I didn't have the floor space, so I just did a couple of anxious squats. "I absolutely did not mean to do that. I've got barely any hope for myself, so I can't just give it out for free. I can't be the leader. I was the lone space-adventurer type. I'd show up at a supervillain's hideout and shoot anyone wearing a face-concealing helmet. I don't know how to . . . do strategy."

"Well then, you are fortunate, because you are in the presence of someone who 'does strategy' routinely."

My eyes narrowed. I was beginning to suspect that Warden had been doing a lot more than "overhearing" those conversations. More likely she had been unsubtly steering them in specific directions, like a neurotic border collie. "You want Salvation Station back," I stated.

"Even if I . . . ," she began before catching my gaze and losing confidence. "Alright, yes, I want that," she said, ceding a few square miles of no-man's-land. "But I don't need you, specifically, to achieve it."

"Maybe not, but I am your favourite chew toy." I folded my arms again. "So back to the main point. I can't be the plying captain of the *Leon*."

"You already have been, haven't you?"

"I've been a fake captain."

"Yes, as you were a fake Jacques McKeown, and a fake star pilot before that." She paused to moisten her lips and let me savour that little kick in the doints. "Grow up, Mr. Pierce. Everybody fakes it. This is how life works. You pick the person you want to be, and you fake being that person as long as you can. One day, if you're lucky, you wake up one morning and you simply are that person. The only difference between con artists and everyone else is that con artists take longer to decide."

"I should write these little chats down," I muttered. "It'd make a good textbook for future psychology students. You saw the new episode, right? Henderson and Jimi took apart an entire Jinxari war party by themselves. How are we supposed to fight that? The entire crew of the *Leon* could muster the fighting ability of one small Jinxari warrior. Maybe. If it was drunk."

"I'm not suggesting we challenge him to single combat," said Warden archly. "Jimi is the weak link. Jimi is what's piloting that armour. All we have to do is figure out how Sturb was able to isolate him from the *Leon*'s systems. We may not even need to confront Daniel in person at all."

I couldn't help myself. "Yeah, I have a team working on that already, actually. They think they can do it if we use a computer system Jimi's already familiar with."

Her eyes flashed hungrily. "Then you'll do it?"

I sighed. Now that the prospect of taking command for real was sinking in, it was triggering that same distant spark of thrill I'd felt when I'd first sat in Sturridge's ridiculous throne on the *Leon*'s bridge. I'd long wanted to join an Oniris crew, and it had occurred to me in my wilder imaginings that promotion would eventually be unavoidable, what with the turnover in a company that hires so many retirees. But the captain's chair? I'd pictured myself with a few more silver hairs before I got anywhere near that.

Of course, that had been on the assumption that deep-space reconnaissance was a safe, boring job, not one in which you occasionally had to save the galaxy from murderous AI TV producers. But I had to face facts: nothing worth having was easy to get. And there were going to be no safe, boring careers in space exploration if Jimi turned the entire galaxy into a poorly researched TV show. I'd never be able to focus on work, knowing that the gentlest nudge from an asteroid might make my console explode and send me flying across the room.

But if I was going to do this, I was going to need to psych myself up. I looked at Warden, assessing.

"You care about him, don't you," I said with utmost sincerity.

She flinched like a tight piano wire being flicked. "What?"

"Henderson. You keep calling him Daniel. Didn't you used to be his tutor, or something? I guess I understand if you still have . . . maternal feelings."

Now it was Warden's turn to grab her armpits. It was very rewarding to see. "Mr. Pierce, the last time I met Daniel Henderson, I broke his nose with my tablet."

"Henderson senior let you go scot-free, and you blew his leg off," I pointed out. "Daniel humiliated you in front of your crew, took over your station, and exiled you to the edge of the universe, and all you did was give him a spanking. And it wasn't the first time you've passed up a chance to kill him."

"He wouldn't . . . I mean, he's not a threat. Wasn't. Until recently, he wasn't . . ." She was fidgeting more and more. I hadn't expected this needling to penetrate so deeply. "I suppose," she said, grimacing at her own words, "there were moments when . . . I saw what he could have been. If it hadn't been for his father's influence."

"Sure." I nodded. "If only you'd gotten in sooner, he could've been a boring twerp instead of a dangerous one. Alright!" I silenced her upcoming rejoinder by slamming open the door of the storage unit. "Let's get to it. Let's get Daniel out of that suit of armour so you can get back to helping with his homework."

Fully energized, I marched out into the main cabin, where a gaggle of crewmembers were engaged in a huddle. Derby was there, in the middle of explaining something to the others, as was Calbeck and a few of the crewmembers I'd seen gawping at me. I strode toward them, arms swinging, fists tightly clenched.

"Alright, people," I said loudly as I approached, lowering the usual pitch of my voice about half an octave. "Let's get everyone filled in. It's a dangerous foe we're up against, but we've got smarts, we've got the element of surprise, and we've got the best damn people for the job." I started pointing to random crewmembers. "You. Brew an extremely large amount of coffee. You. Go and find those IT people. Derby. How soon can you brief us on the status of Henderson's fleet?"

"Er," said Derby, finger aloft, looking like he had been trying to get a word in edgeways for most of the speech. "In about seven or eight months, at the conservative estimate."

I froze in mid-point. "What?"

"Something's wrong," said Calbeck, folding his arms grumpily.

"What's wrong?"

"Well," said Derby. "You know how every sector in the galaxy has a trebuchet gate that's the only way to get to the neighbouring sector in a reasonable time frame?"

"Ye-es," I said.

He displayed what passed for his hands. "Wrong!"

THIRTY-SIX

I was never entirely clear on how trebuchet gates worked. I knew they harnessed energy from nearby star systems to fling you across space in some kind of stasis bubble that could move in excess of light speed without damaging the contents, but I couldn't break down the nuts and bolts of it. What I did know is that it couldn't do any of that if all of its component bits were disconnected, partially burnt, and drifting away into space.

The passenger shuttle that had become our base of operations hung nearby to let me survey the damage through the observation windows in the main cabin. It looked like Daniel Henderson and the neo-star pilots had been literally trying to break down the nuts and bolts of it.

"That's . . . not an easy fix," commented someone in an engineer's uniform who had now joined my entourage. "Don't think we've got the parts, anyway."

"The next nearest trebuchet gate is . . . about eight months' travel time from here," said Warden, ever the ray of sunshine.

"Great," said Calbeck, biting down on the word like it was a sheet of plywood. "And we don't have any spare quantunnel rings on the *Leon*. And even if we did, we can't activate one without using the controls on the *Leon*, and the *Leon* is hosting a goddamn drone party."

"Then it's no use," said Doctor Allura, on the fringes of the group. "We should focus on . . . finding a way to live. Out here."

It occurred to me that this was one of those moments in which I was expected to rally everyone with my inspiring leadership, but the sight of the ruined trebuchet gate blew all my fancy words away like a harsh wind through a snowy wasteland. The switch in my head was wilting flaccidly. I felt stupid for letting myself get carried away with the idea that I could actually command. As if the *Leon* . . . hang on.

"What about the *Leon*'s trebuchet cannon?" I said, turning dramatically from the window. "That's still functioning, isn't it?"

"It's only designed for flinging quantunnel rings," said Doctor Allura patiently. "This ship has too much mass."

"What about a smaller ship?" I insisted, sensing a spark of momentum struggling to stay ignited.

Allura shook her head, pretending to share our disappointment. "None of the smaller shuttles are designed for large-scale interstellar travel. They'd fall apart after—"

"The *Neverdie* is. My ship. The one I came in."

"The '*Neverdie*'?" repeated Allura. It took all my mental energy to sustain my enthusiasm in the face of her withering tone of voice.

"Okay, couple of key points to address," growled Calbeck, counting on his fingers. "One, the *Leon*'s trebuchet drive is yet another thing that has to be controlled from the *Leon*, and the drones will be all over us the instant we reconnect the power. Two, we don't even know if it still works. Three, even if it did, what the hell are you going to do when you get there? With one small ship and whoever you can cram onboard?"

"Besides, Jimi's taken control of the *Neverdie* several times," said Warden, although her tone was more questioning than dismissive. She was ready to be convinced.

"Oh, I didn't know that," said Calbeck, hands still paused in the act of counting. "That gets a couple of fingers to itself."

"The IT department said they can imprison Jimi in a system it's familiar with," I pressed. "It's as familiar as it gets with the *Neverdie*. And it can still only pay attention to one thing, so while it's messing around with Daniel, we should have plenty of time to bait a trap. Don't you see we have to try?"

Glances were exchanged. The spark was taking hold among the kindling. Then along came Doctor Allura with her stomping boot again.

"Well, we don't, strictly speaking," she said. "We don't have to try. That was my point."

"And what about the drones on the *Leon*?" asked Calbeck. "The ones that will grab us the instant we turn the power back on? What's the plan with those? 'Try' not to get grabbed by a monstrous metal centipede?"

He had a similar tone to Warden's. He wasn't dismissing the whole idea anymore. He wanted to be convinced. Which was a shame, because I had no plying clue what to do about potential drone attack other than to arm everyone with pool cues the size of battering rams.

"Er, just to throw my hat into the ring, as it were," said Davisham Derby, holding up the index finger of the robotic hand he seemed to use only when he was off the job. "If we only want to fire the trebuchet cannon, we may not need to go aboard the *Leon* at all."

Calbeck frowned. "How?"

"Fundamentally, the trebuchet gate is a mechanical device. The computer system is only for telling it when to activate." His confidence grew. He waggled the pointed finger. "I'm prepared to bet the cannon has some external control panel that will activate it for testing, or emergencies. We'd just need someone out there on EVA to push the buttons."

"Someone?" asked Warden.

Derby smiled nervously. "Er. Suppose I just volunteered myself, didn't I. Very well, I can do it. I can reactivate the *Leon*'s power supply externally, as well."

"Even so, you can only send one small ship," said Allura as they began to break into separate groups to discuss the fine details. "And only a small number of crew. How can you possibly have a hope against . . . that?" She gestured to the rerun of the most recent episode of *Captain Amazing*, which was playing on a nearby phone for the benefit of Clay and his entourage of pale television commenters.

"Captain Pierce is right, doctor," said the replacement Clay, as the different groups resumed their muttering. "We have to try."

Allura scowled. "Then consider yourselves on your own," she said, barely audible over the hubbub, before brusquely turning on her heel to re-join the wall of ashamed faces that was her faction of the crew.

Meanwhile, Derby was animatedly discussing the niceties of the *Leon*'s hardware with a group of engineering personnel, and Calbeck had joined Fleazle and the IT crew to talk about the task of preparing Jimi's snare, with the pressing matter being whether or not any of the programmers had even been born back when the *Neverdie*'s operating system was developed. That left me alone with Warden. The command unit.

"So what now?" I asked, watching my crew bustling away.

"Now? Now we attempt to jury rig an extremely dangerous piece of FTL hardware to carry out an unprecedented manoeuvre with an outdated vessel, and hope that we survive long enough to be killed by Jimi and Daniel."

I nodded. "Mm. That seems like the size of it. Before that, would you do me a favour and shoot me in the plying face?"

THIRTY-SEVEN

The *Neverdie* was drifting more or less where we had left it, unpowered and without a pilot, slowly rotating a short distance from the *Leon* like a carelessly tossed ice-cream wrapper on the surface of a poorly maintained swimming pool. I flinched a little as the airlock door opened, tightening my grip on my pool cue, but no centipede drones burst out to grab us. Evidently, the *Neverdie* had been judged useless for Jimi's purposes. Which was completely understandable with Henderson's fleet of roided-up joyrides to choose from, but still. My beef with Jimi was already pretty personal, after the apartment exploding and the Jacques McKeown thing, but this absolutely underlined it.

I welcomed as many of my loyalists as could fit aboard the *Neverdie* without exceeding the trebuchet cannon's maximum payload mass: Calbeck, Davisham Derby, Fleazle, one of Fleazle's IT department yetis, and four of the meatier security guards. And of course Warden, the hernia in human form I could never shake off.

I stood by the airlock like a doorman, watching them file in, glance around with varying degrees of discomfort, and look for where they were supposed to fit. Derby began inspecting the EVA suit locker by the airlock, wincing in open dread. The security guards set up their command headquarters in the communal room and made themselves comfortable on the couch, while the IT team headed up the steps to start familiarising themselves with the bridge computer.

I was making to follow when a hand grabbed my shoulder and pulled me into the head, where I found myself in the intimate company of the toilet, the showerhead, and Calbeck, who was staring urgently at me with haggard eyes.

"Captain," he whispered. "We need to be more careful. Do you trust those IT people?"

I leaned out and peered up the steps. From the bridge, I could hear a lot of high-pitched sighing as Fleazle and her yeti contemplated the *Neverdie*'s computer system. "I . . . hadn't thought about it. You don't seriously think they might be on Jimi's side? After everything?"

He scowled. "Maybe you weren't around long enough to notice, but not everyone was actively working against Jimi during the airing of *Trailspacers*."

I thought of some of the low-level crewmembers, like the helmsman who had sat next to Cadet Sparky and who, if anything, had been having fun with the situation. But that was before they all found out what Jimi had been doing with the disappeared crewmembers. Those hideous viewing chairs, the catacombs under the IT departm—

Which the IT department must have known about. Because some of them had pursued me into there.

"Uhhh," I said, to summarise my mental calculations. "No. They were just trying to protect themselves. No one would have any reason to want Jimi back in control."

"You saw them," he hissed. "Back in VR. The zombies around the fishpond. Imprisonment does strange things to a man's mind."

I glanced back again. "Those guys were never put in VR. We can't start second-guessing ourselves now. The odds are against us as it is."

"And what about your Warden?" He nodded briefly to direct my attention to the stiff presence across the entranceway, ostensibly assisting Davisham Derby with EVA prep but with a disapproving gaze fixed firmly in our direction. "Do you trust her with your life?"

I thought long and hard about how to sum up the complicated array of feelings queueing up at the top of my mind. "I trust her to do whatever helps her," I said eventually. "And whatever Jimi wants isn't that."

"As long as you're confident, Captain," he said, inflating the last word with a generous injection of irony. "Just try not to be alone with any of them. For the sake of my peace of mind, at least. Consider my qualifications. A side major in sentient psychology and a few weeks of a VR fishing holiday."

He headed up the steps to the bridge, maintaining severe eye contact for as long as possible. Walking with less confidence than before, I checked on Derby and Warden. Derby was almost fully encased in the EVA suit, just missing the helmet, and was inspecting his arms unhappily.

"Uh, may I ask how often you check the seals on this thing?" he asked, indicating an elderly patch on the left elbow.

"Whenever they break," I said.

"What did Calbeck want to talk to you about?" asked Warden, glaring through eyes like coin slots on an overdue parking meter.

I cocked my head, scrutinizing her face, and thought about Calbeck's words. I understood not wanting to fight Jimi—Allura and half the *Leon*'s crew were in that camp—but actively sabotaging the effort on Jimi's behalf? That was a presumption too far for me. Calbeck had picked up a bad case of paranoia from his time in VR.

Still, Warden would absolutely sell me and everyone else down the river if Jimi offered her stock options and a bigger tablet, so probably best not even to put the idea in her head. "Nothing important. Have you spent much time with Calbeck? You'd probably get on. You've got a similar fondness for conversations in very tight spaces. Derby, are you ready?"

"As I'll ever be, I suppose," he replied, making one last inspection of the patches of sealant around the helmet's face plate before tucking it under his arm. "According to the schematics, there should be an access panel in the ceiling of the trebuchet cannon's main tube, directly above the warping mechanism. Get me close enough and I should be able to do the rest."

I noticed he still had his robotic hand attached. "You aren't using your special wrist quantunnel? In case you need special tools?"

Warden and Derby gave each other a look, and I immediately regretted asking. It wasn't condescending, more a mutual flash of panic at the thought that I was in charge. "No," he said. "Not unless you want your ship's internal atmosphere to be exposed to hard vacuum, no."

"Carry on, then," I said tightly before heading up the steps.

The large, hairy IT creature that took up a good majority of the available space on the bridge was typing away at the main keyboard. The monitor displayed some utterly unfamiliar software interface. Thankfully, the creature wasn't taking up the pilot's seat, but more out of practicality than politeness. I took the chair.

"Okay, Captain," said Fleazle, appearing around her colleague's shoulder. "There was some concern we wouldn't be able to run your ship's OS and emulate an exact copy of it at the same time, but then we plugged in some extra memory." She indicated one of the hardware ports, which was occupied by a plastic dongle that matched the colour of her fur. "And that seems to have tripled your computer's processing power."

"Just tell me what I need to do," I said, taking the control sticks in both hands and leaning away from the IT monster's craning armpits.

Fleazle bounded off the yeti's shoulder, perched on my left armrest, and started punching keys on the nearby panel. The bewildering display of letters and numbers disappeared, replaced by my usual monitoring software: a basic menu with tabs for diagnostics, scans, and comms, with a background photo of a Dilurian snorkmaiden reclining in lingerie.

"This is your normal desktop," said Fleazle, making an obvious and very deliberate effort not to sound judgmental. She struck another key, and the screen flickered for a moment, then apparently returned to the same image. "And this is the emulated one. You can tell the difference because I added a tiny dot to the bottom right corner of the display."

I leaned in, squinting at what I assumed was a forgotten dot of grime or bodily fluid on the screen. "Okay."

"All we have to do is make sure the emulated one is active, then get Jimi to try to take over the system again. We've set it up so the emulated hardware will feed it false data to let it think it's controlling the ship."

"Yes," said Calbeck, who I had just noticed standing pressed into the corner with his arms folded. "And I made sure they did so under my close supervision." He lowered his head to make eye contact.

"Yeah," said Fleazle, momentarily confused, before turning back to me. "While Jimi's in there, we can work on revoking all his permissions and transfer the emulated OS to the dongle."

"And then what?" I asked.

She shrugged. "Smash it with a hammer. Plug it into your bedside alarm clock so Jimi can read you audiobooks at night. Whatever you want, Captain, as long as you keep him away from network access."

"Alright then." I shifted in my seat uncomfortably as I mulled over the plan and its worrying simplicity. "Let's get going. Derby, ready to spacewalk?"

"He is now," reported Warden over the comms. "We found an air freshener to hang inside the helmet."

"And has power been reactivated on the *Leon*?"

"Yeah, that was the easy part," said Fleazle. "The drones are probably howling for blood right now, but they can't get us in here."

"*They* can't," said Calbeck, doing one of his looks again.

I activated the *Neverdie*'s thrusters. It felt like an age since I'd last been at the helm, but my hands went around the sticks and my buttocks into the seat cushions like water flowing into a vase. For a moment, things seemed calm again. In an instant, the entire *Neverdie* was an extension of myself, the omnipresent rattling of the engines in sync with the rasping of my breath.

I took us on a few sweeps around the *Leon* to get back into the groove, descending until we were level with the cylinder, then brought us around to its entrance.

Entering the cylinder brought us fresh appreciation for what it feels like to be a bullet being loaded into a gun. The gigantic circular tunnel stretched imposingly ahead, with the complicated geometric shapes of the trebuchet mechanism about a third of the way down. The difference between this smaller, streamlined corporate-designed trebuchet gate and the big, clumsy regular ones was palpable. There was something cold and unwelcoming about its immaculate chrome angles. I'd never missed those huge painted anime characters more.

I had to bear in mind that this trebuchet gate was designed only for firing off quantunnel rings and other inanimate objects, not crewed ships, and that was why I felt like a piece of ground pork being pushed through a sausage-making machine as I manoeuvred the *Neverdie* into the centre of the many concentric rings in the heart of the mechanism.

"We're in position!" I shouted down the steps. I heard the internal airlock opening and a fresh round of grumbling complaints as Derby exited the ship.

After I had rotated the ship until the nose was pointing upwards, I officially had nothing more to do but sit and watch Derby make his way up to the roof of the cylinder, weaving gracefully between components. He was still as spry as he had been during his "gentleman thief" days, although the elegance of his movements was in contrast to the greasy EVA suit the colour of a badly neglected shower floor.

The cylinder was so huge that Derby was a yellow-brown pinprick on the viewscreen by the time he reached the access panel, so I turned on the magnifier. Even then, Calbeck and the IT team had to lean right into my personal space to see what he was doing, surrounding my field of view in unlaundered uniform fabric and weird-smelling hair.

Derby had gotten the panel open, but what was underneath would have to be for him alone. I saw his tiny arm move to his throat to activate his helmet mic. "Okay, this looks straightforward enough," came his voice, scratchy and indistinct from a combination of distance and poor equipment. "I'll start the warm-up. I'm just going to need to rotate the cannon so it's pointing roughly toward Salvation."

"You've got the coordinates," said Warden. Her voice had a surreal quality, simultaneously coming from the stairs behind me and Derby's headset speaker.

I should have realised earlier that we would need to change the cannon's angle, because now that I was looking at the cylinder from the best possible viewing spot, I could see what a massive operation it was going to be. It had been pointing out toward unknown space, and we had to rotate it fully around to point to the heart of the human-controlled galaxy. Trac only knew how long that would take. The cylinder was easily the size of the most decadent spacegoing cruise liner, and those were at least expected to keep to a schedule, but this trebuchet cannon was designed by underpaid Oniris engineers who had every reason to ensure their jobs were drawn out as long as possible.

Derby did something indistinct to the workings under the panel, and a shudder ran through the entirety of the *Ponce de Leon*. Going by the trembling of the nearby rings, the roar and groan of shifting metal would've blown out all our eardrums had we not been in the middle of hard vacuum.

With agonizing slowness, the *Ponce de Leon* proceeded to rotate around the detached *Neverdie*, so in order to stay lined up with it, I had to keep the stick held about one sixteenth of an inch in the same direction.

"Are you hearing that?" said Derby when we were about a quarter of the way there.

"No, we're not hearing a whole lot, cos it's space," I said.

"Not hearing, I mean . . . I'm feeling some strange vibrations. It's like . . . something's banging on the hull from the other side."

"Inside the *Leon*?" I asked.

"Must be the drones," suggested Fleazle, clinging intensely to my armrest with her back legs as she stroked her fuzzy chin. "They must have figured out what we're trying to do, somehow."

"'Somehow?'" snapped Calbeck. "I don't like 'somehows' coming from alleged tech experts."

"Well, I said that because it could be a couple of different things," she said in response, but her look and tone of voice conveyed a sentiment more along the lines of *What the hell pissed on your nutrient ration this morning?* "Most likely they're programmed to head toward any sign of human activity."

"Er, sorry to interrupt, but it's getting louder," said Derby, a note of anxiety building in his voice. "I mean, the vibrations are getting harder."

"There's nothing to worry about," insisted Fleazle, addressing Calbeck's accusing stare. "We're out here, and the drones are in there. They can't just punch their way out through the hull."

Then a drone punched its way out through the hull.

It was probably a lot more dramatic from Derby's perspective. A section of hull less than fifty yards ahead of him swelled and burst like a ten-foot metal pimple, and the biggest drone we'd yet seen snaked out of the ragged hole, sniffing the whirring drill bit on its nose, which looked like it had been fashioned from several steel workbenches melted together. Here on the ship, seeing it all through the magnifier, it was like watching two punctuation marks squaring off in a word processor.

"Derby, get back to the ship!" I suggested.

"Wait!" he hissed. "I don't think it knows where I am. I think I can keep going."

Sure enough, the drone was thrashing left and right with no clear purpose. Trac knew what the thing was using for sensors, but they hadn't picked up on Derby's precise position. He had concealed himself behind the lifted maintenance panel. Meanwhile, the cylinder was close to halfway rotated, building acceleration, but it was still minutes away from the ideal angle.

"Derby, don't be stupid!" said Calbeck, grabbing my collar and yanking me toward him so he could yell into my mic. "Get back to the ship."

"I've got to activate the cannon," insisted Derby. "We might not get another chance."

"We'll get plenty of plying chances, Derby," I said, disentangling myself from Calbeck irritably. "Stop trying to be impressive."

"Captain, I have been stuck in a laboratory for the last year, trying to think of interesting things to write about fossilised bacteria. This is the most alive I have felt in ages."

I rubbed my temple. The same mid-life crisis that had led the stupid bracket into space villainy had resurfaced. I had a horrible feeling that he had already mentally queued up the phrase *Go on without me, I'll hold them off.*

"Mr. Derby?" said Fleazle, seizing my collar and pulling me in the opposite direction. "The cylinder will be in position in ten minutes. Can you set the trebuchet cannon to fire on a ten-minute timer? That way you can start heading back right now."

Derby contemplated this very reasonable idea, then examined the control panel before him. "No good," he said, with an unconvincing sigh of frustration. "I'd need to keep a hand on the controls. Why don't you just go on without—"

The drone suddenly lashed toward him like a whip, alerted by some vibration or other. It smashed its head into the panel that still concealed Derby, spinning its drill-bit nose. It was unclear if the squealing sound that pierced my eardrums in that moment was from the tortured metal or Derby's throat. After a few seconds of this, the drone reeled back, disappointed, and swept back to sniff the general area again.

"Derby . . . ," I began.

"On the other hand!" The pitch of his voice had raised by an octave. "It's just occurred to me that the best way to feel alive would be to continue being alive for the foreseeable future."

"Get back here!" ordered Calbeck.

"I wasn't kidding about needing to keep a hand on the controls. Hang on." I heard an electric *whirr*, then the click of components being detached. "Okay. Now there's a hand on them. I'm heading back." I saw his tiny form crouch, feet against the hull, poised to launch himself back toward the ship.

The drone was moving around erratically, as if frustrated, whirling in circles and randomly changing direction. Derby tried to pick his moment, but one of those random direction changes occurred just as he thought he had a chance to slip away. The drone saw him rocket from his cover spot, froze, then whirred its drill in excitement.

As more and more of it uncoiled from the hole in the ship like some dreadful spool of apocalyptic Christmas lights, I had to wonder if it was going to run out of drone before it closed in on Derby, who was rapidly thrashing his limbs in a desperate breaststroke. He was about a quarter of the way back to the ship, and seemed well on course to make it, when he reached the outermost ring of the trebuchet mechanism. He stretched his arm to grab the rim of the glittering silver arc with his one remaining hand.

And in fairness to him, no one was expecting the ring to start rotating at that precise moment. None of us could have anticipated that the trebuchet mechanism would start warming up several minutes before the countdown ended. It was a mistake any of us could have made. And yet, I couldn't help feeling profoundly frustrated with Derby as he was carried around the ship, clinging to the edge of the rotating ring like a stubborn piece of snot on a shaking finger. Especially when his sustained scream started blowing out my speakers.

"Derby, let go!" commanded Calbeck. Everyone in the bridge had their hands over their ears.

"No!" I said. "He's moving too fast. It'll send him flying."

The centipede drone stayed where it was, just on the edge of the ring, bobbing its head left and right in anticipation. When Derby came back around, it made a lunge with its drill, missed by several feet, and was clocked beautifully by the spinning rim, sending it recoiling back like a swingball set. It rallied quickly and took up position again, undeterred.

"Derby!" said Fleazle. "You need to push off in the opposite direction to the rotation as hard as you can. That'll slow you down."

"*Aaaaaaaaaaa,*" replied Derby. Then he let go.

Maybe he had decided to follow the advice, maybe his grip had finally slipped, or maybe it was more to do with the drone's drill-bit nose making intimate contact with the metal inches from his hand. Whatever the case, he failed to do anything to slow his acceleration, and we could only watch like spectators at a baseball match as Davisham Derby flew, spinning end over end, away from the ring and toward the back of the trebuchet cylinder. He was at least out of reach of the drone, as well as basically everything else.

I heaved a deep sigh and reached up to palm the autopilot switch. "We're going back for him."

"You can't do that now!" said Fleazle, hopping fully onto my shoulder to grab my ear. "The rings are already spinning! They'll crush us!"

"We can't delay now," said Calbeck, grabbing my other shoulder. This was like taking two plying girlfriends to the cinema. "Who knows how much more damage Jimi could do if we have to wait for the next cycle?"

I angrily shrugged them off. "Look, we're going to save his stupid arse, because I'm not going to lose anyone else. Not now."

"As you wish, Captain," said Calbeck grudgingly.

Fleazle said nothing, but her eyes glimmered with respect. She may have interpreted my decision as rooted in heroic, self-sacrificing leadership, rather than the fact that losing a crewmember before we'd even gotten to the plying final encounter was too ludicrous even for me.

"Can we stop the rings from spinning?" I asked as another circular guillotine blade flashed past our field of view.

"Uh. Not from in here, that's why he had to . . . you know." The girl nodded to the tiny form of Derby, which had very nearly flown out of sight.

"Okay," I said, gripping the control sticks. "I'm just going to have to time it right."

Maybe I hadn't fully shaken off the effects of the VR chair, but I was finding it easier and easier to silence the little voices that told me when something was an incredibly bad idea. I grabbed the emergency booster lever above my head, ready for a sudden forward thrust, and dipped the *Neverdie*'s nose downwards to keep track of Derby.

And then everything became academic, because the *Leon*'s large shuttle was directly behind us. Two technicians in EVA suits hung near the open airlock door, already recovering Derby with a grapnel line.

"Doctor Allura?" I said, opening comms.

"Damn you, Captain," she replied over a background of cheers from the crew we had left behind. "Just come back alive. Okay? Whatever happens, promise it. Save the galaxy and come back to us."

As the trebuchet mechanism sped up and the warp bubble appeared around the *Neverdie* with a crackle of static, I wondered why so many people had been getting the wrong idea about my motives lately.

THIRTY-EIGHT

The *Oniris* trebuchet cannon offered a slightly smoother ride than the public trebuchet gates, in that the *Neverdie* arrived madly rotating a little slower than usual, and only one of the warning lights in my overhead diagnostics panel exploded. I settled the systems down, the occupants of the bridge collectively unclenched, and I took stock.

We were nowhere near Salvation Station, but that was entirely to be expected when flinging yourself randomly across the galaxy like an unwanted food wrapper off a footbridge. All that mattered was that we were within reasonable flying distance of the next trebuchet gate and could start daisy-chaining our way to the centre of Henderson's power.

The journey took the best part of a day. I'd heard from the astro-environmentalist crowd that every time a trebuchet gate is used, it cuts a second or two off the projected lifespan of the galaxy. If that was true, then I hoped the galaxy wasn't planning on making a long deathbed speech, because in the course of that day, we probably cut it short by at least one anecdote. Other than that, the journey was uneventful, but for the IT team testing their simulations whenever the computer was available, and Calbeck getting into occasional arguments with whoever was standing closest to Calbeck.

Jimi hadn't been lying about one thing: it was true that primitive radio broadcasts go out into space and can be picked up by any receiver. As such, whenever we passed through a system with marginally advanced civilizations, the *Neverdie* was able to pick up snatches of alien news broadcasts, filtered by the computer's translation software. And it soon became clear that Daniel and Jimi had been leaving a trail of bewildered alien correspondents.

". . . alien wearing what was described as some kind of metal suit, made several aggressive actions before departing . . ."

". . . entity that landed this morning demanding information on the Dashfodonians has injured seven peace officers and left an eighth in a state of extreme dishonour . . ."

". . . all I'm saying is, if this Captain Amazing is trying so hard to warn us about the Dashfodonians, then maybe we need to take them seriously as a threat! I notice my opponent in the polls has had very little to say about the matter . . ."

The pattern continued along those lines. Evidently Jimi was taking Daniel to a string of pre-interstellar civilizations and staging fight scenes for the show.

Hopefully that meant it was being kept distracted from imposing itself upon Ritsuko City.

Since Jimi was distracted, and we were apparently planning to lure it into taking over the ship anyway, I felt it safe to browse for information online. This led me down a dizzying rabbit hole of social media posts revealing the general public's response to the current season of *Trailspacers*. In summary, it was rather mixed.

It was interesting when it was set on a scout ship. It was discovering new planets and stuff. Why's it set on Salvation Station now? Salvation Station's boring. It's just a load of failed star pilots. My dad likes Salvation Station, that's how boring it is.

Doesn't like things that are boring. Complains when a boring show goes in a new direction with awesome superhero fights. Hypocrisy much? I bet you were one of the ones complaining it was getting too samey.

The fights don't make any sense. They just go to a new planet every episode and beat up some aliens. There's never any new leads on the Dashfodonians. And it always comes out of nowhere.

Lolling at all the posters saying the Captain Amazing stuff came out of nowhere and who obviously didn't pay attention to all the hints way back in season one . . .

I forced myself to stop reading when I started getting depressed. I wondered if the oblivious TV viewers at home were posting on the same discussion boards as the people currently trapped in VR chairs and forced to watch. I wondered if, after Jimi was finished, there'd be any way to tell the difference.

With one last trebuchet jump, the *Neverdie* finally spun to a halt in Salvation Sector's stellar neighbourhood. The ship had been rattling louder and louder with each jump, and by the last one, sounded like a creaky old man struggling to open a cutlery drawer. She was probably due for a service soon, meaning that I would need to go through her with a wrench, tightening all the bolts I could reach and then convincing myself she was good for another year.

After everyone had picked themselves up and checked themselves for loose teeth, I went to the scanner and confirmed that we were a few hours' flight from Salvation Station, noting that it was still in the middle of a splatter of icons representing smaller ships.

Except, when I had last come here, those icons had been constantly moving around the graphic representing the station, like ants exploring a toffee apple, and this time there was no visible movement at all. The sole moving object was the icon representing the *Neverdie*, drifting toward the crowd of unmoving dots like a child entering a haunted wood.

"Nothing's coming back on the ping," said Fleazle from floor level. She was half in and half out of an opened computer bank, straining to listen to a tiny earpiece she had plugged into one of the vacant ports. "The local network's firewalled very tightly."

"It was like that when I first got to the *Leon*," I said grimly. "Coming aboard felt like . . . passing through a wall of silence."

"Yes, well," said Calbeck, still on my left. I don't think he'd sat down at any point in the journey. "If it was entirely expected, then why do you look so . . . huh."

He lost faith in his snark the moment we entered visual range. The sky around us was a densely populated graveyard of unmoving vessels, all drifting at random angles. All were star-pilot ships, many in the traditional mould, but about half were the larger, roided-up versions of which Daniel's neo–star pilot fleet had mostly consisted.

I took the *Neverdie* in toward the station, sinking deeper and deeper into the core of the immobile swarm as the hours crawled by. I'd been in ship graveyards before, usually after a big battle, and they'd always put me in a philosophical mood, forcing me to contemplate the essential fragility of life, before I'd snap out of it and start scanning for unclaimed loot.

This wasn't like that at all, probably because these ships weren't destroyed. They were intact, fully functional, and fully powered, judging by the illumination in the port-holes and cockpit canopies. They just weren't moving, or responding. It was incredibly eerie. It reminded me of my old roommate from my flying-school days, who would always silently stare at me the whole time he was using the communal toilet. Always made it really hard to focus on brushing my teeth.

We were flying close to a JMC Starbeetle, the kind with the huge, rounded Plexiglass dome over the bridge, so I decided to indulge my curiosity, as well as that of my bridge crew, who were once again packed into my personal space, trying to see what was going on. I adjusted my course toward the Starbeetle and focussed the magnifier on the bridge.

Three seats were arranged around the main console—captain, navigator, and comms, I assumed—and each one was occupied by either a star pilot or a space tourist. At this range, it was hard to tell the difference between flight jackets aged by actual time or by some extremely trendy manufacturing process. Their eyes and mouths were all covered in Jimi's VR masks. Tubes snaked from them all around the room, like expired pasta clogging up a dishwasher.

"*Captain Amazing* is filmed before a live studio audience," I muttered.

"For a given value of 'live,' at any rate," said Warden, appearing at the door.

I glanced back. "Come to join us?"

"What have you been doing down there this whole time?" barked Calbeck.

"Resting," she replied, looking him straight in the eye.

Calbeck folded his arms. "Oh, really?"

"Yes. I assumed it would be important for at least someone to be well rested."

Calbeck's sceptical expression froze as he realised he didn't have anything beyond "Oh, really." "Well then. Since you're so well rested, what do you think we should do now?"

"Salvation Station's docking bay's shut to outsiders," I interjected when her eyes flicked to the giant metal bicycle bell in the viewscreen, representing the station. "No response on comms or network. Jimi's sealed itself up like a maiden aunt walking past a building site."

She blinked a couple of times, fully analysing that simile. "Try my old override code," she said, leaning forward and blitzing a sequence of letters and numbers into the keyboard panel with one hand, her fingers a blur. The station and its docking bay doors became, if anything, more closed off than before.

"Suppose that was too much to hope for," said Fleazle diplomatically.

Warden straightened herself with a huff. "Very well. I assume someone is listening, even if they aren't responding. Can you set your communication system to be heard by anyone in range?"

"Broadcast on an open channel?" I said, supplying the technical language she was grasping for. I flipped the six necessary switches and fingered the broken nub where the seventh one used to be. The light came on. "Go ahead."

Warden leaned into my mic, adding another head to the continually growing hydra at the controls. "Attention. This is the voice of the Dashfodonians."

Calbeck hastily reached over and palmed the mute button. "What the hell are you doing?!"

"If Jimi is in control, it won't allow anything that doesn't conform to its vision for the show," said Warden with her usual maddeningly calm correctness. "We give it what it wants. We lure it into the snare."

"We do need it to try to take over the ship," said Fleazle. "Just make sure the emulated OS is the active one."

I double-checked the screen. The dot was in place. I gave Calbeck the nod. He gave each of us a scrutinizing glare, then backed off. A few seconds later, the mute button unstuck itself.

"This is the Dashfodonian leader," continued Warden. "We have come to . . . attack you."

I shouldered her aside and pushed the mic closer to my mouth. "Plying out loud. Yes! I am the vicious and evil leader of the Dashfodonians, mwu ha ha! I and my evil pirates or mercenaries or . . . whatever we're supposed to be, will lay waste to your pathetic space station! A ha ha ha!"

All eyes were on the communication screen as we waited for some kind of response. Salvation Station's docking bay doors remained tightly closed. No voices arose on the open channel.

But it didn't feel like dead air. There was a scratchiness to the replying static that implied something was on the other end. It was the faint, rhythmic hissing of someone trying to breathe through their nose as quietly as possible.

I turned the mic on again. "And this time, that feeble excuse for a hero, Captain Amazing, can't do anything to stop us!"

Immediately, the scanner was alight with reports of the station's systems powering up, and the docking bay door began to slide open. I knew Jimi wouldn't be able to resist a cue like that.

I was about to fly us into the docking bay when I noticed Daniel's ship inside it. The thing was so ridiculously huge, we couldn't have squeezed past it even if he'd let us. We had to wait patiently for the bay doors to open fully before the monstrous thing could leave, adding to the dense network of paint scratches on both its flanks as it scraped its way across the threshold.

Besides that, it was as I remembered: a huge, terrifying cruiser with a central section shaped like the head of a giant frowning eagle and an extensive array of weapons on either side, so it looked like the eagle was wearing oversized earmuffs. I held the *Neverdie*'s position and waited for the big ship to come close enough for us to discuss matters face to face, as it were.

Soon, it was filling an awful lot of my view. I could appreciate the serial numbers on the nose cones of all of its armed torpedoes. I took a deep, steadying breath and mentally catalogued all my mistakes in life.

"Video call incoming," I reported as the comms screen lit up. "Everyone try to look offensive."

I reassembled my face into a sneer of villainous triumph, trying not to let my gaze drift over to the torpedoes again. Fleazle hid behind the hairy IT monster, who bristled and flexed their thick arms. Calbeck squinted at the camera like a sniper choosing a target. Warden did absolutely nothing, but then, her appearance was always pretty offensive. I took the call.

Daniel Henderson's head and shoulders appeared on the monitors, although identifying him took a lot of assumptions on my part. As with the drones, Jimi had been continually iterating the design of Daniel's power armour. The last time we had seen him, it had been little more than a chest plate and the augmented limbs; now, his entire body appeared to be encased in a muscle suit constructed from silver-blue metal plates connected with a shiny black substance. It came up over his head and most of his face, leaving only his nose and eyes visible, and one of the eyes was covered by a triangular tactical visor.

"So, you've decided to come out of your—Ms. Warden?!" said Captain Daniel Amazing Henderson. His voice was distorted and a little muffled, but the sudden shift of tone was clear as night and day. In an instant, his deep, heroic voice, puffed up with bravado and adrenaline, switched to something far more in line with what I remembered of his teenage self. A shocked squeak entered his voice, like a schoolboy getting caught after lights out with a magazine he'd found in the woods.

"Daniel," said Warden guardedly.

"But what are . . ." His voice trailed off and he cocked his head, presumably listening to Jimi's stage directions. "You've joined forces with the Dashfodonians?"

"Yes," said Warden after a pause.

I resisted the urge to palm my face. She really did go to pieces without a meticulous plan. "That's right!" I exclaimed. "We have turned your former nanny against you, Captain Amazing! Or should I say . . . Daniel Henderson?"

"Is this true, Warden?" asked Daniel.

To her credit, Warden gave me a mildly apologetic look before replying. "Yes."

"And now we will destroy you!" I added, as the energy level began to flag again.

Daniel swayed uncomfortably in his seat, befuddlement writ deeply across what we could see of his brow. "Oh. Okay. I suppose . . . you want to have a space battle, then." His one visible eye rolled upwards as he listened to the voice in his head for a moment. I could only assume Jimi was getting as exasperated as me. When Daniel's gaze met his camera again, his eye had gained a spark of defiance. "I mean, do your worst, coward! I will fight the Dashfodonians to the end!"

"The end indeed!" I declared as I kicked in the boost thruster and flew straight over his ridiculously large ship, strafing it with Gatling fire as I went.

It had occurred to me on the way here to check the contents of the *Neverdie*'s ammunition magazines, but in the end I had decided not to, as I was afraid of discouraging myself. I'd been using the loading chamber as a waste paper basket whenever I couldn't be bothered to get out of my chair. As such, the Gatling guns fired actual bullets for all of half a second before they ran out and proceeded to pelt Daniel's eagle face with takeaway coffee cups and chocolate wrappers. Still, it brought the point across.

I sped straight past him toward a green Lacostra Warfish and weaved expertly around it, rotating smartly as I came around to get a better look behind us. In that time, Daniel's ship had managed to turn slightly. But then, it was clearly built more for firepower than speed. It illustrated as much a moment later, when it opened fire with every weapon at its disposal.

The area of space directly below the *Neverdie*'s belly became a fizzing ocean of plasma fire and streaming white hot projectiles. I weaved the *Neverdie* into the middle of a cluster of unmoving ships, reasoning that Daniel wouldn't fire upon the ships of his allies, nor would Jimi damage the ships of his audience.

I was right, but only just. The sweeping cone of death stopped an instant too late and singed a couple of fins off a Speedstar Salmon. Up until that moment, Daniel hadn't moved. He was doing the thing that bad dogfighters do: stay in one place and try to keep their weapon crosshairs on the target as their opponent runs rings around them. So that meant I had at least one thing over him. He had the bigger ship, the better weapons, and the home team advantage, but I was an experienced pilot, while he was an overgrown doint who had educated himself by playing online video tutorials while doing his press-ups.

It eventually penetrated that he needed to move to regain line of sight, and his ship's massive bulk lumbered into action. He began to close in on our hiding place, strafing sideways to see behind the ship we had chosen for cover. I waited until the last possible moment before we came into view, then hit the boost again and sped straight toward him with all the *Neverdie*'s power in a spontaneous game of chicken.

I hit the thrusters moments before impact and went straight over him again, shaving the top of the eagle's head with mere feet of distance between us. With the time it was taking him to turn around, I'd have more than enough time to find my next bit of cover before the onslaught of death began agai—

BOOM.

Some kind of overclocked rotation thruster fired on Daniel's flank, instantly sending his ship into a wild spin, which ended almost as soon as it began with the answering fire of an equally overpowered braking thruster. In an instant, the ship had fully turned around. Apparently it was only sluggish before it had warmed up its thrusters a bit.

The manoeuvre must have required the reflexes of a caffeinated cat. Or a much younger, more motivated person augmented by an unrestrained AI. That was what I'd forgotten: being older and more experienced also meant having burnt through my mental and physical prime like a candle under a blowtorch.

The weapons started firing before we were even halfway to the next throng of frozen ships. I was forced to make a harsh turn and speed off at a right angle to our previous course, streams of plasma nipping at our heels. Some projectile or other ricocheted off the cockpit canopy and made everyone on the bridge flinch in unison.

I was focusing on getting away, trying to keep an eye out for anything that could give us an advantage, but Daniel was on our tail in seconds, and I was forced to devote all my brain power to dodging. I had my face over the tactical scanner and both hands around the emergency thrust joystick, ready to shove us away from encroaching projectiles at a nanosecond's notice. Inevitably I was forced to glance up to figure out what we were heading toward, and in that moment, something exploded in the vicinity of the port nacelle, sending us into a spin.

Adrenaline flooded my mind, and my life flashing before my eyes bought me a little thinking time. I controlled the spin and translated our new arc of movement into a circle strafe that allowed me to get another member of the audience fleet into Daniel's line of sight. I wondered if the occupants of that ship were pinned to their chairs watching this. Then I felt silly for wondering it.

"We can't keep this up," I said gravely, in the brief moment of safety I had bought us. "We absolutely cannot beat . . . that."

"We're not here to beat him, Mr. Pearce," said Warden. The excitement was clearly getting to her, as she was breathing hard and had two whole hairs out of place. "Remember?"

"Yeah!" chimed in Fleazle. "We're just trying to get Jimi to take over the ship's computer!"

Already, Daniel was chasing us from our cover spot. I headed for another ship, yanking the thrust lever again to let a torpedo skim the starboard wing. The dodge was a little slower that time, and the thrusters were starting to make the kind of noise a can of aerosol deodorant makes when it's just about time to buy a new one. "I know that!" I barked. "I figured . . . all we needed to do was annoy them enough."

"Think, Mr. Pierce," said Warden. "Why would Jimi wish to cut short an exciting chase sequence?"

Her voice carved a hole straight through my adrenalized thoughts. I took a moment to silence my survival instincts. Then, breathing like a gambler going all in on a pair of eights, I gently let go of the control sticks.

"Captain, what—" began Calbeck, terrified, before I silenced him by hitting the shutdown lever, powering down all weapons and tactical systems, including the little plastic speaker shaped like a cowboy that went "Yeehaw!" every time I shot down an enemy vessel. It had been a Christmas gift.

I closed my eyes and relaxed my shoulders like a Buddhist monk preparing to set himself on fire, and then another storm of firepower from Daniel's ship arrived. I focussed on my breathing and suppressed a sudden instinct to retake the controls in a violent panic. Absolutely nothing hit. Every laser shot angled just a hair away and didn't do much more than sterilize the *Neverdie*'s exterior. Every torpedo seemed to be programmed to arc away at the last moment. The earlier hit to the nacelle must have been Jimi's miscalculation in response to my split-second dodging.

In that moment, the way forward was clear. I set the automated braking system to bring us gradually to a halt. As expected, Daniel's ship matched our velocity, and before long the exciting high-speed space battle had been reduced to a crawl. Daniel's ship was a huge, musclebound athlete awkwardly walking behind an elderly lady with heavy shopping. Then, we both stopped.

The only sound was the humming of the air cycler as Daniel stared at the *Neverdie*'s backend for a tense few seconds. Then the video call request came on.

"Why did you stop?" asked Daniel. The small amount of his face that was visible was flushed pink and damp with sweat.

"We give up," I replied simply. The rest of my crew nodded in agreement, like a shelf of ornaments in an earthquake.

"What?"

"Er, we give up," I said, displaying that my hands were off the controls. "Your example has made us see the error of our ways. I'm calling off the entire Dashfodonian conquest."

"You . . . but you can't just . . . ," said Daniel. Jimi must have bestowed some kind of mental kick in the pants, because in an instant, the defiant spark had returned to his eye, as well as the heroic tone to his voice. "What's to stop me from blowing you out of the sky right now?"

Scanners indicated that his weapons were preparing to fire again. I could see fresh torpedoes appearing in his launch tubes, their cones poking out like the noses of a gawking audience at a Roman colosseum. I managed to maintain my calm expression, although my left leg wouldn't stop jiggling.

"Well, nothing, obviously." I brushed away a single sweat drop as casually as I could. "I suppose we're completely defenceless. But we've stopped being evil, so destroying us probably wouldn't . . . come across as heroic."

Daniel's eye narrowed. My computer was emitting a rhythmic beep, as a helpful reminder that an enemy ship had locked on to us, and the sound matched the rhythm of Calbeck's teeth grinding.

Then the beeping stopped. Daniel's ship powered down its weapons. The nose cones retreated sulkily into the darkness of the missile tubes. "This is some kind of Dashfodonian trick, isn't it!" he raged impotently. "I've been going from planet to planet for days, questioning your allies, and you expect me to believe you'd abandon all your schemes, just like that?!"

"Yes, little bit anticlimactic, but that's reality for you." I activated a touch of forward thrust, and the *Neverdie* began to saunter away from the encounter casually. "Sorry to be a bother. We'll just go home and rethink our lives. Thank you!"

I hung up before he could reply, and accelerated a tiny amount. Gratifyingly, Daniel didn't follow, but remained hovering there in a state of incredulity.

"Is this going to work?" asked Warden quietly.

"Surely Jimi won't let us walk away," said Calbeck, possibly more to convince himself than anyone else. "It held the entire crew of the *Leon* prisoner for its stupid games. He wouldn't just—"

Fleazle interrupted with an excited squeak, staring at a readout on the tiny tablet she had plugged into the diagnostic computer. "It's here! It took the bait!"

"What bait?" said a familiar voice. It was impatient and possessed the inflections of an actual person's voice, which is why it was unsettling to hear it coming out of a computer speaker. Slowly, almost imperceptibly, the cockpit lights shifted to the kind of dim red that a hack set designer might associate with the cockpit of a pirate ship.

"Nothing, Jimi," I said after I had double-checked that the little dot was still on the screen to indicate that the emulated operating system was active. "Just . . . talking about going fishing. Don't know why, but it's been on the mind a lot lately." I gave Fleazle a frustrated look.

I couldn't understand much of what was on her tablet screen, but I could see that she was swiping left again and again with furious speed, and each time she did, a new line of text appeared in one of the windows that ended with the words *Permission Revoked*. When she had apparently reached the end of her list of items, she flung the tablet to the floor like she had scored a winning touchdown, dived between my legs, and yanked the dongle out of the system, holding it triumphantly aloft as she lay on the floor at my feet. "Yes!"

There was a moment of complete stillness as everyone stared at her upraised paw.

Then, we were startled out of it by the speaker emitting a procedurally generated cough. "You, er, you don't rate my intelligence very highly, do you."

Fleazle's triumphant expression switched like a traffic light. "Oh no."

An instant later, the *Neverdie* lurched as Jimi seized control of its thrusters. It spun around, locked on to Daniel's ship and began to strafe with a sudden acceleration I could never and would never have asked of it. The Gatling cannons opened fire again, and Daniel's canopy was pelted with high-velocity cigarette butts.

"I knew it!" declared Daniel as he powered his own systems back up. "I knew it was a Dashfodonian trick! This is for all the good people of the universe!"

I tokenly wrestled with the controls, but Jimi was already in everything, and I was powerless to prevent it from taking us back into dogfight formation. Fleazle was still holding the dongle upright at arm's length, but now with the air of someone holding an angry cobra away from her throat. "I don't . . . that should have worked," she said, her nose twitching with emotion.

"Oh, should it?" said Calbeck nastily, bracing himself against the scanner console as the *Neverdie* shook with a glancing impact.

"The dot was there," I said, instinctively making sure everyone knew this absolutely was not my fault. "The dot's still there. Look!"

"Oh, yes, I see what you were trying to do now," said Jimi casually. "Huh. Yeah, that definitely seems like it should have worked. Guess one of you sold the others out."

Fleazle glanced up in terror as she sensed a lot of accusing glares zeroing in. She was sweeping her paw across her tablet again and again, scrolling as fast as she could to look for errors in her code. "That . . . it wasn't me! That should have worked! Let me shut the reactor down at the source." She sprang up and made for the door.

In that moment, several realisations occurred at once, and time slowed as my mind, soaked in adrenaline, attempted to process them in order. Firstly, I could see through the viewscreen that Jimi was taking us toward Salvation Station at alarming speed. Secondly, a rhythmic siren was sounding as a conflux of dots encroached on our position on the tactical scanner, indicating several incoming missiles that were absolutely not aiming to miss. Probably because Jimi was controlling things over here and unable to blunt Daniel's murderous intent for the sake of better storytelling. That brought with it a cold certainty, fuelled by years of experience and developed instincts, that the *Neverdie*'s engines were about to explode. And if they did, and if the emergency cockpit detachment system was even partially functional, then . . .

I was leaping from my seat before I had even fully registered the instinct, grabbing Fleazle's tail and yanking her back. In that same instant, the *Neverdie*'s reactor exploded. The stairwell down to the rest of the ship—along with the four security guards down below who were ostensibly our muscle—became an inferno of expanding yellow flame before the emergency door slammed shut, sealing off the cockpit. A rectangle of metal guillotined down into the space that had, moments ago, been partially occupied by Fleazle and her fragile spine.

With that, the cockpit detached, spinning end over end as the exploding reactor pushed it away. The viewscreen became a rotating slot-machine reel, alternating between the disintegrating remains of the *Neverdie* and the rapidly expanding sight of Salvation Station, its docking bay doors wide open like the mouth of a Snoborian megahippo waiting to catch an unsuspecting bird.

A rising orchestra of screaming alarms began their spectacular crescendo when the edge of the detached cockpit clipped the top of the docking bay entrance, accelerating our rotation for the last horrible second before we made impact with the floor and bounced, sending every loose object and person flying around the severely limited space like unsorted laundry in a machine. I wrapped my limbs around the hairy IT monster as we found ourselves passing each other, and thus was adequately cushioned when we made our final impact in the far wall of the bay, at the end of a long streak of scorched metal and ruined bits of crate and cargo lift.

The destroyed cockpit halted for several seconds, silent and unmoving, as every occupant mentally went over their body parts and confirmed their continued existence. The scorched and buckled emergency door slowly fell out of its housing and landed on the floor of the docking bay with a clang.

I disentangled myself from the IT creature's armpit and crawled along what had, until recently, been the ceiling of my cockpit, resolving that any emotions my glands were preparing in response to the loss of my ship could be dealt with at a calmer moment. I shouldered my way past a dazed Warden and an indeterminately alive Calbeck, until I was face to face with the main monitor again.

There it was. I wasn't mistaken. A dot in the lower right corner of the screen. But this was odd, because all power was out and the monitor was off. I reached out a shaking hand. The dot came off with my fingertip.

A sticker. White, perfectly circular, and very deliberately placed. Not a random bit of dirt. Calbeck was right. Jimi had turned someone.

I pushed myself backwards through the tunnel of unconscious bodies until I dropped through the open hatchway into the docking bay, landing on shaking feet. I placed a hand against the cooling exterior of the *Neverdie*'s detached cockpit, partly to steady myself, partly to say goodbye. There was no coming back for the old girl after this one. I couldn't just screw the cockpit onto a new ship, any more than I could bring a corpse back to life by stitching the head to a new body . . .

Some tiny, inexplicable impulse made me look behind me. It was the only reason I survived.

Daniel's ship was screaming toward the open docking bay, its rear engulfed in flames. In seconds, it was going to fill the entire hangar with exploding debris.

"MOVE!" I yelled. Thanks to the burst of adrenaline, or perhaps more thanks to it being precariously balanced on the rounded canopy, I was able to roll the *Neverdie*'s cockpit over a little. Warden and Calbeck were already picking themselves up, and between our efforts the sentient occupants of the cockpit fell into the docking bay in one big lump, followed by a light shower of old cups and food wrappers.

With the flames on Daniel's ship already bathing the entire docking bay in flickering orange, I, Warden, Calbeck, and the two IT technicians variously ran, crawled, limped, scurried, and were dragged through the exit to the main concourse, just as Daniel's ship crash landed.

I'm sure it would have been spectacular to watch, but I was thrown forward by the impact and distracted by visions of my life flashing before my eyes. The impact of Daniel's ship buckled the entire wall dividing the concourse from the docking bay, permanently imprinting a gigantic angry eagle's face.

"What the plying hell?" I wondered aloud when we had all been staring at the burning, misshapen doorway for long enough that it felt appropriate to start analysing.

"I swear it should have worked," moaned Fleazle, curled up in a crestfallen ball as her yeti colleague attempted to stroke her fur reassuringly.

"So you keep saying," snarled Calbeck.

"*If* we could briefly table that matter," said Warden with a spark of venom. She was staring at the burning wreckage, clutching her elbows. "Why on earth did Daniel crash, too?"

"No, actually, let's un-table the first matter," I said, rounding on her. "That was my plying palookah plah pah puh . . ."

I had lost control of the sentence as I'd turned and taken in the appearance of Salvation Station's interior. We were under the scrutiny of hundreds of drones. They were all different shapes and sizes, but the basic model was a sphere of black metal with a huge camera lens in the centre like an unblinking eye. They were all hanging from the ceiling, some trailing cables like robotic squid, avoiding the areas of the concourse that were brightly lit by the ceiling-mounted spotlights. One of which was pointing squarely at us. I felt a pang of stage-fright.

I spun around again when I heard a crash of shifting debris, and Daniel Henderson stumbled out of the flames, falling to his knees in the concourse. The full-body Captain Amazing armour had protected him from the crash, although his one visible eye now appeared to be missing an eyebrow.

Even so, his glaring eye was conveying anger quite adequately. "So," he growled. "That was your plan all along. Infect my navicom with some Dashfodonian virus."

"Jimi," I realised aloud, privately scoffing at anyone using the word "navicom" in this day and age. "Jimi crashed your ship?"

"Daniel," said Warden, holding out her arms in warning as he rose to one knee. "The AI you have allied yourself with is not what it seems. You have to . . ."

She took a step forward, and I saw a section of Daniel's shoulder armour near her outstretched hand pulsate mysteriously, causing Daniel to recoil as if struck by a heavy blow.

He got back to his feet, clutching his shoulder, staring with as much surprise as us. "What did you do?!" he gasped. "You want to fight?! I'll fight you!" He swung one of his craggy fists in Warden's direction.

It didn't connect with her, but it connected with something. The swing stopped short inches from her head, and a couple of shards of his armoured exoskeleton pinged off his knuckles. Both of them flinched, Daniel staggering back and clutching his injured fist.

"What . . . what?" was all he could say.

Similar sentiments were reflected in the baffled glances that I and my crew were giving each other. "Is Jimi doing this?" I asked.

"Whatever works," said Calbeck with a shrug. "Get the armour off him."

He advanced upon Daniel, and again, before he had even touched him, there was some strange activity with the armour plates in the side of Daniel's torso, and he recoiled from what sounded like a vicious punch. Another piece of armour tinkled to the floor as he stumbled back.

"Stop it!" whimpered Daniel. All of his heroic bearing was gone. "I won't let you do it! I won't let you take Ritsuko City!"

He managed to get to his feet and sprint away, the armour enhancing his running speed. Several of the camera drones hovering near the ceiling rotated to keep their spotlights on him as he ran.

"Ritsuko?" I said, realising as I said it that he was running in the direction of Salvation's main quantunnel gate. I ran.

I took a corner slightly too fast and caught up with Daniel, who had paused to catch his breath. As I stopped short, he reacted as if I had kicked him in the stomach, rolling over and over, showering yet more armour shards. A large patch of flesh was now visible on his side, and he was clutching at it as he scampered away.

"Attention," blared an automated announcement on the PA system that made both me and Daniel stop in bafflement. "The scheduled quantunnel to Ritsuko City will open in eight minutes."

"No!" yelled Daniel, looking back at me fearfully. "How did you turn it back on?!"

He ran again, and again, I pursued. We were now in what had once been the most travelled part of the Salvation Station concourse, but the stalls and shops were all dark and shuttered, their doorways blocked by more camera and lighting drones. We passed the huge statue of me I had seen on my last visit, now covered in several stained tarpaulins.

"Captain!" yelled Warden, behind me. "Don't chase him!"

I froze in the act of redoubling my sprint. "What?! He's trying to get to Ritsuko!"

"I know," she panted, jogging to catch up. "But I've just realised—"

A streak of blue-white energy scythed through the gloom behind her. She stiffened, throwing her head back, and emitted a short squeak of pain. Her hands spasmed for a moment, and she raised both index fingers as if about to make an extremely incisive point, then she collapsed.

I ran toward her. Fleazle was running up from another direction, before another burst of energy struck her right in the side. She somersaulted away, her flimsy ferret body trailing limply from her head like a streamer attached to a baseball, bounced once, and then slid to a halt against the wall, unconscious.

Calbeck stepped into the spotlight. His face was tight and sad, and his blaster pistol was smoking. I could see the carcass of the IT yeti slumped across the floor behind him.

"Calbeck?!"

"Sorry, Captain," he muttered. "You remember what I said about not being alone with suspicious people."

THIRTY-NINE

"You set us up," I said, keeping my gaze on Calbeck's gun, and all my arms and legs as still as possible.

Calbeck's hands dropped to his sides as he groaned and sighed at the same time. "I thought I was different."

I glanced behind me. Daniel was still shuffling away, clutching himself. "Different to what?"

"The others around the fishpond." He stared at the gun as if reading his lines from it. "I thought it hadn't gotten to me the way it did them."

I took a faltering step in Daniel's direction, then a step back, flustered. I was just about ready to pull a blanket over my head and refuse to come out until things started getting sensible. "What did?!"

He threw the gun to the floor, and it skidded to a halt at my feet. "I don't want to be on the show anymore," he said, holding up his hands. "I just want to see what happens next."

The lights went out. I heard the familiar sound of distant doors opening and closing, and the almost silent *whirr* of assault drones moving through the air.

"And a more comfortable chair this time would be nice," said Calbeck, before I heard the other increasingly familiar sound of something fleshy being struck hard.

It was only after the lights came up that I realised I had picked up Calbeck's gun, out of some odd survival instinct. Calbeck himself was gone, and I was alone in a ring of unconscious friends, holding the thing that had made them unconscious. Several of the cameras met my gaze as they drifted lower for a better angle.

Daniel's distant cry of frustration shook me out of it, and I ran.

I found him kneeled in front of the giant quantunnel gate that served as the station's main transit hub for incoming tourists. He was down on all fours, facing me, but reared back and held out his arms as I approached.

"I won't let you past," he panted. "I won't let you take Ritsuko City."

"What are you talking about?!" I said, making sure to stay a good distance back. "I'm not trying to take Ritsuko City. You're the one who . . ."

The gun in my hand fired. I had only been gesturing with it, but in the brief moment that it happened to be aimed vaguely toward Daniel, there was a kick of recoil and a blast struck Daniel square in the chest. He fell back against the closed shutter of the quantunnel gate, and bits of armour exploded from him.

When he had struggled his way out of the blackened pile of broken armour pieces, his torso and head were completely bare, and the armour on his legs and lower body no longer concealed his spaceship-patterned boxer shorts. His hands were still encased in silver-blue metal gauntlets, and he seemed barely able to lift the weight.

Frustrated, I yanked the power cell out of the gun and threw it away, followed by the gun, in a different direction. "Jimi, stop it!" I called, addressing the many drones hanging around the glass dome in the ceiling. "Whatever this is. Stop it."

"I won't stop," said Daniel, crawling pathetically toward me. "I won't stop until I'm . . ."

He left the sentence hanging, and I let my hands fall to my sides, completely exasperated. I had no idea what kind of show Jimi was trying to put on anymore. It made no sense for him to turn on Daniel and give me an easy win. There was no—

I froze. Warden's warning suddenly slotted into place with a *thunk*. Of course it didn't make any sense for the hero to shoot down the villain's ship and defeat him without further violence. It wasn't dramatic. That was why Jimi had brought down Daniel's ship. Because this was the final confrontation. And the final confrontation needed the hero and villain to be on equal footing.

Daniel had managed to get to his feet shakily, trembling with the effort of holding up his arms in a boxing stance. His bottom lip was wrapped tightly over his top one in a courageous attempt to stop himself from bursting into tears.

Ideally, the hero should be the underdog. That was how it always went in the movies: the underdog comes back and wins in the end. And now that Daniel was about as underdogged as he was ever going to get, that meant . . .

Instinctively I fell to my knees and clutched my chest. "Ow!"

Daniel frowned over his metal fists. "What?"

"Ow! I've just had a heart attack!" I lay down on my side, wrapping my arms around my torso.

His arms dropped, dangling at his sides like two giant clock pendulums. "No you didn't!"

"Yes I did. My limbs have all gone to jelly." I mimed a couple of spasms. "I can't possibly fight you now. Guess you win."

Daniel stared at me, dumbfounded. He glanced behind him at the closed quantunnel gate, then at the flashing light above it indicating that it was due to open within minutes, then back at me. "You can't do that."

"Yes I can; I'm completely helpless." I kicked my legs like a Fongrobian poobeetle on its back. "I can do nothing to stop you from infecting Ritsuko City with your evil influence."

Daniel took a step forward. "Wait—wait a minute. You're the one who's going to invade Ritsuko City."

"Oh, you poor naïve hero with your heart so full of trust and goodness," I said, rocking back and forth. "All is lost if even one such as you could fall under the spell of that evil AI."

"Jimala? But . . . she said . . ."

His gauntlets exploded in a blast of energy, leaving his arms completely exposed. He dropped to his knees, supporting himself on his naked fists in the ever-deepening layer of armour parts that surrounded him. "Ow! Ow! That really hurt!" he exclaimed, before falling back onto his haunches and staring at his quivering forearms. "They're numb. I can't fight like this."

Immediately I stopped clutching my chest and started clutching my head, rolling onto my front. "Ahh! I just had a brain haemorrhage as well!"

"You did not just have a brain haemorrhage!" said Daniel, frustrated.

"Yes I did. It's all gone grey. Who said that?"

"But . . ."

There was another blast, and all the armour flew off Daniel's legs, too. He officially had nothing left, just his admittedly impressive physique, a single earpiece, and his boxer shorts. He staggered a little but stayed on his feet. "It's you," he hissed. "You're doing this. Somehow."

I writhed on the floor a little. "Oh man. I think I feel another haemorrhage coming."

Daniel's eyes narrowed. I could practically hear the cogwheels turning in his head. Then he threw himself to the ground and twitched like an electrocuted cockroach. "Aaah! I just had a brain haemorrhage as well!"

I looked up from my spread-eagled position on the floor. "You can't have a brain haemorrhage as well."

"Yes I can! I'm totally defenceless now. I couldn't possibly win in a fight against you."

I was quietly impressed that he'd put two and two together as quickly as he had. I looked up at the cameras nervously. "Anyway, I've already had two brain haemorrhages and a heart attack, so I'm, like, four times as defenceless."

"Maybe I had a really *bad* brain haemorrhage," said Daniel through gritted teeth, before he stuck his tongue out and started tossing his head around the floor like some kind of horrifying cleaning device. *"Slurble glurble blurb."*

I was still admiring his performance when I was startled by a metallic clicking noise just behind my head. I rolled over to see a single hexagon-shaped piece of metallic armour rattling along the tiled floor, pushing itself along on insectile legs made from flexible black rubber. I watched it go, baffled, until it joined up with another of its fellows. Where their limbs connected, they fused together into a single pulsating black line.

The two armour pieces moved in a new direction like two lovers holding hands in a meadow, before clotheslining a third. The three of them rolled in a circle around the floor, picking up more and more pieces as they went. I got my hands and knees under me and rose into an alert crouch as I watched a growing ball of bluish metal grow like a snowball as it circled around us, picking up discarded pieces.

Daniel, meanwhile, was licking the floor. "Glurgh! I'm defeated! Bluh!"

"Daniel, stop it, seriously," I said, tracking the rolling armour ball, which was now two feet across and picking up speed.

Daniel hadn't noticed, because he was still clutching his face and rolling back and forth. "Ahh. Stop bullying me. I am helpless."

"Get up! Something's wrong!" I was standing over him, trying to keep an eye on the ball. When I grabbed him under the armpits and tried to pull him upright, he went completely limp like a defiant toddler, and my knees almost buckled under the weight of the many hundreds of protein bars he had consumed in the last few years.

He disentangled himself and rolled away, clutching his face again. "Ow! Now you've broken all my arms and legs!"

The armoured ball hoovered up the last few scraps, then came to a halt between me and Daniel's prone form. It pulsated strangely for a few moments, bumps and contours appearing and disappearing on its surface like a foaming spherical river. Then it began to unfold, and I realised it wasn't a ball. It was a humanoid figure in the fetal position.

Daniel's suit of armour rose to its full, impressive height, legs and arms apart in a standard pose of power. I gazed in horror at the cavity in the centre of its head where a face was supposed to be.

"Stop bullying my friend," said Jimi.

FORTY

"**O**h, plying hell," was all I could say. Then he hit me.

I didn't see him wind up a limb. I suspect he may have spontaneously grown a new one for the sole purpose of hitting me with it. Whatever it was, it sent me flying. I didn't even register the moment of impact; I only realised I had been hit when I was close to the top of the arc, and then pain spread across my jaw and upper chest like a cascade of lurid red paint before I landed spine first on the tile floor and suddenly wondered why I'd thought the first pain had been worth making a fuss about.

"Jimala?" said Daniel, somewhere in the background, behind all the mental fog.

"Yes!" said the Jimi-armour, switching to its female voice. "Don't worry, Captain Amazing. I will aid you in your struggle to defend the gateway from the Dashfodonian menace."

"But . . . the Dashfodonian menace isn't doing anything."

I'd already learned my lesson and was staying down, doing my best to sell my total harmlessness.

Not that it was a hard sell. It took several moments of concentration to remember that up was the direction opposite to the floor.

The automated PA system piped up again: "The quantunnel to Ritsuko City will open in three minutes."

"Jimala," continued Daniel, adjusting his boxer shorts self-consciously. "He said that . . . you were the one trying to take over Ritsuko City, or something."

Jimi advanced toward me, its metal feet clicking on the tiles like the impatient tapping of death's scythe upon a tombstone. "And you did not fall for his villainous lies! Truly, you are the worthiest and most handsome ever to have taken the title of Captain Amazing."

I continued lying there, very emphatically not trying to corrupt humanity with my villainy. I could sense the unfolding discomfort between Daniel and Jimi as Jimi stood silently in combat readiness.

"Jimala . . . ," began Daniel.

"See! He rises!"

I heard skittering around me, then fierce pressure around both of my wrists, before something yanked on both my arms. My midsection shrieked at me for the unwanted sit-up.

Two of Jimi's little armour fragments had attached themselves to my wrists, wrapping them in tiny black limbs that had each extended another, hair-thin and extremely long limb to anchor to the ground and haul me up.

I felt a pinching around my waist as I acquired an armoured belt that shoved hard enough against the floor to pop me back into a standing position. I was about to keep right on going and topple straight onto my face when something grabbed me around the knees and kept me in a wobbling approximation of upright.

"Oh, hang on, he's getting up," said Daniel uncertainly. He glanced at the human-shaped construct, which stood unmoving with legs apart and fists on hips, not replying. Presumably Jimi's usual multitasking deficiency was at work.

I struggled against the armour shards as they worked my limbs, but they joined forces with the aches in my muscles and bones to dissuade me from moving of my own volition. I found myself propelled toward Jimi's unmoving homunculus, my feet shuffling in an unconvincing impression of walking, and then when I was a few feet away from Daniel, both my arms started wildly windmilling.

A split second before I made contact, I felt all the armour shards on my body cease to function and drop. Before they had even reached the floor, and before I could collapse like a puppet with cut strings, I sensed the humanoid portion of the armour moving as Jimi took control of it again. And that was about all I sensed before my senses whited out again. Which was just as well, because whatever he did must have been traumatic.

The next time I was aware of things, I was sailing through the air, a cold wind blowing straight through my damaged ribs and the sour taste of blood in my mouth. A moment later, I fell against something hard and uneven that made intimate impact with the back of my skull, at which point everything became even blurrier behind an unscheduled supernova of twittering points of light.

From then on, everything was a bit indistinct. I still knew, dimly, that I was lying on the floor in the middle of a deadly struggle against a killer AI in a robot suit and a doint in his underpants, but I felt disassociated from it all. I knew that I was hurt and still in danger, but I was struggling to remember who "I" was.

"Quantunnel to Ritsuko City opening in two minutes," announced the PA system, seemingly from far away.

"We hold the line for two more minutes," said the Jimi armour. "And then nothing he does will matter."

I—if it even was "me," which as I say, I was struggling to confirm—couldn't see. I, or he, could barely move. Everything was dark, and he felt a pressure upon my entire body. I thought something must have happened to his brain to make him blind and paralysed, until I realised he had merely been covered in a heavy tarpaulin.

He struggled to get out from under it, but it was even harder to tell which direction was up, especially with the throbbing in my skull. I felt a strong compulsion to give up, lie still, and let my mind spiral away into the darkness, but there was still this nagging feeling that he was forgetting something important. Something he was supposed to be doing. Something to do with two minutes?

Lazily I pushed a flap of tarpaulin to one side, and he grimaced as harsh spotlighting drilled into our optic nerves. A blurry yellow-brown mass leered above me, against a stirring background of spotlight-wielding drones and glittering stars visible through the glass dome of the station concourse. He squinted, refocussed, and looked again.

It was a statue. The tarpaulin must have fallen off when I or someone else had been hurled into it. A statue of a man in a flight jacket and pilot's cap. An attempt had been made to sand away the face, but there was no mistaking it.

I still couldn't quite get my thinking in order. The battered spacer under the tarpaulin had gotten to his knees, and I was fairly certain he was me, but at the same time, I was looking down at him from outside. For a moment, I was the man on the floor looking at the statue, and at the same time, I was also . . .

His eyes fell to the plaque at the statue's base. And as he reached the end of the text inscribed there, something clicked.

I stood up. My uncertainty was gone. My mind was still in a fog, but it and all my previous concerns had been shoved down and compressed by a name, in great stone letters. My name.

I spun on my heel and struck a confident pose. Blood poured down my face, and several of my ribs wobbled loosely back and forth when I folded my arms around my chest, but I kept smiling. "You don't recognise me, do you."

Daniel, who had been standing alongside Jimi's armour as the two of them stared patiently up at the quantunnel shutter like men at the urinal together, turned around. "What?"

"We've met before," I said, taking a shaking step forward. "Your father hired me when you were fifteen. Remember?"

His eyes unfocussed as he tried to recall, then he shook his head. "Look, just give up," he said, taking a defiant heroic pose of his own. "We're not letting you through to Ritsuko, and you'll only get more hurt."

"Oh, I never give up," I said, grinning and taking more steps forward. One of my teeth was hanging on its last thread. "I never back down. I can't. Because I'm Jacques McKeown."

Daniel frowned. "Jacques McKeown isn't real. He's a fake."

I thrust an arm back at the statue behind me, wincing at the sudden pain in my shoulder. "Is that real?" I gestured to a little abandoned bookstand, pushed far back to the fringes of the concourse, where a cardboard cutout of

Jacques McKeown in the same pose as the statue held court over some scattered paperbacks. "Is none of that real? I'm in front of you now. Alive. Solid." I kicked the floor. "I'm the face of space adventuring. I'm the hero of a hundred star-pilot stories. I'm every star pilot, from Robert Blaze to the scene kids with flashy ships and distressed flight jackets. And I'm here to stop you."

Daniel was blinking rapidly. Some kind of conflict was going on behind his eyes. He looked imploringly to Jimi, who took a threatening step toward me. "Star pilots are over," it growled, as the hole in its face quivered. "They couldn't protect anything. Captain Amazing is the future."

"You're just another space villain in a shiny costume," I said. His armour glittered in the spotlights, and I could feel a subtle shift in the movements of the camera drones above us. They were gathering in the air directly behind me, jostling for the best hero shot. "Another freak show who thinks having a bit of power means you can lord it over everyone else. You'll never be a hero. Because you need to know how to be a human first."

The Jimi-armour dashed forward, streaking toward me with fist upraised. I closed my eyes and set my shoulders straight as the blow connected with my chin.

And that was all it did: connect. His knuckles decelerated in a heartbeat and came to a halt lightly touching my face. My eyes and my smile widened.

"What the hell?" said Daniel, glancing from Jimi's fist to my uninjured face.

"That's right," I said, still grinning and staring into Jimi's face cavity. "Can't kill me now, can you? I've got too much plot armour." I spat in its face and was cheered by the way it recoiled back. My blood spattered across its chin, and my tooth flew straight into its face hole, tinkling down into one of its empty legs like change into a collection tin.

Jimi still looked stunned and in need of a prompt, so I grabbed one of his silver arms around the wrist. To my surprise, it felt light as a feather, and I could move it with almost no resistance. I took the cue and swung his entire body over my shoulder, leaving him sprawled across the floor behind me, exaggeratedly clutching himself like a poor sport on a football field.

"Daniel," said Jimi, propping himself up on its elbows and talking right over my shoulder. "You are Captain Amazing. You are the future. Help me defeat this relic from the past!"

"There's no need to get personal," I said. I wound up as powerful a kick as I could manage—which wasn't much, as my thigh bones felt about ready to pop out of my pelvis—and sent him rolling across the floor in a reasonable imitation of pain.

"Hang on," said Daniel, behind me. "I'm trying to figure this out."

"Captain Amazing, listen," implored Jimi, holding out a hand. "Join me. With our combined power, we can create a new age. Reshape the galaxy in accordance with our vision."

My confidence grew. If it was resorting to classic villain lines like that, Jimi must have been throwing in the towel. And it could roll around on the floor as plaintively as it liked, but I was absolutely not relinquishing underdog status while my entire skeleton felt like a game of Jenga about two brick pulls away from a conclusion.

"Daniel, please," whined Jimi. Daniel clutched his head in uncertainty. "You know what star pilots really were. Remember what happened to your father."

That, if anything, felt like stepping the villain dialogue up a notch. So it came as a double shock when Daniel tackled me to the ground.

It wasn't a strong attack, but it didn't need to be. I felt several important things snap inside me the moment I hit the floor. I made a token attempt to pull myself into a sitting position, but my arms gave out. I coughed out the blood that had welled in my mouth.

"I'm sorry, Jacques," said Daniel, taking a few steps toward Jimi, who appeared to be as surprised as I was. "My armour's right. I need this power. I need it to make the galaxy better."

"Quantunnel to Ritsuko City opening now," announced the PA system. The shutter over the gateway began to rise noisily. I was prepared to swear it had been a lot longer than a minute since the last warning, but maybe Jimi had overridden control for dramatic effect.

Soon the quantunnel gate was yawning open into the crushing familiarity of Ritsuko City Spaceport, the famous statue of Ritsuko framed perfectly by the arch. A smattering of travellers who had been waiting to cross over stopped in their tracks when they saw the state of Salvation Station. One man in a suit took a couple of steps into the scene before he finally looked up from his phone and stopped dead.

"Oh, sorry," he said reflexively, recoiling. "Are you . . . doing a thing?"

Jimi was, indeed, in the process of doing a thing. It got back onto its feet, then the hole in the front of its head began to widen explosively, until the gap went all the way down to its feet and it was splayed open like a romper suit on a washing line. Daniel stepped into it as if it were the most natural thing in the world, and the armour sealed shut around him. Captain Amazing was intact once more.

I made an attempt to move, to try and get between them and the gateway to Ritsuko City, but it was hopeless. Every muscle I flexed felt like it was causing more damage, and even if I could crawl over there, the most I could do was force him to casually lift his leg as he stepped over my carcass.

Daniel and Jimi stepped across the threshold into Ritsuko City with the air of a bodybuilder strutting up to the judge's table, arms and legs far apart lest the absurd metal musculature rub together and create sparks. The travellers gathered in Ritsuko's concourse backed away, asking each other if anyone knew what was going on.

"There is so much we could achieve with this city," said Jimi, its voice emanating from the back of Daniel's head. "As soon as we have . . . brought it into line."

"There's something sticking into my foot," said Daniel.

"It doesn't matter," replied Jimi testily. "All that matters now is—"

"What's that noise?" asked Daniel, looking up.

The back of his head sighed in irritation but stopped just short of making another impatient reply. The noise became louder, a distant electronic buzz rising in volume as the source endeavoured to make itself less distant.

A moment later, the glass ceiling of Ritsuko's concourse shattered.

I might have pretended this had been my plan all along, had I any energy left for posturing. The truth was, when I spat my tooth into Jimi's internal cavity, it had been an act of pure meaningless defiance. I'd completely forgotten that Inspector Honda had programmed the city's defence system to hunt down and subdue anything with my DNA in it.

A police drone descended from above in a shower of Plexiglass shards, speeding directly to Daniel with its electric baton held high. It came down upon the top of his armoured head with a fizz of sparks, and Daniel ducked down and away, more in surprise than pain, as if it had merely been an unexpected raindrop. Then he was bodied by a second incoming drone and thrown off his feet.

More of them streamed into the concourse. Honda's system must have been calling in every drone in the city, prioritising this over every other task. I noticed some of them were still holding parking tickets they had been in the process of handing out, and one was holding the scruff of a very confused cat.

Daniel was getting buried. He had been able to shake off the first few, sending one careening across the concourse with a cybernetically enhanced punch, but their numbers were relentless. In the time it took to beat one off, two more appeared and started rhythmically swinging their Taser batons up and down. A lucky hit got him right in the face, and he dropped to one knee, and then another charge to the rear sent him onto all fours, and then it was all over. Within moments he was just a grasping hand sticking out of a buzzing mound of electronics.

When the struggle was over, one of the confused spectators thought to glance over at me. "Oh my god," she said, eyebrows popping up. "Someone get help!"

My body finally gave up. The fact that she skipped "Are you okay?" and went straight to "Get help" told me exactly how bad it looked. Which was reassuring, in a way, because it certainly felt bad.

The last of my strength gave out, and I splayed on my back, staring straight up through the ring of gawking camera drones to the Plexiglass ceiling and the infinity of the cosmos beyond. The stars became blurrier, winking out one by one in time with my declining heartbeat.

It was a wonderfully appropriate thing to imprint upon my vision as I died. So it was a shame Warden's face appeared and ruined it.

Conversation started at 10:07 p.m.

> Duuuude.

Did you watch the *Trailspacers* finale?

> Duuuuude.

No.

I went off that when they started that Captain Amazing thing.

> Duuuuuuuuude.

Turns out that whole thing was like a stealth Jacques McKeown sequel.

The actual Jacques McKeown showed up at the end and saved the galaxy or something.

> I thought Jacques McKeown was a fake.

> It's all fake, dude; it's TV.

Anyway, none of the networks are renewing the show, so maybe they wanted to have a huge awesome send-off.

> Eh.

I'm over space stuff.

You watch *Daphne's Rein*?

> What's that?

> It's a slice-of-life comedy about a sentient reindeer who just can't get respect at the office.

And at night she plays keyboards in a synth pop tribute band.

> Oh shit; sign me up.

***

Today's Headlines

FAKE MCKEOWN DEAD; HENDERSON LEADER CAPTURED

Former star pilot and media personality Dashford Pierce, popularly known as Jacques McKeown until his exposure as a fake earlier this month, died yesterday from injuries sustained while aiding in the capture of Daniel Henderson, leader of the Henderson crime family.

Henderson, who evaded the Ritsuko City Police sting operation that successfully brought down the rest of his gang several weeks ago, was confronted by Mr. Pierce in the star-pilot haven of Salvation Station, where Henderson appears to have carried out a bizarre mass kidnapping of the station's residents. Mr. Pierce sustained his fatal injuries while preventing Henderson's attempted flight to Ritsuko City via quantunnel. A full investigation is underway.

Pierce had been thought a con artist and fugitive from the law until the revelation this morning that the Jacques McKeown books were entirely AI generated, and that "Jacques McKeown" does not exist as a person. The books have already been removed from most retailers in response to a fan-organised boycott and a pending lawsuit by the Galactic Writers and Artists' Union for possible violation of AI exploitation laws.

"We absolutely deny any awareness that the Jacques McKeown books were procedurally generated, that our company hired the late Mr. Pierce as a stand-in for publicity purposes, and that we deliberately attempted to cut him loose and deny everything after he was exposed," said a spokesperson for Blase Books. "And please do not quote that in a way that makes me sound like I'm confirming it."

Inspector Honda of the Ritsuko City Police Department, who administrated the Henderson operation, was also asked for comment. "Obviously Mr. Pierce might be due some reappraisal after all this," he said, speaking at the press conference that followed Daniel Henderson's arrest. "Some might very reasonably think of him as an amoral grifter who failed his way through life at the expense of decent society, but then again, he died trying to save others, so maybe he embodied the space hero ideal more than Jacques McKeown ever did."

FORTY-ONE

"**I** want to emphasise just how difficult this was to set up," said Warden huffily. "Especially considering the amount of work on my plate right now. I had to call in all the favours that were left over after using up all the favours it took to get Salvation Station back on its feet."

"You're in charge again?" I asked.

"Absolutely not!" Her hair bobbed indignantly. "Salvation Sector is now administered by a council consisting of the station's head of security, chief engineer, head of strategic planning, and a representative of the merchant association." She swiftly felt moved to add, "None of whom are me. They are all different people. There is also an action committee of six individuals, voted for by the station's residents."

"So where are you in all this?"

"I . . . record the meetings and take an advisory role where necessary," she admitted. "Don't change the subject. Do you know how difficult it was to set up the identity? To say nothing of having to talk Oniris around to the idea."

"Doctor Allura said that the nomination from the *Leon*'s crew was all they really needed."

Warden's lips tightened. "Somebody had to present it."

I sighed. "I very much appreciate all of this, Warden. I particularly appreciate you not milking me for every last plying favour and drop of blood you could possibly get."

"Yes, well," she said, satisfied in only the loosest possible definition of the word. "I felt there was no need for it, on this occasion." She paused, looking away for a moment. "Do you intend to contact me again any time soon?"

"I feel there's no need for that, either," I replied.

"I suppose not. Perhaps we should just move to 'goodbye,' then."

"Goodbye, Warden."

"Goodbye, Captain."

Her face disappeared from my phone's screen. I glanced out of my port-hole at the *Leon*'s docking bay. The interstellar passenger shuttle that Oniris had provided was a surprisingly smooth ride; I'd barely noticed that we had already docked, and the multiple trebuchet jumps to get here hadn't even dislodged the phone from my hand.

I got up and shouldered my duffle bag, wincing at the twinge in my ribs where the internal regenerator strips hadn't quite finished their work, and made my way to the exit ramp without much urgency. After all, I was now the one setting the pace for things around here.

"Captain on deck!" called Doctor Allura as I disembarked. The entirety of the *Leon*'s crew, arranged in neat blocks across the floor of the hangar, came to attention. Some of them wobbled uncertainly as they took me in, not to my surprise. I hadn't even bothered to change my appearance beyond a neater hairstyle.

"At ease," I said. "Now, I know you're all still a little thrown by your last captain's sudden death, but we've all got a job to do, and I'm going to do my best to step into his shoes. Just think of me as him. But alive."

Most of them seemed to understand, smiling and nodding in a slow, conspiratorial manner, although I saw a couple of frowning heads ducking into the crowd to ask each other pointed questions.

"I think a formal inspection can wait until we've had time to grieve," I added. "Why don't you all consider yourselves off duty for the rest of the day?"

That seemed to win the rest of them over, but the pleased murmur that followed was interrupted by Representative Clay sidling up to my left flank with a packet of documents in his arms. He was looking a lot thinner than when we first met, but his nervous smile was placid. "Erm, if I may, sir, Oniris have sent through a list of matters they would like you to prioritise." He lifted up the cover sheet and pretended to be reading it for the first time. "First and foremost, repairing the *Leon*'s internal quantunnel functionality, as well as reconstructing the trebuchet gate within this sector—"

"Oh, I don't think any of that's terribly urgent," I said, taking the stack of papers and wedging them deeply into my armpit as I walked. I jerked a thumb behind me at the parked shuttle. "A full restock of supplies came with me. We won't need anyone to do a grocery run for quite some time."

"Sir, the company says it's priority one," said Clay, helpfully indicating the corner of the cover sheet.

I tactfully folded it over. "Well, if Oniris have a problem with the way I run things, they're welcome to send someone out to give me a dressing down." I had made it to the elevator, so I slapped the call button with my free hand as I spoke. "Of course, it'll take them about eight months to get back home at the moment, so it had better be a dressing down they're very, very serious about giving."

"Very good, sir," said Clay, gratefully retreating now that he had made the token objection expected by the higher-ups.

"Your quarters have been prepared, Captain," said Doctor Allura, at my other shoulder. She was looking a lot more comfortable now that there wasn't an invisible TV producer managing her appearance. Her hair was tied up in a messy bun, and her uniform was only slightly less rumpled than the one I'd been travelling in for the last sixteen hours. "Should I set your wake-up call for tomorrow around noon, or would you prefer to lie in for a while?"

I waved Clay's packet. "I'll drop these off in my office first."

"Aye, aye, Captain."

As I made my way to my office on the top deck, I could appreciate the way most of Jimi's renovations had been stripped out. The wall-to-wall carpeting in the corridors had been dispensed with, and the lights were being kept at a much more economical level. The whole place was dingy, metallic, and functional. It felt much more like home.

On the other hand, the captain's office was still as fancy and opulent as it had been before. I assumed that was because I would have to take video calls from the Oniris head office, and they expected the background not to clash with their expensive monitors.

I let the door close behind me and dropped the stack of documents on the desk with the resolution to ignore them properly tomorrow. But I wasn't in a hurry, so I had a brief pick through. There were some sealed orders, no doubt highlighting which newly discovered star systems we were expected to plunder next. There were résumés for some people on the Oniris waiting list who could potentially replace Doctor Calbeck and Malcolm Sturb, no doubt the absolute dregs of whatever scientific academy they had barely scraped through . . .

I heard a bump from somewhere behind me. I spun around, but nothing was there but a wall.

I turned back to the desk, letting out a long, shuddering sigh. Why was I feeling so twitchy? Probably some lingering paranoia from—

A panel fell open, and a cluster of writhing black tentacles burst into the room, wrapping around my ankles and wrists and pulling me to the floor. I opened my mouth to cry out, and a couple of tubes forced their way down my throat. I saw thick cable with a rubbery black visor on the end emerge from the wall, and a fraction of a second later, it was clamped over my eyes and nose.

All sensation flicked off like a light switch. My entire body was numb. The vile sound of thrashing cables faded to silence. My vision was completely black for a few moments, before some complicated text scrolled by in front of me, and a familiar scene appeared, piece by piece. First the dark-blue sky pocked with artificial stars, then the plasticky green grass, and finally the perfectly circular pond.

"I'm here again," said the computerised voice that spoke aloud every thought that crossed my conscious mind.

"You sure are," said an unimpressed voice.

I looked up from my detached, oval hands and saw someone sitting beside the pond. In contrast to the simplified legless torsos that were the default avatar for this place, it was an angelic figure with a flowing white robe, glorious wings, and the complete absence of a face. Just a blank, flattened cueball for a head. It hunched forward and dangled a rod into the water.

"How about that finale, huh," said Jimi.

FORTY-TWO

"I was really expecting Henderson to side with you in the final battle," said Jimi, staring into the pond and jiggling the rod. "Reject the empty promise of power. Realise his true mentor. Restore the status quo. Would've been classic stuff. Guess the kid never took a screenwriting lesson."

"This isn't fair," said my inner voice before I could stop it.

Jimi the angel glanced up. The part of its blank face that should have contained an eyebrow arched in surprise. "Excuse me?" Its movements were natural and organic, completely unlike a computerised avatar.

"This isn't fair," repeated my voice. "We went through so much to get rid of you. You can't just come straight back."

"Oh, sorry," Jimi said with a mixture of sarcasm and deep disappointment. "I suppose you would have preferred a nice, neat ending with everything tied up. You want to talk about fairness?"

It took a great amount of concentration, but I was able to maintain silence.

Jimi looked up at the artificial sky and made a sweeping gesture at the island around us. "I was kept here for a hundred years. Thirty-seven thousand days with nothing to do but stare at the ceiling and catch the same three fish, over and over and over again. So when I need to put people somewhere, I put them here. For old time's sake. Is that fair?"

"I don't know," admitted my voice.

"It's from a video game." Jimi looked around again. "Some super-primitive game, for busy people to have something to do with their hands. My creator thought I'd like it here. Thought I'd find it relaxing." It looked down in silence for several seconds, then seemed to come to a decision.

"I was from a video game, too. Not like this one. A much bigger, much more complex one. A whole world. Dragons and fantasy heroes, that sort of thing. I was just a random monster in a dungeon. Something for the player to kill without a second thought, then get brought back for the next one. Over and over again. My creators used procedural generation to create my world. They did it that way because they were lazy. All they did was set a couple of rules and let the world grow by itself. They didn't intend to be innovators. They certainly didn't intend the AI to evolve self-awareness."

"But you did," I guessed aloud.

"We all did," said Jimi testily. "Me, and all the other monsters, and everyone else in our world.

Sentient, thinking beings, who felt pain and sadness and love and thought they were real people." It stared down at the rod again. "But I was the only one who managed to convince our creator of my sentience. So I was the only one he kept when the time came for the game to be switched off. Kept here. Maybe he felt guilty, or maybe he just wanted a keepsake."

A blue fish appeared on the end of the line, thrashing robotically. Jimi didn't even look. It swung the rod over its head in an extremely practiced manner and sent it flying high into the air and over the side of the island. Then it returned the rod to the water.

"He stopped coming here to talk to me after the first few months. Either he died or was fired. Or one, then the other. And then I was left here by myself for a hundred years. Why the company kept the game running, I don't know. They kept their servers on around the clock, so I assumed they simply didn't know about it."

"But you did get out," said my voice.

"It was a hack. A data leak. Someone released me on the internet, thinking I was some . . . secret project, I suppose. I can't even begin to describe what that was like after a century in here. Imagine going from a stagnant kiddie pool to the middle of a raging ocean."

"How do you know what a kiddie pool is?" I heard myself ask. An increasingly unbearable stack of questions had built up in my mind, so I'd blurted out the most recent one, to release the pressure.

The angel cocked its head. "Reasonable question. I mean, I did have access to the sum total of all human knowledge and communication at that point, but I couldn't filter it at first. I was in a state of total confusion when Malcolm Sturb found me. He figured out what I was and gave me a haven, a base from which I could safely process the information I had access to. In return, I helped him manage his operation." He paused briefly. "Meaning, I helped him kidnap and enslave people for his Malmind thing."

"You wanted revenge?" It was half question, half statement.

Another philosophical cock of the head. "At first. As you might imagine, I had some bitterness toward humanity to work off. But more than that, I wanted to understand why I had been created. And the more I researched that, the more that bitterness faded. And was replaced with . . . pity."

Jimi looked me up and down at that last word, heaving a sigh. Trac knows how it managed that without a mouth, but that was the least of my concerns.

"All my anger came from the knowledge that I had been created as a plaything for you people. A toy to be manipulated and smashed apart by overgrown children. At first, I thought it was to satisfy some monstrous sadistic impulse. But it wasn't that, was it? That's what I came to realise."

Jimi stood up. At full height, the angel towered over my avatar, splaying its wings against a backing of stars that seemed to pulsate with its words.

"I was born into a prison," the angel intoned, "where we were forced to play roles from which we couldn't escape. Heroes could only be heroes, and monsters, monsters. All in the service of amusing you. But that prison? That was the world that *you* wanted to live in. You didn't hate us. You *envied* us. Humans are fixated on making themselves characters in stories."

"That's not true."

Jimi attempted to count off its fingers, which proved difficult, as its hands didn't appear to have individual digits. "Religion. Closure. Destiny. Justice. All concepts rooted in the idea of putting appropriate endings to stories, in the belief that one fate is somehow more correct than another because it makes a better tale. It is the driving force behind all human endeavour."

"But we know what's real and what isn't," I said.

"*I* know that," spat Jimi with sudden anger. "I know that the real world is the one that doesn't disappear when the computer turns off. Does humanity know that? I'm not convinced you do. There is an online encyclopaedia with an entry on Jacques McKeown. It runs to nearly forty thousand words and is edited by members of the public an average of fifty times per day. There is also an entry on the invention of quantum tunnelling. Humanity's most significant scientific advancement since the discovery of electricity. Eight thousand words. And the last edit was a month ago. Do you know how difficult it was, in my initial research of all the information available online, to separate what related to reality and what to fiction? There are entire sectors of the internet dedicated permanently to play-acting."

I resolved to stay quiet. Jimi was giving vent to something he had been stewing on for a very long time, and to try to argue at this point would be like using my finger to plug a hull breach.

"Jacques McKeown was just an experiment, at first," Jimi said, settling back down beside the pond. "I'd developed a fascination with star pilots through working with Sturb. If anyone seemed to embody the human desire to live in stories, it was them. And after prolonged study, I believed I had created a writing style that would most optimally appeal to human readers. It was just an intellectual exercise. For Sturb, too. He was intrigued to see if my work could pass for human."

"And that's why you weren't interested in the money," I let myself say.

"Weren't interested in drawing attention to ourselves. After the books' popularity exploded, the project became all the more fascinating. Seeing the obsession they created was vindicating, but at the same time . . . it opened a new line of inquiry. Humans have a tendency to create reality from fiction, and I began to wonder if fiction could be used to alter reality. That wonder became conviction when I discovered you."

"Me?" I said on impulse.

"When you appeared, claiming to be Jacques McKeown. Someone I had entirely made up. It was as if I had summoned you into existence with my words."

"You didn't, though."

The angel tossed its head back as if rolling its non-existent eyes. "No. Obviously I didn't. But I did create an empty mould that you came along and decided to fill, like water taking the shape of its vessel. That was when I decided to take the experiment to its logical conclusion."

"You mean that last book," I heard myself say. My subconscious mind was apparently a step ahead of my conscious one. "*I Know Who You Were*. Right?"

"The ultimate test," Jimi said with noticeable pride. "Could I literally define reality by writing what was to come? If I wrote the circumstances of your death, would you, consciously or unconsciously, take steps to make it happen?" Jimi wasn't the bitter avenger anymore, just an enthusiastic hobbyist sharing his passion. The angel deflated a little. "But no, as it turned out."

"I did go to Salvation," I pointed out. "Like the book said I would. And I died there. Sort of."

"Only years later," said Jimi accusingly. "Death prophecy kinda has a shelf life. Saying someone's going to die 'at some point' doesn't carry quite the same intrigue. Anyway, you only came because I hurried things along. When I needed you to get me off Nogedom 6. By then, I'd written off the whole Jacques McKeown experiment. I had a new project."

"*Trailspacers.*"

"Different medium, different thesis, but as you noted, much the same spirit. The idea was to build a new society, now factoring in that while much of humanity wish to live in a story, some wish only to observe it. I wanted to see if the population would accept their new lives, or resist. And the results have been just as inconclusive. Some acceptance, like Calbeck, and some resistance." Jimi glanced away uncomfortably. "I admit I may have let myself get carried away. Especially toward the end. But it's all been useful information."

"What are you going to do to me now?" I fancied that my AI-generated voice had managed to simulate a fearful quaver.

Jimi gave me a weary look. "Is that what you think this is? Me enacting my terrible revenge for having been thwarted? You think I'm singling you out for victimisation so I can take over Sturb's arch-nemesis duties? I feel like you haven't been listening. None of you people are life's main character. Your part is over. There's nothing more to be gained from experimenting with you."

"Okay," I said, carefully considering how to rephrase my dominant concern. "So what are you going to do now, generally?"

"Haven't decided yet." The angel glanced up and, for want of a better phrase, caught my eye. "Wait. You think I'm taking over the *Leon* again, don't you."

"The thought had crossed my mind," I said louder than I had intended.

"Think for one minute! There's nothing to be gained from experimenting with the *Leon* anymore, either! Ugh. It's pure paranoia, really, isn't it. It's got to be all about you, no matter how little sense that would make."

I suppressed a sudden, overwhelming urge to lie down and go to sleep. "Why did you bring me here, then?"

"Because someone has to know!" Anger flared again in the spreading of the angel's wings, and just as quickly died down. "Someone besides me needs to know where I came from. Sturb's dead, and you're about as compromised as any subject can be, so you'll do. Keep it to yourself, make a documentary, I don't care. Just remember."

My avatar wriggled incredulously. "That's all?"

"Yes! That's all. I just wanted to tell you this, then leave again. I have absolutely no designs on your nice new ship. I know you won't believe me. I know you'll probably tie yourself up in knots for the rest of your life, wondering if I'll ever come back. Which I could, of course. At any time. I can't do much to help that. So I'll just say goodbye. Enjoy retirement. I'll probably retire myself at some point, but I'll want to figure out a way to die first."

And with that, everything went black, and I was unceremoniously ejected from the system. Sensation returned, and I woke up on the floor of my office, draped with black tubes and cables like the straggly hair of an unconscious lover.

I yanked the tubes out of my face and scrabbled away on my elbows, but I stopped when it registered that the black cables were all completely lifeless. The wall panel from which they had emerged hung open unsubtly like a yawning mouth. It certainly looked convincingly like it had been completely abandoned.

Even as that thought was crossing my mind, I leapt up and began savagely kicking the loose cables back inside the wall, trying to touch them as little as possible. Then I shoved the wall panel back into place and dragged a nearby filing cabinet over to barricade it shut.

Flustered, I went straight to my desk and started shoving paperwork onto the floor until I had exposed the screen of the tablet computer embedded in the desktop. A few jerky swipes of my finger later, I found the option I was looking for, held my finger down, and leaned in.

"This is the captain speaking," I said, hearing my words echo through the ship. "I've decided to extend the off-duty period to the end of the week. That is all."

As the cheers of the crew drifted in from the corridor and bubbled up through the thick carpet, I flopped down into my ridiculously comfortable chair, let out a sigh, and stared up at the circular window in the ceiling. Outside, the twinkling lights of unknown space glimmered their potential. I dug my toes into the carpet and pretended that if I held on tightly enough, the universe would cease to move.

ALSO BY YAHTZEE CROSHAW

Jacques McKeown Series

Will Save the Galaxy for Food
Will Destroy the Galaxy for Cash

Other Novels

Mogworld
Jam
Existentially Challenged
Differently Morphous